MESSINANTS

Pyreans Book 2

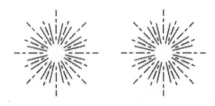

S. H. JUCHA

Published by Hannon Books, Inc.
www.scottjucha.com

ISBN: 978-0-9994928-2-6 (e-book)
ISBN: 978-0-9994928-3-3 (softcover)

First Edition: March 2018

Cover Design: Damon Za

Acknowledgments

Messinants is the second book in the Pyreans series. I wish to extend a special thanks to my independent editor, Joni Wilson, whose efforts enabled the finished product. To my proofreaders, Abiola Streete, Dr. Jan Hamilton, David Melvin, Ron Critchfield, Pat Bailey, and Mykola Dolgalov, I offer my sincere thanks for their support.

I wish to thank several sources for information incorporated into the book's science. Toby's bone replacement (BRC, pronounced brick) originated from the website of EpiBone and commentary by CEO Nina Tandon.

The El car diamond-thread cable concept was borrowed from Penn State Professor John Badding and Dow Chemical Company senior R&D analytical chemist Tom Fitzgibbons, who isolated liquid-state benzene molecules into a zigzagging arrangement of rings of carbon atoms in the shape of a triangular pyramid — a formation similar to that of diamonds.

Despite the assistance I've received from others, all errors are mine.

Glossary

A glossary is located at the end of the book. Some alien names are used frequently. For pronunciation of many of them, refer to the glossary. For instance, Jatouche is pronounced as jaw-toosh, with a hard "j," as are all the Jatouche names beginning with "j."

Patch Death

"Major Finian, we've got a suspicious death," Commandant Emerson Strattleford called over his comm unit.

"Where, Commandant?" Liam asked. It was late evening, and Liam was off duty, which was why he was surprised to receive Emerson's call.

"Locate my device, Major. I'll preserve the scene until your people arrive," Emerson replied and abruptly ended the call.

Liam checked his comm unit for the duty roster and selected a name. When his call was answered, he said, "Sergeant Lindstrom, you're authorized to locate the commandant's position. Contact Sergeant Rodriguez and a forensics team to investigate a death at his location. Send me the reports when you file them."

"Understood, Sir," Cecilia replied. She accessed the JOS station's security personnel database, pulled up the code for the commandant's comm unit, and pinged it. Then she called Miguel and passed on the major's orders.

Emerson stared dejectedly at the scantily clad body of Lily Tormelli. She was splayed across the bed, and her pose suggested she was asleep, except Lily was absolutely still, her eyes open and staring.

The commandant's evening had been flipped on its head. During the years, he'd availed himself of the services of more than a few coin-kitties. Then, ten months ago, he'd met Lily at the Starlight, one of the station's more prestigious cantinas. It was an unlikely pairing. Emerson was a short man with a strident personality, which didn't engender the amorous attentions of women, including service providers.

Lily was Emerson's physical opposite — tall, long-legged, and lithe. But, she was a kind and gentle woman. There was another element to their relationship, which was in addition to the exchange of coin and services.

Lily was addicted to streak. It was a plant-based narcotic produced by the downsiders, the population of Pyreans who occupied the planet's domes.

Emerson was under no illusion that his position as commandant might have been the primary reason for their seemingly chance encounter at the cantina. He wasn't happy to accommodate Lily's habit, but, at the same time, he would have done anything to be with her.

Lily's weekly supply of streak was shipped to Emerson via the El, the elevator car that connected the station to the domes. Addressed to the station's commandant, the package passed through freight customs without inspection.

Knowing there were precious few minutes before security and forensics arrived, Emerson scanned the scene. There was nothing to be done about his DNA. It would be found throughout Lily's cabin. That wasn't his primary concern. He couldn't believe that Lily had taken her life, which the scene suggested. It wasn't like her, and, while the drug was addictive, it wasn't debilitating.

Emerson carefully searched the dresser, nightstands, couch, and chairs in the richly appointed sleeping quarters. There was no indication of pill vials, syringes, or any implement by which Lily might have taken her life.

Peering closely at Lily, Emerson performed a cursory inspection of her body. He couldn't find any indication of trauma. Her skin appeared as flawless as ever.

Emerson did find Lily's comm unit. It was partially tucked under her arm. Using a disposable wipe, he pulled the device free and was surprised to discover it open, the virtual screen projecting above the device. That was an odd thing for Lily to do. She jealously guarded her comm unit. As an independent coin-kitty, her contacts and comm history were incredibly valuable to her and a good many people.

Examining the screen, Emerson saw a message meant for him. It said, "Bitty, I'm sorry. I can't live without my streak, and I don't want to hurt you. I love you."

The commandant used his comm unit to take a snapshot of Lily's screen, then, with a second wipe, he cleared the message. He was about to close the comm, when he halted. Instead, Emerson accessed the device's system controls and selected the wipe function. When the comm unit chimed, marking the end of the operation, he closed the unit and tucked it under her arm, where he'd found it.

Emerson got rid of the wipes by flushing them down the sink. As they rapidly dissolved in the running water, he heard, "Commandant? It's Sergeant Lindstrom."

"Here, Sergeant," Emerson replied, stepping from the bathroom, his voice guiding Cecilia into the sleeping quarters.

"I was told we're considering this death as suspicious, Commandant," Cecilia said, asking for confirmation.

"Investigate carefully and fully, Sergeant. Am I clear?" Emerson replied, his eyes boring into Cecilia's.

"Crystal clear, Commandant," Cecilia responded, snapping upright. A question was on the tip of her tongue, but Emerson quickly vacated the sleeping quarters. Seconds later, she heard the cabin door slide open and close, and she was left alone with the deceased.

With little to go on, Cecilia began documenting the scene. She activated her comm unit with a touch of her thumb. Starting from the cabin's front door, she recorded the entire salon and then moved into the sleeping quarters. She paid particular attention to the body, leaning in for closeups of the limbs, torso, and face.

Cecilia heard the cabin door slide open and Miguel Rodriguez call out, "Security."

"In the sleeping quarters with the body, Miguel," Cecilia replied. "I'm nearly done recording the scene," she added, when Miguel walked into the room.

"Do we have an ID, Cecilia?" Miguel asked.

"Negative," Cecilia replied.

Miguel pulled his DAD, a portable DNA analysis device, also known as a sniffer. He touched it to the dead woman's toe and waited.

The DAD accessed a database, which held the DNA profile of every stationer born aboard the JOS, the Jenkels Orbital Platform, in the past 129 years. The database included spacers, active and retired, and the occupants of the *Honora Belle*, the Pyreans' colony ship. It didn't include the downsiders, who occupied the domes on the planet, much to security's frustration.

"Her name's Lily Tormelli, and this is her cabin," Miguel said, when the DAD returned a match. "She's a registered coin-kitty. How did the commandant say he got word of this death?"

"He didn't," Cecilia replied, closing her comm unit. "All he said to me was make sure that we investigate this death thoroughly. Then he left. More like he ran," she added, flicking a hand toward the door.

"Hmm, strange," Miguel commented.

"Sergeant Rodriguez, forensics is here," Jorge Olas called from the cabin door.

"Sleeping quarters," Miguel shouted.

"Touch anything?" Jorge asked, as his team entered the room. He nodded appreciatively, when he received negative replies. "Anyone else been here?"

"The commandant was here when I arrived," Cecilia replied, "but he left quickly. I didn't get to ask him a single question."

"Odd," Jorge commented, and Cecilia and Miguel exchanged quick glances. That's what they were all thinking. "You two done?" Jorge asked.

"All yours, Jorge," Miguel said, stepping away from the bed.

"What do we have?" Jorge asked, making a cursory examination of the body, as he pulled on gloves.

"We've been told by the commandant to treat the circumstances as suspicious and to check every detail," Cecilia replied.

"Doubly odd," Jorge replied, studying Cecilia's face. Her serious expression told him what he needed to know. "You two want to wait for the cursory examination before I move the body or get my report later?"

"Wait," the two sergeants replied in unison.

A forensics tech pulled a scope, hooked it to a monitor, and began a slow scan of the body from the feet upwards. Jorge hovered over the monitor. When the tech finished, she looked at Jorge, who nodded. She slipped the scope into its sleeve on her belt, and she and a male tech turned the body over.

"Wait," Miguel ordered. "Roll her back." With gloved hands, he slipped out the comm unit from under Lily's body. "You're good to go," he added to Jorge, and the techs rolled the body over.

Miguel scanned the comm unit with the sniffer, but he found only the one DNA profile on the unit, Lily's.

Meanwhile, the male tech employed his own sniffer and was checking the room. In seconds, it beeped, indicating a match. Then, it continued to beep regularly, announcing new matches, until the tech shut down the audio signal.

"Busy woman," Miguel quietly commented to Cecilia.

"Look at her," Cecilia replied. "Beautiful and statuesque. Not to mention that she leases a private cabin instead of working out of a club."

"A lot of coin changing hands," Miguel agreed.

"Lift the hair. Check behind the ears and through the scalp," Jorge ordered. Monitoring the scope's output, he said, "Check behind the other ear."

"Confirmed," the female tech said.

"Sniff them," Jorge ordered.

"Only the deceased's DNA," the male tech replied.

"What did you find?" Miguel asked.

"The woman's been patched ... one patch tucked behind each ear. We found only her DNA on them," Jorge replied. "It's looking like suicide. She could have gotten the patches from med staff, trading for coin or services. I'll know more after a full examination."

While the forensics team went about moving the body to a gurney, Cecilia and Miguel stepped into the salon.

"Check this," Miguel said, holding up the dead woman's comm unit.

"Cleared?" Cecilia said, reading the small system's status window.

"She could have wanted to prevent her client list from falling into other hands," Miguel suggested.

"She's a registered coin-kitty. It's a legal profession, and she lives in a nice area of the JOS. Anyone who wanted to know who her clients were only had to drop a snoop cam in the ceiling, with a view of the corridor," Cecilia replied.

"So why is the commandant telling us to investigate this death as suspicious?" Miguel asked.

* * * *

Early the next morning, Major Finian was in his office, reviewing the sergeants' report and the preliminary forensic analysis on Lily Tormelli. His people had worked late due to the commandant's interest in the case. Emerson wasn't a well-respected man, but that didn't change the way the security and forensic teams performed their jobs. Liam liked to think that was because officers below Emerson's rank set good examples, the likes of who sat in front of him, Lieutenant Devon Higgins.

"What am I missing, Liam?" Devon asked. "This woman has been addicted to streak for years. According to forensics, her entire hair length, every seventy-eight centimeters, tested positive for the drug. More than likely, her supplier cut her off, she panicked, and used some illegal patches."

"When was the last time you heard of a patch death that wasn't administered by the med teams, Devon?" Liam asked.

"Actually, not one, since it became legal to request the procedure for terminal conditions," Devon replied. "Maybe the woman just wanted privacy."

"Possible, but you're forgetting that patches are under direct control of the forensics head," Liam replied.

"Oh," Devon said quietly, realizing Liam was speaking about Margaret O'Toole, which meant that inventory access was tightly controlled. "There was that theft years ago," Devon suddenly recalled.

"Ten patches, seven years ago," Liam agreed. "And there was a spate of suspicious deaths, following the theft, within the following nine months."

"Yes, I recall the basics. Stationers were using the patches, but the postmortems indicated they didn't have any underlying terminal symptoms. Everyone thought that it was the spread of some sort of mysterious space dementia. But, I don't remember the outcome of those cases. I was sitting for my officer's exams, at the time."

"There was no outcome, Devon. Eight of the ten patches were used, and forensics listed the deaths as unexplained suicides."

"So, ten patches are taken. Eight are used immediately. Are you saying the patches that Lily used came from these ten?" Devon asked.

"I checked with Margaret this morning," Liam said. "The two patches on our deceased are from the group of ten that was stolen. And, before you ask, Margaret's inventory of deadly items has been kept in a vault ever since the robbery, and she showed me the electronic methods used to procure and account for them. I haven't a clue how anyone could get two more of them now and neither does Margaret."

"Who sits on two patches for seven years? Are you thinking this woman wrestled with thoughts of suicide for years and finally killed herself after all this time?" Devon asked.

"That scenario doesn't make sense to me, Devon," Liam replied.

"But why do I think that you want us to continue to investigate this as a suspicious death?" Devon asked.

"I was at your desk, when those patch deaths occurred," Liam replied. "I had a theory, at the time, but I didn't have an opportunity to discuss it with the major, who sat at this desk."

"Who was that?" Devon asked.

"The last of the patch deaths," Liam said.

"I think I'll wait to hear your theory before I say anything more," Devon replied.

"In order, the deaths were: a maintenance tech, a prominent JOS businessman, a cantina owner, a freight supervisor, a cantina owner, a coin-kat, a freight unloader, and Major Dorsey. Each death was accomplished by a patch on the neck or behind the ear."

"Which leads me to wonder why this woman, Lily, used two patches," Devon mused.

"I have two guesses about that," Liam replied, leaning back in his chair. "She might have thought the efficacy had been reduced over time and wanted to ensure that the patches did the job. Then again, she might have wanted to ensure that the second patch wasn't left to be used by some unfortunate individual. Putting that aside, there's another reason to pursue this case. Lily Tormelli was Emerson's latest paramour."

Devon narrowed his eyes at Liam. "You've had the commandant followed," he whispered conspiratorially.

"I can't confirm that," Liam replied quietly.

Devon grunted in reply. He appreciated the sentiment. Liam was protecting him from his covert observation of the commandant. There was no doubt in Devon's mind why Liam was doing it. Ever since the discovery of the illegal liaison between Lise Panoy, the downside governor, and Emerson, the pair of men were attempting to figure how they could introduce their improperly obtained evidence to expose the commandant.

"Here's what I can't figure, Liam. I looked up Lily's online ads. She was an incredibly striking woman. How could the commandant afford sessions with her on a regular basis?"

"Who said he paid full price?" Liam asked.

"Her streak?" Devon guessed, and Liam nodded his head. "You think Emerson was facilitating Lily's delivery?"

"We know how tough it is for a streak user to get a regular supply. Distributors keep popping up, and we keep shutting them down. Lily would have been mighty appreciative of Emerson if he could safely deliver her supply," Liam proposed.

"We're sure there are no manufacturing sources for streak on board?" Devon asked.

"There's no evidence of that on either station, and I don't see Harbour, as captain of the *Belle,* allowing it to be produced in the colony ship's hydroponic gardens," Liam replied. "As far as I know, the only source is still the nut of the plumerase tree."

"Have to give it to Earth's bioengineering efforts," Devon said in disgust. "They take a simple fruit, the plum, and figure they can make it better by creating a version with more sugar. They're successful in that, but it turns out the nut can be processed to produce a dangerous narcotic."

Liam nodded in agreement and added, "What I can't understand is why Earth chose to add the seeds to the *Honora Belle*'s inventory, and why the first dome settlers chose to plant the seeds."

"I had a thought," Devon suddenly said. "What if the target of the patches wasn't Lily Tormelli but Emerson?"

"Only thing the DAD found on Lily and her comm unit was her DNA, and that includes the patches," Liam said, sorting through the forensics report to make sure he was correct.

The two men eyed each other, their minds whirling to connect the disparate pieces of the investigation.

"Where do we go from here, Liam?" Devon asked.

"I find it too great a coincidence that Major Dorsey was investigating El cargo shipping at the time of the patch deaths," Liam replied.

"Do tell?" Devon replied, sitting up in his chair, his interest piqued.

"Yes, and that makes me want to investigate the people who've gotten the vacated positions in El custom inspections since the deaths of the individuals."

"But you don't want to look at the other deaths?" Devon asked.

"They might have been obstacles to the distributors' illegal shipping or they might have been innocent bystanders," Liam replied.

"That latter option is cold, Liam. You think someone stole ten patches and used them to eliminate two cargo personnel. Then they killed six others to hide those deaths?"

"The two cargo personnel were numbers four and seven," Liam replied. "They were nicely hidden among the group, don't you think?"

"I'd love to ask Markos Andropov and Giorgio Sestos about this," Devon remarked, with a nasty grin, referring to the former governor of Pyre and his head of security. "Unfortunately, I don't see the pair wanting to extend their seventeen-year incarceration sentences just to please us by answering questions about their involvement in illegal narcotics trade."

Liam matched Devon's grin, as he added. "I'd love to make it life sentences for both of them."

"We do have an alternative suspect," Devon suggested. "The streak shipments are probably small, weekly or biweekly. The ex-governor and his security stooge have been locked up for a much longer time."

"You're insinuating the new governor, Lise Panoy, might have something to do with the streak shipments," Liam replied. "I don't see that. She wouldn't risk her position. Although, she might be willing to cut off the shipments if she found out about them."

"So where does this leave us?" Devon asked.

Liam carefully considered his options and then said, "First and foremost, we've a legitimate reason to investigate the source of Lily's streak. Perhaps, by following this legal line of inquiry, we might find a way to put the commandant in jeopardy, if he was facilitating her shipments."

"Oh, I like the way you think," Devon replied, his grin splitting his face wide.

-2-
Accusations

Lise Panoy, the domes' governor, and the construction supervisor of the impending fifth agri-dome stepped out of their e-trans.

The interconnecting tunnel to the new agri-dome was recently completed and the pair stood at the far gates, examining the work beyond. Encased in vac suits against Pyre's harsh air, caused by repeated volcanic-like surface activity, the workers controlled small, automated digging vehicles to carve out the dome's outer ring.

Unlike the residential domes, the agri-domes were constructed by sinking the support girders and interlinking panels deep into the surface to prevent unwanted gases from seeping into the airspace occupied by the dome. The construction would allow a small amount of porosity, but that was necessary to facilitate water drainage and ground oxygenation for roots.

"The well strikes have been successful?" Lise asked.

"Yes, Governor. We hit a lake bed, deep underground. The pumps will produce enough water to take care of this agri-dome and another, if we wish," the supervisor replied.

"Excellent, and the anticipated completion time for the dome girders and panels?" Lise asked.

"We estimate about seven and a half months, Governor. The YIPS expects to deliver the first set of girders to the JOS within weeks. We'll be ready for them."

"Has the YIPS obtained priority for the shipments downside?" Lise asked.

The Yellen-Inglehart Processing Station would ship its products to the JOS terminal arms. To reach the domes, the material was transferred through the arms to the lower levels of the El car, the freight level. Girders were constructed to precise specifications that allowed them to neatly fit within the El's cargo space.

However, the size of the girder and panel shipments required that no other freight be transferred at the same time. Traditionally, the freighting was done during the hours of midnight to four in the morning, and exclusive access to the El's cargo space required the commandant's prior approval.

The supervisor cleared his throat and ducked his head "I've sent requests, Governor."

"And?" Lise pressed.

"No response from the commandant's office," the supervisor replied. He watched the storm gather in the governor's eyes, and he wished to be anywhere else but standing in front of her. When her comm unit chimed, he could have kissed the caller.

Lise glanced at the caller's ID and signaled the supervisor away with an imperial wave of her fingers. He happily made himself scarce.

"Commandant Strattleford," Lise replied evenly, "I was just speaking about you. My agri-dome supervisor informs me that the YIPS hasn't received your approval for priority freight access to the El for our newest dome's girders and panels."

"Your agri-dome shipments might have to wait, Governor," Emerson replied.

"I presume my recent transfer was to your liking, Emerson," Lise replied, keeping a rein on her temper.

Emerson had demanded an increase in the payments to him after the debacle created by the previous domes' governor, Markos Andropov. The governor's ugly secret of imprisoning a family of empaths was exposed when the eldest daughter, Aurelia Garmenti, escaped the domes, made her way to the JOS, and boarded a mining ship. As events unfolded, Lise failed to keep Emerson apprised of the fine details, which put him in a precarious position with his security staff and many others.

"It's adequate ... for now," Emerson replied tartly. "But you and I have another matter to discuss. A friend of mine committed suicide with two patches."

"I'm sorry to hear that, Commandant, but I don't see how that pertains to our business," Lise replied, confused by the subject change.

"She left a message for me, which indicated the patches were meant for me but she couldn't do it," Emerson replied. His voice threatened to rise to a screech, as it was wont to do, and he worked to prevent that from happening. He was angry, but his overriding emotion was fear, driven by the thought that he'd escaped a near brush with death.

"Commandant, we don't have the capability to manufacture patches. They couldn't have come from downside," Lise argued. Her mind was working overtime, attempting to figure who might have been trying to take out the commandant. Although she hated the little man, she needed him.

"The woman was hooked on streak, Governor. You do make that, don't you?" Emerson replied with heat.

"There are elements downside who profit from that. You know that, as well as I do, Commandant. Who was this woman?"

"Her name was Lily Tormelli, Governor. In her message to me, she said she couldn't live without her streak."

"Obviously, someone threatened to cut off her supply of the narcotic, Commandant. I'll investigate this immediately from this side. This type of stupidity is bad for business."

"You do that, Governor. When you have something useful to tell me, I'll take the time to review the YIPS and your supervisor's shipping requests." Emerson cut the comm, tapped off the monitor's display of Lily's death report, and leaned back in his chair. He didn't know the name of the downsider, who was shipping Lily's streak to the JOS, which meant he had no idea if that individual was the one who had targeted him. Furthermore, he couldn't be certain that Lise Panoy wasn't behind the attempt on his life.

The agri-dome construction supervisor turned from regarding the ongoing work to see if the governor had finished her call. He caught sight of her climbing into what had been their shared e-trans on the far side of the interlock. He let out a deep, long sigh of relief and called for a new vehicle.

Lise arrived at her home and hurried upstairs to her office. Idrian Tuttle and Rufus Stewart were waiting for her, as she requested. Lise stalked across the room to stand in front of them, where she could observe their reactions.

"Which one of you two idiots, or was it both of you, tried to kill the commandant?" she demanded hotly. The reactions she got told her that they weren't complicit. She held up her hands to cut off their protestations. "Enough," she declared. "Sit down."

"What happened, Lise?" Idrian asked.

"Who's a stationer by the name of Lily Tormelli?" Lise asked instead.

"Uh-oh," Rufus said softly. "Lily Tormelli has been the commandant's exclusive coin-kitty for nearly a year."

"She *was* his coin-kitty," Lise replied, pacing around the room. "A got a call from the little man himself. He's holding up our priority El shipments until we find out who got her killed."

"Lise, you have to back up. What happened?" Idrian pleaded.

Lise sat behind her desk and faced the men on the other side. "According to the commandant, his coin-kitty was addicted to streak. He also said she left him a message that implied someone threatened to cut off her supply unless she patched the commandant. Apparently, the woman liked the little man too much. She patched herself instead, and the commandant is angrier than I've ever heard him."

"Over a coin-kitty?" Rufus asked.

"It is what it is," Lise said. She drummed her well-manicured fingernails on her desktop, while she thought. "The commandant isn't going to help us with our dome shipments until we provide him a guilty party."

"Lise, the individual who engineered this doesn't have to be a supplier," Rufus argued. "It could have been the distributor on station. And let's not begin to count the number of people who the commandant has angered."

"That might be true, but we've got to offer the commandant someone," Lise replied.

"Could it be anyone?" Idrian suggested.

"That occurred to me too, Idrian," Lise replied. "But Emerson has some smart people working for him, Major Finian, for one. If we give him an innocent, he'll see through it. No, it's time to uncover some of the streak suppliers, who are operating downside."

"You're probably aware, Lise, that we have a good number of streak manufacturers," Rufus said. "It's a simple process to extract the drug, and a lot of people have access to the nuts. The plumerase fruit is enormously popular downside and topside. We grow the trees in a section of every agridome."

"Not to mention, nearly every significant family, who has a garden, has planted one or more plumerase trees," Idrian added. "They can enjoy the fruit and make some coin by selling the nuts on the side."

"I don't expect to disrupt our economic base nor our families, Sirs," Lise replied, her eyes narrowing, as her thoughts evolved. "Our suppliers will have to give up many of their distributors on station, and we can offer that bunch to the commandant. He can sort it out up there. In the meantime, we'll have a handle on who is producing the drug and making coin, without sharing."

Idrian shared an avaricious grin with Lise. It was the kind of plan he enjoyed. Solve a problem for the topsiders and make some coin at the same time.

＊ ＊ ＊ ＊

"You're in danger of a trip outside the domes without a vac suit," Idrian said, as the two men rode an e-trans away from Lise's house.

Idrian sat behind the console. He'd entered an override code so that the little electric vehicle wouldn't stop for other passengers, as it was programmed to do.

"Tell me about it," Rufus replied, with a snarl. "And I don't want to hear that you warned me."

"Do you still have just the one supplier?" Idrian asked.

"No, I have three now. Demand kept increasing, and the stuff is so profitable," Rufus replied. He rubbed his hands over his face.

"You could suggest to Lise that you run the investigation," Idrian offered.

"Not a chance," Rufus replied. "As far as I know, Lise is already aware that I'm facilitating some suppliers. It's one thing to make a little coin on the side with an illegal process. She doesn't mind that sort of the thing, as long as it doesn't disrupt the broader scheme of things. But, if I offer to manage the investigation, she'll see that as overreaching. I don't want to end up like Markos or worse."

After the men left Lise's office, she called her security head, Jordie MacKiernan, to attend her.

"Jordie, what do we know about streak operations by Idrian and Rufus?" Lise asked when the security chief made himself comfortable on a couch next to Lise's armchair.

"I've nothing on Idrian, and that's not for a lack of trying. Word is that he likes to keep his business dealings legal. The man appears averse to placing himself, his family, or businesses in jeopardy."

"Sounds like Idrian," Lise commented. "He's the dependable sort until he's sure the advantages are wholly in his favor."

"The information on Rufus is mixed," Jordie continued. "He got into the trade about three years ago with a small plumerase harvester. Since then, he's acquired another source and started a small manufacturing lab. My sources say that the lab is producing more streak than the two sources can provide in nuts."

"So, he has more sources than you can identify?" Lise asked, her eyes piercing Jordie's.

"That's the status, at this time," Jordie replied. His tone wasn't apologetic. Lise didn't appreciate weakness, and he wasn't the type of man to exhibit any.

"We have a problem, Jordie," Lise said. She laid out the recent topside events to him, leaving little out. When she finished, she said, "I intend to give the commandant a list of station distributors to mollify him."

"All of them?" Jordie asked.

"Probably not," Lise replied. "I'll need to know who supports them. That will help me decide. Certainly, we want to turn over Rufus' distributors. He'll get the message from that without me having to confront him."

"Do we make an example of anyone?" Jordie asked.

"Yes, I'm afraid so, Jordie. Streak is bad for dome business. A little drug distribution on station can create leverage opportunities, but too much means security will be descending on us. They've had a taste of what they can achieve when they came here, arrested Markos and Giorgio, and obtained convictions. Topsider moods are running against dome independence, and that has to be cooled."

"How will you choose, Lise, and how many?"

"That depends on the details of the suppliers, lab owners, and distributors that you bring me. We're going to trim shipments by about two-thirds, eliminating as few people as possible."

"Disappearances or accidents?" Jordie asked.

"Probably a combination, Jordie. Most important, this is your priority, and you're authorized to spend whatever coin you need. Emerson is sitting on our agri-dome priority shipment approval until he has the information on station streak distributors from us."

"Understood, Lise," Jordie said, and swiftly exited the office.

Two years ago, Jordie believed he was missing out on an opportunity to earn some extra coin. His sources told him of the increased traffic in streak. The problem was that he had no legitimate access to the easy sources, namely the agri-domes. However, Jordie was, if nothing else, a resourceful man. He did have hundreds of informants in the homes of important families and businesspeople. And, each of these families had one or two of the popular plumerase trees in their gardens. It was easy enough to disseminate the word through an intermediary that the kitchen help could make some extra coin by collecting the nuts of the fruit.

The question Jordie was now asking himself was whether Lise knew of his profitable little side operation. Being a man who erred on the side of caution, he chose to believe that she did know. Whether Lise did or didn't know really didn't matter. She'd laid out her position on the matter. The streak trade was bad for dome business, and anything that was bad for dome business was subject to punishment.

Jordie made the decision to swiftly close his business. He'd give word to his security man, Stevens, who had organized the kitchen suppliers, that the business was ended. It was the same low-level security employee who made the rounds to collect the nuts. In the near future, the kitchen help would find no one coming for their supplies.

Jordie briefly lamented the loss of a good security member, but Stevens was too knowledgeable about his side operation. The individual would soon find a quiet place to rest under Pyre's rocky soil, a good distance outside the domes.

-3-
The JOS

Captain Jessie Cinders walked down the exit ramp of the *Spryte*, one of his three mining ships. The *Spryte* was docked on a JOS terminal arm. Its gravity wheel was shut down, which meant the crew were utilizing deck shoes to adhere to the corridors' surfaces and the terminal arm's walkway in the absence of gravity.

Ituau Tulafono, Jessie's first mate, and two crew members, an engineer and a tech, accompanied him. Jessie's ships and crews had abided by the lengthy quarantine instituted by Emerson, Lise, and Captain Stamerson, following their discovery of the alien site on Triton, Pyre's outermost moon.

Still, most stationers worked to avoid contact with Jessie's crews. Some stationers went so far as to make it their business to brace Jessie's spacers and shout at them to board their ships and leave, as if they had somewhere else to go.

Having suffered the stationers' fears and wrath for days, it became standard procedure for Jessie's crews on the *Spryte*, *Marianne*, and *Unruly Pearl* to maintain safety in numbers. Ituau had taken it on herself to personally accompany Jessie anywhere he went. Stationers had only to look at the heavy-boned woman of Polynesian ancestry, with the shaved head and hard expression, to decide to give Jessie a wider berth.

Jessie and his crew swept out of the gangway onto the terminal arm, walking with the telltale spacer's gait of ensuring one foot was down before the other lifted.

"Heads-up, Captain!" Toby shouted.

Three of the *Spryte*'s crew glanced overhead toward the boy floating at the top of the terminal arm and hanging onto a rail. Every terminal arm was equipped with top rails, fastened along its length, for individuals who managed to lose their shoe grip on the deck's special coating.

However, Jessie, having been forewarned by Toby, spun around. It was déjà vu. But, this time, it wasn't sixteen-year-old Aurelia, known as Rules to Jessie's spacers, coming at him. It was a younger, smaller girl. Her face was a study in horror, as she sped toward him. She and Toby had been playing freefall, launching themselves along the terminal arm and performing acrobatic maneuvers.

Jessie caught the young girl in his arms, as he launched off the deck in a backward somersault to lessen their impact. He grabbed an overhead rail short of Toby's position.

"Nicely done, Captain," Toby said, with an infectious grin, his red hair floating around his head. "Just like old times."

"Seems like it, Toby. How's the leg?" Jessie asked.

"Great, Captain. The BRC took. I'm going to be fine. I'd like you to meet Pena, a friend of mine."

Jessie released one hand from the rail and offered it to the young girl.

Pena looked from Toby to Jessie and back, her mouth wide open. "You *do* know Captain Cinders," she said in awe, and then belatedly shook Jessie's hand.

"Pleased to meet you, Pena," Jessie replied genially. "Yes, Toby and I are old friends," he added and watched Toby puff up with pride, the boy's grin widening. "You two, be careful," Jessie said, as he pushed off to touch down on the terminal's decking.

"Hey, Ituau," Toby said, when the first mate passed under him.

"Toby, good to see you again," Ituau replied. The wide-eyed stare the young girl returned Ituau told the first mate that Toby had scored major points.

At the end of the terminal arm, Jessie tapped a plate to call for a capsule. The main engines of the JOS kept the station aloft in its near planet orbit and imparted spin to deliver gravity to its residents. But, the terminal arms were stationary. That necessitated a transfer mechanism between the two structures. A giant ring revolved around the JOS, which connected the station to the terminal arms structure. Housed within the ring were capsules or caps, as they were called, which could exit the ring to pick up passengers from either side. When passengers were loaded, the ring would snatch a cap, transfer it across its breadth, and exit it on the other side.

When the cap arrived, Jessie and his people boarded, strapped themselves in, and the cap was whisked away by the ring. To accommodate the different orientations of the station and terminal arms, the cap tilted midway through its transition. This allowed the occupants to exit the cap into their destination in the correct orientation.

Entering the JOS main corridor, which was heavy with midday traffic, the crew suddenly became their own island, and the stationers flowed around them like waves fearing to touch the shore. Within minutes, the group left the central corridor, lined with the most prestigious of shops, restaurants, cantinas, and sleepholds. Winding through corridors and taking a lift, they made their way to a quiet section of the JOS.

At a hatch-like door, Ituau smacked the heavy red button, and the hatch slid in and aside. They walked into the midday mealtime noise of a heavily crowded cantina, known as the Miner's Pit. It had been Captain Rose's place before he willed it to Jessie.

"Captain," Maggie yelled over the boisterousness of her customers and greeted him with a hug. "Been waiting for you to visit," she added.

"Had business to attend to, Maggie," Cinders said, lifting Maggie and twirling her around once. "I wanted to tell you thanks for your efforts on the *Belle*'s cantina. Your idea saved my crews' sanity at Emperion."

"Aren't you in a good mood," Maggie said, laughing at Jessie's actions, a contrast to his usually no-nonsense demeanor.

"My company and crew have coin in our accounts, Maggie. My people are happy and safe, I might add. No alien infections. What's not to be happy about?"

"Well, Captain, I'd like to wallow in your compliment, but the cantina's idea was Harbour's. I think when she saw spacers relaxing here, she got the idea to have one aboard the Belle. I thought she was trying to set up some kind of competition, but Dingles set me straight, right away."

"Hmm, and it was Harbour who gave you the credit," Jessie mused.

"For an empath, there's a lot to like about that woman, Captain," Maggie replied. "Changing the subject and speaking of reprobates, how's Dingles doing?"

"Acting like he was twenty years younger, Maggie. Harbour and other empaths cured him of his space dementia, and he's busy chasing an empath by the name of Nadine."

"An empath?" Maggie asked in disbelief.

"Yes, believe it or not. Dingles likes to say that spacers enjoy challenges." Jessie eyed the crowded cantina and said, "Doesn't look like a spare seat in the house, Maggie."

"There will be soon enough, Captain," Maggie said with determination and marched off toward a table with three spacers, who were done eating and lounging over drinks.

"Belly to the bar with those drinks, spacers. Captain needs a table for him and his crew," Maggie ordered. The three retirees stood and tipped caps or touched brows toward Jessie. The table was quickly cleaned, and Maggie waved them over.

"Drinks?" Maggie asked. When everyone demurred, Maggie took their food orders on her comm unit, sent it to the kitchen, and returned to her post at the door. She was the cantina's hostess and manager. Years ago, she had sailed with Captain Corbin Rose before an accident took her arm.

Ituau leaned close to Jessie to be heard and said, "Captain, I've been meaning to ask you. What's the plan?"

"At the moment, it's downtime for the ships' crews," Jessie replied.

"Begging your pardon, Captain, but I don't think our people are enjoying their downtime," Ituau said. "The stationers are too jittery about our alien discovery. I notice that our crew members aren't drinking or carousing much. They don't want any trouble with station security. They're making their visits on station brief and returning to the ship quickly after a meal or spending some time with family and friends."

Jessie eyed the other two *Spryte* crew members, who nodded their agreement.

"What's your suggestion, Ituau, if the crew doesn't want to enjoy their downtime?"

"I say we get back to work, Captain. We made some good coin on the Emperion slush. That made everyone happy, and we know we can do it again and again."

"We did have a good time aboard the *Belle*, Captain, whether we were working on the colony ship or on downtime," the engineer added.

"The colony ship was great," the tech enthused. "Fresh food, a cantina, people to meet ..."

"And empaths," Jessie finished for the tech.

"Yeah," the tech agreed with a sigh, which brought chuckles from Ituau and the engineer.

It was a sign of the amazing transformation that a single, sixteen-year-old runaway from a murder charge had wrought on Jessie's crews. His people would always think of Aurelia Garmenti as Rules, a name her young sister, Sasha, had given her.

Prior to meeting Rules, spacers knew little about empaths and their capabilities to read and influence emotions. But, their fears about them were enough to want to keep the empaths at arm's length. In truth, spacers couldn't afford the coin for an empath's therapeutic time.

Jessie's ships were stranded at Triton, Pyre's third, outermost moon, away from resupply from the JOS by the commandant's extraordinary six-month quarantine. It was the powerful empath leader, Harbour, who managed to pull together some spacers and engineers and break the aging colony ship out of orbit over Pyre and sail it to Triton to save them.

Aboard the colony ship, Jessie's crews regularly mixed with the empaths, who were grateful for the presence of the spacers, many of whom worked on the ship's much-needed maintenance. Working with the spacers at Emperion, slinging slush, a primary resource for YIPS manufacturing, enabled the *Belle* to earn some much-needed coin to see to long-awaited capital expenditures.

"Even Sasha?" Jessie asked innocently. That brought his crew's heads sharply up. Sasha was a young empath, one of the strongest ever discovered. Having spent her entire life imprisoned in the governor's house with her mother, Helena, and her sister, Aurelia, Sasha was completely untrained. She tended to have two power positions for her abilities — on and off. There was little middle ground.

"Sometimes you have to take the strange with the wonderful, Captain," Ituau replied with a grin. "I know Sasha means well by her attempts to perk us up, but she could send you loopy for a half hour. Sometimes, after she sent to me, I couldn't remember what it was I was headed to do."

"But you felt good about whatever it was," the engineer said, adding his own grin.

"Okay, I'll talk to Captains Erring and Hastings," Jessie said. "If they concur with your opinions, we'll pack it up, head for Emperion, and make some more coin."

The crew's hearty agreement was cut short, when the food arrived. Expectations of an early launch drove their appetites, and they dove into their dishes.

Jessie had no sooner finished his meal than his comm unit signaled.

Ituau heard the soft, pleasant tones, and she smirked. In all the time she'd been Jessie's first mate, he'd never programmed his comm unit to respond based on who called him. It had been the default chime for everyone. That was until lately.

"Private call," Jessie said, standing, and waving his comm unit.

"Sure, Captain," Ituau said. She pointed toward the manager's office to prevent Jessie from stepping outside the cantina to be alone.

While Jessie made for the office, Ituau and the other *Spryte* crew members shared smiles. Their captain had never married and never had a girlfriend longer than the length of a downtime. He still didn't have a liaison with a woman, unless you considered a business relationship as qualifying. Of all the women who could have captured Jessie Cinders' fancy, it happened to be Harbour, leader of the empaths and captain of the *Honora Belle*.

"Hello, Harbour," Jessie said, when he closed the door to the office.

"Hello, Jessie. Enjoying your downtime?" Harbour asked.

"Yes and no," Jessie replied. "The YIPS notified me that the *Belle*'s slush transfer is complete."

Jessie was using the spacer's generic term for frozen gases. Despite the lengthy quarantine, Harbour and he had reversed his company's impending economic disaster, changing it into an abundance of coin. Rather than sit out their enforced time at Triton, where the alien site was discovered, Jessie's three ships and the *Belle* had sailed for Emperion.

This moon was covered with a deep layer of frozen gases. It was tidally locked in the planet's shadow never receiving the warmth of starlight. The spacers made use of the numerous and voluminous, empty water and gas tanks of the *Belle* to transport the slush.

"We finished the offload, yesterday, Jessie. I received the YIPS payment this morning, and I'll need your account information to transfer your share of the coin."

"Are you intent on giving me your share of the payment, Harbour?" Jessie asked innocently. He could imagine Harbour's shock when she reviewed the enormous amount of funds deposited by YIPS accounting into the colony ship's general account. The *Belle* had limped along for generations on the meager earnings of artisans and, lately, the more generous client payments to the empaths.

"You have your share?" Harbour asked in disbelief.

Jessie laughed quietly. "Here's what I want you to focus on, Harbour. That's only our first haul, unless you want to quit this partnership," Jessie suggested in a casual manner.

"Hmm ... let me think about that," Harbour replied. She waited until she heard Jessie struggle to retract his suggestion that they dissolve their agreement. Then she burst out laughing.

"Don't do that," Jessie declared. "I nearly fell over, thinking you might be taking my facetious suggestion seriously. I started wondering if another captain had approached you with a better deal."

"In time, Captain Cinders, you'll find I'm extremely loyal to the right people," Harbour replied seriously. "But, back on the subject at hand, how did we make so much coin?"

Jessie was still digesting Harbour's comment about loyalty. He'd walked away from more than one lucrative deal in his life because he didn't trust the other individual. He thanked his stars that the personal trait was important to Harbour too.

"Sorry, Harbour, musing there for a second. Uh, prior to negotiating the contract with the YIPS, I did some checking with my sources about the state of business at the JOS and the domes, the backlog of slush at the YIPS, and what the miner captains might be hauling in from the inner belt. I found out the JOS and the domes are intending to expand, the YIPS was already short for slush, and the miners were primarily hauling ore. This told me the YIPS would be desperate for slush."

"Over how much time have you accumulated these sources?" Harbour asked.

"Some of these contacts belonged to Captain Rose," Jessie replied. "Many of them were generated by me and my crew. Every captain needs sources to stay ahead of the competition and to make the best deals."

"How do I go about procuring contacts or sources?" Harbour asked. Her role as captain was new, and she had no formal training as a spacer. Nonetheless, the residents of the *Belle*, some slightly fewer than 3,000 individuals, had elected her to the position, especially when they discovered Harbour intended to rescue Jessie's ships at Triton.

"That's the good news for you, Harbour; you don't have to go looking for them. They'll come to you. You and your ship are valuable assets, and you can choose your associations."

"By that definition, I have one associate. How am I doing?" Harbour asked, her humor slipping out.

Harbour waited for Jessie to respond. As was his custom, silence was his response to her teasing. She patiently waited him out. *One of these days, you're going to go too far,* Harbour thought. *Then, he'll run away.* She despised comm calls as opposed to sitting beside Jessie. For an empath, who could detect a person's emotions, the calls denied her sensitivities — they were tasteless.

Part of Jessie pleaded for him to relent. He was more than a little tired of the isolating role of company owner and ship's captain. "I've heard the man has some rough edges, but he plays it straight. You might have made a good choice, rescuing his sorry butt."

"I thought I did," Harbour said. Her laughter was soft. Having gotten Jessie to emotionally connect with her, she returned to the problems that her people had encountered.

"Jessie, some issues have come up for this ship. We're having difficulties obtaining supplies. With Emerson's most recent decree, none of my people, including Danny and the shuttle, can make the JOS, without the *Belle* going through a decontamination blowout."

"Only the authorities have no idea how to blowout a colony ship," Jessie finished for Harbour.

"Exactly. It's not like a colony ship was designed to do that sort of thing," Harbour said, exasperated with the commandant and his edicts. Both Harbour and Jessie knew that it wasn't just Emerson. Major Finian of JOS security had taken Harbour into his confidence and informed her of the machinations between the commandant and the governor. Subsequently, Harbour had shared the news with Jessie.

"Not to worry, Harbour," Jessie said. "I'll take care of your needs with Maggie."

"Those are the cantina's provisions, Jessie. We need a great deal more material for this ship."

"Again, no problem, Harbour. We'll have two ships, returning to Emperion, with empty holds. Unless you're ordering new ship engines, we can probably handle it. Have Dingles send his list to Ituau. We'll load our ships and be on our way."

"Wait! What about your crews' downtime?" Harbour asked.

"Apparently the crews aren't having as good a time on station as they did on the *Belle*. They're anxious to go back to work, earn more coin, and enjoy the hospitalities of your ship and your empaths," Jessie replied.

Harbour laughed heartily at the thought that the spacers were anxious to visit with her empaths, and Jessie brought the comm unit a little closer to his ear so he could enjoy Harbour's warm, throaty laughter.

"Well, Jessie, I might as well have Dingles get this ship underway. I'll see you at Emperion," Harbour replied and closed her device.

Jessie exited the manager's office, with quick steps.

Ituau spotted Jessie's upbeat body language and gave the other two spacers a heads-up.

"Ituau, expect a lengthy list of supplies from Dingles for the *Belle*. Notify the *Spryte*'s crew that they have three more days of downtime before we launch."

"Did you talk to the other captains?" Ituau asked.

"Negative. This is an executive decision. I'll be ordering the *Pearl* to head for Emperion. The *Belle* is setting sail now. The *Annie* and the *Spryte* will follow as soon as supplies are loaded."

"How long this time, Captain?" the engineer asked.

"Minimum six months, maybe longer," Jessie replied. When the engineer frowned, Jessie asked, "What's wrong?"

"This is getting hard on the crew, especially those who have family aboard station, Captain," he replied.

Jessie looked at Ituau, who nodded.

"Wait one," Jessie replied and hustled back to the manager's office to make a comm call.

"Yes, Jessie," Harbour said, answering his call.

"Harbour, any issues with getting more residents for your ship? Some of my crew might like to bring their families along. They could probably pay a nominal fee for the cabin and the food."

"You tell your people, Jessie, that their families are welcome, and lodging and meals will be supplied for free, courtesy of the *Belle*."

Jessie murmured a thank you and closed the comm unit. Back at the table, he said, "Captain Harbour says that the families are welcome. Spread the word. I'll inform the captains. It might be tight getting them aboard for the trip out to Emperion unless our shuttles can catch the *Belle* before she gets too far out."

"Do you have any idea what Captain Harbour will charge for boarding?" the engineer asked with concern.

"The captain said that cabins and meals will be free," Jessie replied.

Jessie's spacers stared at him with open mouths.

"Free?" the engineer whispered, and Jessie tipped his head in agreement.

You're one lucky man, Captain, Ituau thought.

-4-
Honora Belle

Aboard the *Belle*, Harbour called a meeting in the captain's quarters. The salon's central table could barely hold the number of invitees. Seated to her right was Dingles, whose given name was Mitch Bassiter. Next to him was Nadine, who had once been the oldest *active* empath but no longer.

On Harbour's left sat Yasmin, her best friend. Next to Yasmin was Aurelia and beside her was Lindsey Jabrook, who had been the empaths' protector prior to the captain. Danny Thompson, the *Belle*'s shuttle pilot, and two engineers, Bryan Forshaw and Pete Jennings, occupied the opposite end of the table from Harbour.

Lindsey Jabrook was the miracle attendee, as far as Harbour was concerned. Sasha, Aurelia's powerful and willful younger sister, had stumbled onto the retired empath, who suffered from a lack of empathetic defensive control. The emotions of others crashed in on her, bombarding her, until she had to be isolated in a quiet, but comfortable, cabin of the colony ship.

Sasha had often played a game with her sister. It was called "protect mother," who was Helen Garmenti. Mother and daughter were permanent residents of the *Belle* after being freed from confinement in the ex-governor's house. Sasha, who formed a quick bond with the elderly empath, chose to play the game with Lindsey. Apparently, while protecting Lindsey from various other empaths, the elder empath slowly regained her complete array of powers. How this was done was still a mystery to every empath.

At one point, Harbour had asked Lindsey, "Do you want the position of Harbour back?" It had been the habit of each empath, who assumed the group's leadership, that they adopt the name of the original leader. It was considered a beacon to all young women, who discovered their abilities, to seek Harbour for sanctuary. And it was only women who had the empathetic ability, which manifested in the recessive genes of the XX-chromosome pairs.

"I might have once been head of the empaths, but I was never captain of this ship," Lindsey had replied. "I wouldn't have a clue what to do, in that regard."

Harbour had smiled and said, "Sometimes, I don't think I do."

To which, Lindsey replied, "I heard something from Dingles that I truly believe. You have the spacers' trust. If you tell them what you want, they'll make it happen. That, to me, is what defines a good captain."

Harbour opened her meeting by announcing, "The *Belle*'s general fund has received the YIPS payment for the slush delivery."

"How did we do, Captain?" Dingles asked. He was Harbour's first mate and a highly trained navigator, whose last position was aboard the *Spryte*. Space dementia had claimed Dingles, and Harbour had rescued him from security incarceration and his mental torture.

Harbour sent the amount to the table's comm units and everyone snatched their devices.

"That's some serious coin," Danny said, whistling softly. "Even after we cut it in half to share with Captain Cinders, it's going to be an impressive amount."

"Captain Cinders has his share," Harbour said simply. She enjoyed watching heads snap up and her people eye her.

"There's still the distribution to the residents' accounts," Yasmin reminded Harbour. Every resident of the colony ship received a stipend from the general fund. This had been instituted only after the empaths became the primary means by which the ship earned coin.

"Already done," Harbour replied, smiling. She was prepared to bask in the congratulatory emotions of the spacers and her fellow empaths, but she sensed a disturbance. Turning her head, she located the source. It was Aurelia.

"Aurelia, what's wrong?" Harbour asked.

"I'd like to be happy, thrilled, or something," Aurelia complained. "But I've never handled coin in my life, and I've no idea what this amount means. What can it buy?"

"Nutrients and new plantings for the hydroponic gardens," Nadine said.

"Down payment on a new shuttle," Danny replied.

"More crew," Dingles added.

"Engine parts," Bryan volunteered.

"Cabin supplies and outfitting," Yasmin said.

"More heat throughout the ship," Pete said, when it was his turn, and everyone murmured their approval of that suggestion.

"So, we have to choose which one of these we want to spend our coin on?" Aurelia asked, gazing around the table.

"We can do all of these, Aurelia," Harbour said quietly.

"Then this is a whole lot of coin," Aurelia said, hoisting her comm unit.

"A whole lot of coin, spacer," Dingles agreed, "and we're going back for seconds." He received a soft flush of pleasure from Nadine, and he slipped his hand into hers under the table.

"I imagine most of you have already devised ways to spend these funds, but here's how it's going to work," Harbour said. "You can have sixty percent of the amount that you're seeing. But, you're going to thrash out among yourselves how it's to be spent."

Yasmin signaled to be heard, but Harbour waved her off.

"Before everyone starts asking questions, I'll tell you my issues," Harbour continued. "We might be at Emperion for longer than six months, and I'm expecting some of the families of crew aboard Captain Cinder's ships. Food, cabin outfittings, and heat are high priorities. Hand in hand with those are the needs of the ship to operate independently. We can't land our shuttle aboard Captain Cinder's ship bays. In addition, our shuttle has no collar lock, and it's aging."

Harbour turned to Yasmin, who asked, "How long do we have to put this together?"

"A day or two," Harbour replied. "Focus on what we need for this next trip. Also, presume that our next haul will generate the same amount of coin or more, and you can have eighty percent of those funds."

"Is there something brewing, Captain, that we need to know about?" Dingles asked.

"Captain Cinders is cancelling the crews' downtime. The *Pearl* will launch soon for Emperion, and the *Spryte* and *Annie* are waiting to load our supplies request."

"Problems aboard the JOS?" Danny asked.

"Some," Harbour replied. "But it seems the captain's spacers are missing the comforts of the *Belle*. I suppose the JOS pales in comparison to our hospitality."

Those around the table chuckled or laughed at the thought that spacers preferred to spend their downtime on an aging colony ship rather than the modern space station.

"Dingles, get us underway to Emperion, while this group starts making lists and arguing," Harbour ordered. "After that, you can join them."

"Aye, aye, Captain," Dingles replied, jumping up from the table and making for the bridge.

The group followed Dingles out the door, but Aurelia lagged behind.

"Permission to speak, Captain?" Aurelia asked, when they were alone.

"Of course, Rules," Harbour replied. She'd discovered that when only spacers, officers or crew, were present, Aurelia preferred the name she was first known by them, Rules. She'd adopted her sister's lament against her to protect her identity, as a means of hiding aboard the JOS, while running from the authorities for the murder of her sexual tormentor, Dimitri Belosov.

"Captain, while I appreciate being included in this group, I've nothing to contribute. I don't handle any function on this ship, and I don't know the price of services or things."

"I can't disagree with that analysis, Rules," Harbour replied, which caused Aurelia to frown and consider what she was missing.

Finally, Aurelia held out her hands and said, "I give up."

"At this moment, you're enjoying the role of spacer, Rules, but you'd be the first to admit that your education is sadly lacking, through no fault of your own. What do you see yourself doing in five years, ten years, or further out?"

"I haven't given it much thought —" Aurelia said, before she stopped. "But, it appears that you might have, Captain," she added.

"We haven't spent a great deal of time together, Rules, but it's obvious to me that you've earned the admiration of Captain Cinders," Harbour replied.

"The captain has been gracious —" Aurelia began.

"Stop," Harbour ordered. "You're speaking to me as if I were a normal. Never do that to another empath. You know what you've sensed from Jessie Cinders. Are you going to stand there and invent some explanation to me about luck or generosity concerning the captain's reactions to you?"

"Sorry, Captain," Aurelia replied, transmitting her feeling of embarrassment to Harbour. "It felt wrong to admit to you what I knew about the captain's protective emotions concerning me."

"They would sound that way if you were talking to a normal," Harbour explained. "What you sense from another person is meant to be kept private. Typically, a client-empath session is conducted privately, and the secrecy of their interaction was always jealously guarded. However, you've thrown all that out the hatch."

Aurelia thought to object that it wasn't her fault, but, when she didn't sense any recrimination from Harbour, she held her tongue. *Then again,* Aurelia thought, *you often don't sense Harbour's emotions unless she intentionally leaks them to you.*

"When I first heard from Captain Cinders that you, an empath from downside, were aboard the *Spryte*, I feared for the safety of the sensitives under my care and the status of this ship," Harbour said, placing an arm around Aurelia's shoulder and walking her toward the suite's door. "I couldn't have imagined the wonderful things that would develop from your actions. I've made you a part of this committee, because I see great things for you, Rules, and it's time we broadened your education. I don't mean just about the price of things, although those are good things to learn. You'll be working with a wonderful group of people. Watch and learn how they communicate, resolve their conflicts, and negotiate a final list for submission."

"I hope you'll pardon me for saying, Captain, but this has been a scary conversation."

"The world is a scary place, Rules. It needs good people in the right places to prevent the scary from overtaking us," Harbour said, as she opened the cabin door and waved Aurelia out.

* * * *

Henry Stamerson, the head of the JOS Review Board and a retired mining captain, drained the last of his caf. He closed his comm unit, shutting off its signal to the monitor. He'd finished reading Harbour's explosive documents for the third time. She'd discovered that hundreds of original files had been removed from the *Belle*'s vast library, in the years immediately following the colony ship making orbit over Pyre. According to the ship's charter, this was an illegal procedure.

Lise Panoy had created a furor, when she used information from those files to justify the quarantine after the *Annie*'s crew discovered the alien site on Triton. According to Lise, she'd recently discovered the missing original files in the Andropov library after taking over the governorship. However, Henry and certain security officers doubted that.

During a tense discussion, Lise had agreed to send the files to Emerson. Henry never knew if she had delivered them to Emerson, and the commandant never mentioned them again. The copies Henry read came from Harbour, and she'd never disclosed to him how she discovered there were missing library files nor how she determined which files were missing. Nonetheless, Harbour had uncovered copies of the files and sent them to select individuals.

Despite the evening's late hour, Henry decided to call Harbour. The *Belle* was underway again and had filed a course for Emperion. To an ex-mining captain, it meant the ship would be a hive of activity for many days.

"This is the *Honora Belle*. Beatrice Andrews on comm. Please state your name and your business," Birdie replied to Henry's call.

"Birdie?" Henry queried in surprise.

"Yes. Who's this?"

"Captain Stamerson, Birdie. What are you doing aboard the *Belle*?" Henry asked,

"Earning coin again, Captain, and being useful. It beats sitting in my cabin aboard the JOS and feeling sorry for myself."

"You know, Birdie, after all the time you served on my ship, if you had coin problems you could have come to me for help."

"That was never my way, Captain."

Henry knew that to be true. Birdie Andrews was one independent, tough-minded woman, who made her own way in life. It hurt him to think she was silently struggling, and he had never looked her up to see how she was doing. He wondered how many other retired crew members from his ship were in the same condition.

"How is it, Birdie, working for Dingles and Captain Harbour?" Henry asked.

"Like I struck heavy metal, Captain. The *Belle*'s no mining ship, but this girl can carry anything you need. With Captain Cinders' partnership, we made a good haul of slush to the YIPS."

"So I heard, Birdie. What I wanted to know about are the working conditions."

"Well, I can tell you, Captain, that I have a cabin to myself. No double bunking. The fresh food at every meal is okay, and the cantina is adequate. And then, there are the empaths who we have to contend with. The sensitives know they are dependent on the spacers now that the ship is sailing, which means they never leave us alone. They're always sending us happy thoughts. It's a tough life, I can tell you, Captain."

Birdie worked hard to keep from laughing, while she let the captain absorb her words. It took him a while.

"Single-bunk cabins, fresh food, a cantina, and your personal therapists," Henry repeated slowly. "Is Captain Harbour hiring? I might want to apply for a position." A thought occurred to Henry and he quickly added, "Seriously, Birdie, is she hiring?"

"Recently, Dingles added a few more spacers, and he plans to increase that number after the next haul. And, before you ask, Captain, I gave him recommendations for some of our old crew members."

"Thank you, Birdie. That's more than I've done lately for them, and I'm sorry for that."

"Apology accepted, Captain, and the reason for your call?"

"I'd like to speak to your captain, if she's available?" Henry replied.

"One moment, Captain," Birdie replied, switching the call to Harbour's comm unit.

"Captain Stamerson, nice to hear from you," Harbour said, when she heard from Birdie who was calling.

"I'd like to forgo formalities with you, Captain Harbour, if that's okay with you," Henry said.

"Certainly, Henry, I'm not sure if I'll ever be comfortable being called captain."

"It grows on you, Harbour. Give it time."

"What can I do for you, Henry?" Harbour asked.

"I've reviewed the key documents that you sent me, Harbour," Henry replied. "I never did receive a set from Emerson."

"I didn't expect you would, Henry."

"Why is that? Is this something personal between Emerson and you because of his position on quarantine?"

"That accusation is beneath you, Captain," Harbour replied with a touch of heat.

"Apologies, Captain Harbour. I'm foolishly repeating others. May we return to civility?"

"I can't give you any details, Henry, about what I know without divulging confidences. However, since you've read the *Belle's* documents, ask yourself who stands to lose the most if the colony ship's original directives were implemented."

"Probably everyone who holds a position of power ... the governor, the family heads, the commandant, security officers, and the Review Board members. Come to think of it, the Captain's Articles would need to be rewritten. That would leave you in charge, Harbour."

Harbour heard Henry's chuckle, when she failed to respond to his comments.

"I take it that you hadn't thought that far ahead, Harbour. If Pyreans were to embrace these directives, you would assume the responsibilities for the processes that would lead to the election of our representatives, president, and judges. These elected officials would choose whether to keep the existing security structure or revamp it. They would also be responsible for rewriting the Captain's Articles and requiring the present captains to sign the articles or risk losing access to our stations."

Harbour felt as if she had been slapped upside the head. Her stomach churned at the extent of the upheaval that Henry was suggesting.

"You don't think it's too late to delete these files, do you, Henry?" Harbour asked in a quiet voice.

"I'm sure that Emerson and Lise would agree to that suggestion," Henry replied. He meant to make it a jest, but his voice sounded rather sad.

"But you wouldn't agree to it, would you, Henry?"

"I'm sorry, Harbour. You don't command a ship for more than thirty years without realizing that shouldering responsibility has become ingrained in your nature. I can't forget that I've seen these documents, Harbour, and personally, I think they need to be implemented."

"Shouldn't there be some sort of vote by Pyreans to approve of whether we adopt these measures?" Harbour asked.

"A referendum. Most assuredly, Harbour."

"How do you envision this happening?" Harbour asked, hoping for answers to her concerns. Instead, she heard Henry's laughter. It was so long and hard that he started to choke. She heard the clink of a glass and his subsequent swallows.

"Apologies, Harbour," Henry finally said, clearing his throat repeatedly. "To answer your question, I've no idea how to proceed to move Pyre from our present societal organization to this one intended by Earth. But, I wish you the best of luck, and I'll support whatever you propose."

* * * *

Harbour was so rattled by the implications of her conversation with Henry Stamerson that she sought to talk to the one person who might make sense of it all.

The *Spryte*'s second mate received Harbour's call. "Good evening, Captain Harbour, Nate Mikado here."

"Nate, I'd like to talk to Captain Cinders, if he's awake. If not, don't bother him," Harbour replied.

"He's available, Captain. One moment," Nate replied.

Nate muted the bridge comm, picked up his personal comm unit, and called Jessie.

"Yes, Nate," Jessie replied groggily.

"Captain Harbour on the line for you, Captain. Orders were to contact you anytime she called."

"Switch it through to me, Nate," Jessie said, sitting up in bed.

"And, please, Captain, she didn't want to disturb you, if you were asleep, and I might have intimated that you were available."

"Understood, Nate, give me thirty seconds before you connect me," Jessie replied. He unstrapped his bunk's webbing, slipped on deck shoes, and climbed into a pair of skins, triggering the tiny mechanisms that closed at the back and the extremities. By the time Jessie's comm lit with the transferred call, he was alert.

Harbour spent a good hour talking to Jessie, detailing her conversation with Henry and discussing her concerns.

"Would you sign new articles, Jessie?" Harbour asked at one point.

"If they were fair, yes, I would, Harbour. It would be a small price to pay if it meant removing the likes of the commandant, governor, and family heads from power."

"When I was reviewing many of the documents in the *Belle's* library, I discovered the list of colony ships that had preceded our launch," Harbour said. "According to the logs of this ship's first captain, the *Honora Belle* might have been the last colony ship launched. Conditions on Earth were in great decline. Did you ever wonder what happened to the other colony ships?"

Jessie was taken aback by the question. He had never considered the fates of the other colony ships, and it amazed him that Harbour had. One thought did occur to him. "I hope the other ships fared better than us. We didn't make our original destination. Instead, our fortune delivered us to Pyre, of all places!"

"According to the *Belle's* navigation files, our course was in the opposite direction to the trajectories taken by the first two North American Confederation colony ships," Harbour explained.

"Which means that those ships targeted stars far across the galaxy from our present location," Jessie replied.

"So, talk to me about supplies, Jessie. My head hurts from this discussion," Harbour said.

"Ituau received Dingles' list. Quite the number of items, I might add," Jessie replied. At the moment, he was imagining sitting across the table from Harbour, having dinner and making small talk. It was a pleasant image.

"I apologize for the file Dingles sent her," Harbour replied, chuckling over her recall of its length. "Without being able to step aboard the JOS, there were personal items that my people were requesting."

Jessie laughed with Harbour. "There were so many of those items that I was forced to divide them among the crew and send them out shopping. I've had male crew members buying feminine products probably for the first time in their lives."

Their banter over the next quarter hour did a great deal to ease Harbour's anxieties. When she closed her comm unit, she entertained thoughts of casual moments in Jessie's company. Those musings accompanied Harbour into her dreams.

Q-Gates

The Jatouche tech, Kractik, began her console shift at the Q-gates. She was assigned the position of relief console operator to back up one of the four operators, if needed. It was late in the evening and traffic had slowed at two of the gates. Boredom quickly set in for Kractik, while she stood around, as the operators handled the flow in and out through the other active gates.

To busy herself, Kractik picked up, one by one, the small devices resting on a translucent canopy covering. She ran through each device's test procedures to ensure they were ready for use. When her hand lifted the third piece of equipment, she froze. Barely visible through the milky canopy was the glow of a power light.

Immediately, Kractik called her supervisor, Kiprick, who hurried from below onto the dome's floor. Kractik had removed the remaining tools, and she pointed to the dim light below the canopy. Kiprick slipped the locks of the canopy, which covered the operations portion of the console for Q-gate number two.

The console was signaling that the other end of gate two at Gasnar was operational. Without hesitation, Kiprick called the dome commander and informed him of the emergency. Soldiers spilled out from the level below and surrounded the platform of gate two. They stood at the ready, beam weapons trained on the stage. Kiprick was confident the console's warning of incoming Gasnarians would allow him the necessary time to alert the soldiers to the impending invasion.

Travelers, queuing to return to their worlds and those incoming, looked on in alarm at the soldiers surrounding the gate, which had been inoperable for as long as memories served. Of the six Q-gates operated by the Jatouche, four were in constant use. One was constantly guarded against more incursions by the Colony, even though the last attack was more than twenty annuals ago. This gate, number two, had been inoperative for more than four hundred annuals.

Kiprick hurried below and placed a call to the dome's senior administrator, who, at present, was on the Jatouche home world, Na-Tikkook.

"Pull the data from the console, Kiprick," Jaktook ordered, after listening to what Kractik had discovered. "We must know how long the other end of the gate has been operational."

"At once," Kiprick replied. He placed the administrator's call on hold and used the dome's comm system to connect to the relief console tech.

"Query the console, Kractik," Kiprick said urgently. "When did it first record the far gate was operational?"

Kractik bent over the console and touched panels, tapping in the request. "Point seven three four annuals," Kractik replied in awe.

"How can that be?" Kiprick questioned.

"One moment," Kractik replied. She ran her query again. "Confirmed, Supervisor. Approximately four-fifths of an annual."

"Thank you, Kractik," said Kiprick. He relayed the information to the dome commander, who, after due consideration, retired two-thirds of his force, leaving the same number of soldiers guarding gate two as guarded gate five, which led to the world of the Colony.

Kiprick picked up the call to the dome's administrator and repeated what he'd learned.

"You're sure?" Jaktook asked.

"Kractik is an eminently qualified tech," Kiprick replied. "She ran the query twice, and I've no doubt she varied her input to ensure the console understood her request. As we know, the Messinants designed the consoles to be intuitive of our needs. I believe we can trust the response that Kractik received."

"Understood, Kiprick. Update me if anything changes. It goes without saying that the canopy cover over gate two's portion of the console should be left off and an operator assigned to the station."

"Kractik is due for promotion. I would suggest that she receive the operator assignment to monitor the gate," Kiprick replied.

"She's young," Jaktook objected.

"She's qualified, and she's diligent. Without her efforts, the Gasnarians might have flooded through the gate and caught us by surprise," Kiprick replied.

"I leave the decision to you, Kiprick. Be careful. This news will unsettle His Excellency and his advisors, and they'll want extensive precautions."

"Understood, Jaktook," Kiprick said and shut down his call. He understood Jaktook's reservations. Kractik was his daughter. Despite that, she worked harder than most to demonstrate that favoritism wasn't applicable to her, and he felt he had held her back long enough. He looked forward to promoting her, only wishing it was under more favorable circumstances.

Planetside, Jaktook placed a call to the royal residence, regretting the late hour. He would be disturbing senior individuals, who would be forced to leave the comfort of their pallets and the warmth of their mates.

"His Excellency is asleep," Jaktook was told.

"And Q-gate number two is active," Jaktook replied. There was silence on the other end. Then he heard, "I'll wake His Excellency and assemble the advisors. I presume you'll be in attendance, dome administrator."

"I can be at the royal residence within the hour," Jaktook replied.

* * * *

Jaktook called for a vehicle. The transport organizer tracked Jaktook's movements and had the car arrive at his domicile, as he exited the extensive complex. It whisked him away, and Jaktook took the opportunity to organize his thoughts. Rarely did an administrator hold an emergency session with His Excellency and senior advisors.

At the royal residence, security admitted Jaktook, allowing the vehicle to drop him off underground, where he was checked a second time by personnel. Finally, security escorted him to the royal chambers, which was located on the uppermost floors of the building.

Jaktook stood in an antechamber, waiting to be announced. It was a while before the ornate doors, carved in vine patterns, slid aside and a senior security person motioned him inside. Jaktook crossed the room toward the seated individuals, while trying to prevent staring at the sumptuous furnishings. He'd never been in the royal residence, much less His Excellency's private chambers.

"Ah, Dome Administrator Jaktook," Tacticnok said, rising to welcome Jaktook.

The poor administrator was caught in the middle of what he hoped was a graceful bow to His Excellency Rictook, as he hastily straightened to accept the greeting of the royal family's daughter. Jaktook returned the greeting and took the seat that was offered him.

"Jaktook, let me introduce His Excellency's advisors," Tacticnok said. "To your left is Master Economist Pickcit. To your right is Master Scientist Tiknock, and beside me is Master Strategist Roknick. Now that we're acquainted, please tell us the details of your discovery."

Jaktook related step-by-step the events that had taken place at the dome, as related to him by Kiprick.

"What is your confidence in the accuracy of what you've told us?" Tacticnok asked. It was a testament to the daughter's importance to His Excellency and the Jatouche that she was conducting the meeting. Not only was she the heir apparent, but she was His Excellency's most trusted advisor. His Excellency hadn't spoken, and it was accepted by Jaktook that Rictook probably wouldn't address him.

"Kiprick is a most competent supervisor, Your Highness. It was his daughter, a relief console tech, who discovered the Gasnar gate was active."

"And you say that the console has recorded the Gasnar gate as having been active for the past four-fifths of an annual?" Master Scientist Tiknock asked.

"Yes, Master Tiknock," Jaktook replied.

"Incredible that the console operators didn't observe the change, during all that time," Master Strategist Roknick grumped.

"I would have thought the reason for that was obvious, Master Roknick," Tacticnok replied. "If I'm correct, the console operator group is entirely male."

"I fail to understand your reasoning, Your Highness," Roknick replied.

"It's simple, Master Roknick," Tacticnok replied. "The tech who discovered the lit panel, which was buried under a canopy and a pile of equipment, was female. Obviously, females are more diligent and detailed in these types of duties. As we've discussed, the His Highness is well aware of the potential of our female population even if others are slow to realize their capabilities."

Roknick bit back his reply. This was an old argument that he'd fought many times with His Highness and the royal daughters, especially Tacticnok. To his and other Jatouche senior personnel's frustration, not a single male had been born to the royal couple. Instead, they had four females, and the three younger females were as determined as Tacticnok to break with traditions that seniors believed had served the Jatouche well for millenniums. To make matters worse, His Excellency Rictook wholly supported his daughter's efforts.

"My question is this: Could the Messinants have returned?" Roknick asked. As the strategist, who guided the military commanders, he was anxious to understand if the gate might have been repaired by the ancient race.

"Has anyone heard from any civilization that a Messinant has been seen in recent memory? They've been gone for eons," Pickcit, the economist, objected.

"I'm wondering why the gate has become operational now," Tiknock, the scientist, pondered. "The fight at Gasnar was more than four hundred annuals ago. Could the Gasnarians have recovered?"

"That seems unlikely," Roknick replied. This was the type of conjecture that made him nervous. "The last reports from our soldiers indicated the Gasnarian planet was engulfed in upheavals from the force of our energy weapon."

"I'm familiar with those historical reports," Tiknock said testily. "They also indicated that there were Gasnar ships around the moon, ships capable of preserving life."

"But for the hundreds of years it would take the planet's atmosphere to clear?" Pickcit asked.

"Impossible for them to survive, I say," Roknick declared.

"It was sad that our relations with the Gasnarians came to such a violent conclusion," Pickcit lamented. He saw the loss of economic opportunity to both worlds.

"We didn't start the fight," Roknick said, his tone hardening.

"Advisors," Tacticnok said calmly, and the seniors quieted. She waited until she had their attention before she continued. "We're not here to argue the past or what our ancestors might have done differently. We're here to discuss what the activation of gate two's far point means to the Jatouche. Then we're to come to some conclusion and suggest actions for His Excellency to consider."

Tacticnok received apologies from the advisors. She glanced briefly at the dome administrator. Most individuals, who were in His Excellency's presence for the first time, were usually frozen in posture, with eyes downcast. In contrast, Jaktook was intent on the advisors' words, and, rather than observing passively, his face reflected the approving and disapproving thoughts flickering through his mind.

"So, the question stands: Who could have reactivated the gate?" Tacticnok asked. "Trusted advisors, you've reviewed the historical documentation many times, I'm sure. What were the final conditions at Gasnar? Exactly how was the gate shut down?"

There was a shuffling of feet, crossing and uncrossing. Tacticnok noticed that the frown on Jaktook's face reflected her own.

"The records are vague on that point," the master strategist admitted. "There was only the single gate at Gasnar, which meant the console was to be the focus of the attack, while our soldiers deployed an energy weapon against the planet. The fight was protracted. Several teams were sent before they managed to complete the weapon's set up and fire it. The last team to enter the Q-gate from this side carried an assortment of tools and weapons.

None of those individuals returned, which leaves us guessing as to how they accomplished their task."

"At that time, scientists postulated that if the Gasnarian Q-gate were demolished, it would have been a cataclysmic event," Tiknock said. "More than likely the energy would have surged along the quantum connection, resulting in the destruction of our gate and hence the dome. They calculated that the detonation would have destroyed a good portion of our planet's satellite, Your Highness."

"Doesn't this speak to the Messinants' return?" Pickcit asked. "Who else would have the expertise to repair what our people had cunningly stopped?"

"If only we knew how the gate was finally disabled," Roknick lamented. "The last group to make it back were techs. They brought some of the wounded with them. The dome protected our few remaining soldiers, when our energy weapon was destroyed along with everyone at the deployment site. According to the techs' statements, the last soldiers at the dome were attempting to provide Pinnick, a console operator, with precious moments of protection. It was said that he had an idea how to disable the console. Our dome supervisor reported that after the techs and wounded returned to Jatouche, they anxiously waited and watched. Finally, one of our console operators announced that the Gasnar gate was deactivated."

"I find the construction of the domes and gates confounding," Tiknock, the scientist, said. "Consider gate five. If the Messinants had designed our dome with six separate and distinct consoles, which would individually power each gate, we could have shut down gate five against the Colony's incursions, hundreds of years ago. Instead, one console powers and controls all our gates."

"I agree," Pickcit echoed fervently. "What were the Messinants thinking? This is an ancient race capable of raising an innumerable number of species from forests, deserts, and seas to achieve sentience. And, somehow they envisioned these species intermixing with only peaceful intentions."

"For such an ancient, powerful, and technologically advanced race, the Messinants strike me as unbelievably naïve or full of hubris, take your pick," Roknick added in disgust.

"It appears we're at an impasse as to how we should proceed, now that the Gasnarian gate is operational," Tacticnok stated. "We don't know why or how the gate was activated, but I think it's time we found out. I propose a small team make the trip."

"To accomplish what?" Master Scientist Tiknock asked with interest.

"First and foremost, we must answer the question of who activated the gate," Tacticnok stated firmly.

"What if the Messinants are there?" Pickcit asked.

"That's highly doubtful," Tiknock replied. "I believe that race played geneticists for millenniums with the creatures of many worlds, raising them into sentience. Then they tired of their activities and moved on, leaving all of us to make our own way. No, I'm definitely a proponent of the idea that a new race has discovered the dome and repaired it."

"If Tiknock is correct, we have linguists and sophisticated communication devices that can facilitate a conversation with this new species," Tacticnok offered.

"That's if these aliens give us an opportunity to communicate," Roknick groused. "They could be even more cunning and dangerous than the Gasnarians."

"That seems improbable," Pickcit replied. "Of our six gates, only two connected us to aggressive species. The ratio is even more palatable when you consider the connections of the other races, which have multiple gates."

"I would venture to say that the species who repaired the Gasnar gate is technologically superior, which enabled them to deduce the console's problem and repair it," Tiknock reasoned.

"In which case, it would be better to visit Gasnar before they learn to operate the console and visit us," Tacticnok said. "If they are as superior as Master Tiknock imagines, it would serve us well to play the part of gracious neighbors and greet them first. I'll lead a small team to investigate."

An uproar ensued, at least as much of an uproar as could be demonstrated in front of His Excellency.

Tacticnok waited for the advisors to air their objections. In the meantime, she noticed a toothy grin on Jaktook's face, and she smiled at him.

When His Excellency Rictook raised his fingers a few degrees off his lap, the advisors immediately quieted. He turned toward his daughter, who leaned close to hear her father's whispers.

"His Excellency approves of me acting as the emissary to Gasnar for the Jatouche," Tacticnok announced. "Thank you, advisors, for your precious time at this late hour."

The meeting's attendees rose and waited for Rictook to leave the audience chamber. The advisors were arguing, as they left the royal residence and headed to the subterranean levels, where they could command transports.

Jaktook had let the advisors precede him out of the room. He had no desire to share a car with them to the lower levels. That small delay allowed Jaktook to catch Tacticnok's signal to remain. As he expected, the advisors never looked back to see if he was in their presence.

"Your Highness," Jaktook said, dipping his head politely, when the doors of the audience chamber slid closed behind the advisors.

"In public and in company, that is my address, Jaktook. When we're in private, I'm Tacticnok. I noticed that you didn't always approve of the opinions offered by the advisors."

Jaktook couldn't tell which of Tacticnok's statements threw him off more, or maybe it was all of them. However, he chose to tackle the most dangerous one. "I meant no disrespect Your ... pardon, Tacticnok —"

Tacticnok interrupted the administrator's apology. "Be at ease, Jaktook. That wasn't a criticism. I'm interested in hearing your thoughts."

Tacticnok noticed Jaktook's hesitation, and she sought a means of convincing him of her sincerity. "Here," she said indicating a comfortable lounge for two. "Sit with me."

Jaktook couldn't have appeared more uncomfortable if he had sat on a bed of spikes, but he did as he was bidden.

"I'm not my father, Jaktook," Tacticnok began. "Royalty's formality can be stifling ... personally and publicly. Over time, that has to change. The activation of the Gasnarian gate is an opportunity to show the people of Jatouche that members of the royal household can take a hands-on approach to governing this planet. We don't have to be locked here in this metal tower and protected at all costs."

Jaktook wasn't sure of what sort of response was required of him. On this subject, he opted for keeping his mouth shut.

"What are your thoughts, Jaktook?" Tacticnok asked, staring at him intensely.

"I agree with Master Scientist Tiknock. Those who repaired the gate are neither the Messinants nor the Gasnarians, and they might or might not be technically sophisticated."

"Explain," Tacticnok requested.

"It was a console operator, essentially a tech, who supposedly disabled the gate," Jaktook replied, warming to a subject that he had long considered. He was one of the Jatouche who yearned to ascend to a higher level in society. In his spare time, he researched many subjects, modern and historical. "And time was short. What options do you think he had?"

Jaktook couldn't believe he was treating the royal daughter as if she were a new console operator that he was training. But the expression on Tacticnok's face said that she wasn't offended. She wore a frown, indicating she was deep in thought.

"I think I see where you're leading, Jaktook. With the fight taking place beside him and his comrades dying, the operator would have only moments to accomplish what he intended. And, he wasn't a scientist or engineer. His approach wouldn't have been an attempt to render the console inoperable via its programming. It would have been elementary and direct."

Jaktook smiled and his head dipped approvingly. Tacticnok beamed in reply, but the smile quickly left her face. "How does this answer the question of whether this new species is technologically adept or not?" she asked.

"It doesn't," Jaktook said apologetically. "What it does is make a case for the alternative argument."

"Ah, I understand. If our tech did something simple, which might have had a devastating effect on the nearby soldiers involved in the fight, it would mean the console's repair would be simple," Tacticnok reasoned. "But then the Gasnarians could have made the repair too."

"That's a distinct possibility, but an improbable one," Jaktook replied. "I believe that the Jatouche operator disabled the console, and it collapsed the dome. When the Gasnarians saw their planet disrupted and their dome and gate deactivated, I believe they descended into anarchy and consumed themselves. They would have had no home and no place of refuge. Within a year, they were probably nonexistent as a species."

Tacticnok shivered at the thought of the ugly ending that the Gasnarians met, but Roknick was correct on this one issue. The Gasnarians had started the fight.

The Jatouche were a much more advanced species when the two races met. The Gasnarians were cordial and earnest in their greetings. Over the years, they worked hard to learn the Jatouche culture and master the technology. They became advanced pilots, engineers, and techs, always focused on the technological positions.

Then, one day, the Gasnarians made their move. They flooded through the gate in droves, weapons eliminating everyone. Once they had control of the dome console, they flooded out onto the shuttle base via the transports. Most Jatouche pilots electronically locked the Gasnarians out of their shuttles' bridge controls and died for their sacrifices. The Gasnarians loaded those shuttles that they had commandeered and headed for the Jatouche home world, Na-Tikkook.

To our historians, the Gasnarians' grand plan remains unclear. The invaders were heavily outnumbered. Within a quarter annual, all shuttles were returned to Jatouche control, and the dome retaken. At the time, the predominating thought was that it was simply the Gasnarian nature that was at fault. Their base instincts were compared to dangerous animals, and, despite the genetic manipulations of the Messinants, those aggressive tendencies remained. While they might have pretended to possess polite mannerisms, those merely masked their predilection for domination over others.

Tacticnok shook herself out of her reverie. "I find your ideas refreshing, Jaktook, and I've decided you'll accompany me on our investigation. What do you say?"

Jaktook was severely shaken and squashed any immediate response or visible reaction. He freely admitted he was essentially a passive male, one who was at peace with administrative positions. Flying in the face of that comfortable existence was the offer of a royal daughter to perform a field operation, perhaps a dangerous one. It didn't seem as if he had an option, and he chose to make the best of it. "It would be my honor, Tacticnok," he replied.

"I'm pleased that you joined the expedition, Jaktook," Tacticnok said, rising from her seat, and the administrator hurried to stand.

"I want the tech who discovered the lit panel on board too," Tacticnok added.

"The tech, Kractik, has been promoted to console operator," Jaktook replied.

"Well deserved, I'm sure. Make the necessary arrangements with her supervisor," Tacticnok ordered. "I'll be in touch, Jaktook," she added, as she gestured toward the salon's exit.

-6-
Gasnar

Tacticnok joined her father in his royal sleeping quarters, and the aging monarch dismissed the servants.

"A bold move, daughter," Rictook commented. "The advisors were unsettled."

"How is it that not one of these elevated males thought to suggest we investigate the Gasnarian dome?" Tacticnok retorted.

"Perhaps, they presumed my head-strong daughter would do that anyway," Rictook replied, laying a hand on his daughter's cheek.

Tacticnok smiled at the gentle rebuke, but the fierceness in her eyes quickly returned. "I spoke with Jaktook at length, father. It's obvious that he's studied the events at the Gasnarian dome. His counsel was illuminating."

"What did you learn?" Rictook asked, stretching out onto a comfortable, elevated pallet.

"Jaktook offered an alternative perspective on the capabilities of those who might have repaired the gate based on what we could have done to shut it down," Tacticnok said.

"Interesting analytical approach," Rictook replied. "I didn't find the advisors' arguments for superior beings to be convincing."

"Neither did I," Tacticnok replied. "Jaktook thought the argument for superior beings was weak. He favored the idea that a simple, but effective, shutdown of the console could easily be reversed by a less technologically advanced species. He answered the question of why the Gasnarians didn't repair the dome by saying they would have witnessed the disappearance of the dome itself. With few of them left and the planet's surface becoming uninhabitable, the remaining Gasnarians would have withered like old fruit on the vine."

"A chilling image, daughter."

"Sorry, father. Those were my words, not Jaktook's," Tacticnok replied. "I've requested he accompany me on our passage to Gasnar, and he has agreed."

"Who else do you intend to recruit for your team?" Rictook asked.

"The tech, Kractik, who discovered the gate's activation, has been promoted to console operator. I will take her."

"Who else, daughter?" Rictook asked. His aging, but piercing, eyes stared intently at Tacticnok.

"We will need a competent linguist," Tacticnok added, thinking through her needs. These were the discussions with her father that she relished. He curbed her enthusiasm and tendency for immediate action with questions that made her think before leaping. She glanced at her father and recognized the expression that said he was still waiting.

"That's four noncombatants, when you include me, father. For protection, we'll need four well-trained military personnel to guard each of us." When Rictook nodded his approval, Tacticnok quickly added, "Soldiers who can take orders from a female."

* * * *

In less than one lunar cycle, Tacticnok had worked out the details of the expedition to Gasnar. Master Scientist Tiknock had calculated the hour of their trip based on Tacticnok's request that they arrive at the Gasnarian moon while the dome was bathed in early starlight.

"Are you ready, Jaktook?" Tacticnok asked. Although it was late evening by Na-Tikkook's clock, she was hoping for an enthusiastic response from the administrator that would dispel some of her own fears.

While Jaktook searched for the right response, Kractik piped up, "I'm ready, Your Highness. I can't wait to get started."

The linguist and four guards, who were to accompany Tacticnok, dubiously eyed the young console operator.

"Well said, Kractik," Tacticnok replied, casting a determined expression at her entourage. "After we arrive at Gasnar, if we encounter resistance, by that I mean weapons fire, we must defend Kractik, while she resets the console for our return. If there is no aggressive action, but an alien presence, no one is to move. Stay calm. Jittak, your men are not to raise their weapons or otherwise intimidate them. Our linguist and I will attempt to placate the aliens and get them speaking."

"And if there is no alien presence, Your Highness?" Jittak asked. He was the one officer present. Tacticnok had lost that argument with her father, when she had pushed for four common soldiers.

"Then, we'll have an opportunity for Kractik to collect console information and observe what evidence we can of who might have repaired the gate," Tacticnok replied.

"And the length of our stay, Your Highness?" Jittak requested.

"As long as I wish," Tacticnok replied, her eyes boring into the military officer's until he ducked his head in acknowledgment.

"One more important item before we depart," Tacticnok added. "After we arrive at Gasnar, you'll not address me as Your Highness or show deference to me in any manner whatsoever. It's critical that the aliens not recognize me as an important individual. I'm merely the head of an investigative team. You'll call me by my name, Tacticnok. Am I understood?"

Confusion was written large on every face, but that of Jaktook's. He quickly announced, "Completely, Your Highness. We'll be most casual in address and treatment of you on the other side."

Jaktook's quick smile had added to the others' consternation. It had been ingrained in Jatouche since infancy on how to address and act in the presence of a royal family member, if ever that moment came about. Now, they were being told to drop those decades of habits and act in a most unusual fashion with a royal daughter, who would be in close proximity to them.

Jittak managed to save some face, when he replied, "My soldiers will do as you request, Your Highness, and they'll remember to demonstrate the correct obeisance when we return." He glared at his three soldiers to make his point.

"Let's go," Tacticnok announced, and the eight Jatouche stepped onto the gate's platform. She pointed a finger at the console operator, who dutifully activated the gate's beam. Energy from the platform speared the dome's shield, merged with it, and the Jatouche disappeared.

The console operator glanced at Kiprick, the dome supervisor, who stood beside him. A forlorn expression on the young operator's face indicated that he felt he had done something wrong to send a royal family member into unknown circumstances. In commiseration, Kiprick laid a steady hand on the operator's shoulder. That his daughter accompanied Tacticnok made him no less troubled.

When the Jatouche appeared at Gasnar, it was all the soldiers could do not to raise their weapons in readiness, but no one wanted to disobey Her Highness' directive.

"Well, this is disappointing," Tacticnok said, surveying the empty dome. Her gaze fell on the bodies lying around the dome's floor.

"What do you make of this, Jaktook?" Tacticnok asked, indicating those who died in battle. "The gate has been repaired, but the dead remain."

"Recall our earlier conversation, Tacticnok, about the probabilities of the race not being as superior as the advisors proposed," Jaktook replied.

Concern was exchanged in the expressions shared by the other team members. Evident in the administrator's words was that he had conversed privately with a royal member, and they or he had contradicted the advisors' learned opinions. The expedition was turning out to be surprisingly revealing, in more ways than one.

"The aliens managed to repair the gate, but they were confounded by the bodies in some way," Tacticnok mused. "Unable to decide what to do with them, they chose to leave them."

Jittak's training engaged, and he overcame his reticence to communicate with the royal daughter. "Tacticnok, I would suggest fear was the reason. If I understood what you and the administrator are proposing, then I could imagine a young race, who might be shocked to discover beings unlike themselves. They would see the encumbrances and equipment on two types of bodies and could well imagine a fight."

"Excellent reasoning, Jittak," Tacticnok said. "A young race. Does that not fit your thinking, Jaktook?"

"It does, and Jittak's thought of the aliens fearing the bodies makes sense," Jaktook replied.

"But why abandon something as impressive as a Messinant dome?" Tacticnok asked, gazing around at the civilians for answers.

"What if this young race has managed to travel the stars in another manner, possibly by ship?" Kractik asked.

"Wouldn't that suppose they were a superior race?" Tacticnok queried.

"For that question, I've no answer, Your ... I mean ... Tacticnok," Kractik replied. "It was my thought to convey an idea as to how this young race might have arrived at Gasnar and why they might have had no experience with other sentient species. These bodies would have been their first indication that they weren't alone in the universe."

"That would be frightening indeed," Tacticnok agreed. "Well, come, before Jittak's nerves are stretched too thin by our standing here and discussing aliens." She spared a glance for Jittak and chuckled.

As the Jatouche climbed off the platform, Tacticnok ordered. "Kractik, the console. Jittak, have your soldiers load our dead. Our linguist can accompany them on the return."

While the soldiers began gathering the bodies of their fallen and loading them on the platform, Tacticnok turned to Jakkock, the linguist. "Perhaps on the next trip you'll have an opportunity to use your skills. For now, you're accompanying these bodies to prevent a panic at the sight of them. By now, the dome supervisor will have erected a curtain around the gate two platform, which should limit exposure to the other gates' passengers. Maintain calm and request the transport of the bodies in containers so they remain invisible to journeyers."

"Understood, Tacticnok," Jakkock replied and climbed back onto the platform.

Kractik was busy querying the console for recordings, which would have been compiled as soon as the gate was activated, when Jaktook tapped her shoulder and pointed to the platform. Kractik saw the linguist waiting beside the fallen Jatouche, and she nodded, setting the gate for transmission. She checked a final time to ensure no one was ascending or descending the platform. Receiving Jakkock's nod, she activated the gate. With a rush of light, Jakkock and the Jatouche dead were gone.

"Now the next group of bodies, Jittak," Tacticnok said, while walking toward the edge of the dome. A soldier kept pace with her, his eyes constantly scanning for aliens that he feared would pop up from beneath the dome's floor at any moment. He hoped Her Highness couldn't hear the thunderous beating of his heart.

"The Gasnarians?" Jittak asked, incredulous at the request.

Tacticnok wanted to blurt, "Do you see any others?" However, she knew that the entire investigation was unorthodox, and she curbed her tongue.

"It's our theory that a young race has discovered the dome, inadvertently activated it, and fled, leaving these bodies behind," Tacticnok explained. "It's our duty to teach this race, to lead them, so that they will be valuable future partners. As the more advanced and superior species, we must demonstrate to these young ones a concern for all life. We can start to do that by removing every one of these bodies, ours and those who attacked us."

"As you wish, Tacticnok," Jittak replied, only barely curtailing in time his initiation of a bow. He ordered his soldiers to grab the Gasnarian bodies and load them on the platform. With the linguist having already returned, he felt comfortable sending one soldier with the dead.

"Recall Tacticnok's words to Jakkock," Jittak admonished the soldier. "See that you do the same when you return home."

Kractik waited for Jittak's approval before she sent the soldier and the Gasnarian dead to Jatouche.

Tacticnok was peering through the blue wall of energy that comprised the dome's hemisphere. She felt someone step beside her and nudge her arm. Raised in the rarified environment of the royal residence, Tacticnok was surprised by the intimacy of the gesture. But, when she glanced aside, she saw Jaktook quietly offering her an instrument.

A rush of embarrassment swept through Tacticnok. She had planned this momentous event to demonstrate to the Jatouche that a royal daughter could do more for their people than sit in their metal tower. Yet, she had arrived at Gasnar without a single device to aid her inspection. It told her much about Jaktook that he offered her his instrument out of sight of the others, and she gratefully took it.

"Kractik, air quality?" Tacticnok queried.

Quickly checking the console's environment monitoring, Kractik replied, "Standard conditions for us, as would be expected, Tacticnok."

Tacticnok signaled her helmet's release, and it slid above her face, over her head, and into its sleeve at the back of her neck. Automatically, her suit's air functions were curtailed. Bringing Jaktook's viewer to her eyes, Tacticnok scanned the rocky outcrops that surrounded this half of the dome.

Finally, she despaired of discovering anything and handed the viewer back to Jaktook. "Perhaps, administrator, I'm not the best qualified to observe the dome's exterior for indications of aliens. Tell me what you see," Tacticnok said.

Jaktook scanned beyond the dome. Unlike Tacticnok, who he saw had gazed at the cliff faces, he searched the cliff and cut outlines for anything that might stand out against the brightening horizon.

"There, Tacticnok," Jaktook said, handing the viewer back. He pointed with his arm, and Tacticnok leaned close to sight along it to where the administrator pointed. Her cheek touched his arm, and a small thrill shot through her at the unaccustomed touch of a male not of the family.

Tacticnok played the viewer over the same area. It took her a while to find the device that rested on the cliff edge. She had expected to see something substantial, not the small pile of equipment she found. "What do you think those are?" Tacticnok asked.

"Without examining the instruments closely, I could only hazard a guess, Tacticnok."

"I would welcome your thoughts, Jaktook."

"I believe the structure that projects upward is primitive equipment, designed to collect this star's light to power the instrumentation. Do you see the device with the small round disk on its face?"

"Yes," Tacticnok replied, keeping the viewer to her eyes.

"That would be early technology, which is designed to collect imagery. The aliens might have deserted the dome after activating it, but they put up a means of continuing to observe this place."

"Interesting," Tacticnok said. "Do you think they know the function of the Messinant domes?"

"Difficult to say, Tacticnok, what they thought. This might be their first dome. If so, how were they to know that there would be a second one, which was in quantum entanglement with this one? In the minds of early races, there is ample room for fear and wild imagination, without the knowledge that someday they might acquire."

"Tacticnok, I have the records we require," Kractik announced.

Tacticnok turned and caught Jittak's hopeful expression. "Yes, Jittak, we're leaving. Kractik, set the gate for transmission," she ordered.

Kractik programmed the platform for a delayed activation. She waited until everyone was in place, and then she tapped the console's panel and hurried to join the others. The platform's energy spiked, melded with that of the dome, and sent the Jatouche home.

7

Aliens

When Rictook received word that the last of the investigating team had arrived at Na-Tikkook's dome, he breathed a sigh of relief for the royal daughter's safe return. He wasn't the only one. The people were well aware of Her Highness' intentions and worried, while she was gone.

After arriving home, Tacticnok took the initiative to organize the review of the records collected by Kractik. She requested Jaktook, Kractik, and Jittak accompany her on the shuttle flight planetside.

In the shuttle's hold were the dead recovered from the Gasnar dome. The bodies would be examined by medical scientists, who would report on anything of value to the military.

The day after landing, Tacticnok convened a meeting at the royal tower. It was held one floor below the royal chambers in a room dedicated to data reviews. Comfortable pallets and lounges ringed an array of monitors. Consoles provided techs an opportunity to display a host of different types of recorded information.

Jaktook ordered a transport and collected Kractik and Jittak, who had never been to the royal tower. He tried to project an air of confidence to his comrades, although he didn't feel it. Royal guards led the threesome from the transport level to the tech presentation room.

On the entrance of Jaktook, Kractik, and Jittak, Tacticnok rose immediately to welcome them. She could see their nervous demeanors and sought to ease their concerns by making casual introductions with her father's advisors. Unfortunately, the senior individuals, with their taciturn responses, didn't help the situation.

In order to disturb the advisors' complacency, Tacticnok directed her team to various positions. "Kractik, you'll control the replay of the Gasnar console data. The tech seated there will show you the controls. Jittak, please sit there." Tacticnok pointed to a place between two of the senior advisors, who were forced to spread apart and make room for the military officer.

"Jaktook, join me," Tacticnok added, sitting on a raised pallet and patting the space beside her.

While Kractik received instructions from the console tech, Tacticnok reviewed for the advisors what the team had found at the Gasnar gate.

"You're sure of your assessment of the monitoring equipment?" Master Scientist Tiknock asked.

"I'm sure," Jaktook replied. "As curator of the city center's historical technology wing, Master Tiknock, you're familiar with early optical devices. I've spent many hours perusing that fine display of ancient technology. At Gasnar, I observed examples of primitive instrumentation: an optical device, a solar power array, and a transmission tool."

Tiknock preened at the compliment and graciously nodded his acceptance of Jaktook's assessment of his Gasnar observations.

Well done, Jaktook, Tacticnok thought.

Unbeknownst to anyone but Tacticnok, Rictook sat quietly in a nearby room reserved for his exclusive use. He was able to monitor the meeting room's conversation and observe any data the participants watched. He chose to stay apart from the others in order to allow the individuals a free exchange of ideas without his royal presence intimidating the non-advisors.

Another reason for Rictook's isolation was that he was proud of his daughter, and he wanted her to have this moment. Although he was unsure of what next steps the Jatouche should take, he had no doubt that Tacticnok would provide an abundance of suggestions.

"Ready, Your Highness," Kractik called from the console.

"Begin," Tacticnok ordered.

The meeting's participants saw the imagery start with a brief flash of light before dust and debris occluded the visuals.

"I've never seen this conducted on such an incredible scale," Tiknock said, "But, I imagine, once the dome was energized, the sensors detected material on the floor and emergency procedures were initiated."

When Jittak, who was sitting beside the aging scientist frowned at him, Tiknock added, "After centuries of being open to celestial dust, the dome cleaned itself."

Jittak nodded his thanks. It was a note to Tiknock that those who made the trip to Gasnar, brave as they were, did not have the tremendous knowledge possessed by the advisors. But, rather than feel superior, he decided to instruct the young ones as best he could. No doubt there would be other expeditions to Gasnar, and he, for one, would certainly not be among them.

"Bipedal and four limbs," Master Strategist Roknick observed, when the dome cleared. "Cumbersome-looking suits," he added.

Tacticnok glanced at Jaktook and offered him a quick smile. The administrator had correctly offered the idea that the race, which activated the dome, might be young and technically inexperienced.

"I don't understand. What are these antics?" Jittak asked after the group watched the aliens test the dome's screen with a tool, then spread out and search the console, the dome's floor, and the space beyond.

"These aren't antics. They're confused," Jaktook explained. "They have no idea what they've initiated, and they're now enclosed in a Messinant dome, with no concept of its operation."

"Kractik, move the imagery forward until you see a change in their methods," Tacticnok ordered.

The participants watched the imagery speed past. Time was compressed as the aliens tired of their search and lay down on the dome's floor to rest. When their activity resumed, one of the aliens removed its helmet in panic. Shock was obvious on the faces of the other aliens, who rushed to that one's side.

"Why are the aliens frightened by removing their helmets?" Jittak asked.

"Much of Jaktook's conjectures have been most accurate," Tiknock said, tipping his head to the administrator. "These aliens had no idea the Messinants supplied breathable air when the dome was cleaned. The one who removed the helmet had run the suit's tanks empty. It removed its helmet, because it was suffocating. It expected to die."

Tiknock's words stunned the group. For millenniums, the Jatouche led lives that were well-protected. The only dangers had come from the Gasnarian invasion, which was repelled, and the occasional incursion by the Colony through gate five. To the relief of every Jatouche, soldiers and technology had contained the Colony's attempts to gain a foothold in the dome.

"This is akin to watching dumb beasts struggle to escape a crevice in which they've fallen and can't escape," Master Pickcit commented. "If I didn't know they would eventually free themselves, I'd stop watching."

"I'm most sorry for the angst these aliens felt, but does anyone else find this particular race as visually unappealing as I do?" Roknick asked.

Tacticnok bristled at the comment. "And how do you think we would appear to them, Master Roknick?" she asked.

"Perhaps, Master Roknick would prefer the company of the Colony," Pickcit offered. He spoke his comment in jest, softening it with a light tone, but his steady stare said that he too found Roknick's comment to be unwarranted.

From that point in the imagery, Kractik hurried it forward again. The aliens removed their helmets, searched the dome again, and lay back down to rest. More time passed before one of them stirred, shook another awake, and that one hurried to the edge of the dome.

"Why is that one waving its limbs and waggling its digits?" Jittak asked.

"I would surmise that it's some form of primitive communication to an individual outside the dome, who has discovered the missing comrades," Tiknock offered.

"If their comrades were nearby, why didn't the aliens call for help? Doesn't every race know how to communicate through the dome's energy wall?" Roknick asked. "The Messinants left instructions in the console on how to construct the devices to do that."

"Master Roknick, I don't believe you've been following the essence of our conversation," Tacticnok said firmly. "It has been proposed by my team members that the alien race we've discovered is a young one, far less advanced than us. Furthermore, this might be their first evidence that they're not alone in the galaxy. They're at a loss to understand what they've encountered."

Tacticnok deliberately left out the part that Jaktook was the one who had proposed the idea. She didn't want the advisors focusing any resentment on the administrator. *I will apologize to Jaktook later,* she thought. It took her aback that she intended to offer her regrets to a nonroyal for an insignificant slight. *But that's what's required,* she admonished herself mentally.

Kractik advanced through the imagery. By now, the participants were totally engrossed in trying to understand the aliens' actions. They directed Kractik constantly. At times, she would reverse the imagery's advance and move to a different perspective.

In the other room, Rictook smiled at the intense discussion, and took a moment to acknowledge his decision to remain apart from the meeting.

"Is that alien ill?" Jittak asked, when he witnessed one of them collapse.

"Kractik, where are we on the timeline?" Tacticnok asked.

"Using Gasnar time, Your Highness, the aliens are entering their planet's third rotation of being trapped inside the dome," Kractik replied.

"Unless their suits recycle fluids as efficiently as ours, they would need a constant supply of water," Roknick suggested.

"And I've not seen them take any fluids," Tacticnok noted.

"None," Pickcit agreed.

"They're becoming dehydrated. That's why the one alien collapsed," Tiknock reasoned.

"It's good to see the others care for the one who's in trouble. It does speak to the compassion that they exhibit for one another," Tacticnok said.

"The fallen one might be their leader, and they would risk retribution if they didn't care for that one," Roknick countered.

Kractik forwarded the imagery again until Tiknock interrupted her.

"Aha, there," Tiknock exclaimed, pointing at the display. "Kractik, if you would? I need a close view of the console."

Kractik manipulated the dome's imagery. This was one of the many incredible features of a Messinant dome. When activated, the hemisphere recorded all motion within it — from every perspective point of the dome.

It was also one of those secrets that the races who used the gates had been unable to unravel.

Kractik sought an eye-level view to the left of the alien, who was investigating the console. She froze the image and glanced at Tiknock, who bobbed his head in appreciation.

"See there!" Tiknock said excitedly. "A telltale double spiral. The Messinants know this species."

"This is perplexing," Jaktook said.

"Isn't it?" Tiknock agreed.

"Explain," Tacticnok requested.

Tiknock graciously indicated with a hand that Jaktook should go first.

"We can see that this young race has no experience with a Messinant dome," Jaktook said. "Yet, the console holds a record of their genetic identity. Otherwise, the dome's egress-ingress panel wouldn't have activated. But, if the Messinants knew of this race, why didn't they build them a Q-gate?"

"It's possible the Messinants never uplifted this race," Tiknock proposed. "These aliens might have been discovered by the Messinants after they exhibited sentience."

"Considering the length of time the Messinants have been gone and this species' weak technological achievement, wouldn't there have been ample time for the Messinants to build them a gate before they could have been observed?" Pickcit asked.

"Difficult to say, Master Pickcit," Jaktook replied. "Perhaps the Messinants observed traits about these aliens that caused them to have reservations about building them a Q-gate."

"It could have been as simple as the alien's home world had no available satellite on which to build," Jittak offered.

The group murmured their agreement of the possibilities. They were developing many more questions than answers.

"If this race has no experience with Messinant domes and they are now at Gasnar, how did they get there?" Tacticnok asked.

In the next room, Rictook leaned forward in expectation of the answer to that question. This was one that he wanted asked, and he commended his daughter for thinking of it.

"I believe, Your Highness, the only plausible answer is that this race has found a means of traveling between the stars without gates. In which case, it means they have ships that can make the journey," Tiknock reasoned.

"Kractik offered us this very concept," Jaktook said, nodding toward the tech. "However, I would qualify your response, Master Tiknock. If this group were to possess ships that could travel between the stars at will, then their technology should be much further advanced. I believe you're correct about your assumption that they've accomplished the arrival at Gasnar by ship. But, do you recall the proposal by Gitnock?"

"Yes, Jaktook," Tiknock replied. "If memory serves, Gitnock offered the concept that we could expand our civilization to other star systems by virtue of colony ships. It would be a costly construction project, and the effort's outcome might never be known."

"Explain in more detail, Jaktook," Tacticnok requested.

"Colony ships would have been huge vessels. They would have sailed to another star for centuries. The Jatouche would have lived aboard for generations or be kept in some form of hibernation until they arrived. Then they would have attempted to develop a new world."

"What happened to this idea? I don't recall it," Tacticnok replied.

"The concept was proposed hundreds of years ago, Your Highness," Tiknock replied. "It's commendable that Jaktook has knowledge of it. Essentially, the idea went nowhere."

"The concept was fraught with multiple problems," Jaktook explained. "We had the gates and could travel to the stars without risking our people aboard ships that might never safely make landfall."

"It sounds incredibly dangerous," Tacticnok said. "And this is how you're proposing these aliens arrived at Gasnar?"

"My concern," Pickcit interrupted, "is why these aliens would have chosen to take on such an incredible gamble with their futures? What conditions existed on their home world that they would build these ships and launch them into the unknown? More to the point, if those conditions were extremely unsettling, a society in turmoil, did they bring those difficulties with them?"

"This species might be technologically inexperienced, but they managed to cross the vast distances between stars. That makes them a most resolute species," Roknick added, "which could make them more dangerous than the Gasnarians."

"I take your meaning, Roknick," Tiknock remarked. "Here are these aliens, investigating a foreign site, with their bodies festooned with weapons, and they evince no concern for their ailing comrades."

Roknick glared at Tiknock, but the master scientist merely chuckled in reply.

Kractik hurried the imagery forward. They watched the aliens converse with their arms and digits, rest, wait, and converse some more. Eventually their comrades gained entry to the dome, and the entire group left. Soon after, the dome's recording of events ended.

"Kractik, confirm the timing of these recordings," Jaktook requested.

"The dome was activated and, within a few rotations, it was abandoned some four-fifths of an annual ago," Kractik replied. "Without any more activity, the console contained no further recordings."

"The aliens have been waiting and watching, all this time, to see what activating the dome had initiated. I wonder what they think of what they've just witnessed with our visit," Jaktook mused.

* * * *

"I would hear your thoughts, daughter," Rictook said.

The meeting's participants had returned to their work or homes, as the case might be, and Rictook and Tacticnok had retired upstairs to the royal chambers.

"I was wondering, as we came up here, what our reactions might have been if we had discovered what these aliens found," Tacticnok said, reclining on a comfortable pallet that was raised above the floor and which offered an armrest and pillow at one end.

Rictook eased onto his pallet, taking a few moments to adjust his position. When supported, he sighed, regarded his daughter, and said, "You're referring to an inactive dome, undoubtedly covered in hundreds of annuals of stardust, with the dead of two different species on the deck."

"That's what I'm imagining, father," Tacticnok replied.

"Probably not much different than what you witnessed in the console's recordings. The true question is: Would we have had the ingenuity to reactivate the dome?"

"I can't help thinking of the incredible fear they must have felt when the dome was energized, and they realized they were trapped inside. Yet, they remained calm and found a way to exit themselves through the use of the console and with the help of their comrades," Tacticnok said.

"You admire them," Rictook remarked, and Tacticnok tipped her head in agreement. "Give me your advice, daughter. What should we do?"

Tacticnok had been thinking on this ever since she set foot on the base of the Gasnarian dome. Every piece of evidence added to her conviction that there was only one possible course of action. But Tacticnok was her father's daughter, and he was the ruler of the Jatouche. As such, he must be presented with all viable options.

"I see three courses of action, father," Tacticnok began. "We can wait and hope that the aliens never realize the purpose of the gate and never learn to operate the console. There is every reason to think they'll be satisfied with monitoring the dome for fear of what it might represent."

"Do you think that is a viable option, daughter?"

"No, father. These aliens are adventurous and curious, and they're not without skills. Eventually, they'll overcome their fear, and they'll learn to activate the Q-gate. Then they'll appear here at Na-Tikkook, and we'll be forced into a reactive posture. I don't recommend that."

"And the second?" Rictook asked.

"Master Roknick holds a hostile opinion about the aliens. If we trust his instinct, we should command the Gasnarian dome, while we are able."

"And your opinion of this line of action?" Rictook asked.

"In the short term, it would guarantee there would be no intervention from these aliens into Jatouche space. In the long term, they'll see our actions as an invasion of their territory. They might not have weapons now, but our incursion will guarantee that they develop them. By the time they come for us, their anger will run deep, and they'll attack with a vengeance."

Rictook leaned back, considering the potential outcomes of such an option. "My primary concern would be that if the aliens attack the Gasnarian dome with sufficient weaponry power, they might destroy the Q-gate. I fear what the energy flashback might do to our end of the gate. We could lose our entire dome and the links to the alliance worlds," he mused.

"That has been the concern of scientists for every militaristic action taken by the enemies of the alliance," Tacticnok agreed. "Consider this, father. If we take this option of attacking first, there's the possibility that the aliens take back the dome without destroying it. With the bitterness they'll hold, we'll never be allowed to return. To them, we'll always be their Colony."

Rictook shuddered at the thought of becoming a sentient race's nightmare. "Which means, more than likely, one day they'll learn to use the gate and attack Na-Tikkook. Then, we'll have two enemies appearing through our gates."

Rictook sipped on his fruit juice drink. "I await your third option, daughter, and hope for relief from these dark thoughts your words have engendered," he said.

"The third option, father, is to visit the Gasnarian dome and show ourselves. We take provisions and use the dome's facilities, while we wait," Tacticnok replied.

"And what would this team do, while it waits?" Rictook asked. He was careful not to speak using the same word his daughter had used. He wasn't ready to include her in the team.

"Our team would know they're being monitored. Their purpose would be to gesture to the aliens to meet with them," Tacticnok replied.

Rictook felt it was time to discuss the one point he'd been evading. "I presume you'll propose to me that you should lead this expedition."

"Father, you know this first meeting will be crucial. The encouragement to the aliens to speak with us must carry the right tone. There must be no intimidation. The greeting must be warm and cordial. Once language translation is established, communication must be clever and exacting. It would be foolish to give away too much information about our race. A careful balance must be struck between hospitality to the aliens and concern for our citizenry. Whom do you see, father, who can be responsible for those measured steps over a period of time?"

This was his daughter's response that Rictook feared. It was a succinct prediction of the intricate steps that would need to be taken during first contact and would require a firm but delicate guiding hand. Worse, Tacticnok was right. Rictook could think of no other to lead the team.

8

Emperion

The *Honora Belle* and Jessie's three mining ships rendezvoused at Emperion, Pyre's second moon. The medium-sized moon was covered tens of meters deep in frozen gases, which were in great demand by the YIPS to power its processes and whose final products were critical to every ship, the stations, and the domes.

This was the second run to Emperion for the partnership of Jessie and Harbour. During the first operation, the crews had spent weeks designing a method of sucking up the slush with heat pipes, loading transfer tanks attached to shuttles, offloading them outside the *Belle*'s bays, maneuvering them into the bays with small vehicles, and pumping the pressurized gases from the transfer tanks to the *Belle*'s tanks.

The colony ship's lower decks were outfitted with row upon row of dry tanks, which had held water and gases for the 50,000 colonists who'd made the journey from Earth. Those tanks had long been empty. This made them the perfect containers for Emperion slush. In contrast to Jessie's single slush-carrying transport, the *Pearl*, the *Belle* could carry hundreds of times more product than Jessie's ship.

For the first venture, the primary limitation was the scarcity of supplies to keep the operation going. That wasn't a problem now. At the JOS, Jessie's ships had loaded extra crew, families, and supplies from the list compiled by Harbour and her people. After making Emperion, it took days to ferry the people and supplies from Jessie's ships to the *Belle*. The transfers included two young teenage empaths whom security had reported to Harbour.

When the ships had reached Emperion for the first time and restarted the six-month quarantine clock, the mood was somber but hopeful. It was the opportunity of crew to spend their downtime aboard the colony ship and enjoy the new cantina that relieved the long months. Even spacers working on the *Belle* considered it downtime. They could retire to comfortable cabins and relish the fresh food grown in the colony ship's extensive hydroponic gardens.

The enormous payout of YIPS coin in return for the delivery of the *Belle* and *Pearl*'s slush into personal accounts had transformed the crews' expectations. Every ship was a hive of energetic activity. Once again, Jessie divided his crews between slinging slush and supporting Dingles' ever-growing list of needs. Jessie's spacers found themselves helping Harbour's people open deactivated hydroponic gardens, supporting the artisans' decorating of cabins, and performing maintenance duties.

The spacers' spouses and partners, who had transferred to the *Belle*, found active lives, and, if the children thought they were to be spared activities, they were seriously mistaken. Several residents were engaged to open classes. There was a wealth of talent to pull from, including techs, engineers, spacers, horticulturists, and many more.

Many of the disenfranchised, who had spent years aboard the *Belle*, unable to earn livings on the JOS or the YIPS, discovered they were in demand again. The list of tasks was endless — more systems online; more people to accommodate; more food to grow, cook, and serve; children to educate and provide daycare; a cantina to run; and entertainment to provide. Slowly, the colony ship was resurrected and transformed — a near derelict becoming a home.

Unlike the first trip to Emperion, when weeks were lost to the design and engineering efforts to accommodate the slush transfer, this time the operation was fully underway in less than a week. And, the best part of all, the *Belle* and Jessie's ships were alone at Emperion.

For the most part, Pyrean mining ships were single-owner, captain ships. The captains needed a guaranteed haul. So, they chose to make for the inner belt and a load of ore, always hoping for a rich metal strike. Jessie and his spacers knew that it was only a matter of time before the other mining ships attached tanks and made for Emperion. Jessie calculated and shared with Harbour that they had one or two more runs, which would be eight to sixteen months, before the competition showed up.

"Good thing there's more slush than thousands of ships could carry," Harbour had remarked.

"Generous of you to speak up for our competition that way," Jessie had remarked. "Now, I want you to think about the price of slush when those competitors begin offloading their slush at the YIPS."

"Oh," Harbour had uttered.

* * * *

Harbour stood with a group of spacers in the *Belle's* cantina. The spacers held drinks in their hands, while Harbour enjoyed a green, a mix of herbs, vegetables, and other ingredients that replenished an empath's sensitivities.

The spacers wore their odd assortments of downtime gear. Underneath the gear were the ubiquitous skins, body-fitting unitards that protected the wearer against the chill of life topside, stations or ships. Spacers often possessed basic black skins. To differentiate themselves from stationers and announce their independence, they covered their skins in choice pieces of fabrics during downtime — colorful vests, a decorative hat, or a print skirt, to name a few items — and it often made no matter whether male or female which items they wore.

Harbour's stand-up table was surrounded by other spacers, who were accompanied by spouses or partners. Residents who had wholeheartedly adopted the spacers were in attendance too. They could be differentiated by their choice of clothing, casual layers of fabric, most of them woven from plants grown in the hydroponics gardens.

The residents had formed a band, of sorts, for some live entertainment. The instruments were a hodgepodge of items scavenged from the ship. And, it must be said that they weren't too bad. They maintained a lively rhythm, if not a little too much enthusiasm in their performances.

What everyone was enjoying was the new ambient air temperature. Ever since Harbour had come to the *Belle*, which was as a young teenager when her powers had reached an intolerable level, she had dressed in many layers to ward off the chill. Now, with more systems coming online, coin in the general fund, and reaction mass in the tanks, there was an opportunity to raise the air temperature by seven more degrees, and Harbour took advantage of it, much to everyone's appreciation.

"I want us to think about this ship's escalating need for reaction mass," Harbour said to her group of spacers.

"You thinking of adding more people, Captain, or are we turning this ship into one of them fancy spas like on the JOS?" Dingles asked.

"I'm thinking of independence, Dingles," Harbour replied. "For the foreseeable future, this ship has been permanently quarantined because security can't figure a way to perform a blowout on it. Now that the commandant has realized we're transferring personnel between Captain Cinders' ships and the *Belle*, he's issued another edict that all of us are quarantined for another six months."

"Good thing we intend to be out here for longer than that," Danny Thompson, the *Belle*'s pilot, replied, hoisting his drink, and the spacers cheered and chased down some of their own.

"Seriously, Captain, you thinking of buying some of the YIPS propulsion mass after they've processed our slush?" Bryan Forshaw, the propulsion engineer of the *Belle*, asked.

"Does seem a little ridiculous, doesn't it?" Harbour commented. "What would it take to process Emperion slush aboard the *Belle*?"

More than one spacer choked on his or her drink. They loved their captain. She possessed every characteristic they could wish for regarding a leader — someone who cared for the crew and someone who put coin in their pockets. But a spacer, she wasn't. Harbour had never trained as one and had never worn a vac suit, which meant she'd never walk on a moon or outside a ship in an airless environment until she achieved the ratings.

"Captain, you risk spreading this ship in little pieces all over Pyrean space," Bryan replied, after he'd cleared his throat. "Processing frozen gases is dangerous business."

If Bryan thought he'd managed to curtail Harbour's idea, he was sadly mistaken. It was the fact that Harbour wasn't a spacer that she didn't think like one.

"Fine," Harbour replied. "We don't process it inside the *Belle*. We process it outside."

"Outside where, Captain?" Dingles asked, thinking he'd missed a crucial part of the conversation.

"Over Emperion, at our own processing station. We build a mini-YIPS," Harbour replied, as if it were the simplest thing in the world to do.

"Captain, there's an old saying about learning to walk before you run," Dingles replied. "We've earned a good amount of coin, but we'd need a great deal more before we could design and construct our own processing plant."

"Understood, Dingles," Harbour replied evenly. "Now listen carefully. I'm serious about having access to a supply of reaction mass that doesn't require us sitting off the YIPS and buying our own product back. If you don't like my idea, come up with alternative ones."

Harbour received a round of assent from the table. They recognized that Harbour was thinking ahead for them, even if some of her ideas were a little unrealistic.

Sensing the mood shift in her spacers, which hadn't been her intention, Harbour chose to bring up a lighter subject. "By the way, I've not been able to decide what to wear over my skins during downtime at the cantina. Any suggestions for me?"

"Um, captains don't tend to join the crew when it comes to that tradition," Dingles said.

"Well, there's always a first time," Harbour rejoined.

The male spacers ducked their heads or found somewhere else to look, and Birdie broke out laughing.

"What?" Harbour asked. She detected embarrassment from the men and unabashed amusement from Birdie.

"I believe our males have already made their opinions known on that subject, Captain, more than a little while ago. It seems they appreciate your skins as they are," Birdie replied.

"Oh, so you like Makana's designs, do you?" Harbour asked, with a straight face.

A *Belle* artisan by the name of Makana had decorated Harbour's flat-back skins with silver filigree that came off the shoulders and down the outside of the arms. It also initiated from inside the arms at the wrists, ran up under the arms, and then down past the outside of the hips to the ankles. It was beautiful work, and it wonderfully accented Harbour's figure.

Harbour could sense the waves of mortification from the men, and she deliberately kept a neutral expression on her face.

Birdie was unsure how to respond. In her mind, she received pulses of bubbling humor that she recognized Harbour was sharing with her. Joining in the moment, Birdie replied, "Yes, captain, the men are very appreciative of anything that's well designed."

That did it. The two women cracked up. Despite the men's mortification, they laughed good-naturedly at themselves and toasted their captain.

Harbour detected a rapid shift in Dingles' emotional output. His comm unit had chimed, and he'd glanced at the message. A frown furrowed his brow.

"Captain, maybe you and I should visit the bridge," Dingles suggested.

Harbour heard the casual manner in which Dingles spoke, but the angst pouring off him was palpable to an empath. She made her excuses to the spacers, and, after passing through the cantina's doors, they walked briskly toward the colony ship's bridge.

"Problem?" Harbour asked.

"Don't know, Captain," Dingles replied. "The message requested my presence on the bridge and asked that I hook on.

"I've heard that phrase used before," Harbour said, recalling times when Dingles and Ituau Tulafono, Jessie's first mate, used the phrase. "Seems to be spacer shorthand."

"It is, Captain. Between spacers, it requires the listener to drop what they're doing or saying and follow the speaker's lead. The correct and only expected response is *aye, latched on.*"

"Looks like I'll need to add learning the lexicon of spacer shorthand to my long, long list of things to learn about being a captain and a spacer," Harbour replied, with no little chagrin.

"Little steps, Captain. Everything will come with time," Dingles replied.

"That works, Dingles, if circumstances allow me the time."

Dingles had no reply for that sentiment. He knew some of what his captain was dealing with concerning the commandant and the governor. That was enough for him to appreciate the complex and powerful machinations arrayed against the colony ship. As he quick marched toward the bridge beside Harbour, he sincerely hoped that the text to him had exaggerated the seriousness of the situation.

"Report, Monty," Harbour ordered, as she strode onto the bridge.

"Captain," Michael "Monty" Montpellier replied hurriedly, jumping up. He'd expected only Dingles to respond to his text. The ex-third mate and retired spacer was a new hire. He'd wanted to join the *Belle*'s first excursion but personal obligations prevented him. Dingles had promised to pick him up if there was another opportunity.

"I've been on duty for second watch a few hours, Captain," Monty explained. "I was going through my checklist of required bridge routines and logging my observations. I got to the last one, and that's when I discovered that."

Monty stepped aside and pointed to a small monitor off to the right side of the extensive bridge operations area.

Soon after Jessie had set up the monitoring equipment overlooking Triton's alien dome, Dingles had assigned the array's output to a central monitor of the *Belle*'s bridge operations. Over time, when nothing changed on the screen and as more and more of the colony ship's functions were brought online, the output of the Triton dome monitor was relegated to smaller and smaller monitors off to the side. Finally, the array's output was nearly hidden from view.

Harbour and Dingles crowded close to the small monitor.

"Uh-oh," Dingles muttered.

Harbour stared at the image of the blue energy field that formed the alien dome. The platform, console, and highly carved, metal deck were as Jessie and his team left them nearly a year ago. The only difference in the otherwise unchanging image was that the bodies were gone.

"Dingles, check the log of the first watch," Harbour ordered.

Dingles took a seat at the panel used by the ship's officers. He pulled up the log from the first watch. "The Triton dome monitor was checked three and a half hours into the watch. No change was reported."

"Is there an image record with the entry?" Harbour asked.

Dingles pulled up the entry and the attached image. "Aye, Captain, bodies are there," Dingles replied.

"Pull the array's recording from the last entry until now. I want to replay it to a small audience in the captain's office tomorrow. You'll be joining me." Harbour started for the bridge exit and then stopped. "And, Dingles, I want that array's signal output on a central monitor, and I want it left there."

Dingles found his response of, "Understood, Captain," attempting to catch Harbour's retreating back.

"Dingles," Monty said, after Harbour left. "I'm not up on what Captain Cinders and his crew found and did on Triton, except that it was all about aliens. What I'd like to know: Is it possible the bodies disintegrated with age, and that they're gone because they're just so much dust on the deck?"

Dingles looked at Monty and shook his head, a worried expression on his face.

"I was afraid of that," Monty replied. "Thanks for the honest answer."

Once in her quarters, Harbour snatched the comm unit off her hip. She placed a call to the *Spryte,* Jessie's ship.

"Captain Harbour, Nate here," the second mate replied.

"Nate, is Captain Cinders available?" Harbour asked.

"The captain is downside on Emperion," Nate replied. "Word is the crew turned in early, what with it getting dark. Captain Cinders is expected back aboard the *Spryte* at first light. Is there a problem, Captain?"

Harbour ignored the question and asked one of her own. "Nate, do I have the correct list of people who investigated the dome? Captain Cinders, Darrin, Belinda, Rules, Tully, and Hamoi."

"That's correct, Captain," Nate replied, a sinking feeling forming in his gut.

"Please communicate, at the earliest moment, to Captain Cinders that I'm requesting those six individuals aboard the *Belle* for midday meal," Harbour said.

"Midday meal, Captain?" Nate asked, perplexed at the invitation.

"Yes, Nate, an important midday meal," Harbour replied and ended the call.

Everyone who Harbour was requesting was downside, except for Darrin, who was aboard the *Annie*. There would be a crew member awake in the shelter, who would be monitoring comms. Nate called the shelter and left a message for Jessie.

* * * *

Jessie woke from a good night's rest. That normally wouldn't be the case after a shuttle ride down to Triton and hours walking and hopping around in a vac suit, while inspecting the slush processes. He rolled up from his cot, stuck his feet into deck shoes, and eyed the shelter crew. Most of them were either finishing breakfast or cleaning up. He was late.

The reason for his restful sleep and the crews' good mood sat upright on the next cot. Sitting in her customary cross-legged position, Rules was doing her best to prep the crew for the day's hard work that was to come.

Jessie heard from Yohlin Erring, the *Marianne*'s captain, that it would come to a fight if anyone was to ever slight Rules. That went double if security attempted to take her from them, as they were intending to do, if offered the opportunity.

Mining was hard work; space mining was harder. Spacers aged prematurely from the wear and tear on their bodies. Rules couldn't help her crewmates in that regard, but she could ease their perceptions of the aches and pains. Rules was one of the most powerful empaths ever discovered, and she was only a teenager.

Belinda Kilmer, who Rules had cured of space dementia, brought a tray of hot food and drink to Jessie's side.

"Sleep well, Captain?" Belinda asked.

"You can wipe that smile off your face, spacer," Jessie growled. "You know we all did." Jessie glanced toward Rules, and she flashed a bright smile at him. "That goes for you too, spacer!" Jessie added.

The crew's response ranged from snickers to guffaws, and Jessie was forced to shake his head and grin. His tough demeanor hadn't convinced anyone. Much of that was due to Rules' influence, but the crew knew his complaints were so much camouflage.

Jessie quickly worked through his breakfast, and Belinda picked up his tray for recycling. That's when the spacer, who had been on comms duty during the night, flashed Jessie's comm unit. Reading the message, Jessie felt the contents of his stomach roil, and he worked to keep his food down.

Aurelia sensed the shift in Jessie's mood. Her eyes darted to him, and, just as quickly, the sheltered crew focused on Jessie too.

Jessie put a false smile on his face. "Apologies, everyone," he said, glancing at Aurelia, "I should have read the entire text before I reacted."

Aurelia took the hint and resumed her broadcasting, which slowly took effect on the crew. But, she wasn't fooled. Jessie's concerns were still detectable.

"Looks like some of us are invited to midday meal at Captain Harbour's table," Jessie said. "How fortunate a precious few are?" Jessie punctuated his statements with the lift of a single eyebrow, and the crew jeered and laughed at his antics.

While the crew used the facilities and prepared to return to work, donning their vac suits, Jessie carefully and quietly notified Belinda, Hamoi, Tully, and Aurelia that they would be joining him for the meal.

It was Belinda who asked Jessie, "Is Darrin invited too, Captain?"

When Jessie nodded, Belinda tucked her lower lip between her teeth.

"Cheerful expression for the crew, Belinda," Jessie quietly admonished.

Jessie and his spacers trekked to the *Spryte*'s shuttle and lifted for the *Annie*. He called Captain Erring to let her know he needed Darrin for a visit to the *Belle*.

"The spacer network is way ahead of you, Jessie," Yohlin replied to his request. "Selecting the crew members who were trapped with you in the dome is akin to broadcasting a distress signal. Did Captain Harbour give you a reason for your special meal?"

"No, it could be a celebratory affair," Jessie posited.

"And that's what you believe?" Erring asked.

"No, but it's what I'm hoping is the reason," Jessie replied.

"What did we do to deserve to be the ones to discover an alien dome?" Yohlin asked rhetorically.

"Because we're the most intrepid of Pyrean miners?" Jessie offered, which generated a chuckle from Yohlin.

"Darrin will be suited and waiting in the airlock when you dock your shuttle, Jessie. I can't wait to receive your post-meal message."

Jessie picked up Darrin and made the *Belle* with a half hour to spare. By the time they cycled through the airlock, dumped their vac suits into lockers, and made their way to the captain's quarters, they were on time.

"Thank you for coming on such short notice," Harbour said, by way of greeting Jessie and his spacers. She stepped aside to indicate the table, which was well-laid with dishes, cutlery, and drink glasses.

Jessie had hoped to have a private word with Harbour before the meal, but it looked like she had other ideas.

"This looks fabulous, Captain," Belinda announced, passing Jessie and gently nudging his arm.

"Absolutely," Darrin agreed, and greeted Dingles before taking a place beside the *Belle*'s first mate.

Aurelia held her hands out to Harbour, and the two empaths shared a brief exchange, which brought warm smiles to their faces. Aurelia had sought to detect Harbour's underlying emotions, but, as was the captain's custom, her broadcasts were tightly controlled.

"Captain Cinders," Harbour said. Her tone was an earnest entreaty to Jessie to join the others.

"Thanks for the invitation, Captain," Jessie replied graciously. He gave Harbour the slightest of smiles and took a place at the table.

It was obvious to Jessie and his crew that Harbour had gone to extraordinary lengths to make the meal a pleasurable affair. The setting was pleasant, but it was the food and drink that overpowered the spacers' senses. Meals aboard the *Belle* provided spacers with the rare treat of fresh food instead of their preserved meals. But, the people who had prepared this meal had outdone themselves, and the quiet at the table, except for the clinks of utensils and the occasional murmur of appreciation, was a testament to the spacers' enjoyment.

When the dishes and glasses were cleared, Harbour rose and said, "If you'll come this way, I have something to show you."

Jessie's crew glanced toward him, but he walked purposefully toward Harbour's study, which she'd indicated.

In the study, Belinda commented, "This is nice, if not a little ..."

"Dark," Harbour supplied. "I've been reviewing the records of the *Belle*'s voyage. Every captain in the rotation was male. I believe this study was designed with their tastes in mind."

The guests sat in comfortable seats, while Harbour remained standing. Dingles positioned himself to the side of Harbour's desk and busied himself accessing something on his comm unit. A large monitor slid up from inside Harbour's desk. It faced the seated individuals.

"Last evening, it was reported that there was a change in the image from the Triton dome," Harbour said. "Dingles and I looked at the array's output, and there was a change. Dingles pulled the recorded material from the bridge's first watch entry and it indicated no change."

Jessie raised a finger to interrupt, but Harbour lifted her hand partway. "No one else, including me, has seen the recorded output of the array. I thought it only fitting that this group discover it together with Dingles and me."

Harbour nodded to Dingles and took a seat beside Jessie.

"I've set the recording to fast forward until motion is detected," Dingles said, as the image of the Triton dome, as Jessie and the crew had left it, popped on the screen. The image appeared static, except for the occasional trickle of dust that fell in front of the vid's lens.

Then light flared from the platform, merged with the dome, and eight figures appeared, bathed in bright blue light.

"Oh, for the love of Pyre," Darrin managed to gasp out.

When the energy from the platform diminished, the figures held their positions, frozen in a strange tableau.

"Well, now we know the platform's purpose isn't for entertainment," Jessie remarked.

"Out of thin air ... a gate," Tully, the survey engineer, marveled.

"Incredible," Hamoi, the tech, agreed. "I wonder if it's quantum coupled or if there are multiple destinations."

"Spacers, I think we need to focus on the aliens who've appeared, for now," Belinda admonished. "You can debate the fine points of the fabulous technology later."

The group watched in fascination as the aliens spread out. Jessie immediately picked up on the leader, and he kept his eyes on that one.

"They're recovering both sets of bodies," Harbour commented, when the second group was loaded on the platform. The Pyreans watched the energy of the platform couple with that of the dome, as each group left. They saw first one alien, a second, and then a third approach the edge of the dome. The darkened helmet on the one that Jessie had identified as the leader slid over the alien's head.

"Well, now we know what the little ones look like rehydrated," Darrin commented.

"Furry," Belinda added.

"A smart one," Jessie murmured. There was no doubt that the third individual had spotted the monitoring equipment, using some sort of device to study it, and pointed it out to the leader.

After more minutes of viewing, the last group of aliens boarded the platform, and an individual at the console hurried to join them before the group disappeared in a glow of bright blue energy.

In the study, silence ruled, before Harbour finally turned to Tully and asked, "What did you mean about a gate?"

"Gates were a theoretical proposal by physicists as a means by which people could travel between the stars. The concept postulated that two gates would be quantum entangled, and, as such, would always exist in a sort of intimacy with each other that would negate the enormous distances that they might be apart," Tully explained.

"Essentially, travel between quantum-coupled gates would be instantaneous," Hamoi added, his excitement showing.

"I would suggest that the concept isn't so theoretical," Harbour said, turning around in her seat. She stared at the dome's bare deck, now devoid of bodies. She couldn't get the little aliens' furry faces and large eyes out of her mind.

"Well, there is one good bit of news. We don't have to worry about contamination from the dead bodies anymore," Darrin quipped. His delivery was dry, and no one laughed.

"I made a call to aliens," Hamoi said in wonder, reflecting on his activation of the console.

"Don't sound so proud of yourself, spacer," Darrin reprimanded. "Didn't you notice the four individuals who constantly guarded the other four, or, perhaps you thought those were compound sprayers they held in their hands?"

Quiet returned to the study, but the silence was soon interrupted by Jessie's questions, "Why nearly a year? We know there was a fight at the dome, and it was destroyed during the struggle. These aliens, the little ones, must have been the visitors to this world. Regardless of whether they were the aggressors or the aggrieved party, they should have wanted to know immediately who had activated this end of their gate. So, why wait a year to return and take a look?"

"It does cast the little aliens in the more passive role," Harbour reasoned. "Maybe they knew immediately that this gate was active, and they were ready to repel the attackers who they expected to flood through their end of the gate. Then, when no one came, they decided to take a look. It was an extremely cursory visit, and they left nothing behind."

"That we know of," Hamoi said.

When the group turned to look at Hamoi, he added, "I'm just saying that they had a tech at the console the entire time. Who knows what that individual programmed into the console for this gate to do? Maybe this dome is set to monitor us."

9

Broadcast

Jessie and Harbour excused their people to resume their duties. The pair of them sat in their same chairs in the study, staring at the image Dingles left on the monitor. It was a dome swept clean of dust by the site's activation and, now, swept clean of bodies by visiting aliens.

Neither captain had thought to ask the spacers to keep what they saw to themselves. It wasn't the way either of them operated. But Harbour had instructed Dingles to block comms to Pyre: the stations, the ships, and the domes. Jessie had issued the same instructions to Ituau and Captains Erring and Hastings. For the moment, they had containment of what had been seen by those at Emperion.

"We don't have much time to make a decision, do we?" Harbour asked.

"A day, at most. After that, those at Pyre will be wondering why they can't reach us, and that might create more problems than we can handle," Jessie replied.

"More problems than that?" Harbour asked, gesturing at the monitor.

"I don't think there's a bigger problem than that," Jessie replied, tipping his head toward the image of the alien dome.

"Did you ever wonder if we were alone in the universe, as the only intelligent species I mean?" Harbour asked.

Jessie mulled over the question and then replied, "Prior to discovering the Triton dome, I'd given it much thought. I think I didn't dwelt on the subject because I was too focused on my work. And you?"

"Never gave it much thought either. I can't imagine I'd find anything in the *Belle*'s library," Harbour mused.

"What?" Jessie exclaimed in mock surprise. "No files labeled 'In case of aliens, read this!'"

Harbour laughed and slapped Jessie's shoulder, and he grinned unashamedly back at her. Harbour felt her power rise, and she hurriedly curtailed it before it could slip out.

Jessie's face became still, and he stared at Harbour. "It tries to get away from you, doesn't it?" he asked.

"Because our power is a part of our personality, empaths have to be ever vigilant. When we relax, we openly broadcast our emotions. It kind of takes the fun out of being around normals," Harbour replied.

"Maybe it doesn't have to always be that way," Jessie said.

It was Harbour's turn to stare at him.

"I've watched the *Annie*'s crew with Aurelia," Jessie finally said. "Her powers coupled with her personality are a win-win situation for them. They revel in their wakeup calls. You can hear the creak and pop of joints, as they rise, but they wear these goofy expressions, as if none of it mattered."

"Your tone says you don't approve," Harbour said.

"For them, I'm happy," Jessie allowed. "I just don't know if I could ever get used to it."

"You feel that you would never know when you're being manipulated," Harbour surmised.

"Something like that," Jessie replied.

"I imagine that without much training, Aurelia is broadcasting to the entire ship or shelter," Harbour offered, "which means that you received her ministrations. Did that bother you?"

"It's different with Rules," Jessie replied, shifting to the crew's name for Aurelia.

Harbour had noticed that Jessie often did this. In his mind, Aurelia was the young girl who had become Pyre's political pawn, but Rules was his crew member. To Jessie, there were definitely different associations attached to the two names.

"You're saying that you can trust an empath. It just depends on the individual," Harbour said. She arched an eyebrow at Jessie, who caught it, but turned to observe the alien dome image rather than reply.

Jessie understood the point Harbour was trying to make. To him, there was a vast gulf between a young, naïve girl, with a big heart, and a mature woman, responsible for the safety of thousands and captain of a colony ship.

"What do you intend to do about it?" Harbour asked.

Jessie was still working on the distinctions between the two women and was caught off guard by the question. "What?" he asked.

"About the aliens who came and went," Harbour said, pointing to the monitor. She sent the slightest amount of power, carrying her humor to Jessie. She hadn't meant the aliens, when she asked him what he was going to do, and she'd enjoyed his moment of confusion. Jessie's reactions demonstrated to her that he could accept a relationship with one empath, albeit on a simpler emotional level. The challenge for Harbour was that Jessie thought of Rules as a comrade, and she hoped to play a more intimate role.

Jessie felt the tickle of mirth, a contrast to Harbour's neutral expression, and he grinned at her, catching what she'd done. "Yes, the aliens," he said and nodded, turning back to the monitor, even while he continued to smile.

"I think we have only one option," Jessie said, after a moment of consideration.

"Broadcast Pyre-wide, as is our duty as captains," Harbour finished for him. "Afterwards, we can talk about what we're going to do about them."

Jessie's mouth fell open to hear Harbour quoting the articles. She grinned at him, tapped his shoulder, and headed for the main salon.

"Not funny," Jessie called after her, and he heard her mellow laughter.

＊ ＊ ＊ ＊

Birdie set her cup of caf beside the bridge comm panel and belched appreciatively. Food aboard the *Belle* was a continual delight to the aging spacer. But better than the food was the company of spacers, once again. And, if that wasn't enough, life couldn't have become more interesting.

Birdie composed her broadcast that would alert all of Pyre, the stations, the ships, and the domes, to the forthcoming message from Captains Harbour and Cinders. When complete, she angled one of the colony ship's enormous antennas in the direction of the JOS, ensuring the beam was wide enough to encompass the YIPS. There was no guarantee that the ships working the inner belt would receive the transmission, but the spacer rumor mill would take care of that soon enough.

Tapping a comm panel icon, the announcement was sent. Birdie picked up her caf cup, chuckling into it before she took another sip. Life had become pure pleasure to the aging spacer.

A few minutes before the appointed hour, Harbour and Jessie stepped onto the crowded bridge.

"It seems a great many of your ship's systems are in need of monitoring, Captain," Jessie commented drily to Harbour.

"Big ship ... a lot of systems," Harbour replied, in kind.

At the entrance of the captains, the spacers had crowded to the bulkheads to stay out of their way and hoping not to be thrown off the bridge. That's when Jessie noted that a few faces belonged to his crew members. He winced and heard Harbour's snicker.

"A lot of systems," Jessie murmured, by way of apology, after realizing his gaffe.

Dingles was seated next to Birdie, and he readied the array's imagery that would be sent as part of the broadcast.

On the hour, Birdie opened the comm system for the Pyre-wide broadcast. She hand signaled Dingles, who did the same to Harbour.

"This is Captain Harbour, with Captain Cinders," Harbour announced. "We're calling from the *Honora Belle* with another critical message for Pyrean citizens. At the end of our communication, we'll broadcast a vid record to authenticate what we're saying."

Harbour tipped her head toward Jessie, who picked up the narrative. "A year ago, my crew discovered an alien site on Triton, which we told you about in our broadcast then. We left the dome and the alien bodies on its decking that we found there. In an effort to understand what the dome's activation meant, I ordered a monitoring array planted, overlooking the dome."

"In order to better facilitate the site's monitoring," Harbour added. "The *Belle* upgraded the equipment's ability to transmit to the colony ship no matter the distance. Yesterday, nearly a year after the array was set up, it recorded something vital. A group of us watched eight aliens arrive inside the dome, recover the bodies of the dead aliens, and leave the same way they came."

Jessie continued the announcement. "It's tough enough to accept that we have proof that there are aliens in the universe. We understand how scary that might sound to everyone. But, on top of that, it's equally important to understand how the aliens came and went. It wasn't by ship. What you'll see in the vid is a bright light shooting up from what we call the platform. It merges with the dome and then the aliens appear. They exit the same way. According to our engineers and techs, they believe the purpose of the dome is to create a gate between worlds. It's a method of instantaneous transport."

"We don't know what the aliens' appearance means to us," Harbour offered. "As Captain Cinders said, it's a great deal to absorb. We'll continue to monitor the dome, and we'll update Pyre, if conditions change. The vid record of the events at the dome will follow immediately. The *Belle* out."

Birdie cut the bridge audio pickup, and Dingles began transmitting the vid record.

* * * *

In downside houses and offices, aboard ships, and in station shops, cabins and cantinas, Pyreans crowded around monitors to watch the vid of the aliens appearing and disappearing within the dome. Every part of the event was mind-boggling. There were aliens. They could travel instantaneously between the stars, and they didn't look like humans. They were short and furry.

Rufus and Idrian had independently heard and watched the broadcast. Soon afterwards, they were contacted by Lise to attend her. Now, they were listening to her on a comm call with the commandant.

"Do you think they could have faked the recording?" Emerson asked.

"To what end?" Lise replied.

"To scare everyone away from Triton," Emerson supplied.

Lise took a breath and blew it out. *Idiot,* she thought heatedly. "Why would they want that?" she asked.

"They might have found something valuable on Triton, and they want it all for themselves," Emerson replied.

"You do recall that the *Belle* and Cinder's ships have spent the entire past year at Emperion and sailing between that moon and the stations. If they'd found something of intrinsic worth at Triton, why aren't they there?"

Emerson didn't have an answer for that. The vid recording had rattled him to the point where he couldn't think straight. Previous to witnessing the aliens' appearance, he had plans that arranged for a comfortable life, just as soon as he caught the person who tried to kill him. But those plans seemed inconsequential in the face of the *Belle*'s recording.

"Commandant, get hold of your faculties," Lise said firmly. "This is a perfect opportunity for us. The populace will want a strong hand to guide them. We can make a case for a united Pyre and a single leader!"

Anger seeped into Emerson's mind, pushing aside the fear that had resided there since the viewing. "And I suppose that leader would be you, Lise?" he asked.

"Who else is qualified?" Lise replied smoothly, without missing a beat. "And I'll need a dependable commandant to keep order in security and ensure that only our enemies are investigated."

Finally, Emerson's brain was fully engaged. He didn't trust Lise. There was a part of him that wondered if Lise wasn't behind the intrigue to have him killed by Lily Tormelli, his coin-kitty. "I believe we have unfinished business, Lise. You owe me a list of streak distributors. Take care of that first, and then we'll talk about the future leadership of Pyre." Emerson quickly ended his call downside.

"He hung up," Lise announced, throwing her comm unit in disgust on the desk.

"Lise, it might be premature to push for a change in Pyrean leadership," Idrian suggested. "Everyone is shaken to the core about what the *Belle* recorded."

"You should hear yourself, Idrian," Rufus laughed harshly. "All I've heard from frightened individuals are words that speak of the vid recording, what the *Belle* recorded, or the colony ship's transmission. Not one of you has the guts to say aliens. So there are aliens. So what?"

"And that doesn't bother you at all?" Idrian asked, incensed by Rufus' attitude.

"You saw the same recording I saw, Idrian," Rufus replied. "Kick that sharp mind of yours into action. The dome is a gate, okay! Cinders explained that the platform was the receiving and sending part. It accommodated a small group of furry creatures."

"What's your point, Rufus?" Idrian asked.

"Just exactly how are the little furry things supposed to bother us?" Rufus retorted. "They arrive at the Triton dome, without a ship. That means they can't get off the moon."

"They could bring supplies through and build a ship," Idrian proposed.

"Which would take them how long?" Rufus shot back. "And how would they move the ship's massive engines from inside the dome to the assembly location. If anything, we have a lot of years before they're a problem for us, if ever."

Idrian thought on what Rufus was saying, and it occurred to him that there was a hole in Rufus' logic. "You're probably right, Rufus," Idrian replied calmly, settling casually into his chair's back. "That is, of course, if no one goes to help them."

Rufus started to object, but he was cut off by Lise's whispered, "Oh, for the love of Pyre." Lise's eyes were locked on Idrian, as she added, "Those fools at Emperion."

"They wouldn't," Rufus objected.

"They would," Lise riposted.

-10-
Distributors

"I don't know what's worse … thinking about those aliens who appeared at Triton or knowing what Emerson's doing with Lise Panoy," Lieutenant Devon Higgins remarked, when he finished playing the latest recording of the commandant's downside call for Major Liam Finian.

Devon had been ordered to secretly record Emerson's communications, when Liam first suspected intrigue between the commandant and then-governor Markos Andropov. Those suspicions had proven to be correct. Even though Markos and his head of security, Giorgio Sestos, were arrested and convicted of their crimes, Devon had never stopped the illegal recording of Emerson's downside calls.

"We can't do anything about the aliens," Liam replied. "Let's focus on the commandant. He's still after the streak distributor's list, which means he's never stopped running his own investigation into Lily Tormelli's suicide. And, as long as Lise Panoy's expedited shipping request is on hold, she'll acquiesce to his request."

The two security officers were ensconced in Devon's office, with the door locked and the wall of window glass darkened.

"I feel like I'm sitting on a rich ore strike but don't have any means of extracting the metal and making some coin," Devon complained. "What's the good of knowing the game the commandant's playing if we can't use it against him?"

"Would you rather be kept in the dark?" Liam asked.

"No," Devon replied dejectedly.

"Maybe we're going about this all wrong," Liam mused. "If we can't introduce these recordings, then we need to think of another way to put the commandant in jeopardy."

"What's your idea?" Devon asked.

"I don't have one, but I'm thinking we might have someone who would," Liam replied. "Call Sergeant Lindstrom in here."

"You sure you want to involve someone else, Liam? We could be risking Cecilia's career."

"Do it, Devon. We'll approach the subject sideways. Maybe we can get her help indirectly."

After Devon made the call, the men returned to the subject of the Triton aliens, postulating what they might do next.

"I'll tell you what scares me," Liam said. "It's the two captains at Emperion."

"You're referring to Harbour and Cinders."

"Yes, absolutely," Liam replied. "There's a strange synchronicity at work between those two. It's like you put together two people who shouldn't fit, but somehow, they energize each other. If the aliens appear again, I'm wondering if they can resist returning to Triton."

"I've a different take, Liam," Devon replied, leaning back in his chair and smiling. "If the aliens return, I can't think of two better people to go out there and greet them than Harbour and Cinders."

"That's true," Liam acknowledged. "Hopefully the aliens won't eat them."

Responding to a rap on the door, Devon checked his hall vid feed, signaled the door to unlock, and admitted Sergeant Cecilia Lindstrom.

"Am I going to hear one of the commandant's downside calls?" Cecilia asked, after she closed the door and heard the lock snick.

"Sideways approach, huh?" Devon said to Liam. In reply, Liam wore an expression that looked like he'd tasted something sour.

"Sergeant, what do you know?" Liam asked, indicating a seat for Cecilia.

"If you're asking if I've listened to the commandant's calls, I haven't, Major," Cecilia replied. "I presumed I was invited to Lieutenant Higgins' office to hear the latest one, due to the timing."

"The timing?" Devon asked.

"Yes, Sir," Cecilia replied. "When the commandant links with the downside connection, he always calls the same number. As soon as he makes a connection, your link code is added to the call, but it's in passive mode."

Liam and Devon shared looks of trepidation.

"If you two are afraid that you're risking your jobs for illegally spying on the commandant, I wouldn't worry," Cecilia quickly said.

"You're going have to explain this carefully to us, Sergeant," Liam said.

"You must remember that I was trained on comm systems and code enforcement, Sir," Cecilia replied. "In addition, I was involved in the investigation and arrest of the governor."

Liam nodded his understanding, and Cecilia rushed on. "So many things about the Andropov affair never fit together for me. Then there were your attitudes toward the commandant, Sirs. You were, at best, cordial but never friendly or helpful. That's when I decided to do a little investigation of my own and found the commandant calling two numbers downside. It took me a while to cross-trace the numbers, because the downsiders aren't in our comm records. But, I finally identified them as belonging to Markos Andropov and Lise Panoy. After we arrested Andropov, the commandant's calls continued to Lise Panoy."

"Lise Panoy is the governor, Sergeant. Why wouldn't the commandant talk to her?" Liam asked, testing Cecilia.

"Now she is, but she hasn't been in the years that the commandant's been calling her," Cecilia replied.

"Years?" Devon mouthed silently, and Cecilia affirmed the length of time with a tip of her head.

Liam cleared his throat. The conversation was taking so many unexpected turns that it was difficult keeping his focus, but there was one subject that he definitely had to pursue. "Sergeant, if you found out that Devon's comm code was linked to the commandant's calls downside, why couldn't others discover the same thing?"

"In the first place, Major, they'd have to be looking for it. People make twenty to thirty comm calls a day. Multiply that times the number of Pyreans, and you have an idea what's going through the JOS comm servers. The only people who have access to these records are security, who require a warrant. Except for present company," Cecilia added, with a quick grin.

"Continue without the side comments, Sergeant," Liam replied sternly. The fact that someone was aware of Devon and his illegal monitoring had shaken him.

"Sorry, Sir," Cecilia replied. She wanted these two officers, whom she deeply respected, to know that she would support them. Belatedly, she was realizing how nervous they were about what she knew.

"Sirs, the data that I've described are in two different applications. Security personnel would have to search the comm connection logs for that specific pair. Then they'd have to access the server switch logs to see if there were ancillary code connections to that pair, at that time. In addition, accessing the server logs is only allowed by seven security staff and every one of us must log into the server, and our code is attached to anything we review. I've made sure that no one else is looking at what I've been observing."

"Quite inventive of you, Sergeant," Devon commended. "However, your access code is attached to these records, and you have no warrant. That places you in a great deal of jeopardy."

"It would, Sir, if my code were still there," Cecilia replied.

Liam stared hard at Cecilia, who shifted uncomfortably in her seat. He'd decided to promote her during their efforts to arrest Markos Andropov, impressed with her skills and maturity. This conversation had enabled him to see that he'd underestimated her, and he burst out laughing.

"Aren't we a threesome?" Liam declared, when he regained his breath. "Okay, Sergeant, you're on board. Obviously, you know the dangers, based on the protections you've taken. The lieutenant and I have a host of recordings of the commandant conspiring with Lise Panoy on many subjects. But, as you cheekily pointed out, they're illegal."

"Could I ask the type of subjects that we're talking about, Major?" Cecilia asked.

"Quick summary, Sergeant," Devon replied instead. "The commandant supported Andropov's dethronement with Lise Panoy. He's running a secondary investigation to discover the streak distributor who pressured Lily Tormelli."

"Why?" Cecilia asked.

"We heard the commandant tell Lise that Lily left a message on her comm unit. It was to Emerson, and it told him that she couldn't hurt him and couldn't live without her streak. The commandant erased the message."

"The commandant knew Lily?" Cecilia asked, looking between the officers.

"Lily was the commandant's coin-kitty for most of a year. Emerson believes Lily was pressured by her streak distributor. She could either patch the commandant or lose her streak supply. She chose not to hurt the commandant."

"Wow," Cecilia whispered.

"The commandant has Lise chasing down the downside streak suppliers to learn their JOS distributors," Liam said.

'The commandant has that much sway over the governor?" Cecilia asked, in confusion.

"Lise needs a new agri-dome, which requires approval of expedited shipping via the El. Emerson has been sitting on that until he gets what he wants," Devon explained.

"Quite the pair," Cecilia commented.

Liam and Devon glanced at each other. They both liked Cecilia, and it seemed a shame to divulge everything they knew, but there was no value in holding back now.

"Sergeant, those are our minor concerns," Liam said quietly. "Lise Panoy wants to use the present anxiety over the appearance of the aliens to make a move to become the de facto leader of Pyre."

"No," Cecilia replied.

"Afraid so," Devon said, with regret.

"No, Sirs. I meant to imply that there's no way that's happening, if I can help it," Cecilia declared hotly, and the men chuckled.

"Then we're in complete agreement," Liam replied. "However, there's even more going on. It concerns the *Belle*, or more specifically Harbour, and it has the commandant and the governor scared. We've learned that original documents were taken from the colony ship's library, but that's all we know. Captain Stamerson is in the loop, but he's not sharing."

The two security officers waited for Cecilia's reply. When she offered none, they thought they had burdened the sergeant with too much information, and they shared expressions of chagrin.

Despite the presence of senior officers, Cecilia tucked her legs to her chest and wrapped her arms around them. A single thumbnail rested against her front teeth. This was Cecilia's favorite position, which she assumed when wrestling with a problem. Cecilia stayed curled for several minutes, and, uncharacteristically, the officers remained quiet.

Finally, Cecilia unfolded her legs, looking from Liam to Devon and back. "The way I see it, we can't ever use the recordings you have, correct?"

The men nodded.

"Then, the question I'd like to ask is: Should we be trying to keep tabs on the commandant, or should we be trying to prevent the illicit liaison between the commandant and the governor?" Cecilia asked.

"Both, if we could," Liam replied. "If not both, then the latter would be the more preferable. Let's start with that one. What's your idea?"

"I was thinking we could sow a little discord," Cecilia replied, with a grin. "What if the next time the commandant calls the governor, a call tracer is placed on her comm unit?"

"How could that be done?" Devon asked. "We won't get access to the commandant's unit."

"It would have to be done in real time," Cecilia replied. "I could set up a piece of code on the comm servers. Then, when the server detected the next time the two connected, I would be pinged. After I responded, it would all happen automatically."

"What's your exposure, Sergeant?" Liam asked.

"I would receive a notification when the piece of code was downloaded. I would then go back into the servers and erase my footsteps," Cecilia replied.

"Everything you're saying is supposed to be impossible," Devon objected.

"The Review Board's warrant system created the holes, Sir," Cecilia replied. "Before that process was added, the comm system was secure. You still need the warrant code to legally secure a full record of the calls and messages. What I'm doing is acting surreptitiously intervening as a third party on the call."

"Do you know if anyone else can do this?" Devon asked.

"Three or four others in security have the basic skills, but I don't think they've put them to use," Cecilia replied.

"Why's that?" Liam asked.

"I would have seen their tracks," Cecilia said.

"How did you come by these skills?" Liam asked, his eyes narrowing.

"The information has been passed down through generations, Sir," Cecilia replied. "It was one of my ancestors who created the warrant system. He was a little paranoid about the power structure of the domes and security. He knew the ways that the comm system might be manipulated and taught it to his son, who became a security comm operator. That information was passed to his daughter, my mother, who taught it to me."

Liam and Devon stared at Cecilia, who lifted a single eyebrow at them.

"Wow," Devon whispered. "The things you don't know."

"Okay, Sergeant," Liam said, gathering his thoughts. "What happens when Lise Panoy gets this code?"

"What would you like to happen?" Cecilia asked, and the two officers grinned at each other.

* * * *

Lise Panoy sat at her desk, reviewing the list that Jordie MacKiernan, her chief of security, had delivered.

"Is the list complete?" Lise asked.

"No, Governor," Jordie replied. "The information quality varies. I'm relatively sure that we've located every streak manufacturer, and we've identified the vast majority of significant nut suppliers, but we've yet to gather all the names of the little ones, of course."

"The little ones?" Lise asked.

"The household suppliers," Jordie replied. "My investigation has revealed that nearly every household with one or more plumerase trees in the garden is acting as a supplier. We just don't know who those people are within the households. They could be the gardener, the cook, the home owner —"

"I get it," Lise said, holding up a hand to interrupt Jordie. "What about the JOS side of the list, the distributors?"

"That's where the list is most incomplete, Governor," Jordie replied. "Without having an opportunity to interrogate the manufacturers, I can't tell who's receiving what they're shipping topside. You indicated earlier that you weren't interested in me taking any hands-on action."

Lise drummed her nails, while she thought. "And I'm still not, Jordie," she eventually said. "If I gave you another two weeks, could you improve on the names of the JOS distributors?"

"Not significantly, Governor, unless you approve the snatching of a few manufacturers and allow me to persuade them."

Lise quickly sorted the list on her monitor. The number of manufacturers was double what she thought it would be, and the list of nut suppliers was lengthy. The last group, the JOS distributors, had only six names. She returned to the list of manufacturers. They were family heads, except for two names.

"We haven't any more time, Jordie. I need the commandant's approval for the expedited El shipping, and he wants the distributor names."

"If I might suggest, Governor? The commandant has no idea of the extensiveness of streak production and distribution. I, myself, was unaware of it. If we supply him with these six names and tell him that's everyone, then what reason does he have to doubt it?"

"He'll probably doubt its completeness simply because I'm the one sending it to him," Lise said quietly but harshly.

"In which case, if we sent him a list with twenty names, Governor, he'd think the same thing."

Lise stared hard at Jordie, who smirked. "That's quite true, Jordie. I applaud your twisted thinking. Okay, the investigation is over. Time to trim the plumerase supply chain."

"Understood, Governor, how would you like me to proceed?" Jordie asked, pulling out his comm unit, accessing the list, and ready to note Lise's instructions.

"Let's start with the two manufacturers, the ones who aren't family heads," Lise said, leaning back in her chair and staring at the fresco on her ceiling. "I need a message sent to my associates who've ventured into foolish business practices."

"No disappearances then ... something a little freakishly accidental at their manufacturing sites," Jordie suggested.

"Yes, that would do it," Lise replied, continuing to admire the delicate painting. It was an idyllic landscape of old Earth, a scenic valley in autumn colors, with a river winding slowly through it.

"And the nut suppliers?" Jordie asked.

"They need trimming the most," Lise replied, never taking her eyes off the ceiling. "That's too many people for accidents, and it's probably not necessary to remove even the majority of them. Once the two manufacturers encounter their tragically needless accidents, the family heads will get the message. Select a fifth of the suppliers. Some of the largest ones and show them the dome exits. Make it quiet, and do it in a narrow time window. Rumors will fly, and we'll add our own to the mix to decry the illicit streak operations to the domes' population. People will presume it to be a struggle for streak trade dominance, and I'll announce a crackdown. Then you can arrest another fifth of the suppliers, who will quietly be judged and sentenced, with the same result as the others."

"Anyone you specifically have in mind, Governor?"

With a sigh, Lise broke her attention away from the fresco and focused on the list. She tagged a multitude of names and sent the list to Jordie. "Those individuals aren't to be touched."

"Understood, Governor. When do you want me to start?" Jordie asked.

"The manufacturers ... as soon as you're ready. Wait a few days and then the suppliers. Take them out in one night."

"That's fourteen people, Governor. My security team can't handle that many people in one night. If I bring new people on too quickly, we risk exposure."

"What's your proposal, Jordie?"

"Either make fewer disappear in one night or spread them over two nights," Jordie replied.

"Let's make it the first option, Jordie. I'm sure the family heads can put two and two together and get my message once two manufacturers and a handful of suppliers are eliminated."

"Yes, Governor. Anything else?" Jordie asked.

"No, Jordie, start when you're ready," Lise said.

Jordie excused himself and was nearly to the door, when he heard, "Oh, Jordie, was there a reason you didn't include your name in the nut supplier's list?"

Jordie turned around and quietly cleared his throat before he replied, "I wanted to give you the most up-to-date list, Governor. I closed my business two weeks ago and eliminated any connection I had to plumerase nut collection."

"I had noticed Stevens' absence from our security team. Thorough of you, as I would expect, Jordie," Lise said, and sent him out the door, with a shooing of her fingers.

Jordie softly closed the door behind him and paused. His heart was beating fiercely. *You dodged a trip out a dome's airlock on that one,* he thought. *Best you stick to security, Jordie, and leave the business opportunities to others.*

Suspicions

"Governor," Emerson acknowledged, after he closed the office door to take Lise's call.

"I've just sent you the list of distributors that you've been requesting, Commandant," Lise replied. "Now, I want my expedited shipment schedule approved."

"Not so fast, Lise," Emerson said. He muted her call, while he checked the message she'd sent.

"Is this a joke, Lise?" Emerson asked angrily, when he resumed the call. "Do you expect me to believe there are only six streak distributors on the JOS?"

"You asked for an investigation into streak shipments from this end, Emerson," Lise shot back. "We've uncovered six major pipelines to the JOS. Had you considered the possibility that these six individuals might have a good many people working for them? They might be the leaders of distribution chains." She mentally thanked Jordie for alerting her to this possible response from the commandant and providing some alternative replies.

"You have your list, Emerson. Do I get my approval?" Lise pressed.

"When, and if, one or more of these people are caught distributing streak, then you'll get your approval, but not before then," Emerson replied.

"At least, tell me if you know these stationers," Lise requested.

Emerson eyed the list on his comm unit. He mumbled the names out loud, as he read. "None of them are familiar to me, Lise. It'll take some time to set traps and catch them either receiving the streak at El customs or distributing it."

"I expect to hear from you immediately afterwards, Emerson. Don't disappoint me," Lise said sharply and ended the call.

Lise flipped the comm unit aside and returned to reviewing the reports on agri-production. The delay in the new agri-dome start would mean that food suppliers would turn to the JOS to make up for the shortfalls. Once those contracts got established, Lise knew they would tend to stay in place, and she hated the idea of more coin flowing from the domes to the station.

A thought occurred to Lise, and she picked up her comm unit. She thumbed the device, expecting to access the virtual screen, but nothing happened. Disgusted, she tossed it aside and called her personal attendant.

"Governor?" the woman asked from the doorway.

Lise started to reply, but her strong sense of paranoia, which had served her so well, rose up. "Send me Tinder," Lise requested.

"Ma'am," the attendant replied and hurried away.

Moments later, Tinder, the governor's comm tech, tapped on the doorframe, and Lise motioned him inside.

"Check my comm device, Tinder, and check it carefully," Lise ordered.

Tinder glanced at Lise, while he was reaching for the device. The look on the governor's face was all he needed to be sufficiently warned. He unzipped a small case that he was never without, extracted an analytics tool, and plugged it into the governor's comm unit. He extended her device toward her, and she thumbed it for him.

Tinder set Lise's comm unit on the desk and examined the small screen on his analytics tool. Code was scrolling quickly past, and he murmured to himself. It was a habit he couldn't break, and Lise ignored him. Tinder was one of the best comm specialists in the business. He was born on station, and she'd lured him away from the JOS with the offer of a nice salary, a house, and a dedicated girlfriend for two years. As it was, Tinder and his temporary girlfriend had become partners.

"Uh-oh," Tinder said abruptly, and Lise turned from her reports to eye him. "There's a sniffer on this comm unit, Governor."

"The device is never out of my possession, and it's never left open, Tinder. How is that possible?"

"The only other means of accessing your device, Governor, would be while you're online, either messaging or speaking with someone. Who did you last contact, Governor?" Tinder asked, buried deep in thought, while examining his analytics tool. When Lise didn't answer, he glanced at her, noting her face was carved stone. "My apologies, Governor. That was a foolish question."

"What can you tell me about the conditions under which this piece of code found its way onto my comm unit, Tinder?" Lise asked, leaning back in her chair and thanking her stars for heeding her suspicions.

"To insert code like this, which is elegant, by the way, could only have been done via the JOS comm servers. It would have to be done on the fly, while you and the other individual were connected. Two points to note, Governor. The first is that this action would require access by security personnel, and the second is that an amateur placed it."

"Explain the inconsistency, Tinder ... elegant code but an amateurish operation," Lise requested, her eyes narrowing, as thoughts churned in her mind.

"Whoever created the code to accomplish the sniffing routine produced something that is practically undetectable, unless you suspected it was there. It would operate in the background for a period of time and then erase itself. Clever work, Governor," Tinder enthused.

"But?" Lise prompted.

"During the call, there would have been an actionable program, a small snippet, that would have directed where to place the code on your comm unit. Only the code didn't go where it should have gone. Instead it was placed in the general properties folder, which is what screwed-up the comm unit's operations. It doesn't make any sense."

"Hmm," Lise mused.

Tinder stood and slipped his hands in his pants pockets, where his fingers could fidget unnoticed. Having finished his work, he was unsure what to do next. He could hear the tapping of Lise's nails and knew enough to wait and to wait silently.

"Are you sure that removing the piece of code you've spotted will restore my comm unit without any further problem, Tinder?" Lise asked.

"Absolutely, Governor. That's the only item added since your device was last scanned three days ago."

"Remove it, Tinder, and keep it safe," Lise ordered.

Tinder yanked his hands from his pocket and set to work. In less than a minute, he was done and handing Lise's device to her. She thumbed it, and the virtual screen appeared.

"Tinder gathered his analytics tool, stuffed it into his case, stood up, and placed his hands behind his back.

"You may go, Tinder," Lise said perfunctorily, as she turned back to her reports. "Oh, and Tinder, that piece of code and where you found it is to be kept private. Do you understand me?"

"Absolutely, Governor. Totally private, absolutely," Tinder stammered, while trying to make a hasty exit.

Lise stared at her monitor before her mind focused on what happened to her comm device. *You're an idiot, Emerson, and you've made a big mistake, for which I'll make you pay,* Lise thought.

* * * *

Liam, Devon, and Cecilia choked and wheezed, they were laughing so hard. Devon paused the latest exchange between Emerson and Lise to allow everyone to catch their breath. This time, the three of them met in a small conference room in a quiet section of security. They didn't want to be seen together again in Devon's office with the door locked and the glass darkened.

"This is a stroke of luck," Devon said, when the laughter died down. "We had no way to intercept the governor's message, but the commandant accommodates us by reading the list for us during the conversation."

"It's a bad habit of his," Liam said. "I've been in his office, when he's reading text on the monitor, and, invariably, he mutters the words he sees."

The threesome listened to the remainder of the recording from Devon's comm unit. Then the lieutenant immediately deleted it and scrubbed the device's log entry. The original file was in a safe place, with the other recordings, on a security server under a false name.

"Six names," Cecilia said. "Does that sound like a reasonable number?"

"Hard to say," Devon replied. "It could be like the governor suggested. Six key individuals distributing to a bunch of their frontline people."

"I think it was more a matter of timing," Liam mused. "Emerson's failure to approve Lise's expedited shipping means the agri-dome is running far behind its construction schedule." When the other two individuals regarded him with expectant faces, he continued. "If the agri-dome fails to come online in time, it means a short supply of food in the domes. Suppliers will make up the difference by purchasing from the JOS."

"Or maybe even the *Belle*," Cecilia suggested. It was her turn to become the focus of the others, and she added, "According to my sources, Cinders' ships loaded a huge amount of material to revive more of the colony ship's hydroponic gardens. It's possible that the *Belle* could ship the extra production downside."

"Won't happen," Liam said, shaking his head. "For one thing, Lise won't allow Captain Harbour to gain an economic foothold in the domes. She'll prevent that by keeping the specter of alien contamination foremost in downsiders' minds. Then there is this other thing among Harbour, Lise, and, Emerson."

"You think it's a power play by Captain Harbour?" Cecilia asked. She didn't like the idea that one of the people she idolized was imitating the two individuals she hated.

"That doesn't fit," Liam replied. "I think Harbour is acting more as a disruptor. She's probably trying to do the same thing as the three of us, preventing Lise from consolidating her power, with Emerson's help."

"Too bad we can't join forces," Devon added.

"I don't think that would be smart," Liam rejoined. "It works better if there are two separate attacks. It'll be harder for Lise and Emerson to figure out who's working with whom."

"So, what do we do with the information we have?" Cecilia asked.

"We have to get to some or all of these distributors on Lise's list before Emerson finds a way to do it without our involvement," Liam stated.

"Without warrants, what will be our excuse for the surveillance?" Devon asked.

"Oh, didn't I tell you, Sirs?" Cecilia asked, in mock surprise. "I received an informant's message about illicit drugs arriving on the El from downside."

"Seriously?" Devon asked.

"Well, I *will*, as soon as I get to a kiosk, from where I can send it anonymously," Cecilia admitted, grinning.

"That works," Liam said, adding his smile to those of the others. "We have an open case with Lily Tormelli, which the commandant has requested we thoroughly investigate. Now, we've got this potential lead, which might allow us to track the source of the woman's streak."

"I'll need to order an intercept on El cargo storage and the landing pad," Devon said, working his way through the process. "Sergeant, after you receive your text message from this helpful source, forward it to me with a request for surveillance. I'll send you the approval, and you can assign personnel to the tasks."

"Understood, Sir," Cecilia replied. "Knowing our targets, it should be easy to monitor the vids via our recognition applications. I suppose we're also looking for which crew members are assisting them."

"Yes," Liam agreed. "On another matter, Sergeant, did the code get placed on Lise's comm device?"

"Yes, Sir," Cecilia replied.

"What type of information are we expecting from it?" Devon asked.

"None, Sir," Cecilia replied. "I decided it was too risky to use a straightforward attack."

"Then what did you do?" Liam asked, his curiosity piqued.

"In our last discussion, you indicated to me that fomenting relations was the preferred course of events," Cecilia replied. "I decided to indict the commandant in the governor's eyes. I selected some sniffing code from my personal work and, during the call, I had the server implant it on the governor's comm unit in such a way as to make the device inaccessible."

"How does that help us?" Devon asked.

The governor has a comm specialist, Tinder, who's one of the best. He'll locate the code in a heartbeat, and he'll explain to the governor that it's smartly written code that's been placed in the wrong folder."

"But, this Tinder person will know it was transmitted via security's servers," Devon objected.

"Yes, he will, Sir, but he'll also be telling Lise that it was ineptly placed during the call," Cecilia explained.

"Ah, I get it," Liam said. "It was security's resources that were involved but not necessarily security comm personnel, who would know how to do the job properly."

"Just so, Major," Cecilia replied. "The governor should see the commandant's inexperienced hands all over the attempt."

"Oh, that's good," Devon said gleefully. "That's so sneaky, I don't know how to classify it. Sergeant, I'm glad you're on our side."

"Proud to be considered part of the team," Cecilia replied, with an expansive air of accomplishment.

* * * *

Liam, Devon, and Cecilia moved as quickly as the number of hours in a day allowed. None of them clocked their overtime, not wanting to alert the commandant's coin-pinching fingers.

What surprised the threesome was the rapidity of visits by the mainstream distributors. One of them was showing up daily to collect a package.

"Now, it makes sense to me," Devon said, after reviewing some of the initial recordings with Cecilia. "Smaller packages shipped in large containers are more easily missed by inspectors. These little amounts can be slipped in cargo crew members' overall pockets. Then they casually meet the distributors on the passenger landing pad."

"No wonder the custom inspectors have rarely alerted us to a seized shipment," Cecilia had added.

In little more than a week, the six distributors had been identified, accepting packages from cargo crew, which had been removed from the holding areas without passing through customs inspection. Security's next phase of operation swiftly followed.

Cecilia and Sergeant Miguel Rodriguez waited near the El's passenger exit into the JOS. Devon monitored the handoff of streak to a distributor. He watched the individual walk up the exit arm and queue for transport via the station's ring.

"The distributor's boarding the next cap," Devon sent, which the sergeants picked up on their comm-dots, discreetly hidden in their ears. The lieutenant sent an image to their comm units to identify the man.

Cecilia and Miguel were dressed as stationers, lounging around the exit corridor, as if they were meeting El passengers. Both wore common-appearing skins, so as not to attract attention. When the distributor stepped out of the cap, the sergeants bracketed the individual, and Miguel whispered, "Security. Keep walking, cross the main promenade, and enter the side corridor. Cooperate and it will go easier on you."

As it was, the stationer was stunned at being caught after two years without so much as a hint of trouble. He complied, walking woodenly between the security personnel.

In swift order, security swept up four men and two women, who had been on Lise's list. Then they arrested the three cargo crew members, who were complicit in the illegal trafficking.

It was at this point, when Liam filed charges against the distributors, that his operation came under the scrutiny of the commandant. Liam and his people had been able to stay steps ahead of Emerson's parallel investigation because the commandant wasted time attempting to obtain warrants against the distributors. The Review Board had refused to issue them to the commandant. There was insufficient evidence of the distributor's complicity, and the Review Board wasn't about to take the word of the downside governor, as to the distributor's guilt.

Cecilia had gathered only two other security personnel to help her with the surveillance. They were people she could trust, and the small group monitored the efforts of Emerson's second team, who were recording imagery from the identical vids in the El landing pad and inspection areas. It had been a race to capture proof of the operations that could compel the Review Board.

Emerson's eye-opening moment came when he presented his vid evidence to the Review Board.

"I'm not sure what's going on in security, Commandant, but the Board issued warrants for the arrest of these six individuals days ago," Captain Henry Stamerson, head of the Review Board stated, with more than a little ire.

"That's not possible, Captain," Emerson declared. "This is the first time I've presented this evidence."

"Agreed, Commandant," Henry replied. "It was Major Finian who requested the warrants earlier, and they were granted."

Emerson was livid, as he stalked away from the captain's office. He didn't wait until he returned to security before he called Liam.

"Major, if you're aboard the JOS, you'll be waiting for me outside my office by the time I get there," Emerson had shouted into his device, and passersby stared open-mouthed at him.

When Emerson arrived, Liam stood where requested. Emerson signaled the door open with his comm unit and closed it once the men were inside. He was furious that he couldn't slam the door, an action he'd seen in old vids.

"Sit, Major," Emerson ordered, his strident voice reaching for upper octaves. "Why wasn't I included in your investigative loop? This is another key occasion when you've failed to keep me informed of your actions. I've a mind to put you on report, Major, and if you're not careful, you'll find yourself demoted in rank."

Liam sat quietly eyeing the commandant. He couldn't make up his mind whether to accept Emerson's berating or let the commandant know that he'd had enough.

"Well, what do you have to say for yourself, Major?" Emerson demanded, when he failed to produce the apology he expected.

"I was thinking that Lise Panoy would love to hear that you'd demoted me, Commandant," Liam replied. His calm demeanor was gone, and he stared hotly at Emerson, whose mouth hung open.

"What do you mean by that?" Emerson demanded angrily. He attempted to appear enraged by Liam's comment, but concern had crept into his eyes.

Liam regarded Emerson and made up his mind. As he rose from his chair, he said, "Only that the two of you are so friendly that I'm sure the governor would be delighted to know that you'd removed a potential obstacle from her path to Pyre domination."

"Get out, Major, before I have you up on charges for insubordination," Emerson screeched.

Liam exited Emerson's office in carefully measured steps, without saying another word. The glass door slid closed behind him, and he was able to catch Emerson out of the corner of his eye, as he walked away. The commandant sat heavily in his chair, stuck his elbows on the desk, and buried his face in his hands.

Looks like it's going to be an open fight from now on, Commandant, Liam thought. He couldn't perceive the outcome of the struggle that he had initiated, but he didn't regret declaring which side he was on. *I wonder if this is how Harbour feels,* he pondered.

Ituau Tulafono, the *Spryte*'s first mate, settled into her bridge chair aboard the mining ship. She'd returned from three days of downtime on the *Belle* and was feeling relaxed. Her comm panel chimed, and she tapped her board. "Ituau of the *Spryte*," she said.

"I'd say good morning, Ituau, if you're operating by JOS time," Evan Pendleton, the YIPS manager, said.

"We are, Evan. How goes it at the YIPS?"

"Business is booming, Ituau. That's why I need to speak to Captain Cinders. Is he available?"

"Affirmative, Evan, switching you now."

"Hello, Evan, how can I help you?" Jessie asked, after Ituau transferred the call.

"How goes the work at Emperion, Captain?" Evan asked.

"Better than last time, Evan. The transfer process is more efficient, and we've prepared more tanks aboard the *Belle*. Why?"

"Do you have a return date planned yet, Captain?"

Little alarm bells sounded in Jessie's head, and he smelled opportunity. "I don't think there's any hurry for us, Evan. The *Belle* is an extraordinary place for downtime. My crews love her. Too bad the commandant's edict kept you from visiting last time she was at the YIPS. Anyway, Captain Harbour and I are thinking we might be out here for another three months."

"Three months?" Evan repeated. His voice nearly squeaked, and Jessie bit back his chuckle.

"At least three," Jessie replied.

"You couldn't return sooner?" Evan asked.

"Don't see any reason to do that, Evan. Is there something you want to tell me?"

"Okay, Captain, here's the problem. Business is booming, and I'm starting to run low. In two months, metal ore processing at the YIPS will come to a halt without more slush. What will it take to get you to bring the *Belle* to the YIPS within the next thirty days?"

"Make me an offer, Evan. But, remember, the *Belle* is Captain Harbour's domain. As her business partner, I'll be happy to present any offer to her that I feel is valuable."

Evan wasn't fooled by Jessie's posturing. He knew that once Jessie accepted his offer that the *Belle* was as good as on its way. When it came to business, Jessie led the partnership.

When Jessie finished his negotiations with Evan, he placed a call to Harbour.

"We've got an excellent opportunity, Harbour," Jessie announced.

"Wonderful, Jessie. I'd love to hear it ... say over dinner at eighteen hundred hours?" Harbour replied.

"You don't want to hear it now?" Jessie asked.

"I've got my hands full right now, Jessie. It'll have to wait until this evening."

"See you for dinner," Jessie replied, and tapped his desk console connection off.

"One can see you're extremely busy, Captain," Yasmin said, hoisting her green high.

The three empaths, Nadine, Lindsey, and Yasmin, who were meeting with Harbour, snickered and laughed.

"You take your opportunities where you find them," Harbour replied. She smiled at her friends, but there was a serious look in her eye. "The tenor of Jessie's voice told me that his proposal is a business opportunity. That part I'm interested in hearing, but I want to be able to read him. A shift in economics is a potential lever in Pyre's political environment, and I want to be aware of the possibilities."

Harbour's fellow empaths sensed her seriousness, when Harbour shut down her emotional broadcast. Previously, the conversation had been about changes in the *Belle* to accommodate future families and their needs: education, healthcare, nutrition, and more. The exchange had been friendly and open, which allowed the four empaths to share their feelings about the subjects.

That Harbour was seeing every business decision in light of its effect on the future of Pyrean politics was becoming more evident every day to the spacers, empaths, and residents aboard the colony ship. And, the captain was unapologetic about it.

The day passed quickly for both captains, and Jessie was soon landing aboard the *Belle* and exiting his shuttle. Outside the bay's airlock, Jessie shucked his vac suit, with the help of crew, who hung it in a cabinet's harness for him.

At the door to the captain's quarters, Jessie knocked politely, and the door was promptly whisked open.

"Captain Cinders, how nice to see you again," Nadine said. "Please come in."

Jessie walked into the salon, noticing the table was set with elegant dishes and crystal glasses, which belonged to the original captains of the colony ship. Yasmin stood behind a chair and was motioning him to it.

"Thank you, Nadine," Jessie replied cheerfully.

"Captain Harbour will be right with you, Captain," Yasmin said. Then the two women left, quietly closing the door behind them.

When Harbour entered the salon from her sleeping quarters, Jessie quickly stood. Harbour was wearing the skins decorated by Makana, which outlined her attractive figure. Her hair, which was longer than any spacer wore, curled around her neck and onto her shoulders. It glistened in the muted light.

In contrast, Jessie felt undressed. He was wearing his usual attire of dark skins and a pair of clean captain's coveralls. He couldn't remember the last time he felt embarrassed by what he wore.

"Special occasion that I'm not aware of, Harbour, an anniversary or birthday?" Jessie asked.

"No, just dinner, Jessie. By the way, we're serving ourselves tonight," Harbour replied casually, as she took her own seat. "I'm preferring to keep business proposals private until I've had time to consider them," she added.

There was a moment or two of small talk, while they served themselves from the main dishes and carafes. A silence ensued, while Jessie relished the colony ship's fresh food.

Jessie was in the middle of a tasty salad, when Harbour asked, "What's this business proposal?" She meant to throw Jessie off and read his emotions. Part of her hated doing it, but another part wanted to understand her role, and by extension the *Belle*'s, in the growing Pyrean economy.

Jessie wiped his mouth and put down his utensil. "We've been offered a bonus from the YIPS to deliver the *Belle*'s load of slush within the next thirty days." He picked up his drink and hoisted it briefly in Harbour's direction before he relished a mouthful of sweet-tangy fruit juice.

"That's it?" Harbour asked. "Nearly seven months ago, we took the greatest load of slush to the YIPS that it had ever seen. Are you telling me that they're running low again?"

Jessie took another bite of his salad before he launched into his explanation. "When we delivered the first load, the YIPS was already behind in delivering many of its products. Remember that much of our slush is processed to provide the fuels that run the processing station. With our loads, the YIPS was able to catch up with backorders, but continued growth has created greater demand, and the YIPS is, once again, struggling to deliver."

"Growth from where? Be specific, Jessie," Harbour requested.

Jessie took the opportunity to finish the last couple of bites of salad and wash the food down with another sip of drink. He couldn't put his finger on what was driving Harbour's questions, but it was a side of her that he hadn't seen.

"You know about Lise's agri-dome expansion and the new terminal arms for the JOS," Jessie said, and Harbour nodded. "There are two other factors driving YIPS demand. First is investment capital. Certain stationers are doing financially well with downside trade. They've got coin to invest."

"Is there a place or industry where that coin is going?" Harbour asked.

"Yes, mining," Jessie replied. "Most mining ships return a modest profit with hauls of even common aggregate, especially if they have the equipment to do some basic processing onsite. Then there are the captains who hit the rare or heavy metal deposits. They can bring enormous profits to the owners. All in all, it's a safe investment, if there's a qualified captain and a good ship. The owner has the added bonus of sitting comfortably aboard the JOS, while the captain and crew take the risks."

"What's the second factor?" Harbour asked. She had continued to work her way through the meal, while Jessie talked.

"The next is a critical factor for topsiders and downsiders," Jessie replied. He'd picked up his utensil but placed it back down. "The downsiders are building another agri-dome, but they also need more habitat domes. In addition, the JOS is running out of cabin and entrepreneurial space."

"Doesn't that mean more opportunity for us?" Harbour asked.

"Yes, in the interim, but not in the long run," Jessie replied.

"How so?" Harbour asked, slicing into some roasted vegetables and savoring them. She could detect Jessie's longing. He was hungry and wanted to eat, but she was intentionally keeping him from doing that.

"The domes, the JOS, and the investors are competing for the YIPS output. In addition, the investors are pressuring the JOS to focus on more terminal arms for ships rather than expanding cabin and shop space. Word is that three of the ships planned to be built will be patterned on the *Pearl*."

"They'll be coming here," Harbour said.

"Yes, although they won't be serious competition. No, the real problem is the YIPS. It can't keep up with demand, even if there were two colony ships delivering slush and twice as many mining ships delivering ore. The YIPS needs to expand."

"Is that a challenge? Can't they just add on?" Harbour asked.

"The process won't work that way, Harbour. You can add more tanks and bays here and there to handle deliveries, but you can't insert more smelting furnaces into the existing system, without curtailing output.

Essentially, what the YIPS needs to do is create another processing station. That's an enormous undertaking, which will take a couple of decades."

"And the YIPS will be competing against the domes, the JOS, and the investors for their own output," Harbour surmised.

"Exactly," Jessie said.

"So, who wins in this competition?" Harbour asked.

"The question might be: Who loses?" Jessie replied. "Now, you understand some of the reasons for the recent political machinations. These various individuals are looking ahead and trying to position themselves to control the direction of expansion. The domes are trapped on the planet with only one means of moving people and goods. They're dependent on the JOS, and the downsiders hate that. That goes double for the governor and the family heads. The JOS needs the domes, but what if a second personnel station is created?"

"Where would it be?" Harbour asked.

"Most likely in a higher orbit, and it definitely won't be tethered to the domes. Travel between the JOS and the new station will be limited to shuttles, which the downsiders might or might not own, depending on the mood of stationers and, especially, the commandant."

"A second station. Imagine that?" Harbour mused. "Well, we certainly want to earn our bonus for early delivery," Harbour said, as she rose. "Let me know the schedule for completing the slush transfer and removing your spacers. Please ensure Aurelia is aboard the *Belle* before we sail. Now, if you'll excuse me, I have some work to do."

Harbour paused in the study's doorway and partially turned to Jessie. "Please enjoy the remainder of your meal, Jessie. In the future, if you're able to stop by more often, we might have more time to discuss things other than business."

Jessie watched the door close, cutting off his view of Harbour's figure. *Well, you've been scolded, Jessie Cinders,* he thought and laughed quietly to himself. He dug into his food with gusto, finished his meal, and left.

Having time for one drink in the cantina, Jessie chatted with some of the spacers and residents before he caught a shuttle that was distributing spacers aboard their ships before dropping down to the moon.

After shucking his vac suit and walking the gravity wheel, Jessie found Ituau grabbing a late-night snack in the galley.

"Nate on duty?" Jessie asked.

"He's downside, Captain. You're back early. Thought you'd be enjoying an extended dinner," Ituau commented and displayed a knowing smile.

"Dinner ended quickly after the business discussion. You might say I was reprimanded."

"No wonder," Ituau replied and stuffed the last of her hot sandwich in her mouth. It was the tease of the *Spryte*'s crew that no one should get between Ituau and the galley at breaktime without expecting serious bodily injury.

"Where's your sympathy for your captain and employer, I might add?" Jessie feigned indignation.

"When was the last time you were aboard the *Belle* ... *with* Captain Harbour?" Ituau asked.

"I was there three or four weeks ago, inspecting the newly refurbished tanks that were coming online."

"Did you and the captain cross paths?"

"Not that time," Jessie admitted.

"So, when did you last see the woman?" Ituau pursued.

"Okay, seven weeks ago or so, I was in the cantina with some spacers, and Captain Harbour was there," Jessie riposted.

"Hopeless," Ituau commented, finishing the last of her drink in one continuous swallow. "No wonder the woman treats you like a business partner and nothing more," she added.

Jessie thought to object, wishing to assert his status as captain, but Ituau's comments had added another layer of rebuke on top of Harbour's treatment of him. *This is why I stay away from relationships*, Jessie thought. But he wondered if he avoided long-term associations with women by preference or because he wasn't any good at them.

"Well, Ituau, I've something to keep you occupied, so you won't worry so much about me. We're pulling out. I want a schedule to finish transferring everything to the *Belle* from downside that we've extracted.

Then move our people around, so the colony ship can sail. After we get the *Pearl* topped off, all ships will follow the *Belle*. By the way, we get a bonus for any slush delivered to the YIPS within the next thirty days."

"I like the sound of that. What about Rules, Captain?"

"Back to the *Belle*. Captain Harbour's orders," Jessie replied, exiting the galley and heading for his cabin.

* * * *

"You don't want the *Pearl* to sail ahead, Jessie?" Leonard Hastings asked. Jessie's three ships had caught the *Belle* a couple of days out from the YIPS, and the enormous vessel was decelerating.

"Not this time, Leonard," Jessie replied, stretching out on his couch, while he talked via comm with his captains.

"Any particular reason, Jessie?" Yohlin asked.

"Some of the conversations I've had with my business partner make me think that she's more interested in leveraging her newly acquired status than in making coin," Jessie replied.

"You think she'd throw our deal with the YIPS?" Yohlin asked, with concern. She'd been developing investment plans with the additional coin she saw herself earning from the next four trips to Emperion.

"I don't think she'll go that far, Yohlin," Jessie replied. "Harbour has an agenda that surpasses business. My intention is to give her room to play her hand. I don't want us to be adding adversely to the mix by pushing for our needs."

"I hope you're right, Jessie," Yohlin replied. "This is the best deal we've ever had, and I'd hate to see it lost because of the woman's willfulness."

"Careful, Yohlin," Leonard admonished. "You're speaking about the duly elected captain of our colony ship, whose actions not only saved our sad butts but provided the wherewithal to make the coin from the Emperion slush in the first place."

"Apologies, Leonard, you're right," Yohlin replied. "I'm worried all this coin will slip through our hands."

"Yohlin," Jessie said. "Harbour wants the income from these shipments as much as the rest of us. She has plans for it. My point is that her plans aren't the same as ours ... they're bigger, much bigger."

A day and a half later, as the four ships neared the YIPS, Jessie's concerns materialized. He was on a conference call with Harbour and Evan Pendleton, the YIPS manager.

"Wonderful to see the two of you and your ships," Evan said enthusiastically. "Captain Harbour, as soon as you reach a stationary position at the transfer point, my people are standing by to begin pumping. Captain Cinders, we can accommodate the *Pearl* simultaneously on terminal arm one."

Evan quietly cleared his throat before he continued. "Of course, you'll need to follow the commandant's requirements. That's blowouts for Captain Cinders' ships, and no *Belle* personnel are allowed to leave their ship."

"You know that makes no sense, Evan," Jessie replied. "None of us have been to Triton in more than a year, and my crews have been mixing freely with the *Belle*'s."

"I'm sorry, Captain Cinders. Those are the commandant's orders. I hope the bonus helps the situation," Evan said. His tone was extremely conciliatory. If the captains could see him, they would notice the wringing of his hands.

"I don't think so," Harbour said.

"Begging your pardon, Captain?" Evan replied, hoping he'd not heard her correctly.

"I'm inclined to sail back to Emperion and dump this slush back on the surface. What about you, Captain Cinders?" Harbour asked.

"Now that you mention it, Captain Harbour, I'm inclined to agree with you," Jessie quickly added. "It seems we're not appreciated. I mean, here we are delivering this much-needed slush for every Pyrean, and we're treated terribly inhospitably."

"Please, Captains, let's not make any rash decisions," Evan urged. "Perhaps this should be a conversation that you have with the commandant." He couldn't conceive of Harbour returning to Emperion to dump the ship's slush, but, then again, he considered that she was an empath and maybe they thought differently from other people.

"I agree with you, Evan," Harbour replied. "Wait one."

Birdie muted the comm call and looked up at Harbour.

"Birdie, get me the commandant, priority one," Harbour ordered.

Dingles covered his smile with a hand. A priority one call from a ship's captain required the commandant on the comm instantly. If unavailable, the decision passed to Major Finian, his second-in-command.

"Commandant Strattleford, please state the emergency," Emerson intoned officiously

Harbour signaled to Birdie, who added the commandant's line to the conference call.

"The emergency is yours, Commandant Strattleford," Harbour announced forcefully. "You're on the comm with Captain Cinders and Evan Pendleton. We're being told that your previous orders of blowout and restrictions still apply."

"Those are conditions necessary to ensure the safety of Pyrean citizens," Emerson stated.

Harbour would have loved to have been in Emerson's office, at that moment. Realizing that she wanted to hurt him caused her to tamp down her anger.

"Uh, Commandant, Evan Pendleton here. The captains' objections are valid. They've not returned to Triton in a year, and the crews have been mixing."

"In which case, it might be best to quarantine all four ships," Emerson replied.

"You're right, Captain Harbour, we aren't appreciated," Jessie said. "I'm ready to order my ships to reverse course." He was happy Emerson and Evan couldn't see the grin he wore.

"Reverse course to where?" Emerson asked, confounded by the turn in the conversation.

"Captain Harbour has indicated that she'd prefer to dump her load of slush on Emperion rather than accept your conditions, Commandant," Evan stated hurriedly, the pitch of his voice rising.

"That's a bluff, Mr. Pendleton. Get a hold of yourself. There's no way these captains would forgo the amount of coin they're about to receive," Emerson stated confidently.

"You're right, Commandant," Harbour said evenly. "It *is* a bluff. But, I'll tell you what I will do if you don't rescind your directives. I intend to reverse course and station this ship about fifty-thousand kilometers out. Then I'm going to make daily broadcasts to all of Pyre. I'm going to make the case that I'm sitting on a huge load of slush that the YIPS desperately needs, but I can't deliver it because of you. And I'm not going to state your crazy reasons. You'll have to explain them over and over to every stationer whose path you cross."

"I can see those concerned stationers now, Commandant," Jessie said. "There are the investors, who want the terminal arms built and who want their ships built. Then there are the residents, who will worry that the station's generators or drive engines will shut down for lack of reaction mass. You'll be a busy man."

"I think you're forgetting about the commandant's friend, Captain Cinders," Harbour said conspiratorially.

"Oh, you mean Governor Panoy," Jessie said in mock surprise. "That's true. She'll be wondering why her agri-dome construction material isn't forthcoming. Yes, you're going to be an extremely busy man, Commandant."

Jessie was hoping that Harbour said nothing more, and she was thinking the same thing about him.

It took Emerson a while to succumb. He'd muted the comm line, while he trashed his office in anger. He'd have been happy to let Harbour try her broadcasts. He thought he had the superior position ... Pyrean citizenry safety. But the mention of Lise Panoy's reaction to the holdup of her agri-dome had done it.

"The directives are rescinded," Emerson announced tersely. He was about to cut his end of the call, when he heard Harbour say, "We'll need that in writing to both of us, Commandant. Furthermore, you'll make a Pyre-wide announcement of the same message."

When Emerson failed to respond, Jessie asked, "Is that a yes, Commandant?"

"Fine," Emerson replied hotly, cutting the call.

"Evan, Dingles tells me that we'll be stationary in a little under thirteen hours," Harbour said pleasantly. She used sign language to indicate to Birdie to end the transmission to the YIPS, and Birdie acknowledged the request in the same manner.

"Well played, Captain Harbour," Jessie said, knowing her bridge crew was listening. "I don't think the stationers are going to welcome us with open arms, but at least we won't be guilty of defying the commandant's directives."

"We still have a couple of challenges, Captain Cinders. The *Belle* isn't capable of docking on a JOS terminal arm, which we don't want to do anyway with Rules on board. I'm sure the commandant hasn't forgotten about her. But, at least, I can have Danny load our shuttle with passengers and supplies, which will make it more convenient for your crews."

"My ships can take on the heavier things you need, Captain. Ituau has Dingles' new shopping list. Remind your people to travel in small groups if they venture aboard the JOS. Cinders out."

-13-
Stamerson

The YIPS unloaded the *Belle* and the *Pearl*. Afterwards, all of Jessie's ships docked at the JOS, and the crews spent some downtime on the JOS.

More of Harbour and Jessie's spacers encouraged their families and partners to transfer to the *Belle*, which was stationed off the JOS orbital platform. The lure of free room and board encouraged many, but it was the stories of a comfortable environment and the camaraderie of spacers, empaths, and residents that convinced most to make the transfer.

Danny Thompson, the *Belle*'s shuttle pilot, was busy ferrying stationers and their personal property to the colony ship. Nadine, Yasmin, and Lindsey acted as the greeting parties, settling the stationers into their cabins, familiarizing them with the colony ship, and finding them useful outlets for their skills.

Sasha Garmenti, Aurelia's sister, eagerly volunteered to help the adult empaths with the new residents, but every woman politely refused. The last thing they wanted was to have the stationers step off the shuttle and be welcomed by a young empath, who would deluge them with inordinate waves of good cheer. With Lindsey's tutelage, Sasha was improving her control, but when she got excited, those skills were suddenly forgotten.

The YIPS payout from the *Belle*'s first slush haul had shocked Harbour. It was much more than she had expected. This time, she anticipated a more generous deposit in the colony ship's general fund, and she wasn't disappointed. The bonus and extra tanks ensured the deposit of an enormous amount of coin. The total made Harbour smile; it made the *Belle*'s residents giddy. The bounty of their free room and board was considerably improved by ever-fattening stipends.

Harbour communicated to Dingles, Danny, and her engineers of the amounts available to them from the general account. They set about spending it with a will — more crew, maintenance supplies, and much-needed equipment upgrades. The best expenditure, as far as the spacers were concerned, was the expansion of the cantina, which Maggie of the Miner's Pit oversaw.

Danny and Bryan met with a well-known ship architect to discuss shuttle designs that would suit the *Belle* and still be capable of collar docking with Jessie's ships. To the designer's surprise, Danny paid his fee in full and specified that the project was now his priority.

On the morning of the sixth day after the *Belle* took up station off the JOS, Harbour boarded Danny's shuttle for the station. It was her first return to the JOS since the vicious attack on her by Terror, aka Terrell McKenzie, an ex-security corporal. Her nerves jangled, as she climbed the shuttle's steps.

Dingles, who was behind Harbour, saw her shivers, and he whispered, "It will never happen again, Captain." In reply, he felt gratitude sweep through his mind.

Once the shuttle docked, Harbour stepped onto the terminal arm, surprised to be surrounded by a phalanx of spacers. She presumed they were aboard for personal reasons. Determined hostility poured off the spacers, and Harbour gathered her power and settled them. She witnessed fists relax, fingers open, shoulders slump, and steps ease.

When Harbour reached the capsule, Dingles requested that she wait. A group of spacers went first. Harbour and Dingles, with more spacers, followed in the second capsule. Then the remaining spacers transited the ring in the third cap. Once assembled on the other side, the group marched down the main corridor, taking up two-thirds of its width. Stationers gave way, crowding against storefronts.

Every stationer was well aware of what had happened to Harbour at the hands of Terror McKenzie, and most of them could understand the spacers' reactions. They were making an announcement — you'll not touch our captain again.

The first time Harbour had visited the JOS after her election to the captaincy, she'd been embarrassed to be accompanied by a few spacers.

Now, the much larger number of them that surrounded her gave her a sense of comfort.

Dingles saw Harbour's steps shift from tentative to confident, her stride opening. *That's right, Captain*, he thought. *You've taken good care of us, and we intend to do the same for you.*

When the group entered a side corridor, they filled its width, and stationers stepped into doorways to let Harbour and her spacers pass.

While Harbour and the *Belle's* spacers headed for their destination, Cecilia followed Liam's directions on her comm unit, odd as they were, to reach a clandestine meeting. She hadn't been told any more than to be at the location marked on her station map at the appointed time and to tell no one.

Cecilia glanced at her map. One more corner and she should arrive at her destination. She made the turn and slowed her walk. A group of spacers crowded the hallway.

"Sergeant, this way please," a tall, weathered spacer said. He touched an embedded, red button, and a hatch, which was set into the wall, slid aside.

Cecilia nodded to the spacers, as she passed. In turn, they tipped their caps, hats, and various other headgear to her. Inside, she was greeted by a woman with a prosthetic arm.

"Welcome to the Miner's Pit, Sergeant. I'm Maggie, the manager. What can I get you to drink?"

"Water, please," Cecilia replied, as she recognized Liam waving to her from a far table.

Cecelia made her way to the table and stood at the edge.

"This is the Sergeant, whom I spoke of earlier," Liam said to Harbour, introducing Cecilia.

"My thanks, Sergeant, for your efforts in freeing Aurelia's family," Harbour said, rising and extending her hand.

Cecilia politely replied, a moment before her mind was awash with appreciation, and she couldn't help the grin that stretched across her face. Next, she was introduced to Captains Stamerson and Cinders. As she sat down, she tipped her head toward Devon, who rounded out the table.

Maggie sat water in front of Cecilia, who eagerly gulped some to wet her suddenly parched throat. Then Maggie disappeared into her office, closing the door firmly. With the hour too early for the Miner's Pit to open, the members at the table had the cantina to themselves.

"An unusual assembly, to say the least," Henry Stamerson commented. He was glancing around the table, but when Jessie and Liam directed their gazes toward Harbour, he turned expectantly to face her.

"This meeting has no official standing, Captain Stamerson," Harbour said. "We expect you to take no action, either as the head of the Review Board or as a private citizen. The people around this table have been instrumental in discovering critical information that it's time to share. Major Finian, why don't you start?"

Liam took a sip of his water. He wasn't sure that Harbour's idea to share with Captain Stamerson was a good call, but he was tired of sitting on his knowledge with only two other security people on his side. He began by laying out why he decided to record the commandant's calls.

Henry was shocked to discover he was being made a party to illegal comm recordings, but he held his tongue. The major's suspicions weren't any different than his own. "What did you learn, Major?" he asked.

Devon played three of the most pertinent recordings for Henry, which is when the captain understood the critical nature of the meeting. He heard definitive proof of the commandant conspiring with the governor to foster sway of the domes over the stations. As an ex-spacer captain, he was sickened by Emerson's actions. But, before that emotion could take root, Henry experienced a sensation of calm. He glanced at Harbour. The corner of the empath's mouth quirked in a smile before her face smoothed again.

Next, Liam detailed the suicide of Lily Tormelli, the commandant's involvement with her, the suspicion that Lily's patches were intended for the commandant, and the squabble between Emerson and Lise over the JOS streak distributors.

"No wonder the commandant seemed perplexed when he requested warrants and I told him that I'd already issued them to you," Henry said. "It was opportune that you received that informant's message, Major," he added.

"Yes, it was," Liam replied, schooling the expression on his face. "The relationship between the commandant and the governor seemed to be souring, and we decided to help its deterioration." Liam laid out how the comm system had been used against Lise, and what they suspected Lise would think of the tinkering with her device.

"From the perspective of a Review Board member, I can't even begin to total the number of misdemeanors and criminal acts that have been perpetrated," Henry said. That the captain didn't appear angry gave Liam some relief.

"My turn," Harbour announced. It took a little longer for her to tell the story of the *Belle*'s missing library documents. She ended by asking Henry, "Did you find out if the original files that matched the copies I gave you were handed over to the commandant?"

"It took a while to get Emerson's cooperation, but I got access to what Lise uploaded to security," Henry replied. "There were no matches. If Lise possessed the original files, she's keeping them."

"I don't wonder," Harbour replied. "Those are explosive documents. She's hoping no one else has copies."

"I'm losing the thread here," Devon said. "What's so critical about these missing library files?"

"They're the original plans for the Pyrean government, or wherever the colonists made planetfall," Jessie said. "The architects of the colony ships ensured that the ship's captain, who would oversee the landing, had the authority to direct the election of the new government leaders ... president, representatives, and judges."

"It's my belief that the domes' founders stole those files from the *Belle*'s library so that they could set up their own political structure, without the yet-to-be-revived colonists becoming aware of what had been usurped from them," Harbour explained.

"If I'm understanding this correctly," Cecilia said, "these files repudiate our entire political structure ... governor, commandant, and, pardon me, Captain Stamerson, but even the Review Board."

"No apology necessary, Sergeant," Henry replied. "You're correct in your understanding. Captain Harbour and I have discussed this very thing.

And, here's the interesting point," Henry added, leaning forward, placing his forearms on the table. "If Pyre's citizens wanted to implement the directives in these files, it would be up to the captain of the *Belle* to govern the process until the directives were satisfied. In other words, Captain Harbour would temporarily become Pyre's leader."

Around the table, heads turned to stare at Harbour, who looked as if she was going to be sick. A snicker escaped Cinders' lips.

"Wow, President Harbour," Cecilia commented softly, trying out the title.

"Please don't say things like that, Sergeant," Harbour urged.

"So where do we go from here?" Liam asked.

"I've heard nothing so far that can legally be brought against the commandant or the governor," Henry commented. "Major, you arrested the streak distributors, correct?" he asked.

"Yes, Captain, along with three cargo crew members who aided them," Liam replied.

"Is there anything in what they've told you that incriminates Emerson?" Jessie asked.

"The cargo crew are talking, but they haven't much to say," Devon replied. "They earned coin sneaking the packages past inspections. Apparently, they didn't care to ask what the packages contained, as long as they got paid. As for the streak distributors, they're not talking."

"Has the commandant impeded the investigations into streak distribution or the Tormelli suicide?" Henry asked.

"Negative, Captain," Liam replied. "He's run a parallel investigation into both. It's unorthodox, but entirely within his purview."

"Then, at this point, we're at a stalemate," Henry concluded. "We know of the nefarious activities of the commandant and the governor, but the evidence is illegally obtained. It can't be presented before the Review Board. If you did," Henry said, eyeing Liam, "it would mean your career and anyone else who aided and abetted you in the collection of that information."

The expressions around the table were desultory, except for that of Harbour, who wore a satisfied smile.

"Something I'm missing, Captain?" Henry asked.

"For now, Captain Stamerson," Harbour replied. "I believe your analysis is correct, as far as the Review Board is concerned."

"What else is there?" Liam asked.

"The court of public opinion," Harbour replied. "I think we have to expose to Pyrean citizenry the egregious aims of the governor and the commandant's complicity. It will be difficult, and we must be careful."

Various expressions of grins, smiles, and smirks bloomed on faces, and Harbour could sense the emotional lift in their minds. She glanced at Jessie, who tipped his head to her.

The meeting disbanded after Harbour informed the group that she would coordinate the next meeting via a conference call. "I suggest that Major Finian be my single point of contact. He's the most exposed, at this point, and can shield everyone aboard the JOS. He'll arrange a place where all of you can communicate with us for the call," Harbour said, indicating Jessie and herself.

As the group departed, Jessie whispered to Liam, "I've a small cabin that I use for my downtime. I'll code the entry lock for you. Use the cabin for the conference call."

Liam nodded and thanked Jessie.

"Headed to your ship?" Harbour asked Jessie, as they exited the Miner's Pit. When he said yes, she waved at her spacers and replied, "Care to join my retinue?"

"I'd be delighted, Captain," Jessie replied gallantly.

"Form up, you excuse for spacers," Dingles shouted.

"Latched on," the spacers replied in unison and with gusto.

The closest crew members stepped aside for Harbour and Jessie to occupy a place in the middle, then the group headed off with purpose.

"You travel in intimidating style, Captain," Jessie commented, noticing that the spacers who surrounded them weren't wearing downtime apparel, except for headgear. It gave the appearance that they were on duty, and their duty was protecting their captain.

"I'm hoping this is a one-time thing," Harbour replied quietly.

"After everything that's transpired in the past year, my thought is that you'd better get used to this," Jessie replied. "I've rarely seen spacers behave like this. I'm reminded of Captain Erring's comment of what her crew would do if someone made a foolish move against Rules."

"Who knew empaths could be so beloved?" Harbour remarked. She laughed, when she said it, but Jessie thought there was an underlying meaning.

Return to Gasnar

Tacticnok thought that having convinced her father, Rictook, to let her lead the team back to Gasnar meant the greatest hurdle was over. Instead, the ruler had said that the conditions under which she returned must be approved by his advisors. For that pronouncement, she faced a never-ending stream of arguments with the masters over the steps that should be taken. Her team sat quietly, as the discussion unfolded.

"Your Highness, as a financial advisor, you know that I never recommend war or aggression, as my first choice," Master Pickcit said. "Trade ... trade has benefits, where war costs lives and funds, robbing us of the opportunity for growth. In this case, I don't see the value of returning to Gasnar and engaging in dialog with these creatures ... your pardon ... these aliens. The array that Jaktook and Master Tiknock identified at the Gasnarian moon is found in Jatouche ancient history. In all humility, Your Highness, I ask: What's the value in developing a relationship with these aliens, while they're so primitive?"

"I can't disagree with your analysis, Master Pickcit," Tacticnok replied evenly. "But the purpose of our visit isn't for economic reasons. It's to ensure that a young race, who has access to one of our Q-gates, becomes a good neighbor and a supporting member of the alliance, no matter how long it takes them to develop their technology."

"There is, perhaps, a more important reason for going," Master Tiknock said. He'd been quiet for much of the meeting. During the many days since Tacticnok's visit to Gasnar, he'd had several discussions with Jaktook, the dome senior administrator. The young Jatouche fascinated him. He exhibited the curiosity and thinking of a master, but not one who was focused on a single discipline.

"Enlighten us, Master Tiknock," Tacticnok encouraged.

"Remember, it was our people who disrupted Gasnar," Tiknock continued. "Our weapon delivered enough energy into the planet's surface layer to ensure that the release of it would require an abundance of annuals. Surely, it must be our responsibility to determine that the planet has become habitable, once again. If that isn't the case, we should consider what might be done to ease the planet's condition."

"To what purpose?" Master Roknick asked. As the advisor expressing negative ideas, the master strategist was proving to be the worst of the lot, and Tacticnok was slowly losing her temper with him.

"It is a tenet of the alliance that its members ensure that young races receive the benefit of our technology if catastrophe threatens their development. Life in the universe is precious and must be protected, if at all possible," Tiknock replied. "We put the prosperity of this species at risk by what we did at Gasnar."

"We didn't attack the Gasnarians; they attacked us. We owe them nothing," Roknick declared.

"We're not speaking about Gasnarians, Master Roknick," Tiknock pointed out.

"I still say we owe these aliens nothing," Roknick grumped. "The Messinants didn't build the Gasnar gate for them. They're interlopers. If we leave them alone, they'll move on to a more habitable planet."

"What if they can't, Master Roknick?" Jaktook asked.

"Can't what?" Roknick demanded.

"We acknowledge that this race has inferior technology, and we wonder why the Messinants didn't build them a gate. We have many questions about them and few answers," Jaktook replied. "Why do we assume they have choices? What if their appearance at Gasnar was a desperate action on the part of their species to survive? In short, what if they arrived at Gasnar and are trying to make the best of it because they can't move on?"

"Our young friend's reasoning is valid," Tiknock acknowledged. "And it underlines my point. We damaged the planet that these aliens might be desperately clinging to and facing no further options. The alliance would regard their situation as desperate and requiring our help, would it not?"

"It would, Master Tiknock," Tacticnok acknowledged. "And, advisors, imagine if the circumstances of these aliens became known to the alliance, which it eventually will. And, imagine if it also became known that we refused to help, especially when it was noted that we created the hardship for them. Yes, we were attacked, Master Roknick," Tacticnok said, holding up an imperial hand. "But it isn't the Gasnarians trying to live on that planet now."

"As the economic advisor, I've nothing further to add to this discussion, Your Highness. If I may?" Pickcit asked, motioning toward the door.

"Thank you for your input, Master Pickcit," Tacticnok replied.

When Pickcit was excused, he bowed his head, his age preventing him from paying any deeper deference to Tacticnok, and departed.

"It seems I'm expected to be the voice of reason," Roknick said, glancing briefly at Tiknock. "However, Your Highness, I'm not so willing to abdicate reason to your exuberance. His Excellency has commanded us to ensure that you have our best guidance. Not only does that require that we give you our advice but that you partake of it."

"I'm listening, Master Roknick," Tacticnok replied, her temper fraying further.

"If you're intent on this foolhardy mission, I must insist that you take a suitable contingent of soldiers to protect you. Furthermore, I insist on the majority of them preceding you through the gate." Roknick lounged on his pallet, his smug expression making him appear as if he'd scored the winning point in some important game.

"We're going there to entreat them, not intimidate them, Master Roknick," Tacticnok objected.

"I wasn't in favor of the limited protection you had for your first visit, Your Highness. You were most fortunate not to run afoul of the aliens, and I compliment you on keeping your visit short. However, Master Tiknock, Jaktook, and you have made the argument that the equipment you spotted was being used to monitor the dome. Undoubtedly, the aliens have seen you, and there's every reason to believe they'll be waiting for you."

"Weapons weren't in evidence in the console's recording," Tacticnok argued.

"That doesn't mean the aliens don't have them, Your Highness," Roknick replied. "Consider that it's only Jatouche soldiers who carry weapons, and no other members of our race. The aliens, who were trapped in the Gasnar dome, might be explorers, scientists, miners, or anyone else but soldiers."

"All the more reason not to appear festooned with weapons, Master Roknick. That could set off a fight that ends our mission before it gets an opportunity to start," Tacticnok shot back.

"You're saying, Your Highness, that you would prefer to be captured by the aliens rather than resist and give yourself an opportunity to return," Roknick challenged.

It was all that Tacticnok could do not to lash out at the master strategist. She caught Jaktook's motion out of the corner of her eye. His hand made a slow, slashing motion, a negation. She bit back her anger, searching for a worthy response. Something her father said about intractable individuals, who insisted their voices be heard, came to her.

"Your advice is noted, Master Roknick, and I believe it to be wise," Tacticnok said, dipping her head in acknowledgment of its value. "I see now that this team might be in grave danger without a leader of your caliber to accompany it. I thank you for volunteering."

Roknick snapped upright on his pallet. "I did no such thing, Your Highness. There are military leaders, young ones, who are more qualified to be effective field commanders."

"Well, Master Roknick, if you're not accompanying us, then I think we can conclude that you've exhausted your advice. You may leave us now."

If Roknick hadn't been panicked by the royal suggestion that he make the journey to Gasnar, he might have realized that Tacticnok hadn't accepted his advice. Instead, he bowed hastily and quickly made his exit.

Jaktook, Kractik, and Jakkock stared expectantly at Tacticnok, unsure of her emotional reaction to what had transpired. They certainly weren't ready for her gentle laughter.

"Quite effective, Your Highness," Tiknock said, chuckling. "Master Roknick will probably reach his humble abode before he realizes that he never received your agreement. As for my input, Your Highness, it's also complete," Tiknock said, rising. "I believe that we must contact these aliens, not merely to greet them, but to offer our help in restoring their planet to a healthy balance."

When Tacticnok excused Tiknock, he bowed from the waist and said, "I bid this group a good evening." As he passed Jaktook, he laid a companionly hand on the younger Jatouche's shoulder. It was a gesture that Tacticnok noted.

* * * *

Tacticnok weathered her father and her advisors' objections. On a late evening, which would coincide with the Gasnar dome bathed in the light of its star, her team assembled. It was the same eight members as before. The only difference was the amount of gear that was stacked beside their gate and would follow their voyage.

"Is everyone ready?" Tacticnok asked.

Some nodded and some murmured their reply. All in all, it spoke volumes about the more intense level of fear this time. The soldiers, led by Jittak, knew the dome was being observed, and they anticipated the aliens waited to overwhelm them. After that, they could only imagine the primitive forms of punishment that would spell their fates.

"Courage, my friends," Tacticnok said. "Don't let your imaginations run away with you. Remember how many races have joined the alliance. I'm confident that this young species might be another honorable one. As before, while we're at Gasnar, I'm merely Tacticnok, the team leader."

Tacticnok signaled her helmet to close and climbed onto the platform with alacrity. She hoped her actions would indicate her confidence. The remaining team members stepped beside Tacticnok, and she checked that the soldiers held their weapons at rest. The console tech energized the gate and sent Na-Tikkook's royal emissary across a vast distance of space via the Messinants' incredible technology.

The arrival at the Gasnar gate was accompanied by the same mix of anxiety and disappointment as the first time for Tacticnok. Had she asked, she would have found that she was the only one who felt those emotions. Everyone, but Jaktook, was breathing sighs of relief. As for Jaktook, he was severely disappointed.

"Kractik, open the egress ramp," Tacticnok ordered. "Then, after our equipment has arrived, prepare the console for our return, with a short delay once initiated."

As Kractik signaled the dome's wedge-shaped ramp aside, the platform's beam flashed, and a pile of gear appeared. There was no rush to remove it. Even if the Jatouche at the far end of the gate tried to send anything, individuals or things, the gate wouldn't operate. Somehow, the Q-gates' synchronicity prevented a sending from one end if anything occupied the platform on the other end. Alliance scientists had been unable to determine how the Messinants accomplished this feature. However, every race was intent on discovering this and many others of the domes' secrets.

Tacticnok walked to the edge of the dome, with Jaktook alongside. This time, she carried her own viewer and a few more devices that she thought might come in handy. She signaled her helmet, which retracted over her head and into her suit. With the viewer to her eyes, Tacticnok focused on the ancient array. Small lights were on, indicating to her that it was in use.

"The aliens' monitor is active," Tacticnok said, with enthusiasm.

"Much as I wish to meet these individuals, Tacticnok, we must prepare ourselves for disappointment," Jaktook replied.

"Explain," Tacticnok requested.

"We've seen imagery of the aliens visiting the dome nearly an annual ago. We see an array that they probably set up at the time. But, they're not here now, and there's no sign of further activity ... no individuals present, no equipment around, and, most important, no ships above."

"Do you think they could have left Gasnar?" Tacticnok asked, deflating.

"I think that we should consider that possibility, Tacticnok," Jaktook replied. "It won't change our plans, but it does mean that we should set a time limit on how long we're prepared to wait for the aliens to meet with us."

Tacticnok loosed a sigh and turned to the waiting team members. "Everyone below," she ordered. "Hang your suits up in the domiciles. Then, Jittak, have your soldiers unpack our supplies."

The small team set about preparing the dome for an extended visit. Below deck, in the central corridor, carvings, which were undecipherable to the uninitiated, were activated to open doors. The glowing carvings, which were on every surface, hid in plain sight a variety of operational triggers that couldn't be identified unless the console's manuals had been deciphered.

The Messinants took steps to ensure that every race, which they'd uplifted, progressed to a certain level of sentience before they could use the gates. The domes were not situated off the home worlds, but the races were challenged to learn the consoles' basic operations and discover the domes' manuals.

In one room off the corridor, the team doffed their suits and hung them up in cabinets. Beds were left extended from the walls. Jittak and his soldiers sniffed in disgust. They were prepared to accommodate the taller Gasnarians. The soldiers touched glyphs on the walls to retract the beds. After a short period, while the beds and pallets were cleansed, laser beams scanned the soldiers, and the beds extended out the required distance to accommodate the shorter Jatouche.

While the soldiers hurried to the dome's deck to unpack supplies, Kractik and Jakkock, the linguist, prepared the primary room. It held equipment that operated as a kitchen of sorts. If the manuals were read, the operations were simple, if not intuitive. There were tables and chairs for eating and holding meetings. But, for this visit, the furniture wouldn't be utilized.

On the platform deck, Jittak and his soldiers unpacked crates, stacking the empties to the side. They were careful to maintain an unobstructed view between wherever Tacticnok stood and the aliens' monitoring array.

Sleeping pedestals were extended and locked in place. Then they were covered with pallets and pillows. Jittak arranged them in a three-quarter circle facing the exposed exit wedge. Tacticnok's pallet was placed on the end of the arc, closest to the distant array. To Jittak, it seemed an odd arrangement, but he'd given up trying to anticipate Tacticnok's needs. He wasn't even sure what he was supposed to do if the aliens showed. As a soldier, he felt entirely out of his depth with the steps of first contact.

In a discussion with his mate, Jittak had lamented that he couldn't understand why a greater number of soldiers, with a more seasoned and higher-ranked leader, wasn't accompanying Her Highness.

"Don't you trust Her Highness' decisions?" his mate had asked.

"How could I judge that?" Jittak had wailed. "The Jatouche haven't met a new race in over a millennium. There's no one alive to guide us. And, every race we met had learned to operate their console and gate. When we greeted them, it was on even terms. But these aliens are technological infants."

"So, my mate, you have no idea what to do. Then you must trust Her Highness. It's that simple."

His mate's advice hadn't settled well with Jittak, but it appeared he had no alternative other than to do just that.

When all was ready, Tacticnok waited until Kractik and Jakkock brought trays of food and drink to the team, who rested on their pallets.

"Sit up, hold the trays in your laps, and your drink cup in your hand," Tacticnok requested. "Jaktook bring your tray here."

Tacticnok walked to the dome's edge. Facing the array, she said, "Everyone, when I raise my cup, do the same in the direction of the alien's equipment. Jaktook, please hold your tray up."

Tacticnok hoisted her cup, and her team did as ordered. Then Jaktook and she returned to their pallets, and the team consumed their meals.

"I believe I am beginning to understand your methods, Tacticnok," Jittak said, while he ate. "We appear as nothing more than simple travelers stopping by to consume a meal and requesting our hosts join us."

"You understand correctly, Jittak," Tacticnok replied.

"It's the aliens' interpretation that concerns me. Do you think they understood that the food we offer isn't us?" Jittak asked.

One of the soldiers coughed, his food suddenly sticking in his throat, and he quickly swallowed most of his drink to wash the impediment down.

"I don't think you're giving these aliens enough credit," Jaktook replied. "Every alliance member journeys via the Messinants' gates. These gates have offered enormous benefits for every race. Which one of them has chosen to travel to another star by ship?"

Jittak nodded his understanding of Jaktook's argument.

"I can't conceive of any species daring to do what they've done or conceiving of how they've done it," Jaktook continued. "But I'm sure of one thing. These aliens have nothing in common with the Gasnarians, and, I, for one, am anxious to meet them. My greatest concern is that they're no longer here, having sailed on to find a more hospitable home world. Tomorrow, I'll assemble the long-range scope. It's my hope to see some activity on or around Gasnar."

Tacticnok could see the effect that Jaktook's words had on the team. It calmed them and gave them an alternate perspective. She glanced at him, admiration shining in her eyes.

-15-
They're Back

"This might sound a little odd," Jessie said. He was working late at his desk aboard the *Spryte*. He'd called Harbour, not really expecting her to be awake.

"I'm an empath, Jessie. Our entire life is odd compared to normals," Harbour replied. It might have come across as harsh, except she ended her words with a warm chuckle.

The sound of Harbour's mellow laughter was one of the reasons Jessie had called her. He missed that sound. In two days, their ships would sail for Emperion, and it would be another blur of six to eight months of hard work moving slush. That Jessie didn't make time for his own pleasures was one of his bad habits, but this was a tough one to break after so many years of entrenchment.

"I wanted to invite you to dinner tomorrow evening," Jessie said.

"Why is that odd, Jessie?" Harbour asked.

"I was wondering if we could dine in your quarters," Jessie said, feeling a little awkward about his proposal.

Harbour burst out laughing. "And why shouldn't you prefer to dine aboard the *Belle*, Jessie? That just shows your superior taste in atmosphere, food, and company, I might add."

"Shall we say seventeen hundred hours?" Jessie suggested.

"I'll see you then, Jessie," Harbour replied, cutting the call. She placed her comm unit on the bedside table. It was programmed to chime, at all hours, for a few special callers, such as Yasmin, Dingles, and Jessie. She turned over, pulled the covers up to her neck, and fell into a deep sleep filled with pleasant dreams.

The next day passed swiftly for Harbour. There remained one day before the *Belle* launched for Emperion, and there was a tremendous number of last-minute details to accomplish. She did ensure that she informed Nadine of her dinner guest.

"A business conversation with the captain?" Nadine asked, projecting a bit of annoyance.

"Captain Cinders requested we meet," Harbour replied.

Nadine perceived the pleasure that leaked through Harbour's blocks.

"The captain asked you to dinner?" Nadine said. "Well, well, our captain dining with a normal for the pleasure of it."

"And look who's talking," Harbour riposted. "As if you and Dingles aren't one of the coziest pair of empath and normal aboard this ship."

"Dingles is critical to this ship's operation. As such, I'm ensuring his mental health by taking a personal interest in his care." Nadine's serious expression lasted a few seconds before she burst out laughing, and Harbour joined her.

"Seriously, Nadine, how does it work for the two of you?" Harbour asked.

"It's new territory for both of us, Harbour," Nadine replied, slipping into the familiar. "On the one hand, Dingles appreciates empaths, especially after what you did for him. To me, he's a breath of fresh air, like walking into one of the hydroponic gardens. I want to share what I feel with him, but I don't want to worry him that I'm always broadcasting."

"So, what do you do?" Harbour pressed.

"We've arranged simple signals. It was Dingles' idea. He's borrowing from his years as a spacer. My default condition, as he calls it, is that I'm not sending when I'm in his presence. We have to agree, usually with a quick hand signal, that an exchange is welcome."

"That way the two of you know when you're about to have a therapy session," Harbour replied, nodding her understanding. "Anytime other than that?"

Nadine's moment of embarrassment quickly passed. She knew Harbour was anxious for the information. "We use the signals in bed. It's easier than talking about it, at those sensitive moments, which happen more frequently than I would have thought possible. For his age, the man is amazingly ... active." She smiled and held up her hands, as if to say, you asked.

If Nadine was expecting Harbour to laugh, it didn't happen. Instead, Harbour stared thoughtfully into space. "Talk about a relationship fraught with problems, Nadine. You have my sympathy, or perhaps you don't need it."

"Not for me, sister," Nadine replied, grinning. "With the right man, so many things are possible. Don't worry about your dinner, Captain; it'll be our pleasure."

Much later in the day, Harbour was meeting with a group of residents and a few new engineers, who were responsible for opening two more hydroponic gardens and deciding what to grow. One of the engineers, Darby, who was an experienced biologist, wanted to work on creating new cultures for the protein vats to vary the colony ship's output.

"The *Belle*'s library has an extensive list of recipes for proteins, Captain. I've no idea what some of these things would taste like, but I'm anxious to try," Darby said.

Harbour gave him permission to resurrect two of the protein vats to experiment with recipes.

"Any of these items that you might be partial to trying, Captain?" Darby asked.

Harbour saw the list appear in her comm unit. It was dizzying in its length. "You choose," she replied. "We'll use the cantina as the testing ground. If the spacers hate your choices, I'm sure they'll let you know."

Darby briefly blanched. "Perhaps, I should ask our spacers to choose what they wish me to create. It might be safer that way."

Harbour chuckled. "My thought exactly, Darby." At that moment, her comm unit chimed, and she glanced at it. "Sorry, must go," she said to the group and left the meeting. As important as the dinner was to her, the needs of the day had consumed her time. She had less than a half hour to get ready, and she was a good ten minutes from her cabin, deep in the lower levels of the colony ship.

"Dingles, I need you," Harbour called via her comm unit.

"Here, Captain," Dingles replied.

"Captain Cinders will be inbound to the *Belle*," Harbour said.

"Not to worry, Captain. His shuttle is on approach. The captain will be on time," Dingles replied, pleased to put his captain's mind at rest.

"But I won't be," Harbour said tensely.

"Understood, Captain. How much time do you need?"

"Not too much, Dingles. Maybe fifteen or twenty minutes past seventeen hundred. I know Captain Cinders likes to be prompt."

"That he does, Captain. I'll take care of it. Anything else? Would you like to know our hand signals or would you two like to work those out for yourselves?"

"Do Nadine and you share everything, Dingles?" Harbour exclaimed. She was becoming breathless, hurrying through corridors. Residents, spacers, and empaths were startled and worked to evade her. Harbour attempted to smile to indicate there wasn't a problem, but she wondered if it didn't appear more like a grimace.

"Pretty much, Captain. Keeps the relationship real interesting," Dingles replied.

"How about you take care of your duties, First Mate," Harbour retorted.

"Aye, aye, Captain," Dingles replied.

Harbour could hear Dingles' muted snicker before he ended the call. She couldn't help but smile and thank her stars for rescuing the man from a deadly sentence in security confinement. Space dementia would have surely claimed Dingles' sanity and then his life, if he had faced incarceration.

Harbour made her cabin and burst through the door, startling the three empaths setting the table.

"I thought maybe you decided to teach the captain a lesson and stand him up," Yasmin commented drily.

Rather than vocally reply, Harbour offered Yasmin a taste of her pique, as she hurried on to her sleeping quarters. In her haste, the other two empaths, Lindsey and Nadine received what she sent. As the sleeping quarters' door closed, they grinned at one another.

"Be careful of your tongue, Yasmin," Nadine warned. "This isn't a simple occasion for Harbour."

"Agreed," Lindsey echoed. "I haven't seen Harbour flustered like this for longer than I can remember."

There wasn't much time for Harbour to do more than shower quickly. She left her hair dry and wound it on top of her head, pinning it in place with a piece of Makana's jewelry. Digging through a small box of keepsakes, she pulled out a pair of long, delicate earrings. Her mother had pressed them into her hand, when security came to take her away and ship her off to the *Belle*.

Harbour had never worn the earrings, out of anger with her mother for letting go of her. Now, many years later, it seemed appropriate to forgive her mother and wear them. She slipped on her best pair of skins and applied a delicate amount of makeup with a mist mask.

Standing in front of a full-length mirror, Harbour eyed her reflection. She was never one to laud over her genetic gifts. This time, the image of the mature woman, with her graceful curves and captivating face, stared back at her. *I need all the help I can get*, Harbour thought, accepting the mirror's image.

When Harbour returned to the salon, the table caught her eye. It was incredibly well laid out, and her friends stood silently by.

"Thank you," Harbour said, and hugged each one of them.

The women filed out, as Jessie approached the cabin. It was Nadine who noticed that he came by way of the bridge and not the main corridor that would be the usual approach from the bay. *Dingles, you clever man,* she thought. *I must show you my appreciation tonight.*

Jessie smiled at the women and entered the salon, closing the door behind him. "Evening, Harbour," he said, adding, "It's a beautiful table."

"I'll let the women know that you appreciate their efforts," Harbour replied, "and thank you for the invitation to my own cabin." She smiled at her jest.

"A man must be prepared to make sacrifices for the good of his stomach," Jessie replied, as he and Harbour sat at the table.

The pair chatted, while they served themselves. They discussed a length of stay at Emperion, the number of tanks they should fill, and the expected coin from the payout. The conversation was easy, and neither of them was admitting how much they enjoyed the company of the other.

While the captains' dinner was underway, the bridge was a hive of activity. The effort was duplicated throughout the *Belle*, with the ship preparing to get underway in the morning. That meant hundreds of systems were undergoing final checks.

Birdie was about to make a comm call, when a flash of blue caught her eye. The bridge crew halted in mid-motions to view the central monitor, the one receiving the broadcast from Triton. Seconds passed, as the events unfolded at the dome before Birdie grabbed her comm unit and called, "They're back, Dingles."

"Who's back?" Dingles asked.

"The aliens at Triton," Birdie replied.

Dingles rushed to the bridge in time to see the aliens, having descended the platform, at work unloading crates. "Birdie, reset playback from the recording to when they first appear. I'll get the captain." As Dingles rushed to the captains' quarters, he thought, *Harbour's going to hate me for interrupting her dinner.*

Harbour was about to bring up the subject of Dingles and Nadine. It was her way of letting Jessie know that a relationship between an empath and a normal was possible. But, the urgent knock at the door interrupted her.

"Enter," Harbour called out, trying to keep any annoyance out of her voice.

"Captain, my apologies for intruding, but you're needed immediately on the bridge," Dingles announced.

Harbour could detect the anxiety sweeping off Dingles in a rush, and she jumped up from the table. "Come, Captain," Harbour said to Jessie, and she hurried after Dingles.

When Harbour and Jessie made the bridge, Dingles said, "Captains, the dome was activated moments ago. Birdie, start the playback."

Harbour, Jessie, Dingles, and the bridge crew were transfixed as they watched the scene unfold at the dome.

When one alien approached the edge of the dome and the helmet slid away, Jessie commented, "That one was here before, doing the same thing. I think it's focusing on our equipment array."

"How can you tell it's the same one, Captain?" Dingles asked.

"By the coloring of the face, tawny fur, and the ridge along the skull's top has a reddish tint. At least, I think it does. It's hard to tell hues looking through the blue energy field of the dome. I think it's wondering if the array is still there. They have to be curious about who activated the dome." Jessie chuckled, which eased some of the tension on the bridge. "I bet they're wondering where the heck we are."

"Captain Harbour, am I reading this wrong," Birdie asked, "or do the aliens look as if they're setting up a permanent camp?"

"Looks like it, Birdie," Harbour agreed, as they watched the aliens return from below decks, unpack crates, and set up pedestals and pallets.

"What does everyone else see when they look at the group now?" Jessie asked, after the aliens were divested of their vac suits and had finished setting up their cots.

"What do you mean, Captain?" Dingles asked.

"When we've not been saying alien, we've been saying creature or it. Looks to me like there might be genders," Jessie replied.

"Undoubtedly, Captain," Harbour stated emphatically. "I thought that part was obvious. Two females and six males."

"Absolutely," Birdie chimed in.

Jessie and Dingles exchanged glances.

"Identified by ..." Jessie asked, leaving the question open.

"Stature and coloring," Harbour promptly supplied. "The two females are more diminutive. The males are broader and heavier. And, of course, the females have prettier coloring."

Birdie and two other women snickered. One female crew member tried to hide hers by coughing.

"Okay, assuming you're correct," Jessie allowed. "Then it's the female who's inviting us to dinner," he said, gesturing at the monitor.

After extending the invitation and finishing their meals, the aliens turned in for the evening, adding masks over their faces against the glare of the dome.

"That's odd," Dingles said. "Obviously, there are rooms below, although I didn't hear about them from Aurelia. But, they left their vac suits below and they prepared meals down there. Yet, they intend to sleep on the dome's deck with that incessant blue light. It doesn't make sense."

"Yes, it does," Harbour replied. "We're looking at the overtures of first contact. The female, who is leading the group, is demonstrating that she has nothing to hide. She's made the offer of food and drink. Furthermore, the same number of them arrived as last time, and they're waiting on the upper deck. They're not hiding. They want us to be comfortable about coming to speak with them. That invitation is emphasized by leaving the deck wedge open."

The entire bridge stared at the sleeping forms of the aliens for a few minutes before Harbour said, "Captain Cinders, I think we should have an after-dinner drink and talk."

"Agreed," Jessie said.

"You're going, aren't you?" Harbour asked, after Jessie and she were seated at her salon's table. The remains of their dinners were cold on their plates, but the centuries-old brandy warmed their stomachs.

"I don't think we have a choice, Harbour. One of us has to go, and, last time I checked, you aren't vac-suit rated," Jessie replied. "And, after all, I need the practice. I'm just getting the hang of responding to exotic females," he added, grinning.

Harbour detected the genuine happiness exuding from Jessie, but she was far from content with his decision. "What about the *Belle* and *Emperion*?" she objected.

"I'm thinking we can do both, Harbour. The *Belle*, the *Spryte*, and the *Pearl* go on to Emperion. Ituau can command the *Spryte*. I'll join Yohlin on the *Annie* and take her ship to Triton."

"With what intention?" Harbour asked.

"Staying alive," Jessie responded, an eyebrow arching and a mouth quirking to underline his attempt at humor.

"Seriously, Jessie," Harbour shot back, and Jessie could feel an intense mix of emotions from Harbour.

Jessie held up his hands in apology. "Sorry, poor joke. In the past year, I've gotten used to the idea that aliens exist in the galaxy. It makes me wonder how many other civilizations exist, and I, for one, would love to know what sort of technology they possess. We must have looked like idiots at the dome, stumbling around, activating it, and then desperate to get out. Here they come, traipsing in and out like we'd go through an airlock. It's obvious that they regularly transport through these domes."

"Do you think they might have more than one of these gates where they come from?" Harbour asked.

"Good question," Jessie replied. "All I know is a lot of our people have been sitting over top of this choked planet, wrestling with a lack of space, and there are aliens on Triton who might possess the wherewithal to help us. Isn't that worth the risk of meeting them?"

"And say what, Jessie? I mean, how good is your alien speak?"

"Don't look at me!" Jessie exclaimed in pretended horror. "I'm counting on them to carry the metal. They're the technologically advanced individuals."

"Who's going with you?" Harbour asked.

"That's an easy one," Jessie replied. "You remember the aliens' first visit? The second female, the one with the brown crown and the muted gold face, ran over to the console. She was there for a while. I'm betting that she downloaded imagery recorded by the console after the dome was activated. This type of structure is too important not to have some sort of monitoring capability. I think the aliens have already seen us, and they're fully aware that we're the technological newbies. That's probably why we're receiving the invitation."

"Then, I take it your plan will be to imitate them, and the same team will accompany you that they saw in the recordings, if that's what they pulled from the console," Harbour supposed.

"Yes. It should demonstrate that we received their message and are replying in kind."

"I would say that's an appropriate and intelligent response, unless they capture you and haul you back to wherever they come from," Harbour replied, her eyes narrowing at Jessie.

"I'll be taking Rules," Jessie replied.

"I expected that," Harbour replied simply. "No telling how an empath might be valuable."

"Do you think she can affect them as an empath?" Jessie asked. He wanted to take Aurelia because she was one of the original team, but he hadn't considered her role as a powerful empath.

"Jessie, they're bipedal, four-limbed, and symmetrical, and they're obviously intelligent creatures, which means they think. The method of their invitation displays sensitivity to creatures, namely us, that they've probably never encountered, which tells me they have emotions. Assuming all that, Aurelia might be a tremendous asset."

"On another note, I don't want to delay our launch," Jessie said, getting to the practicalities of tomorrow, which made him more comfortable. "You can bet that the rumor mill is cranking. There's going to be a tremendous number of questions from Pyreans with few answers. Once our ships are underway, I would advise you to broadcast the recording."

"But not speak about where the *Annie* is going," Harbour supposed, "although the JOS will recognize the ship's trajectory soon enough."

They sipped on their brandy, mulling over their thoughts.

Jessie set his empty glass on the table, examining the reflected light in the brilliant crystal, and said, "I'll talk to Aurelia before I leave, and I'll transfer her to the *Annie* tonight."

"Do you think that's wise?" Harbour asked, concerned that security might arrest her.

"I'll make it a ship-to-ship transfer. We won't step foot on the terminal arms," Jessie assured her. He couldn't think of anything else to say, though he was loath to leave. Prior to the announcement of the aliens' arrival, he'd been enjoying himself. He couldn't recall when he'd felt so relaxed in the company of a woman for a dinner date.

Jessie stood up, extended his hand, and said, "Fill the *Belle*, Harbour. I'll be along shortly."

"See that you do, Jessie," Harbour said, shaking Jessie's hand. Her hope for an intimate dinner had been turned on its head. More critical matters had intruded, and it made her desires feel trivial. However, deep inside, she was unwilling to place her hopes aside. At the door, Harbour said, "One more thing, Jessie."

Jessie turned toward Harbour, and she wrapped her arms around his neck and planted a deep, passionate kiss on him. "If you want more of those, see that you make it to Emperion,'" she said, her voice husky.

-16-
We're Coming

Jessie left Harbour's quarters in a bit of a daze. It wasn't just the kiss. Along with it, he'd received Harbour's intense feelings of concern for him. The many times that Aurelia had shared her emotions with him, the crew had felt slightly clinical. Harbour's emotions were nothing like that. They were deep, complex layers of desire, hope, and fear for another.

As Jessie walked the corridors, his mind slowly lost the effect of that sending. He had a desire to turn around, kiss Harbour, and ask for more. When he kept walking, he thought, *You're a bigger fool, Jessie Cinders, than I ever considered.*

Jessie wasn't allowed to dwell on the subject much longer. His path was suddenly blocked by Aurelia.

"I heard the aliens are back. You're going, aren't you?" Aurelia demanded.

"You guessing or you know?" Jessie asked.

"Know," Aurelia replied. "When I mentioned aliens, I read a mix of excitement and trepidation from you. I translate that as what you're feeling about meeting the aliens."

"Yes, I'm going," Jessie admitted.

"Then I'm going too," Aurelia said, as if it was a foregone conclusion.

"Rules, you wait for the Captain's invitation," Jessie replied, exerting his command authority.

"Maybe we should ask the *Annie*'s crew if they want to sail without me, especially when they learn the ship's headed to Triton," Aurelia replied hotly.

"That sounds like a threat, Rules. Captains don't like threats from their crew members. It creates distrust."

"You trust me, Captain," Aurelia replied, confident of her words. "Maybe you're afraid to take me into dangerous circumstances."

Jessie smiled at Aurelia, reminding himself that he was talking to a teenager. "Harbour and I have already discussed you. You're going. Just wait for the captain's invitation," Jessie said, cuffing her lightly upside the head. "Get into your vac suit. We're taking the *Spryte*'s shuttle and docking aboard my ship so that we don't enter the terminal arm. Meet me at the bay. We'll be aboard the *Spryte* about an hour or so before we transfer to the *Annie*."

"Aye, aye, Captain," Aurelia replied, with a broad grin. She fairly skipped away, and Jessie shook his head in amazement. Two years ago, he couldn't have imagined having any dealings with empaths. Now, two of them had become entwined in his life, and they couldn't be more different. Yet, he dearly didn't want to return to the past.

Jessie and Aurelia had the company of *Spryte* crew, as they returned to the ship. Following spacer protocol, they were all closed in their vac suits. It allowed Jessie to communicate privately with Aurelia, who sat beside him. He tapped Aurelia's leg and signaled with his fingers the comm channel she should select.

"Yes, Captain," Aurelia replied, after she switched from the ship's general channel.

Jessie heard the calm, crew-member voice that Aurelia exuded. Gone was the teenager from the *Belle*. In her place was the spacer role Aurelia had adopted with a will.

"Not a word to anyone about my intention to sail the *Annie* to Triton, Rules," Jessie said, using the name that the spacers were fond of calling her. "That's an announcement for the captains to make to their crews."

"But, if you're aboard the —"

"Hook on, spacer," Jessie growled.

"Aye, latched on, Captain," Aurelia replied. She reminded herself that much of what Jessie and Harbour intended to do was over her head. She satisfied herself with the thought that she wasn't going to be left out of the trip to Triton. *Get your head on straight, spacer,* she thought.

Once aboard the *Spryte*, Jessie retired immediately to his cabin. That Aurelia was among those who got off the shuttle tweaked the crew's interest, but they couldn't seem to engage her in conversation, which piqued their curiosity even more.

Jessie hooked his comm unit to his desk monitor, thumbed open the device, and accessed his Dissemination of Assets, which was filed with security. The record directed security how to disperse his company, coin, and possessions in the event of his death.

In Jessie's last iteration, he'd left his company to Yohlin, Leonard, and Ituau, who would be promoted to captain of the *Spryte*. Any of his possessions aboard the *Spryte* would become the property of Ituau. The Miner's Pit would be left to Maggie. His belongings in his JOS cabin would be sold off and the coin added to his personal account. No one owned a cabin aboard the station, they were all rented. Space was too precious to allow people to hoard empty cabins.

Jessie made one important change to his record. Now, his personal account would be transferred to the *Belle*'s general fund. A smile crossed Jessie's face, as he recalled Harbour's kiss. *Yeah, I'd like more of those,* he thought and chuckled.

"Ituau, if you're still awake, and, even if you're not, get your lazy butt to my cabin," Jessie called over his comm unit.

Several minutes later, Ituau rapped on the cabin door before entering. "You wanted to see my large self?" she asked, grinning. The entire crew was in a good mood for several reasons. Their personal accounts were generously inflated by the recent payouts, and they were going back to Emperion for a third run. And, Rules was aboard. While she might not be talking about why she was there, she was broadcasting good cheer.

"Sit down, Ituau," Jessie said, indicating the small table centered in the main cabin.

"You'll be taking the *Spryte* to Emperion. As of this moment, you're promoted to acting captain." Jessie had to raise a hand to forestall Ituau's questions. "Keep your ship's crew busy and work with Yohlin and Leonard to get the *Belle* filled as quickly as possible. I estimate that we'll have two more good hauls of slush, little more than a year, before I think competitors will be dropping in at Emperion. Plus, at this rate, I think we'll be keeping the YIPS tanks full, and that will allow them to catch up with demand. Then, you know what that means."

"There goes our bonus and the price of slush," Ituau replied. She burned to ask questions, but Jessie was intent on rolling out what he had to say in his own good time.

"One more thing, Ituau. I've reviewed my Dissemination of Assets and wanted you to know what I've recorded."

"Captain, now you're scaring me. Word has it the aliens are back. This is what this is all about, isn't it? You're going to Triton."

"Announcements on that subject will be forthcoming, Ituau. Let me return to my Dissemination of Assets. On the report of my death, you'll be elevated to captain and will have a third share of the company with Captains Erring and Hastings."

Ituau stared at Jessie, tears in her eyes. Jessie felt uncomfortable with Ituau's emotions. She was his hard-bitten, first mate, his right hand.

"That's all," Jessie said, as if the dismissal would end the conversation.

Instead, Ituau stood, crossed the meter of intervening space, and grabbed Jessie in a hug. Her size and strength blew the breath out of Jessie. He heard her harsh, choked whisper in his ear. She said, "You get your butt to Emperion, when you're done with the aliens, Captain. I don't want the *Spryte* that way."

Ituau left before Jessie could say a word, leaving him alone with his thoughts. He couldn't remember the last time he felt so vulnerable. "See what happens when you start trying to live," he muttered. "Life gets better, and then it gets precious."

"Nate, conference call with my captains," Jessie said, over a call to the bridge.

Nate had a quick glimpse of Ituau, when she passed by. Years ago, a disagreement between the two of them was settled by fisticuffs. He was assured that he could take a woman, and she'd disabused him of that notion. After that altercation, he'd become her greatest supporter. To see her emotionally unsettled disturbed him, and, like Ituau, he had questions for the captain but no opportunity to ask them.

"Captains Hastings and Erring on the line, Captain," Nate reported and switched the call from the bridge comm to Jessie's device.

"Slight change of plans for tomorrow's launch," Jessie said, without preamble. "Same time, but different order of business. Leonard, you'll make for Emperion with the *Belle* and the *Spryte*. I've made Ituau acting captain. I'm transferring to the *Annie* with Rules. We'll be headed for —"

"Triton," Yohlin finished for Jessie.

"Going to say hello to those visitors?" Leonard asked.

When Yohlin heard Leonard's chuckle, she retorted, "What's so funny?"

"Don't get your skins in a twist, Yohlin," Leonard replied. "I'd be happy to change captaincies with you."

"And have two men advising each other what to say and do with the aliens? Not on your life, Leonard. There needs to be a woman along to bring some common sense to this fool's errand."

"I believe you just called our illustrious company owner a fool, Yohlin," Leonard remarked.

After a pregnant pause, indicating Yohlin was reconsidering her hasty remarks, the two men broke out in laughter.

"Enough, you two," Yohlin declared. "I'm taking Jessie to Triton, and that's that."

"What's the plan at Triton?" Leonard asked.

"Harbour and I discussed this in detail," Jessie replied. "Tomorrow, you'll see a broadcast from the *Belle* after the ship launches. It'll show the aliens' initial hours in the dome. It's clear they're trying to entice us there, and many subtle actions they've taken signal a nonaggressive stance. My intent is to respond in kind. I believe they have vid of us after the dome activated. To imitate their gestures, I'll take the original crew down with me."

"You'll need a shelter and a search rover downside," Yohlin remarked.

"Minimum footprint," Jessie replied.

"What about contamination?" Leonard asked.

"Good question, Leonard. I've been giving that some thought, and I've a theory. We know now that this dome is a gate, as the engineers call it, to another world or satellite circling a faraway star. We've seen two body types on the deck before these little aliens removed them. My thinking is that we've discovered a network of these gates. The real question is: Who built them?"

"I'm confused, Jessie. How does this side trip into the origin of the gates answer the question of contamination?" Yohlin asked.

"I thought you said a woman would add balance to the expedition, Yohlin," Leonard commented. "If you've not the patience to listen, how are you supposed to help?"

Yohlin could hear Leonard chuckling. "Smart mouth," she muttered.

"While I don't know the answer to the question," Jessie continued, "I think whoever built the domes already thought through this problem and many other issues. Think about it. Hamoi's DNA sample triggered the egress-ingress function. How was that accomplished? Unknown. But, it indicates a heck of a lot of forethought and detailed execution. This is stuff that's so far past our capabilities that I can't even begin to imagine how it was accomplished."

"You're willing to risk your life on those suppositions, Jessie?" Yohlin asked.

"Think of the alternatives," Jessie replied.

"The alternative is that we don't go. The aliens get bored, and then they go home," Yohlin shot back.

"I think what Jessie means, Yohlin, is what will the aliens do if we don't go to Triton?" Leonard asked.

"I was hoping they'd go home, but I'm pretty sure that's wishful thinking," Yohlin replied.

"In time, I think the aliens could transport enough workers and supplies to create something that would impact us ... a shuttle or a weapon. Recall the crater on Triton. I don't think we want to wait to find out if these aliens aren't peaceful. Better to discover that now."

"Why does it have to be you, Jessie?" Yohlin asked.

"Time's a wasting, Yohlin. The sooner we get there, the better, and we've got the experience. Besides, who else would make the trip? The commandant?"

At the mention of Emerson's name, Yohlin and Leonard laughed outright.

"Point taken," Yohlin replied. "When do you transfer, Jessie?" she asked. "And do you want to speak to your volunteers when you arrive?"

"After this call, I'm coming over, Yohlin. It's a shuttle transfer in order to stay out of the terminal arms. Precious cargo."

"The crew will be happy to see Rules," Yohlin noted.

"Everyone is happy to see Rules," Leonard commented.

"Isn't that the truth?" Jessie added. "Yohlin, have the four crew members standing by. I'll talk to them in your quarters."

Jessie ended the call, packed a bag, and signaled Aurelia to meet him at the vac suit room. He made his way around the gravity wheel to the bridge. Nate was in a discussion with Ituau. It was obvious that Nate was frustrated by the lack of answers forthcoming from the first mate.

"Nate, Ituau is acting captain. Follow her orders, as you would mine. You're headed for Emperion. Get the *Belle* loaded with slush."

Jessie's intense stare allowed Nate only one reply, which he gave, "Aye, aye, Captain."

"Ituau, I need a shuttle transfer to the *Annie*, two passengers," Jessie said.

"Understood, Captain," Ituau replied.

As Jessie walked away, he could hear Ituau.

"Don't stare at me like the captain lost his mind, Nate," Ituau said. "Jump to it. Get that shuttle prepped and get him a pilot."

Jessie grinned, as he worked his way around to the vac suit room. Aurelia was already wearing hers, except for the helmet, and she helped him don his suit.

In short order, they were reversing the process, hanging up their suits in the *Annie*'s vac suit room. Jessie received nods and appropriate comments, as he made his way to Yohlin's quarters.

In contrast to the crew's reaction to him, Jessie could hear the warm greetings delivered to Aurelia. Within moments, he could feel Aurelia's uplifting broadcast. The girl couldn't help it. Her entire childhood life was spent in a nicely furnished cage, with minimal interaction with others, except for her mother and her sister. To be so graciously accepted by these roughly worn spacers was a treat to her, and it was one that she repaid every minute afforded her.

At the captain's quarters, Jessie said to Aurelia, "No more sending until this conversation is over."

"Understood, Captain," Aurelia replied, and Jessie felt the pleasant sensation drop off. It was similar to a switch being thrown.

Inside, Jessie received the crew's polite acknowledgments. However, Belinda Kilmer, the second mate, who Aurelia saved from encroaching space dementia, hugged the girl warmly. Darrin "Nose" Fitzgibbon, the first mate, laid a friendly hand on Aurelia's shoulder, as he greeted her. Tully, the survey engineer, and Hamoi, the tech, did the same.

If not for the lessons of the older empaths aboard the *Belle*, Aurelia would have been unable to prevent her power from responding to the presence of the crew members who had adopted her.

Jessie, Yohlin, and the crew crowded around the cabin's table.

Jessie was drawing breath to speak, when Darrin said, "I hope the aliens have a means of communicating with us, Captain. I don't think Kasey's sign language is going to cut it, this time."

Jessie looked around the table. The crew members regarded him with expectant faces, and Jessie glanced at Yohlin, who raised her hands in resignation. With the spacer rumor mill at work, the team had quickly assimilated the reason for the meeting. More than that, they'd already decided to go downside with him.

"For the record, this is a volunteer mission," Jessie said.

"How much food and water do we take?" Belinda asked. "If I remember correctly, we ran a little short on the latter, last time."

Belinda's face appeared innocent, but Jessie knew her comment was tongue-in-cheek and aimed at him. He'd been the one trying to reserve his suit water for the others, which had nearly cost him his life.

"Three full days' worth," Jessie replied. "After that time, we should have established enough rapport with the aliens that returning to the shelter for more supplies won't disturb them."

"Exactly how do we establish a rapport, Captain?" Tully asked.

"Simple," Jessie responded. "We stand there like the technologically inept species we are and let the more sophisticated sentients teach us." Jessie grinned, as the crew nodded their heads in agreement with the plan.

"Works for me," Darrin commented. "What about air, Captain?"

"We each take a single spare tank. I'm counting on the dome supplying decent air. However, to be sure, I want two atmosphere test devices with this team, at all times. If, for some reason, we find after we enter the tunnel that the air doesn't agree with us, then we're out of there."

"Speaking of the tunnel, Jessie," Yohlin said, "I take it the shuttle's dropping on the backside of the dome and the rover will approach the entrance across the plain."

"Exactly, Captain," Jessie replied. "But I believe the plain is the front-side approach. Only backward aliens approach the dome through the rocky cut, thinking it's the front door."

Jessie's joke had Yohlin frowning and the crew laughing.

"The *Belle* will be broadcasting the Triton recording tomorrow," Jessie said. "You'll definitely want to watch it, and your captain will record it so that you can view it several times, which I recommend. Look for answers to questions like: Who's the leader? Who are the males, and who are the females? Who's the console operator? Who's closely allied with the leader? Do you see weapons?"

When there were no questions, Jessie said, "Okay, everyone, back to your duties."

-17-
Broadcast

After spending the first night sleeping on the dome's deck, the Jatouche were woken by noise created by Jaktook and Jittak, as the administrator and the military officer unpacked crates and assembled Jaktook's scope.

"We've demonstrated our presence," Tacticnok announced. "Take our pallets below and set them up in a room apart from the meal room."

While the team hustled to complete their tasks, Tacticnok walked to the edge of the dome and examined the cut that led to the rear of the dome. Then she marched to the other side and swept her viewer across the plains, hoping for a sign of the aliens.

"I'm tired of calling you, aliens," Tacticnok muttered. "Come here and announce yourselves properly so that we might know you." With a sigh, having seen nothing, she lowered the device and returned to where Jaktook was working.

"I can be of help," Tacticnok said to Jaktook.

Jittak was stricken at the thought that a royal member might engage in manual labor, but Jaktook flashed his teeth and nodded toward two small crates a meter from his feet.

"Those two need unpacking. Be careful of the instruments, they're delicate," Jaktook said.

Jittak's expression turned to horror. A dome administrator was giving orders to Her Highness and telling her how to proceed. What made it worse for the officer was that Jaktook was ignoring him and his attempt to warn Jaktook of his breach of etiquette.

"What do I do with it?" Tacticnok asked, holding up the piece of equipment.

"It's slid over the barrel's front. You'll see the groove on the inside of the sleeve. Align it with the fine ridge on the barrel and slide it until you hear a click," Jaktook replied.

Tacticnok peeked into the scope's part that she held, located the groove, matched it to the instrument's guide, and slid it carefully forward. Her tufted ears twitched forward, listening for the sound of it seating. When the device clicked in place, she smiled triumphantly at Jaktook.

"Well done," Jaktook said. "The next item is the power convertor. It will sit at the base of the scope. The short lead connects to the scope, and the long lead connects to the console."

Tacticnok nodded her understanding and dug out the transformer. She laid it at Jaktook's feet, deliberately brushing a bare arm against his lower leg. Then she uncoiled the long lead until it reached the console's base.

"What next?" Tacticnok asked, delighted to be included in the work.

"We need Kractik on the console," Jaktook replied.

"I'll get her," Tacticnok said. Setting aside royal decorum, she ran to the open wedge and down the ramp. The freedom she was enjoying was exhilarating.

"You forget yourself, administrator," Jittak said with heat, when Tacticnok was gone. "You can't order a royal member around, as if she were your servant."

"And you forget your instructions, Jittak," Jaktook replied calmly, as he continued to work. "You think yourself so in control of your thoughts and actions that when the aliens finally arrive, you'll do nothing to give away Tacticnok's esteemed position. One moment you're treating her with deference and the next you'll be required to behave as if she's nothing more than a team leader. Are you that good?"

Jittak glared at Jaktook. Unfortunately, he couldn't argue with the administrator's reasoning.

"To make matters worse, you won't be helping Her Highness either, Jittak," Jaktook continued. "If you treat her as a royal daughter, she'll act in that manner and give herself away. So, I ask you, which of us is doing her the disfavor?"

Tacticnok bounded up the ramp, with Kractik behind her, which stifled Jittak's reply. Kractik picked up the lead destined for the console and walked to the rear. Unlike Jittak, the console operator had fully adopted Tacticnok's role as team leader. As Kractik stretched out coils and walked the lead to the console's rear, she jabbered on about what she was doing, educating her new supervisor, as requested.

"There are several choices available to us, Kractik," Tacticnok said. She was on her knees beside the console operator and staring at multiple ports exiting the console's rear.

"According to the manuals, it doesn't matter, Tacticnok. The Messinants have designed their equipment to test any device connected to it. The console will determine what our transformer needs and deliver the necessary power."

Tacticnok shook her head in amazement.

"I completely understand your reaction," Kractik sympathized. "When I studied the manuals, I was amazed by the incredible technology. After a while, it became overwhelming. You have to focus on what you need to do and save wondering about how the Messinants accomplished all this for later."

Kractik inserted the lead into an open port. Tacticnok flashed a grin, patted her on the shoulder, and left to join Jaktook. *Father is not going to believe me,* Kractik thought, replaying in her mind the touch she'd received from the royal daughter.

Jaktook and Jittak completed the scope's setup. It was powered, and Kractik busied herself over the console's panels. The subtle hum of the transformer was overridden by the beep from the scope, indicating systems' checks were complete. Jaktook hurriedly operated the tracking and focusing mechanisms. His sighting window on the distant Gasnar planet was closing and he wanted to record as much imagery as possible.

Using the scope's screen, Jaktook chose a viewing angle that encompassed the entire planet. Slowly increasing the magnification, he was able to spot the two enormous stations, a host of small ships, and one giant one.

"The aliens haven't abandoned the planet," Jaktook said. "They're still there, and if these constructs are any indication, I believe they've been here for a while."

Jittak crowded close to Jaktook's left for a better view. Tacticnok did the same on the right, grasping the administrator's elbow to steady herself, while she leaned in to view the small screen.

"Where is the great ship going?" Tacticnok asked.

"Kractik," Jaktook called out. "Console's calculation on possible trajectory and destination of the great ship."

Kractik tapped several panels, before she replied, "We need a little more viewing time, Jaktook. Keep the scope steady and the ship within the viewing frame."

While they waited, Jaktook studied the image. A small dot caught his eye and he shouted. "Kractik, in the lower left of the screen, there's a small speck. It seems to be moving our way. Track that one too."

"Acknowledged," Kractik yelled back. She'd set the small object for the console's calculations, when a panel glowed. It contained the information Jaktook sought for his initial request.

"Administrator, the console indicates that there are three satellites orbiting Gasnar," Kractik announced. "We're on the largest of the three and the farthest from the planet. The great ship appears to be headed toward the second satellite in the company of two smaller ships."

"What about acceleration and present velocity?" Jaktook asked.

Kractik stared at the panel and scrolled down the information. "Regretfully, Jaktook, both are abysmal. It will take the great ship nearly a tikar to reach its destination, allowing for deceleration if it's to take up a stationary position."

"A tikar to reach the second closest satellite," Jittak said in disgust. "The aliens would do better to get out and push."

"That speck is identified, administrator," Kractik said, interrupting the conversation. "It's a ship, and your thought is correct. It's headed this way."

Jaktook operated the scope's control and placed the small dot in the center of his screen before he magnified the image to the extent the ship filled the screen. Jittak pushed close to examine the image in minute detail.

"I don't see any evidence of weapon tubes or ports," Jittak said, with relief.

"I would classify it as some sort of freighter," Jaktook added.

"Then they're explorers, adventurers," Tacticnok announced happily. "When will they arrive, Kractik?"

"According to the console, this ship is accelerating much faster than the great ship," Kractik replied. "Even though it has a much farther distance to travel, it will be here in less than a tikar."

"Should we leave and return later before they arrive?" Jittak asked. He envisioned waiting comfortably at Na-Tikkook until the aliens got close. Instead of a simple response, Tacticnok stared coldly at him. Gone was the young female, who, moments ago, was happily learning to assemble a scope. The royal daughter, who eyed him now, was telling him that he'd overstepped his mark.

"Recall, Jittak," Jaktook said amiably, attempting to defuse the moment. "The aliens have an observation device trained on this dome. They're coming in response to Tacticnok's invitation. If they were to see us leave, it's possible they would simply turn around and head back to their planet."

"Apologies, Your ... Tacticnok," Jittak replied. "My judgment was in error." That he had to correct his address and halt his bow told Jittak how right the administrator was regarding his treatment of Tacticnok. *Use the tikar to practice, you fool, before you endanger a royal member,* Jittak thought.

"Jaktook, I wish to see evidence of their civilization, their structures, their enclaves," Tacticnok said, grasping Jaktook's arm again in appreciation of his intervention. "View the planet in closeup," she requested.

Jaktook manipulated the controls and the magnification, zooming in on the planet and playing the view slowly across the face of Gasnar.

"What have we done?" Tacticnok asked in horror, when she'd seen much of what Jaktook displayed.

"Our weapon appears to have disturbed Gasnar's surface to a much greater degree than our scientists calculated," Jaktook said with sadness. "Eruptions should have subsided more than a century of annuals ago. By now, the air should be clear and vegetation regenerating across the entire planet."

"Look at them," Tacticnok said, her voice rising in anger. "They're living in domes and using that archaic device to travel from below and get free of the planet's gravity."

Jittak wanted to remind Tacticnok that it was a war started by the Gasnarians that the Jatouche were forced to fight to eliminate their enemy. But his recent misstep caused him to keep his opinion to himself.

Jaktook pulled on the tuft of his chin. It was a sign Tacticnok recognized as the bloom of an idea in the administrator's mind.

"Talk to me," Tacticnok requested.

"There might be a means of helping the aliens, if first contact and subsequent negotiations go well," Jaktook said thoughtfully, and he received a generous, toothy smile from Tacticnok.

* * * *

"Ready, Birdie?" Harbour asked.

"Ready, Captain," Birdie replied.

Harbour had announced her upcoming vid broadcast a half hour before. Based on the types of broadcasts she'd made from the *Belle*, she was fairly confident that if individuals could get to a monitor, they'd be glued to it.

"Send it, Birdie," Harbour ordered.

Birdie tapped her comm panel and said, "We're broadcasting, Captain." She gestured toward a monitor that displayed the *Belle*'s output via its strongest directional antenna. The imagery started with the dome in its quiet state a few minutes before the bright shot of light from the platform merged with the shell. The presentation concept was Dingles' suggestion.

"I think it will be a bit more dramatic, Captain," Dingles had said.

"I think you're becoming a bit more dramatic," Harbour had rejoined.

"A little spice in life goes a long way," Dingles replied, grinning, and Harbour had laughed at his reference to his relationship with Nadine.

"Notify me, Birdie, when we get to our stop point," Harbour said and left the bridge. She saw no point hanging around the bridge for the next two hours, while the aliens set up their camp.

When the stop point was three minutes out, Birdie placed a call to Harbour. "Do you wish to make your announcement via the bridge or over your comm unit, Captain?"

Enjoying a green with other empaths, Harbour chose to use her device. She hadn't been able to accomplish any significant work. The entire contingent of the *Belle* had their faces plastered to their monitors, watching the replay of the aliens.

"You're on, Captain," Birdie said, when she stopped the vid.

"This is Captain Harbour. While the *Belle*, *Spryte*, and *Pearl* are sailing to Emperion for another load of slush, Captain Cinders has taken the *Annie* to Triton. It's obvious to anyone watching the dome vid, that the aliens are inviting us to meet. Captain Cinders has every intention of accepting that invitation. I'll update this broadcast when something definitive is known and when our intrepid captain makes contact. Captain Harbour out."

Harbour spared a glance for Yasmin, as she cut her connection with the bridge. Yasmin was smiling, but her eyes held a touch of fear, and Harbour sent reassurance.

* * * *

"Do something, Emerson," Lise ground out. She was livid, after watching the *Belle*'s broadcast. "Request an injunction against Captain Cinders."

"On what charges?" Emerson asked.

Harbour's final address had hardly ended, when Emerson's comm unit signaled that Lise was calling. He had half a mind not to answer. But lately, Lise had abandoned any attempt at charm. Something had happened in their relationship, which he was unaware of, and it was better to keep her close until he could discover what irked her. With the streak distributors arrested and convicted, he'd put the death of Lily behind him, although he continued to wonder who had tried to kill him. At the moment, his overarching aim was not to jeopardize his monthly stipend.

"I don't know, Emerson. Think of something. That's why I'm paying you," Lise retorted.

"What, Lise, like charge him with alien contamination? We tried that, and it hasn't worked so far."

"Emerson, Captain Cinders is out there representing Pyre. He's acting as if the people elected him as their representative."

"Lise, it's not as if I can stop him. I don't have access to a ship that can make Triton, and I've no jurisdiction to commandeer a ship in order to chase after him. That action's forbidden by the Captain's Articles."

"Forget you and your foolish articles, Emerson," Lise railed. "I don't think you comprehend the magnitude of the situation. This action by Cinders in combination with Harbour's files are enough to get people thinking that a change is needed. And, I can tell you one thing, the new political organization they envision won't include you or me. So, you find some way to press charges against Captain Cinders with the Review Board. Arrest the man and lock him away when he returns. And, you make sure to smear him publicly."

"Lise, if Cinders goes to Emperion next, that's supposing nothing happens at Triton —"

"We can only hope," Lise interjected.

"What I meant to say, Lise, is that it'll be seven-plus months before Cinders makes the JOS."

"I don't care if it's two years, Emerson. Get it done. Incarcerate the man. If he's successful, the populace is going to make him a hero. That's exactly the kind of thing that you and I don't need."

After the comm call with Lise, Emerson worked furiously to lay up a charge sheet. By the afternoon's end, he was on his way to meet with Captain Henry Stamerson, the head of the Review Board.

"I'm laying charges against Captain Cinders," Emerson announced officiously, when he was admitted to Henry's office.

"What statutes has the captain violated?" Henry asked, while he opened the sheet on his monitor that his comm device had received.

"For one, Captain Cinders has not been appointed as Pyre's representative to meet with the aliens," Emerson replied.

"What proof do you have that the captain is acting in that capacity?" Henry asked.

"He's going to meet the aliens, Captain. What else would he be doing?" Emerson challenged.

"Saying hello?" Henry supplied. He kept his face neutral, but inside he was laughing.

"But in what capacity is the question," Emerson replied, his voice rising.

"In that regard, I have no idea, Commandant, and apparently neither do you. Unless you have proof that Captain Cinders is acting in a capacity other than as a private citizen, this charge has no foundation. And, as to the second charge, the captain won't be violating your quarantine order if he joins the *Belle* at Emperion. I imagine that more than six months will pass before he returns to the station. I see no reason to grant the filing of these charges against Captain Cinders. Good day, Commandant."

The office door closed behind an irate commandant, and Henry chuckled. He knew that Emerson pined for the opportunity to slam a door to demonstrate his anger. He'd lamented the absence of swinging doors many times. Instead, Henry's door slid closed, with a quiet hiss, as it did for everyone.

Henry silently thanked Harbour for arranging the meeting at the Miner's Pit. It had allowed him to establish a close contact with Major Finian, who had given him a heads-up about the commandant. Apparently, the major and his lieutenant had again monitored the conversation between Emerson and Lise. The early warning allowed him to be prepared for Emerson's requests, and Henry had thoroughly enjoyed sending the commandant packing with his bogus charges.

-18-
Triton

The *Annie* made Triton, and Captain Erring directed the pilot to maintain a fixed orbital position above the plains that fronted the dome.

Yohlin approached Jessie, while he was donning his vac suit. The expression on Yohlin's face made Jessie pause to allow her an opportunity to speak.

"You know how I feel about you going down there," Yohlin said. "So, I'm not going to repeat myself. But, I'm warning you, Jessie Cinders, if you get yourself killed down there by the aliens, I'm going to be angry at you for the rest of my life."

Before Jessie could reply, Yohlin stalked off. He glanced at Aurelia, who smiled gently and sent encouragement.

The shuttle was prepped with the search rover, the shelter, and extra equipment. It was crammed so full that many of the auxiliary crew rode atop the gear, while Jessie and the dome crew sat inside the rover.

Once the shuttle landed on the moon, the pilot opened the rear cargo hatch and Hamoi backed the rover off the vessel. Jessie's dome crew stayed with the shuttle to help in the shelter's setup, which was their critical backup site. The light faded, as the last preparations were completed, and the crew hustled inside, doffed their vac suits, set the tanks charging, and enjoyed hot meals.

Aurelia's excitement was palpable. It took Belinda three reminders to get the teenager to dial down her broadcast. However, by morning, Aurelia was sending at full strength again.

"Let's get underway," Jessie announced soon after breakfast, "before we forget why we're here and sit on our cots all day wearing stupid expressions."

Aurelia's chagrined expression preceded the curtailment of her sending. But, if Jessie hadn't said anything, donning her vac suit would have reminded her to clamp down on her power.

Hamoi climbed aboard first, entering the rover through the tight, one-person, rear airlock. He would be the driver. Jessie went second to take the navigator's position beside Hamoi. After that, the crew entered by seniority until Tully motioned Aurelia to precede him.

The shuttle had set down a mere 3 kilometers from the dome's entrance, which made the transit a short distance. However, the surface was littered with boulders and depressions. Per Jessie's orders, Hamoi took his time navigating around the obstacles.

Jessie used the ship's coordinates to zero in on the tunnel entrance and directed Hamoi when he drifted off course. When they arrived, the crew exited, each of them carrying their spare tank.

At the doors, Jessie touched the access plate and stood back, as the dome's mechanisms cleared the small buildup of dust. When the doors slid open, the crew piled into the airlock and waited while it was pressurized.

"What have you got, Tully?" Jessie asked.

Tully held up a finger, while he watched the readout on his atmospheric tester. When the output settled, "Slighter in oxygen content than we need, Captain, but it's all good."

"Two sentient species from different worlds, but both require nearly the same gas mixture," Hamoi said over the open comm channel. "This place creates more questions with every visit."

The Jatouche witnessed the descent of the shuttle the day before, its engine flares starkly lit against the black of space. Tacticnok ordered Jittak to put his soldiers on rotation during the night, to monitor the dome's entrance.

"Do you think these aliens are nocturnal?" Jittak had asked. When Tacticnok stared at him, without saying a word, Jittak tipped his head in apology, "Foolish question," he said.

The Jatouche had consumed a morning meal, when a soldier hustled into the room and announced that the tunnel doors had been activated.

The team rushed from the room, the last out closing the door, and raced up the ramp.

"How many?" Tacticnok asked, when she saw Kractik reach the console.

After a few taps on the panel, a visual projected above it. Kractik's lips moved, as she counted. "Six," she replied.

"The same number as before, even though the size of the alien's ship indicates it could carry many more," Jaktook noted to Tacticnok. His eyes were bright, silently acknowledging the brilliance of her idea to transport the same number of Jatouche as the aliens had seen on their monitoring array.

"Weapons," Jittak asked anxiously.

This time, Kractik took a little longer to study the projection. "I'm not a soldier, Jittak, but nothing they carry resembles a weapon. They have spare air tanks and small square devices. None of the devices have barrels or are hooked to energy sources."

"How do we arrange ourselves?" Jaktook whispered to Tacticnok.

It dawned on the royal daughter that she hadn't thought through this part. *Don't intimidate them,* she thought.

"Jittak, place your soldiers in a line here," Tacticnok ordered, pointing to a spot equidistant from the entrance ramp, the console, and the platform. "Kractik, remain at the console. Prepare for a transit." She stepped in front of the middle of the soldiers and said, "Jaktook, Jakkock, Jittak, stand on either side of me."

"Do we smile?" Jittak asked.

"You saw the aliens, as we did, did you not, Jittak?" Tacticnok asked. It was a rhetorical question and Tacticnok hurried on. "You saw their heads and their teeth. Imagine you are them, and I greet you in this manner." Tacticnok flashed her teeth, which were accented by sharp incisors on the upper and lower jaws.

"I would be intimidated," Jittak replied. He turned to his soldiers and announced, "Neutral expression at all times. If in doubt, do nothing. We have no idea what facial expressions or gestures will frighten them." When he turned around, Tacticnok nodded her approval.

The dome granted access to Jessie and his team, and they dropped their spare tanks inside the inner airlock door. He led his crew along the corridor, its surfaces glowing with blue symbols. The ramp at the end of the corridor was down, inviting them to the upper deck. In single file, they trooped up the ramp and stopped, as they came face to face with the aliens.

Jessie ordered his suit to shut down. He popped the seal on his helmet and removed it, and the crew followed suit.

The two species stared at each other: furred and unfurred, short and tall, tailed and tailless.

Tacticnok touched her chest and uttered her name, while she focused on the alien, who stood in the forefront of the group.

Jessie attempted to repeat the female's name. Apparently, he failed, because it produced chittering among the aliens. One of them, a male to the female's right, whom Jessie had seen keep the leader company, hissed and the aliens quieted.

Tacticnok repeated her name slowly, touching her chest again.

This time, Jessie caught the means by which the female produced her sounds. Rather than try to think of the female's name in his language, he imitated the means by which she produced her name, which was by a quick, repeated clicking of the tongue against the back of the teeth and the roof of the mouth. His efforts earned him a quick view of sharp canines before the female quickly covered them.

Tacticnok repeated her name, and, this time, she pointed carefully toward him.

Without thinking, Jessie replied, pronouncing both names. *Slow steps,* Jessie thought, thinking he should have matched the female, who only gave him a single name.

"This one is entitled," Jittak whispered to Tacticnok. "He carries two names."

"We don't know that," Jaktook whispered back. "It might be common for these aliens to possess two names and the entitled have three."

Tacticnok hissed to quiet them. She spoke the alien's name, as best she could, and the alien obliged by repeating it slowly, which helped for her second try. *They're gracious,* she thought.

Jaktook tipped his head toward Jakkock to follow him. He stepped forward and indicated the leader's helmet. Then he walked around the aliens to the ramp and waved to them to follow.

There was hesitation on the part of Jessie's crew.

"Captain?" Darrin queried.

"We're here," Jessie replied. "Let's be polite."

The Pyreans trooped behind the two Jatouche, who led them down the ramp and stopped at what appeared to be a flat wall.

Jaktook touched a glowing glyph and a door, its outline invisible to the eye, recessed and slid aside.

"It looks like we have to learn these aliens' language," Hamoi commented.

"That's supposing that this is their language," Tully replied.

"Are you implying that this language belonged to the large aliens, whose bodies we saw the first time on the deck, Tully?" Belinda asked.

"Or neither of them," Jessie offered. When his crew stared at him, he added, "What if it's a language common to the domes?"

"Then who put them here?" Darrin asked.

"That's an excellent question, Darrin," Jessie said and followed the two aliens into the room.

Jaktook swept his hand across a row of lockers, each carved with a single symbol. It was the same symbol on every locker. He pointed to the symbol on the first locker, held up his hand, and placed it over the symbol, without touching it. Then, he indicated the leader's hand.

Jessie thought he understood what was requested of him, but, when he reached to touch the glyph, the small alien uttered a sharp click of his tongue. Jessie pulled his hand back and watched the alien pantomime pulling off a glove. Jessie released his glove, yanked it off, and touched the symbol. In response, the locker door popped open. Inside, metal hooks and straps were ready to receive the vac suits.

"Open a locker and hang up your suits," Jessie ordered, as he unlocked his other glove and proceeded to divest himself of his vac suit.

Jaktook and Jakkock waited patiently for the aliens to store their cumbersome suits. However, when they spotted the figures of Belinda and Aurelia, they quickly offered to help hang their equipment.

"Alien male chivalry," Darrin remarked, watching one of the small individuals struggle to help with the women's heavy suits.

"I would love a translation guide for these carvings," Hamoi remarked," if they belong to these aliens."

As the humans exited the room in the company of the aliens, Aurelia remarked, "No time like the present to find out."

"Rules," Jessie cautioned, when he saw her tap the shoulder of the little alien who had helped her.

Jaktook turned at the alien's touch. The female indicated the glyph that opened the doorway, and she was gesturing toward him. He frowned and considered that the alien was requesting the symbol's name. Before he could reply, she fanned her hands at the many symbols decorating the walls and, again, pointed at him.

"No," Jaktook replied, shaking his head and holding up his hands in negation. He tapped Jakkock's shoulder and touched his chest, saying, "Jatouche." Then he waved his hands at the wall, as the alien had done, and said, "Messinants."

"Hamoi, you might be right," Jessie said. "Our hosts are the Jatouche, and it looks like they didn't build the domes. The Messinants did."

The eyes of the Jatouche briefly fluttered and their bodies stilled.

"Rules, I felt you broadcast," Jessie accused. Slowly, the Jatouche resumed their natural movements.

"Sorry, Captain, it slipped out," Aurelia replied apologetically. "Their nature is so gentle and generous, and I reacted to it."

The Jatouche led Jessie and his crew up the ramp. It struck the Pyreans that their hosts, who were technologically far superior to them, weren't the most evolved race. It made them feel incredibly inadequate.

Jessie watched the aliens, who had accompanied them below, jabber excitedly to Tacticnok. There was a great deal of head pointing and eye rolling. When they were finished, the female leader approached Jessie. Tapping her temple, she indicated his head and pointed to her head.

"Sorry, Captain," Aurelia whispered from beside Jessie, when she realized what drove the female's curiosity.

"Don't be, Rules," Jessie replied. "I've been thinking that we've little to offer or compete with these aliens and the Messinants, whoever they are, but your powers might give us an edge."

"Agreed, Captain," Belinda whispered from behind Jessie, "While I can't read alien expressions, the two male Jatouche appeared to be easily susceptible to a small amount of Rules' sending."

Jessie touched his temple and shook his head negatively. Then, he laid a companionly hand on Aurelia's shoulder and spoke her given name.

Tacticnok was fascinated by this turn of events. Jaktook and Jakkock were convinced of some sort of mental exchange from one of the aliens, and now the leader was telling them it was a female, called Aurelia, who possessed the incredible empathetic capability. Tacticnok repeated her gesture that she'd given the alien leader, Jessie Cinders, to the female, Aurelia.

"Captain?" Aurelia asked.

"Give her a taste, Rules," Jessie replied. "Something pleasant and soothing, but not too strong. I don't want to see her falling on her butt."

Despite the strange circumstances, Aurelia couldn't help giggling at the image of an alien dropping to the deck, emotionally overwhelmed.

"Captain, be aware that I can't focus on a single individual in close proximity to others like this. That's something Captain Harbour can do, but I don't have the control, yet."

"Well, Rules, let this be your gift of first contact to an alien leader and her associates," Jessie replied. "Have at it," he added, gesturing with his hand toward the aliens.

In preparation for what was to come, Tacticnok backed up to stand with her team. She grasped Jaktook's hand, and he flashed his teeth at her.

Aurelia called on her power, carefully forming her thoughts. She wanted her sending to be sincere and full of hope. When she was ready, she eased the gate open, letting her emotions out. Sharing her wish for a fortunate future with aliens was a tantalizing moment for Aurelia, and it widened her gate.

First Tacticnok and then the rest of the team closed their eyes. Their bodies swayed as Aurelia's emotions triggered ancient memories of less hectic times before they were uplifted by the Messinants.

Jessie was transfixed by the aliens' reaction to Aurelia. He'd felt much stronger impressions from her, which meant that the Jatouche were highly susceptible to her power. "Okay, Rules, enough," Jessie whispered.

"No, Captain," Belinda hissed. "Rules, ease off slowly," Belinda directed. She was the one spacer who was most familiar with the teenager's power and the uncomfortable feelings that resulted when that power was suddenly truncated.

Belinda's words penetrated Aurelia's focus, and ever so slowly she shut down her sending.

Jessie watched the aliens come out of their emotional trip. They chittered excitedly among themselves, except for one of them. Jessie made note of his coloring. He was the male with the watchful eyes, and he definitely didn't appear to appreciate Aurelia's demonstration.

"Jaktook, help me convince these aliens to cooperate with Jakkock," Tacticnok urged. "Our linguist must program their language into our translators, as quickly as possible. I have many urgent questions to ask them."

Tacticnok sent a reluctant Jittak and his soldiers below to reclaim pedestals and pallets and bring them on deck. When the soldiers were gone, Jakkock and Jaktook motioned to the humans to approach the console. Hamoi, who needed no urging, left the group in a hurry, arriving first.

"A fellow tech," Kractik chittered to her teammates, recognizing the gleam in Hamoi's eyes.

Jakkock connected his device to the console. It would be used to build the language translation application. But, first, the linguist need extensive input.

Kractik accessed a small panel, scrolling through a menu and diving into submenus. She was aware of the tech alien watching her every move, and she stood slightly aside so that he could see well. When she was ready, she nodded to Jakkock. Unfortunately, the linguist seemed a bit daunted by the new aliens, and Jaktook seized the opportunity to start the process.

"Jessie Cinders," Jaktook said, waving the alien leader closer.

Jessie took a position between the female at the console and the alien who'd called to him. The male went through a pantomime of moving his hand like it was speaking, pointing to Jessie, and indicating a small panel beside the female console operator. Jessie nodded his understanding.

An image appeared above the panel, floating in air. Jessie eyed it and said, "star." The male alien flashed his teeth and nodded enthusiastically. The female tapped her panel and another image appeared, and Jessie named that one. The process of language identification was off and running.

Jessie had the luxury of naming items with single words and counting. He was taken through hundreds of images, and it occurred to him that the female didn't have to search for the next one. They came quickly, one after another, as if they were programmed. *The mysterious Messinants,* Jessie thought.

Kractik continued to display images until she reached the end of the session.

When the screen blanked, it confused Jessie. He was ready for more.

Jaktook, who'd stood aside during Jessie's session, touched the leader's dark body covering, which extended from head to toe. When the alien turned his way, Jaktook waved his hand over Jessie's group and indicated the console.

"Nose, you're up next for Jatouche education," Jessie ordered. "No swearing or expounding on the nature of the thing you see. Look at it and call it by its name. Everyone, after Nose finishes we proceed in order of seniority, relieving one another. That seems to be our hosts' intent. Rules, you're last."

While Darrin began his session at the console with Kractik and Jakkock, Jessie motioned Tacticnok aside. Immediately, the male, who kept close to her, followed in her wake.

When the three stood together, Jessie touched his chest and said, "Jessie," then he pointed to the male.

"Jessie Cinders," Jaktook acknowledged, wishing to show that he understood the alien leader's proper address.

"No," Jessie replied, waving his hand in negation. "Jessie," he repeated.

"The leader wishes you to use a familiar. Oblige him, Jaktook," Tacticnok said.

"Jessie," Jaktook repeated.

Jessie repeated his name and pointed to the male and heard, "Jaktook." Jessie was a bit more successful with that name. He was getting the hang of using his tongue against his mouth parts to imitate the sounds rather than attempting a human pronunciation.

Jaktook bobbed his head, and said to Tacticnok, "The leader learns quickly."

When Jessie had their attention, he went through a lengthy pantomime, indicating that they needed food and would have to exit the dome and return to their base camp for it. Having no way to indicate time, he decided to forgo that aspect of his charade.

The alien leader, Jessie, was repeating his strange hand waving, when it dawned on Tacticnok what he was trying to express. She waved her hands in negation, ordered Jaktook to accompany her, and started down the ramp.

Jessie beckoned the remainder of his crew to follow.

In the corridor below, Tacticnok touched a glyph.

Jessie turned to his crew and said, "I hope everyone's memorizing these symbols ... the one for our vac suits and this one." Jessie didn't wait for answers, but simply followed Tacticnok into the room. He watched the female leader access a small cupboard and pull out a set of disposable plates and utensils. In front of a small dispenser, she pulled a lever and a brown, thick paste spooled onto a plate. She stuck a utensil in the pile and offered it to Jessie.

Jessie took the plate and sniffed the paste. "Jatouche?" he asked.

"Jatouche," Tacticnok repeated, adding an indecipherable phrase and waving her hands in negation. "Messinants," she added.

"Captain, you can't test that," Belinda stated firmly. "One of us has to do that."

"I've the least seniority," Aurelia said, volunteering.

Hamoi quickly spoke up. "That might be true, Rules, but then we discovered you can mesmerize our hosts. Now, I'm bottom crew member." He reached for the dish, and Jessie reluctantly handed it to him. Sniffing it, he said, "Has a nice scent." He spooned a small portion into his mouth, swirling the paste around and waiting for an adverse reaction before he swallowed it. After it went down, he said, "Has a slightly salty, nutty flavor. It's not too bad, but, all things considered, I'd rather be dining aboard the *Belle*."

"Wouldn't we all," Tully commented.

Hamoi took his plate over to the table and seats that had come from the wall, when Jaktook touched a set of glyphs. Tacticnok opened a second cabinet, pulled down cups, filled one from a dispenser, and hurried to place it in front of Hamoi.

"Thank you," Hamoi said, and Tacticnok flashed her teeth, expecting the alien had spoken some sort of customary response. He sipped lightly on the liquid and announced, "Water, with a dash of minerals." Then, he took a deep swallow to wash down the paste.

Tacticnok and Jaktook left the aliens in peace. They had observed Jessie and his team wait and watch their member's reaction to the dome's food supply. When the aliens were satisfied, they gathered their plates, utensils, and cups to serve themselves.

On the way up the ramp, Jaktook commented, "They're cautious, and they wouldn't let Jessie eat first."

"An important man to them," Tacticnok replied. "I believe him to be the captain of the ship that you observed sitting above this satellite."

"Surely, a captain would be too precious to risk in a first contact," Jaktook objected.

"In our culture that would be true," Tacticnok replied. "But who knows how these things are done in theirs."

In the meal room, Belinda, around a mouthful of paste, asked, "What do you think, Captain, about things so far?"

"Do you mean would I think that we'd be talking into a console, as it spooled hundreds of images at us, like it was a piece of advanced planning to help aliens meet each other, and would I think I'd be sitting here eating Messinant nut paste? The answer would be no. Otherwise, they're going unexpectedly smoothly. Although, I'm wondering what we're going to do when it's our turn to learn the Jatouche language," Jessie replied.

19

Comm Updates

When Jessie and his crew ascended the dome's ramp, Darrin had finished his turn at the console, and Belinda replaced him.

"Rules, take Darrin below and feed him," Jessie ordered.

"Aye, aye, Captain," Aurelia replied.

"We're eating?" Darrin asked Aurelia dubiously, as he followed her down the ramp.

With little else to do, Jessie and his team sat with backs against the dome's platform and dozed. There appeared only enough pallets to accommodate the Jatouche, and they were loath to usurp any of them.

When Belinda finished her turn, she woke Tully and indicated the console without saying a word. Tully stood, stretched, and sauntered over to the console, curious as to what images he would get. Belinda took Tully's place and promptly fell asleep.

Tully was surprised to find that he wasn't getting simplistic images. Instead they indicated actions, and he described what he saw. At other times, he saw a scene play out between creatures that engendered an emotion, and he did his best to elaborate on the subject.

Since arriving in the dome, Jessie and his crew had shared their names with four of the aliens, who had been delighted, in every case, to reciprocate. Not surprising, four of the aliens weren't introduced.

"It's my take, Captain," Darrin offered, "that those four, whose names we haven't heard, were probably the ones we saw on the first visit. And both times they've come here carrying the same kind of weapons we saw on the dead bodies."

"Probably a type of beam weapon," Hamoi surmised. "They require an energy pack, of some sort."

"There's probably a third door below, which we've not seen, a room where their suits and weapons are kept," Belinda finished. She had the same concerns as Darrin.

"Casually gaze across the dome, and you'll find one of those four watching us," Jessie directed. "He's the one with the small scar on his forehead to the right of his ridge hair. He's definitely the security leader, probably an officer."

By the time it was Aurelia's turn at the console, the teenager received the most complex of the visual scenarios. Not more than a few minutes into her session, she held up her hands in defeat and woke Jessie, and he followed Aurelia back to the console.

Aurelia swirled her finger in reverse at Kractik, who recognized the universal tech gesture and started the submenu again. After each scene played, Aurelia swirled her finger forward, and Kractik moved to the next scene.

"Captain, I'm out of my depth," Aurelia said, after a few scenarios played. "I haven't the life experience, much less the wisdom, to describe some of these things accurately, and I don't want to screw up what the Jatouche are learning. I think maybe Hamoi and I should be excused from this process going forward."

After viewing a few of the console's complex imagery, which Aurelia had been shown, Jessie could understand the young girl's reticence. Even he felt challenged to properly describe the scenes. The first one had been that of a vicious-looking carnivore taking down a delicate herbivore and tearing its flesh, while the animal twitched and mewed. He asked himself how he would describe it. Would he try to keep it simple, detailing the action, or would he add his emotional reactions?

Kractik perceived Jessie, the alien leader, would replace Aurelia, the alien who could share her mind, in the rotation. She spoke her concern to Jakkock, who called a halt to the process, for the day. Meals would be taken and rest would follow.

However, seeing the language lessons were shut down, Jessie mentally shifted priorities, and he had an idea. It was Jessie's thought that the

Messinants had designed the domes to do much more than he could conceive, and he was about to test the boundaries of Messinant technology.

Jessie touched the console operator on the shoulder to catch her attention, and the little female alien bared her teeth in reply. It was time for another of Jessie's pantomime, and Kractik watched with keen interest, as Jessie waved his arms, drew shapes, touched his face, and pointed above. During Jessie's third version, Kractik grinned, whirled to the panel, and set about tapping on her panels.

Kractik set the console to monitor comm traffic and waited for a call.

Jessie peered over Kractik's shoulder, feeling as if he were an instructor hovering over a student or a father over a young daughter. It was difficult to accept that these diminutive aliens, with their polite gestures and nonthreatening appearances, were the ones who were capable of massive planetary destruction. He had come to the conclusion that Triton's huge crater and Pyre's volatile surface were partially, if not entirely, due to their efforts. *Don't forget, they defeated their enemy,* Jessie thought, remembering the larger alien bodies he and his crew discovered on the dome's deck.

Kractik didn't have too long to wait before the console detected a call from the ship overhead to a nearby location, which Kractik presumed was the aliens' base camp. With quick touches, which scrolled a menu down, she selected a submenu item, and the console locked onto the signal and identified the signal mechanics. As communications ensued, the console identified the two signal sources and labeled them on a small map detailing the moon, dome, ship, and a fourth point beyond the tunnel's entrance.

When Kractik was ready, she pointed to the ship and then to the base on the moon's surface, her brow furrowing, as she awaited the leader's response.

Jessie couldn't understand the symbols that annotated the four locations that the console projected, but he could read a map. His finger touched the icon that hovered above the moon's surface.

"Captain Erring here, identify yourself," Yohlin replied.

"Doing anything useful, Captain, or just sitting around on your butt?" Jessie asked. His recognition of the console's power was both exhilarating and terrifying, and he had a moment's concern for its effect on Pyrean society.

"You know ... hanging out on the bridge and waiting for my fool of an owner to call and update me," Yohlin replied. She felt a tremendous sense of relief at being able to banter with Jessie.

"Yeah, I hear he's the irresponsible sort," Jessie said, chuckling.

"All kidding aside, Captain, you're not relaying through the shelter, and your comm unit can't reach the ship. What's going on?" Yohlin asked.

"A console tech, Kractik, has identified our signal sources. I'm calling from the dome," Jessie said.

"Who did you say?" Yohlin asked.

"The aliens have difficult names to pronounce, Captain. Just use your tongue and mouth to imitate the sounds I make, and you'll do a lot better," Jessie replied. "Anyway, Captain, this is a quick update for you. The dome is providing air, water, and food, of a sort. We have the necessities. We're undergoing some sort of language teaching process, which I don't totally comprehend, but I'm leaving it to our hosts to guide us. Within this alien group, called Jatouche, we've got four friendly emissaries, one security officer, and three of his reports. The friendlies appear to be in control."

"Are the four security Jatouche carrying weapons?" Yohlin asked, with concern.

"Negative, Captain, vac suits and weapons have been stored. We've discovered there are rooms along the main corridor."

"None of you ever mentioned doorways," Yohlin said.

"Didn't see them," Jessie replied. "You touch a glyph to open a door, which is downright invisible."

"The Jatouche must be incredible engineers," Yohlin commented.

"Actually, they aren't the most technically advanced race. Apparently, an alien race by the name of Messinants built the domes and the gates. Somehow, the Jatouche learned how to operate their dome. I think that's part of the Messinants' grand plan."

"What? Learn to walk and talk, perfect space travel, and then find the dome, get access, and discover wonders. Is that what you mean?" Yohlin asked.

"Something like that," Jessie replied. "At some point, I'm hoping the Jatouche will teach us how to do this for ourselves."

"And who will own that incredible power?" Yohlin asked.

"That's the ugly question, isn't it?" Jessie replied, his voice nearly growling in disgust. He had visions of the commandant and governor maneuvering to claim the dome. "Let the shelter know that everything's okay here. They're probably worried."

"Not really, we're all enjoying the downtime," Yohlin quipped. Then her voice shifted dramatically. "Before you go, Jessie, will I be able to call you?" she asked.

"Haven't learned that part, yet, Yohlin," Jessie replied, understanding the anxiety he heard in her voice. "When I do, I'll let you know. Cinders out."

Wondering if the reverse technique would work, Jessie touched the icon on the projected map, and the call was truncated. Kractik chittered in acknowledgment of his intuition. Jessie felt like he was on a roll, understanding the enormous capability of a dome, and decided to push his luck. He held up a single finger, hoping he was signaling Kractik to wait one. Then he hurried toward the ramp, hand signaling his crew to remain calm. The Jatouche looked in alarm at Kractik, who replied she thought there was no need for concern.

Jessie searched the glyphs along the main corridor. It took him a few moments to locate the one he needed. Inside the room, he accessed the first cabinet, where he'd stored his vac suit. Buried in a suit's inner pocket was his comm unit. He carried it as a matter of habit. In this case, he'd stored it, figuring that once inside the dome it would be useless.

With the device in hand, Jessie closed the cabinet, exited the room, and hurried back to the console. Both teams watched him with interest. Jessie thumbed the comm unit open. Much to his relief, the catalog of Pyrean ships was still in memory. He hadn't accessed the list in years, simply because he knew every ship's structure by heart. There in the list was the

Honora Belle. With a touch on the projected screen, the colony ship's image appeared, and Jessie showed it to Kractik.

The console operator, Kractik, chittered excitedly to the members of her team, announcing her discovery, as she quickly accessed the records from Jaktook's scope observations.

Jessie watched an image of the *Belle* pop up over the panel, replacing the previous four-point map. He mimed calling the ship, but the female console operator frowned.

Kractik was unsure whether the huge ship, which the alien leader desired, would operate under the same comm conditions as the ship that had brought him to the Gasnar moon. In Jatouche, there were strict standards for such things, but who knew how technologically primitive aliens operated. She had the console locate the ship, which it accomplished quickly. Then she requested the console ping the ship, using the signal standards identified earlier, and received an affirmative response.

* * * *

Birdie watched an icon on her comm panel light. It indicated an incoming call, but, before she could activate it, the icon blinked off. As that was a common occurrence, she thought no more of it. Before she could make herself comfortable in her bridge chair, the icon lit again. This time, she waited a few seconds to ensure the caller was serious before she tapped it to access the comm.

"Things must be getting pretty casual on the *Belle* if the bridge crew can't answer the comm in timely fashion," Jessie said, with mock seriousness.

"Captain Cinders, apologies," Birdie said, sitting upright. "Is the *Annie* inbound?" Birdie glanced at Dingles, who shook his head negatively after eyeing the navigation panel.

"We're still in the dome, Birdie," Jessie replied. "And no need to apologize, the dome's console was the first contact you probably saw on your board. There's some amazing technology here."

Kractik heard the change in the leader's voice. It was more animated than she'd heard when he spoke to his team or the Jatouche. His teeth were consistently exposed, which indicated some sort of emotional expression. She glanced at Tacticnok, who had approached the console, hearing the same things as Kractik. It was female intuition. The alien leader was a male, and all his actions and intonations spoke of an impending communication with a female of worth to him.

Tacticnok circled her finger around her face and pointed to Jessie. Kractik nodded her understanding and tapped furiously on her panels.

While Jessie was chatting with Birdie, his head and shoulders appeared on one of the bridge's central monitors.

"Uh, Captain, did you know that we can see you?" Birdie asked.

Jessie self-consciously swept a hand over his short hair, as he said, "That doesn't surprise me, Birdie. I was telling you about the incredible capabilities of this dome. Our hosts are showing us fascinating things on the order of about one an hour. It makes you dizzy."

"Captain Harbour," Dingles sent over his comm unit. "You've a call from Captain Cinders."

"Transfer it to my device," Harbour replied, excited to hear from Jessie and assuming he had left Triton.

"You'll disappoint the bridge crew, Captain," Dingles replied, trying to contain his humor. "They're enjoying the strikingly sharp image of the captain on a primary bridge monitor. He looks happy."

Dingles' call ended abruptly, and, within moments, Harbour had covered the distance from her quarters to the bridge. Dingles decided not to make mention of the calm that a captain should always exhibit in front of crew.

Harbour glanced at the bridge crew, most of whom were grinning. She composed herself, having nearly called out to Jessie in her excitement at seeing him. "Captain Cinders, you appear to have survived your initial encounter with the aliens. How is it we can receive a visual image from you that appears to be originating from the dome?"

Tacticnok and Kractik watched some of the intensity fade from the alien leader, and they exchanged knowing glances. *An important female to you, Jessie Cinders, but not your mate, yet,* Tacticnok thought sympathetically.

"We're making great progress, Captain," Jessie replied. Had the Jatouche not switched to a visual comm, he would have had an opportunity to talk to Harbour with only his crew listening. That would have been a marginal improvement. *It's probably better this way,* Jessie thought, giving in to the pressing needs of the moment.

Jessie gave Harbour an update similar to the one Yohlin received.

When Jessie was finished, Harbour asked, "What's your expectations about how long you'll be there?"

"That's in flux, Captain. At this point, we're teaching the Jatouche our language."

"And when is it your turn to learn theirs?" Harbour asked.

"Good question," Jessie replied. "I'm hoping they'll solve that part too."

"Can we call you?" Harbour asked, after seeing Birdie pick up her comm unit, put it to her ear, and point to Jessie's image.

"Captain Erring asked the same question, and I don't have an answer. I only minutes ago figured out that we can use the dome's console to communicate to our ships. And this is before we've learned to talk to each other. We've managed to exchange names, but, after that, we've been reduced to images and elaborate pantomimes. At least, that's what I'm doing. The Jatouche are patiently watching me while I go through my comic exercises."

"I'm sure the Jatouche find your antics adorable, Captain. I know most spacers do," Harbour replied. Her heart warmed at the broad smile Jessie returned.

"Yeah, I hear that a lot," Jessie said. For a brief moment, Harbour and he connected again. It was an intimate touch in the midst of the oddities of recent events.

"How goes the work, Captain?" Jessie asked.

"We've just started, but it's our third time out. Our people know their jobs well, and we've begun filling tanks ahead of schedule," Harbour replied. "And you'd be proud of Ituau. She's keeping the *Spryte*'s crew in line. They might actually be happy to see you return."

Jessie chuckled at that one. "We're about to shut down for the day, Captain. Been a long one. I'll make a report at the end of tomorrow's work. Cinders out."

Harbour had drawn breath to say more, intending to say anything to extend the conversation, but Jessie's image had disappeared from the monitor.

There were a number of bridge crew who wore various degrees of commiseration for Harbour on their faces.

"Good to know the captain and his crew are safe," Harbour said perfunctorily and left the bridge.

In the dome, Jessie laid a hand on Kractik's shoulder, patting it gently. He smiled, not caring whether his touch or smile were correct behavior for the little alien. The console operator extended her arm and patted him in return.

Observing the interplay at the console, Tacticnok and Jaktook exchanged glances. She called Jessie's name, gesturing for him to follow Jaktook and her. In turn, Jessie signaled his crew to follow.

Below deck, Jaktook accessed the room where Jessie's people stored their vac suits. The other half of the room appeared bare, but, as usual, it contained symbols, evenly spaced along the wall about a meter and a half from the floor.

Jaktook indicated to Jessie that he should touch the first glyph. When the captain did, a beam from the symbol scanned him, and a platform, complete with pallet and pillow, slid out from the wall. It floated a meter above the floor, held aloft by its attachment to the wall.

"No blanket," Darrin noted.

"But the pallet is warm," Aurelia said, running her hands across its surface. "I like that," she added.

Tacticnok motioned to Belinda and Aurelia, and she led them to the rear of the room. Another carving accessed a small room beyond. Hamoi intended to follow, but, as soon as the females stepped over the threshold, Tacticnok closed the door.

Jessie caught Jaktook's attention and pointed to the closed door. In reply, Jaktook went through the motions of washing. To make his point, Jaktook leaned toward Jessie, sniffed, and issued a soft growl. At the end of his pantomime, he pointed toward Darrin's genitals, which caused the first mate to take a quick step back.

The room's rear door slid open and Tacticnok exited, motioned to Jaktook, and the two aliens left the humans to their own devices.

"Food or facilities?" Jessie asked.

"Food," Darrin and Tully replied in unison.

"Facilities," Belinda and Aurelia, replied in their own chorus, and Jessie and Hamoi grinned at each other.

"Captain, boys, come with us. You won't believe these facilities," Belinda said, and stepped over the threshold.

When the crew crowded into the small room, they found it bare. Aurelia pressed a glyph and a sink slid from the wall.

"Where's the faucet and controls?" Tully asked.

"Doesn't have one," Aurelia replied. "You get slightly warm water every time."

"And here," Belinda continued with a flourish, as she touched another symbol, "are your facilities."

"All this technology, and we get a hose for a toilet," Hamoi commented in disappointment.

"Au contraire, my young technician," Belinda said. "Wait 'til you use this one. It's not your average hose." She grinned and left the men wondering.

For her part, Aurelia touched a glyph on the rear wall and another door slid open, with a second threshold. "This is your shower," she announced. "You won't see an outlet anywhere. We looked. But, there are three symbols. From left to right, they are wash, rinse, and blow. Seems to me, we can strip off these skins, get a wash for us and them."

"Now, if you men will leave, we would like to use these wonderful facilities," Belinda instructed. She shooed them out the door, closed it, and grinned at Aurelia. Immediately, the women began stripping out of their skins.

"I still say we should've eaten first," Darrin grumbled, sitting on the edge of his pallet.

"Knew there was a reason you weren't married or with a partner, Darrin," Tully commented.

"It's not like we need the facilities immediately," Darrin shot back.

Jessie rose off his pallet, leaned over toward Darrin, sniffed, and growled like Jaktook had done. Tully and Hamoi broke up in laughter, and Jessie grinned at Darrin.

When the women joined the men in the sleeping quarters, they were smiling ecstatically.

"I want one of those," Belinda quipped.

"Which part?" Tully asked.

"The whole thing," Aurelia replied, and the women laughed.

One by one, Jessie, Tully, and Hamoi visited the facilities. Each were grinning and smiling at the women, when they returned.

Darrin was last. "Guess it's my turn," he said.

"Please," Belinda pleaded, and Darrin entered the facilities to the sound of his crewmates' chuckles.

When Darrin returned, he said, "Now, can we eat? I'm starving. I can even handle another plate of brown paste."

The group moved to the meal room, and Belinda bade the men sit, while Aurelia and she served them. It was easier than having everyone crowding the tiny kitchen.

"Good news, Darrin," Belinda called out, when she operated the dispenser. "It's not brown; it's green."

Aurelia swiped a finger into the paste and added, "Has a fruity taste but still has the consistency of the brown stuff."

"Fruity, nutty, I don't care. Bring me a plate," Darrin demanded.

Aurelia stuck a utensil in the paste, grabbed a cup of water, and hustled to the tables and chairs, which the men had slid from the walls. She deliberately passed close to Darrin, who reached out for the food.

"Here you are, Captain," Aurelia said sweetly, as she sat the food and water in front of Jessie. "A first mate is second in the presence of a captain, Darrin. You should know that," Aurelia added.

In quick order, Aurelia delivered a second serving to Darrin and continued until Belinda and she carried their food and water to join the men.

"Interesting day," Tully commented.

"Full day," Belinda added.

The crew fed on their green paste and waited for Jessie to speak. "A remarkable day," Jessie finally said, after washing down his bites of green paste with a sip of water.

"Tomorrow, do we continue with the console pictures?" Hamoi asked.

"We'll see that part to the end," Jessie replied. "Then we'll have to see what our hosts have in store for us."

"What do you think the Jatouche want?" Belinda asked.

"That was the question I was asking myself all the way out here," Jessie replied. "But, after meeting them, I'm now asking: What is it that we want?"

"What do we want, Captain?" Aurelia repeated.

"Unless we're prepared to risk another generational voyage in the *Belle*, Rules, we're stuck with this system and our messed-up planet," Jessie said. "We've established a strong enough foothold that we're growing our population, running out of space on the JOS, and straining our resources. At some point, we're going to have to limit our growth."

"But we can build more domes," Aurelia objected. She looked around the table, but her companions, except for Jessie, wouldn't meet her gaze, and the captain's eyes were sad.

"Growing the domes means more power for the governor and the families, Rules, and they'll choose who can live planetside," Jessie explained. "On top of that, an agri-dome has to be added for every two or three dwelling domes. That takes time, and it takes coin. The JOS and the spacers would have to finance the buildout with no guarantee they would be able to inhabit the domes when they were finished. More than likely, it would lead to a serious confrontation. And, don't forget, our means of traveling between topside and downside is one thin little diamond thread, which the El rides on. It's a tenuous connection."

"But, who would dare cut it?" Aurelia asked.

"When things go sideways, people do stupid things," Belinda said, gently touching Aurelia's forearm.

"So, you think the Jatouche would help us with our messed-up planet, Captain?" Tully asked.

"Maybe they can and maybe they can't. If they can't, maybe they know someone who can," Jessie answered.

"I knew it," Hamoi said excitedly. "You think the Jatouche might have other gates, don't you, Captain?"

"It's occurred to me, yes," Jessie replied, smiling at Hamoi, who beamed, as if he'd been vindicated.

20

Breakthrough

After morning meal, Jittak requested a private conversation with Tacticnok, and he was disappointed that Jaktook included himself without invitation. To his further displeasure, Tacticnok didn't object to the dome administrator's presence. In fact, it appeared to him that the opposite was true. Tacticnok welcomed his counsel, which meant Jittak was forced to keep his opinion on the matter to himself.

"Tacticnok, I see danger for us with these aliens. I think we should abort this mission and exit immediately," Jittak stated tensely.

"State your reasons," Tacticnok demanded. She couldn't have been more pleased with the progress they were making, and she felt an urgency to help with the planet's environmental calamity.

"It's the alien called Aurelia," Jittak replied.

"But she gave us nothing but pleasure," Tacticnok objected.

"Pleasure or not, Tacticnok, we were incapacitated while she communicated with her mind. Her technique makes us vulnerable. They could overpower us, and we wouldn't be able to resist," Jittak argued.

"In that regard, Jittak, you must consider the possibility that the alien leader is lying and all of his people are capable of rendering us into a somnolent state," Jaktook stated calmly.

"You make my point for me, Jaktook," Jittak replied. "Worse, our home world would be at risk if these aliens ever used the Q-gate and visited Na-Tikkook."

"No, Jittak," Jaktook objected strenuously. "I point out to you the difference between unreasonable fear, which jumps to hasty conclusions, and the courage to trust until faith is validated."

"We'll be staying, Jittak," Tacticnok stated with determination and ending the conversation. "But, I take your point. As soon as the language base is finalized, I've many questions to put to these aliens, and we'll learn much more about their nature. We'll discover if trust is warranted."

"Tacticnok, the aliens are awake and have been in the meal room for a long while," Kractik reported.

"Probably discussing whether they can trust us or not," Jaktook commented, and Jittak glared at him.

"The two of you will stop your arguing," Tacticnok commanded. "Until I say different, we work with these aliens to discover their nature and what they value. Am I understood?" When she received agreement from both of them, she said, "Come. I wish to be on the deck to welcome them, when they begin their day."

Jessie and his crew trooped up the ramp. It was similar to the first day; the Jatouche were arrayed in two rows.

"Morning, Tacticnok," Jessie said, and received a greeting in reply. Tacticnok motioned toward the console, and Jessie said to his crew, "I'm up first. If anyone discovers they haven't a clue how to reply to the scenes they've been shown, feel free to alert me."

And so the day passed much the same as the first for Pyreans and Jatouche. One by one, the *Annie*'s crew gave up on the console's scenes. Aurelia had bailed the day before. Today, Darrin was the first to give up, followed by Belinda. When Tully threw up his hands, it left only Jessie and Hamoi.

Jessie was concerned about Hamoi, wondering if the young tech was accurately responding to the scenes. He stood behind him and observed Kractik change the display. Hamoi would chat to the console and signal when he was finished. To Jessie's surprise, Hamoi was imaginative in his descriptions of the scenes. He would begin with the basics, graduate to impressions, and then wax lyrically on the subject.

Grinning, Jessie returned to the rest of the crew, who sat in the same positions as yesterday, braced against the platform. "Hamoi's better at this than any of us," Jessie commented, as he resumed his seat.

Left to the efforts of Jessie and Hamoi, the rotations at the console became grueling. Everyone broke for a midday meal, enjoying another plate of brown, nutty-tasting paste.

"Why are you smiling, Hamoi?" Darrin asked, while they were seated around the dining table.

"I'm having fun," Hamoi replied.

"How can you make sense of some of those images?" Belinda asked.

"You're trying too hard," Hamoi replied. "If you think this is about language, it isn't." Hamoi noticed Jessie's stare and sought to amplify his statement. "I thought that was obvious to everyone. Late yesterday, when Rules abandoned her turn, she talked to me about what she saw. It seemed to me that the console was no longer interested in collecting vocabulary, grammar, and such."

"You're speaking of when the scenes began showing those unusual actions?" Jessie asked.

"Exactly, Captain," Hamoi replied. "I think the Messinants programmed the console to help one group of aliens learn about the nature of another race."

"By doing what?" Belinda prompted.

"By showing us scenes that prompted us to share our thoughts and feelings. Didn't you notice some of the more gruesome ones?" Hamoi asked.

"I see your point, Hamoi," Jessie said. "If we had found those ugly scenes enjoyable, even titillating, it would have warned the Jatouche of our dark natures."

"Oh, for the love of Pyre, what if we fail the test?" Darrin moaned.

"I don't think it's a pass-or-fail system, Darrin," Jessie said, trying to calm everyone's anxiety. "It's probably more a matter of gradation. Let's hope our score rates their help."

After midday meal, Hamoi took the first shift at the console. When his turn ended, Jessie was next. He was on his eleventh scene when he gave up. The images had become so abstract that he was at a loss for words to describe them. Jessie signaled his submission to Kractik, and Hamoi eagerly jumped up to take his place.

Unlike the previous rotation process, Kractik kept playing scene after scene for Hamoi. One hour became two and then three. Eventually,

Hamoi's eyes blurred, and his mouth dried. Finally, he lost focus, and Kractik stopped the console's operation.

Hamoi walked woodenly over to the platform and slumped down. His enthusiasm was gone. "Sorry, Captain," Hamoi said. "I ran out of fuel, couldn't focus. It felt as if the images were intentionally stressing."

"They might have been doing just that," Jessie replied. "Since this morning, you've had me thinking about what the Messinants intended to measure with this operation, over and above recording our language."

"Such as?" Belinda asked.

"Patience, perseverance," Jessie replied.

"And I failed," Aurelia said dejectedly.

"It won't be a matter of the success or failure of any one of us," Jessie said. "The console is examining us as a race. And, you," Jessie said, clamping a hand on Hamoi's shoulder, "might have scored extra points for us."

Jaktook stood beside Tacticnok, as Jakkock finished the transfer of the language database and species analysis results from the console to his translation device.

"They exhibited fortitude," Jaktook said quietly.

"For a young race, they did well," Tacticnok agreed," but let's wait to see what Jakkock tells us."

Jessie and his crew watched the Jatouche descend below deck.

"They can't be leaving," Darrin said. "That way's out," he added, hooking a thumb at the platform behind him.

"It's probably time for them to assimilate our language and make a decision about us," Jessie replied. "Well, we know where to retrieve our vac suits, sleep, and eat. I think we're free to do anything of that nature until they're ready to talk to us."

"Or they leave. In which case, we could spend several lifetimes trying to figure out how to follow them," Hamoi commented in a desultory fashion.

* * * *

The Jatouche reclined comfortably on their pallets, while Jakkock finished compiling the translation software. Hours later, when he completed that aspect of his duties, he commented quietly, "Phase one complete." Then he resumed his work, which was the analysis of the responses to the console's images.

Jakkock's programs analyzed various aspects of the six aliens. The console rated each speaker, producing displays of language dexterity and their natures — aggressive to passive; empathetic to emotionally neutral; intrigued by suffering to averse to it.

Late in the evening, Jakkock lifted his short muzzle to Jaktook to indicate his efforts were complete. It was left to Jaktook to wake a sleeping royal member. He lightly touched Tacticnok's shoulder, but it didn't wake her. Emboldened, he gently stroked her arm, and she murmured softly. When Tacticnok came awake, she smiled at Jaktook before she fully realized her whereabouts. Then she abruptly sat up, and commanded, "Report," to cover her lapse.

"Jakkock has finished his work and is ready to present his summary," Jaktook said.

"Water, please?" Tacticnok asked, which gave Jaktook an opportunity to leave her presence and act in a subservient fashion — all to hide the indelicate moment.

"Ready when you are, Jakkock," Tacticnok said, accepting the cup from Jaktook and taking a few sips.

"In language, the aliens are competent," Jakkock began. "There is sufficient complexity to indicate highly developed social skills. However, there is a lack of descriptive quality when it comes to common planetary scenery."

"Then these particular aliens aren't recent arrivals," Jaktook ventured.

"Explain," Tacticnok requested.

Jakkock lifted his analysis device off his lap and set it aside. "This analysis indicates that these aliens have been here long enough that we're speaking to descendants of those first to arrive. I would estimate multiple generations have passed. Jessie Cinders and his associates have never seen a forest in full bloom, delicately colored skies, or star rises over a planet's normal atmospheric horizon. Perhaps in recorded form, but the data indicates that they probably haven't personally witnessed them."

"Understood. Proceed," Tacticnok said.

"The language translation software deems an approximately eighty-two percent accuracy factor for our initial conversations, Tacticnok," Jakkock said. "I advise caution to ensure that new terms introduced by the aliens are closely questioned. Furthermore, items common to us will not have equivalencies in their language."

"So simpler speech is better," Tacticnok said, her head tipped in thought.

"Yes," Jakkock replied. "Now to the analysis of their nature. They're direct in their speech, often blunt. What I find illuminating is the similarity of their scores. When each individual was shown scenes with a common purpose, their descriptions had a great deal of commonality. There is little guise in their thinking."

"You're saying, they're honest in thought and speech?" Tacticnok asked.

"Perhaps these six are," Jittak interrupted. "Who knows about the rest of the species?"

Tacticnok leveled her gaze on Jittak. "I would hear Jakkock's analysis without your conjectures, Jittak. There will be time later to share your general negativity."

Jaktook, who was within Jittak's eyeline, was careful to keep a neutral expression and glance aside. Tacticnok's rebuke surely had stung, and he had lost favor with his men. If they were to leave and return a third time, Jaktook thought that Jittak might not be allowed to accompany them.

Jakkock waited for Tacticnok to look at him before he continued. He was of a similar mind as Jaktook. The officer had overstepped himself more than once and risked the ire of a royal family member when they returned to Na-Tikkook.

"What of the aliens' propensity for aggressive behavior?" Tacticnok asked, trying to mollify her remonstration of Jittak.

"It isn't inconsequential," Jakkock stated, which perked up the ears of the entire Jatouche party. "Let me explain," he said quickly to quiet the fears, which were evident. "It's highly directed. In other words, their language doesn't indicate that they're aggressive, as such. However, if they sense an injustice or detect a wrong being committed against another, especially the weak, their language suggests that they will be quick to take action."

Jittak's eyes pleaded with Tacticnok, and she replied, "Ask."

"Does your language analysis, Jakkock, indicate the extent to which these aliens will go to achieve justice?" Jittak asked.

"I interpret the data as they would probably exhibit a low to moderate response. Interestingly, it's the younger members who have the lower response levels toward injustices. Jessie Cinders exhibits the greatest desire to hold those responsible for their poor behavior."

"Perhaps, you should learn to be nice to Jessie Cinders, Jittak," Jaktook suggested, which earned him a severe glance from Tacticnok. Jaktook received her message clearly. It was, "Don't antagonize the officer."

"We could listen and question your analysis all evening, Jakkock, but you're the linguist. You're the expert. I would like your summary," Tacticnok requested.

"It must be understood, Tacticnok, that these individuals are but a small sample of the population. To make generalities based on testing only six of them is to risk making grave errors," Jakkock replied.

"Your cautions have been heard, Jakkock. I don't intend to embrace them as a whole. We'll continue to take small steps, if your analysis indicates it's safe to proceed. Is it?" Tacticnok asked.

"All things considered, Tacticnok, these aliens might, one day, become our favored allies," Jakkock pronounced.

Jaktook and Kractik beamed. Jittak frowned, and his soldiers maintained neutral expressions in the face of his displeasure.

Tacticnok digested the statement, as if she was mulling the possibilities, but inside she was overjoyed. She had hopes for this species after watching the original imagery of them trapped in the dome and the recent days' initial interactions. Something told her to have the courage to come to the Gasnarian moon, and now the Messinants' tests and Jakkock's analysis were proving her intuition correct.

"Sleep now," Tacticnok ordered. "We'll need sharp minds for tomorrow. Jakkock, program the ear wigs." With that, Tacticnok lay down on her pallet, the hint of a satisfied smile on her face.

The remainder of the team hustled to finish what needed to be done, and turn out the room's lights, which issued from the seams where the walls met the ceiling.

Jakkock kept a small light on, which was attached to his pallet, while he programmed the number of ear wigs he required for tomorrow. Having recorded images of the aliens, he'd modeled ear wigs to fit them, having brought thirty of the devices from Na-Tikkook. He would upgrade the ear wigs of the Jatouche and program the thirty in his case. The aliens would require six.

* * * *

In the morning, Jessie woke the crew early. By his estimation, the Jatouche would soon be ready for them. At least, he hoped they would still be present. The thought that an intelligent alien race had tested them and found them wanting, was too painful to consider.

The crew cleaned up, trudged to the meal room, and consumed their morning's light blue paste, which had a mixed berry flavor.

"I'd give anything for a meal aboard the *Belle*," Tully commented around a mouthful of purplish paste.

"Echo that," Darrin added.

"Fresh food, yum," Hamoi said.

"Finish your paste," Jessie ordered. "Get your heads around the upcoming meeting, if we're going to have one. I haven't got the slightest idea how we're supposed to learn the Jatouche language, and we should all be hoping that we don't have to figure that out."

The crew was dropping plates and cups into the recycler, when Jaktook entered the room and gestured for them to follow. The Pyreans followed the Jatouche down the main corridor, and Jaktook stepped through a third doorway.

"How many rooms are laid along this corridor?" Aurelia asked.

"The better question might be: How many levels does the dome have?" Jessie replied.

Inside, the humans came to a halt. Unlike their humble rooms, the Jatouche occupied a much more elegant room that included a lounge area, an expanded kitchen with multiple dispensers, and subdued lighting.

"Looks like we've been bunking in newbie quarters, and now we've been invited to the Starlight," Belinda commented, referring to the cantina where the wealthy stationers hung out.

Jakkock hurried forward. Jaktook took a small case from him, which Jakkock popped open and removed a small ear wig.

"Ooh, jewelry," Belinda commented. The ear wigs had highly polished finishes so that they weren't easily misplaced when removed.

Jakkock held the first one toward Aurelia. He thought the young female would be the most likely to adopt the device because of its appearance.

Aurelia glanced at Jessie, and he tipped his head in approval. She bent her knees and turned her head for Jakkock, who chittered in delight, and slipped the ear wig into her ear canal.

"I want one," Belinda said, stepping toward Jakkock and copying Aurelia's movements. Jakkock happily applied hers.

When Jakkock turned toward the males, he received a different response. Jessie held out his hand to accept one, and, after that, the remainder of the males did the same thing.

Jakkock stepped back and nodded to Jaktook, who briefly cleared his throat to attract the aliens' attention.

"Jessie Cinders, may I present Her Highness Tacticnok," Jaktook said.

21

Pyre's Reprieve

There were gasps from the Jatouche, who were unprepared for the unveiling of their royal daughter, but it was intentional on the part of Tacticnok.

For the humans, it was a strange sensation to hear the aliens' sharp, high-pitched language immediately followed by the monotone translation issued by the ear wigs.

When none of the aliens responded to Jaktook's announcement, Tacticnok glanced at Jakkock, who was busy monitoring his equipment. He signaled that the audio translation had been issued.

Jessie hand signaled a query to his crew, but he received only negative signs. Hoping he understood how the ear wigs would work, Jessie said, "Apologies, Jaktook, but we don't understand the significance of Tacticnok's title."

"Don't you possess royal members, who rule your citizens, Jessie Cinders?" Jaktook asked, relieved to know the ear wigs and their programs were working.

"We have leaders, but none possess this title," Jessie replied, a frown forming on his face. It felt to him as if the introductions were off to an awkward start.

It was obvious to both groups that the translation program wasn't finding equivalents for some terms.

Rather than let the day's communications get bogged down by trivia, Tacticnok said, "I'm pleased to be called Tacticnok by you and your kind, Jessie Cinders."

"Welcome to Triton, our third moon, Tacticnok, though you probably have your own name for this body," Jessie replied amiably, happy to stick to basics for opening comments.

"We did have another name, Jessie Cinders, but we'll want to adopt your names. Triton, it is. And, how do you call your planet?" Tacticnok asked.

"Pyre," Jessie replied.

"Does this word have a meaning?" Jakkock asked.

"It means material for a fire or burning," Jessie replied.

Tacticnok briefly dipped her head but chose to say nothing.

"How do you call yourselves?" Jaktook asked.

"We're humans, and those of us who live in this system are called Pyreans," Jessie explained.

"Please, Jessie Cinders, sit with us," Tacticnok offered, waving a hand at the lounge, which could accommodate a variety of body types.

"You said you have leaders, Jessie Cinders," Tacticnok said, after everyone was comfortable. "Explain this to us."

Be careful, Captain, Darrin signed.

Understood, Jessie signed in return.

This was the question Jessie had feared, and he chose to be honest rather than found the first exchange with aliens on a lie. He replied, "Tacticnok, our society is small in number. Even so, we're divided. A female rules the planet's domes. A male rules the stations above, and a captain leads the great ship."

"You say two rule, but one leads," Jaktook noted.

Clever one, thought Jessie, who had hoped the distinction wouldn't be challenged. "The two leaders, who rule, have taken their positions," he replied. "But the great ship's captain was elected."

Tacticnok glanced toward Jakkock, when the translation program failed, and he shook his head.

"Jessie Cinders, we don't have this word elected," Tacticnok said.

"Elected means to be chosen by the humans who inhabit the great ship, which we call the *Belle*," Jessie explained.

"An honored position to be chosen to lead," Tacticnok commented.

"You heard me speak to the *Belle*'s captain, Tacticnok, via the console," Jessie said.

The female you covet, Tacticnok thought. She wondered if this was affecting Jessie Cinders' portrayal of the humans' leaders.

A thought suddenly occurred to Jessie, and he decided to act on it. "Tacticnok, you've felt Aurelia's emotional sharing. We call her kind empaths. Captain Harbour leads all of Pyre's empaths, and she is a powerful one."

"More powerful than Aurelia?" Jittak asked.

Aurelia could sense the Jatouche's fear, and she signed a warning to Jessie.

"In truth, she is, Jittak," Jessie replied. "But you won't find another human who possesses more of the virtues that recommend us to you. She's spent her adult life protecting other humans, especially those not favored by our society."

Jessie's answers about Pyre's leaders left the Jatouche confused as how to proceed, and Tacticnok excused Jaktook and Jakkock to speak privately. Jittak decided he should be part of the conversation and joined them.

"The way forward is challenged by these humans' lack of a unified society," Tacticnok said, whispering.

"I'm more concerned about the leader of the great ship, Captain Harbour," Jittak said, deflecting Tacticnok's point. "She'll be more dangerous to us than Aurelia, who I judge to be a youth. In addition, this captain leads a group of empaths."

"Are we not more dangerous to them, Jittak?" Tacticnok challenged. "We brought energy weapons to their world, and these humans carry none."

"If I might interject," Jakkock said. "The Messinants' program indicates great consistency among these six humans, and they've been judged to be lacking in guile. If we wish to accept the Messinants' analysis, then we can believe Jessie Cinders' argument in support of the human called Captain Harbour. She must be a female of great value to those she leads." By reminding his fellow Jatouche of the data's origin, Jakkock raised the specter of the seemingly omniscient Messinants.

"Agreed," Tacticnok said, making up her mind. "We'll speak to Jessie Cinders, and he can communicate to Captain Harbour."

A muted growl escaped Jittak's lips, and Tacticnok leveled her gaze at him until he ducked his head in apology.

When the Jatouche returned, Jessie said, "Tacticnok, I've a few questions of my own. Who was here before us?"

"They were called the Gasnarians," Tacticnok replied. "The planet you call Pyre we know as Gasnar."

Hamoi signed to Jessie, *Ask about the fight.*

"Why do you waggle your fingers at each other?" Jittak asked, suspicious of what he couldn't understand.

"It's called sign language. An associate of mine, Kasey, was born deaf, and he was required to learn it in order to communicate with his parents until he was much older, when his hearing could be repaired," Jessie explained.

"Humans can't repair an infant's disabilities?" Jakkock asked in disbelief.

"Not this kind," Jessie replied. "Kasey taught me the technique. It's how we managed to escape the dome the first time we were here."

"Yes, we saw you using these odd motions," Jaktook enthused. He was happy to have an anomaly seen in the dome's recording explained.

"So, it's a secret language," Jittak challenged.

"It doesn't have to be," Jessie replied, his voice hardening. He felt a tap on his back from Belinda, who sat beside him, and he lightened his tone. "I'm sure Kasey would be pleased to teach it to you, Jittak ... that is, if you ask him nicely."

There was a tittering among the Jatouche when they received the translation.

"After all, Jittak, a security officer, such as yourself, can never have too many assets," Jessie added.

When Jittak received the translation, his mouth fell open. The alien leader had unmasked him, and Jittak wondered how he'd done it.

Jessie ignored Jittak and turned his attention to Tacticnok. "I was about to ask you: Was there a fight with the Gasnarians?"

Tacticnok's eyes narrowed at Jessie, and he realized he'd been disingenuous in starting this subject. "Let me rephrase that," he said.

"There seems evidence of a fight between the Jatouche and the Gasnarians ... dead bodies and a massive crater on this moon."

This time, it appeared Jessie had caused the Jatouche consternation, and it was his turn to eye Tacticnok, daring her to be as truthful with him, as he'd been with her.

"In short, Jessie Cinders, the Gasnarians knew us for hundreds of annuals," Tacticnok said. "One day, they attacked us at our home world. The fight lasted annuals, and the Jatouche ended it here at Gasnar."

"Jessie Cinders, how did humans arrive in this system?" Jaktook asked. This was one of his burning questions.

"Fifty thousand of us slept aboard the *Belle*, while we traveled between the stars," Jessie replied.

"There was no gate where you came from?" Jaktook asked.

"Our home world is called Earth, and we had no gate. By the time our ship left the system, we had explored it in its entirety," Jessie said.

"In the corridor, I was told the symbols on the wall were placed there by the Messinants," Aurelia said. "Who are they?"

"An ancient race, who have been gone for more years than the Jatouche have had records," Jaktook replied. "They were the masters who built the domes and the Q-gates."

"How did the Jatouche learn to use the domes?" Tully asked.

"Over much time," Jaktook replied. "It took many generations to discover that the console contained the answers to our questions. The Messinants had left them for us to discover."

"Something isn't making sense to me," Belinda said, looking from Jaktook to Tacticnok. "You say that the Messinants built the domes and left instructions for you. But, you also say that they were gone before you had written records. How is that possible?"

"It's unclear," Jaktook replied, holding his small hands aloft. "It's thought that they continued to monitor their work."

"What do you mean by their work?" Belinda pressed.

"The Messinants uplifted the Jatouche and many other races," Tacticnok explained. "Wherever they were successful, it appears they built a dome so that the species, when they attained rudimentary space travel, had a means of connecting with other sentient races via the domes."

"Does anybody else understand the term uplifted?" Hamoi asked, scanning his crewmates.

"The Messinants experimented in genetic manipulation of target species. Their intent was to accelerate the process by which a species gained superior intelligence and speech," Jaktook said.

"So, the Messinants uplifted the Jatouche," Hamoi asked, wanting to confirm his train of thought.

"Yes," Tacticnok replied.

"Is there a way to tell if humans were uplifted?" Hamoi asked.

"No, there isn't," Jaktook replied. "Although, the fact that Earth did not receive a gate from the Messinants is an indication that your species probably evolved naturally."

Hamoi started to ask another question, but Jessie signaled him to wait. In the same manner, Jaktook drew breath to speak, and Tacticnok touched his knee. It was obvious to her that Jessie Cinders was about to shift the conversation. Much of what she saw indicated that he was a male who preferred action to discussion.

"Where do we go from here, Tacticnok?" Jessie asked. When Tacticnok frowned, Jessie rephrased his question. "What steps do you intend to take next?"

"We'll be leaving soon for our home world, Na-Tikkook, Jessie Cinders," Tacticnok replied. "The decision to help your species must be offered to my father, His Excellency Rictook."

"By help, are you referring to how we might learn to operate the dome so that we could visit your world?" Jessie asked.

"That is one manner by which the Jatouche might be of aid to you," Tacticnok replied.

"What are some of the other ways?" Jessie said, hoping for more.

"Before I answer that question, Jessie Cinders, I'd speak with one of your leaders," Tacticnok said. She let the statement hang in the air and watched the bodies of the humans tense. *You have no love for those who took their positions,* Tacticnok thought, affirming her suspicions. "I'd speak with Captain Harbour," she said and saw the humans ease.

The entire body of Pyreans and Jatouche trooped to the dome's deck and ringed the console, and Kractik placed a call to the *Belle.*

Jessie's face appeared on the bridge monitor, when Birdie accepted the comm.

"I would speak with Captain Harbour, who represents all empaths and who is the leader of the great ship's humans," Jessie intoned in his best lyrical manner, hoping to convey the importance of the moment.

"I'll request Captain Harbour's presence," Birdie replied, trying to play Jessie's game.

"Captain Harbour to the bridge, now," Dingles called quietly on his comm unit.

"On my way, Dingles," Harbour replied.

"Captain, be aware, Captain Cinders is talking strange. I've the feeling that you'll need to follow his lead," Dingles added.

Dingles whispered to Birdie, who announced to Jessie, "Captain Harbour's presence has been requested. She'll be with you momentarily."

The wait was nearly a quarter hour, while Harbour made her way from below decks. She arrived rather breathlessly and took several minutes to breathe deeply and compose herself. When ready, she said in a strong, clear voice, "This is Captain Harbour."

"Captain Harbour, I've the honor of translating for Her Highness Tacticnok," Jessie said.

Harbour glanced at Dingles, who shrugged his shoulders.

"I'd be pleased to listen to Her Highness Tacticnok," Harbour replied.

The console's view widened, and the *Belle*'s bridge crew was treated to a crystal-clear view of Jessie, his crew, and the Jatouche.

"With our new ear wigs, Captain Harbour, we and the Jatouche are able to understand one another," Jessie said, trying to subtly warn Harbour that her comments would be understood. Harbour tipped her head down ever so slightly, signaling Jessie she'd understood.

"We're grateful for the opportunity to meet Jessie Cinders and his five companions. This has been a historic first contact," Tacticnok said, which Jessie translated.

"I've every confidence in Jessie Cinders and his people, and I'm pleased that you found them valuable representatives of our species," Harbour replied. The thought occurred to Harbour that Jessie had probably been speaking in this manner for a while, and she marveled at what he'd accomplished.

"I've understood from Jessie Cinders that you came by your position in an unusual manner," Tacticnok said.

Jessie smiled, as he repeated the question, and that expression was echoed by Jittak, who was hoping that Tacticnok caught the leader in a lie.

Harbour racked her brain for what Tacticnok might be referring to or what Jessie might have told her. Then it occurred to her that Jessie wouldn't have embellished the truth. He tended to speak plainly, if not bluntly.

"I had the honor of being elected by the residents of the *Belle*," Harbour replied. "Does Her Highness Tacticnok understand what that means?"

Tacticnok nodded, and Jessie affirmed that she did. Out of the corner of his eye, Jessie saw Jittak deflate.

"We too have been honored," Tacticnok said. "We've received a gift from Aurelia."

It occurred to Harbour what was transpiring, during this call. The aliens had met Jessie and his crew and had heard many things from them. Now, they were seeking to confirm some of that information. "You're speaking of Aurelia's empathetic capabilities," Harbour replied. "I hope you weren't overwhelmed. She's young and still learning to control her power."

"It was a most pleasant sensation," Tacticnok replied. "It must be difficult to be a leader of one so powerful that she can overwhelm even you."

Harbour smiled. It was a test, and she decided to push back. "It does not become Her Highness Tacticnok to pose such falsehoods. Jessie

Cinders would have told you who I am. I'm captain of the *Belle* and its many residents. I lead the empaths by right of my greater power and my willingness to put their welfare first. Now, let this be an end to the games or I'll request Jessie Cinders abandon communications with you."

Tacticnok bowed her head in apology. It didn't seem to require a comment, so Jessie kept silent.

"Jessie Cinders can share with you our discussions," Tacticnok said, "but before we leave, I wish to offer my sorrow for the conditions you've suffered on Pyre."

"You've no need to apologize," Harbour replied and then halted in mid-sentence. So many things fell into place from discussions with Jessie and her engineers. Her eyes narrowed at the monitor's image, and she dearly wished to be present in the dome and bring her power to bear on the alien leader. She was sure her years of reading clients would serve her well. Changing her tone, Harbour said, "It's not your fault, or is it?"

When an answer wasn't forthcoming from Tacticnok, Jessie turned from the console to face her. In no way was he a judge of alien expressions, but those worn by Tacticnok, Jaktook, and Jakkock were too easy to read. It was guilt, pure and simple.

"The fight, the battle, here at Triton. The crater. You had some sort of powerful weapon," Jessie accused.

"We did," Jaktook replied, when words seemed to have escaped Tacticnok. "We were fighting to prevent the Gasnarians from getting access to the dome. At first, our beam weapon was used to defend this satellite by preventing their ships from landing shuttles. But the Gasnarians began landing on the far side of this satellite from our installation. Knowing that our position was untenable, it was decided to target the planet."

"Explain exactly what you did," Jessie growled, his temper getting the best of him.

Belinda thought to say something to calm Jessie, but she hesitated. Instead, the entire group of humans and aliens felt a pleasant sensation of sympathy and concern. Aurelia's sending had less power than the previous occasion, and it enabled the Jatouche to enjoy the feeling, without succumbing to it. For Jessie, it tickled the many times he'd benefitted from Aurelia's ministrations, and he relaxed into it. After a few minutes, the sensation subsided.

"Apologies," Jessie said to the Jatouche. "I was rude."

"A valuable individual to have ... a female to calm tempers," Tacticnok said, reaching out a small hand to Aurelia, who grasped it gently. She nodded to Jaktook, requesting he respond to Jessie's request.

"Information regarding our final battle on this satellite isn't complete," Jaktook explained. "Our soldiers were fighting to hold the dome, while a group manned the weapon emplacement. After the planet was targeted, it was locked on continuous fire, while the soldiers attempted to defend it. Some of our soldiers attempted to exit the dome before the Gasnarians could make their entrance. They were caught trying to make their escape through the gate. Then the Jatouche console showed this gate to be inaccessible. We didn't know what happened to our soldiers, and we learned nothing more until you activated the dome.

Tacticnok's eyes pleaded with Jessie, and she said, "The fate of our weapon was unknown to us, Jessie Cinders. Our soldiers told us that they thought the Gasnarians would have destroyed it soon after it began autofiring. Our scientists told us that it would have caused only minimal damage to the planet. But, when the Gasnarians never reactivated the dome, we anticipated those conjectures were wrong."

Harbour couldn't follow what the Jatouche were saying without Jessie's translations, but she knew him well enough to recognize his demeanor, which said it wasn't an appropriate time to interrupt him. *The pleasantries of first contact might have taken a turn for the worse,* Harbour thought.

"How long ago was this?" Jessie asked.

"More than four hundred annuals by the Na-Tikkook timeline," Jaktook replied.

Jessie deflated. *Of all the rotten luck,* he thought. *We have to make planetfall on the site of a major conflict between aliens, and we inherit the mess.*

Tacticnok caught Jessie's attention and swung her eyes toward the console.

"Captain Harbour, the upshot here is that there was a long-running fight between the Jatouche and the previous inhabitants of Pyre called the Gasnarians," Jessie summarized. "The final battle happened here on Triton. The Jatouche were using some sort of beam weapon to defend the dome and destroy Gasnarian ships. The beam weapon was turned on the planet. I think that's what has caused the planet's massive surface upheaval and polluted the atmosphere."

Harbour would have loved to have locked eyes on the Jatouche leader, but Tacticnok's expression indicated she was already feeling ashamed for the suffering of the human colonists.

"Is it a quality of the Jatouche that they believe in correcting their actions, when they know they've harmed others?" Harbour asked.

Tacticnok's head snapped up, and she flashed her teeth. "It's a well-known quality of the Jatouche, Captain Harbour."

"Then I look forward to hearing from Jessie Cinders how the Jatouche can help us," Harbour replied. She felt that this was a good point on which to end the discussion with the aliens and signaled Birdie to cut the call. "Did I just ask the aliens for help?" Harbour said to herself. The wide-eyed stares of the bridge crew seemed to indicate that she had.

"Can you help?" Jessie asked Tacticnok, after Kractik motioned that the call had been terminated.

"Do we have the technology? Yes, Jessie Cinders," Tacticnok replied. "Do we have the equipment? No. They will have to be designed and constructed ... some elements by us and some by you, to our specifications. This will take time."

"Well, we aren't going anywhere," Jessie said with a sigh. "For better or worse, this is our home now. You mentioned earlier that your father must approve any help we receive from the Jatouche. Does he have the authority?"

There was some chittering between Tacticnok, Jaktook, and Jakkock.

"Jessie Cinders, Her Highness Tacticnok is the daughter of His Excellency Rictook, who is the supreme ruler of the Jatouche," Jaktook explained, understanding that humans did not have the same societal organization, as did they. "His word is law. If he approves Tacticnok's request, it will be done."

"And will you request this, Tacticnok?" Jessie asked, pressing for confirmation.

"Oh, yes, Jessie Cinders," Tacticnok replied with enthusiasm. "Have no concerns. My father will hear me."

The gleam in Tacticnok's eyes exuded confidence, and Jessie felt as if he could jump up and cheer in celebration. What almost made him break into a smile was the thought that he couldn't ever remember celebrating in that fashion. Then again, it wasn't every day that you met aliens and discovered that they might be able to help you recover your ailing planet.

"How will we learn what's transpiring?" Jessie asked.

"I'll send reports, Jessie Cinders," Tacticnok said. "Kractik will come with an escort and call Captain Harbour. Will she encounter other humans?"

"My ships are the only ones that would make the journey to Triton, Tacticnok," Jessie replied.

"You possess multiple ships?" Jaktook asked, his eyes wide in amazement.

"Three," Jessie replied.

"A human of substance," Jaktook murmured.

"Some," Jessie said quietly.

And a modest human, Tacticnok thought.

"We'll be gathering our supplies and leaving now, Jessie Cinders," Tacticnok announced.

"We'll be doing the same," Jessie replied. "I want to thank you, Tacticnok, for the courage you exhibited when you chose to come through the gate to meet us, and, whether you can help us or not, thank you for trying."

Jessie held out his hand to Tacticnok. The soft gasps of the Jatouche were audible, but Tacticnok flashed her teeth and laid her small furred hand, with its dark brown pads lining the palm and fingers, into Jessie's. When his closed gently on hers, she did the same, although hers could only partially encompass his.

The exchange of teeth by the two aliens seemed to be a common gesture.

Jakkock extended the case of ear wigs to Jessie. "In hopes that you'll need them, Jessie Cinders," he said.

Jessie nodded his thanks to Jakkock and turned to the alien leader, "Until we meet again, Tacticnok," he said.

"I expect we will," Tacticnok replied.

"Pack it up, crew," Jessie said. "We're out of here."

Jittak ordered his soldiers to do the same, and the two groups descended below to recover their vac suits and their gear. Jessie and his people prepared to leave by the dome's entrance, while Tacticnok's team assembled their equipment on the platform.

The Pyreans had just exited the dome, when a flash of blue light in the fading twilight caught their attention.

"I was going to say, Captain," Darrin said, over the general comm channel, "that this experience was probably the most incredible thing I could imagine. However, I'm going to reserve judgment."

"Yeah, especially if the Jatouche return," Belinda shot back.

"I'm anxious to learn more about their technology," Tully enthused.

"Me too," Hamoi said, his excitement evident.

"You're quiet, Captain," Aurelia commented.

"I'm thinking I've no idea how this is going to work out if the Jatouche return," Jessie said. In the quiet that followed, Jessie called the shelter. "Base, this is Captain Cinders. Ready the shuttle and start breaking down the shelter. We're out of here and headed for Emperion. We've got slush to move."

-22-
Rictook

His Excellency Rictook was delighted to see the safe return of his daughter in the company of the entire party. And, as he expected, Tacticnok wasted no time requesting an audience with him and his advisors. However, in this regard, Rictook wasn't to be rushed. He allowed time for his advisors to receive and analyze the reports from the intrepid team.

On the fourth day after Tacticnok's return from Triton, which the Jatouche were now calling the Gasnarian satellite, she met Jaktook, as he arrived at the lower levels of the royal residence.

"No security?" Jaktook asked, looking behind her.

"I ordered them to wait above," Tacticnok said.

Jaktook assumed that Tacticnok was taking the opportunity to cue him to the strategy they would adopt at this critical meeting. Instead, they rode the lift in silence. The only notable moments were the occasions when Tacticnok's hand brushed his. The sensations made the fur on his forearm rise.

"We can begin," Tacticnok announced, when the advisors joined Rictook, Jaktook, and her.

"If I may, Your Excellency," Roknick, the master strategist, said, "I think it's clear that we can't ally ourselves with the humans. It's too dangerous. The reported subjugation of our team by the one called Aurelia is proof of that."

"It wasn't a subjugation, Your Excellency," Tacticnok replied. "It was a sharing."

"According to Jittak's report, the team was immobilized, while the human, Aurelia, was communicating with her mind," Roknick riposted.

Rictook raised his hand ever so slightly off his thigh, which stilled Tacticnok's reply. He asked, "How did it feel?"

"It was wonderful, Your Excellency," Tacticnok replied. Next to her, Jaktook nodded his agreement.

"I must point out, Your Excellency, that Aurelia is considered a youth among the humans," Roknick continued. "The leader, Jessie Cinders, told Tacticnok that the captain they spoke to was more powerful and ruled many of these so-called empaths."

"Captain Harbour doesn't rule. She leads," Tacticnok said, pleased to be able to correct Roknick.

"Explain," Rictook requested.

"The humans have no royalty," Tacticnok replied. "According to Jessie Cinders, their society is divided."

"Divided how?" Rictook asked.

"The domes on the planet have one leader. Those on the stations above have another. And Captain Harbour leads those who live aboard the great ship that brought these humans to Gasnar ... I mean Pyre," Tacticnok explained.

"And there is another example of the danger of associating with these aliens, Your Excellency," Roknick shot back. "These humans have no need of weapons. They have the power to enthrall us. In addition to that peril, they're divided. We could find ourselves in the middle of their society's upheaval. Who says that these other two leaders will welcome us as supposedly did Captain Harbour?"

Rictook's hand lifted again, and he turned his gaze on Pickcit, the Master Economist.

"On the face of the team's reports, I see no immediate economic advantage in an alliance with these humans, Your Excellency," Pickcit said. "They'll require a great deal of time to lift their technology, without support from us, and, if we extend that support, it'll be without recompense for us."

Tacticnok was crestfallen at the thought that two of her father's key advisors were voicing negative opinions, regarding a liaison with the humans.

"On the other hand, Your Excellency, we must consider the long-term opportunities," Pickcit continued. "Have we heard of any other race, but the Messinants, who have traveled between the stars? Obviously, it was crudely done, but, nonetheless, it was accomplished. Such an incredible feat bodes well for the humans' future development. The questions we must ask ourselves are: Do we wish to form an alliance with the humans now and develop them as business partners or do we wish to isolate them from us and see them become our future competitors?"

Rictook's eyes strayed overhead, while he considered Pickcit's words. When he was ready, he glanced at Tiknock, the master scientist.

"Your Excellency, I possess a duality of thought similar to Master Pickcit," Tiknock said. "The Pyreans, as they prefer to be called, have a woefully underdeveloped technological base. Yet, they traveled between the stars, arriving in the hold of this great ship to a planet that we, unfortunately, destroyed of life. Despite the enormous obstacles, they managed to gain a foothold on the planet and in its orbit. I'm astounded by their resiliency."

Tiknock took a moment to consider his next words before he resumed.

"Every race we've met was developed in the protective, natural fold of their home world," Tiknock said. "They were afforded the opportunity to mature gradually and reach for space in the due course of time. These humans, however, were forced to accept the ravaged planet that we bequeathed them. Against all odds, they survived, built stations, constructed ships, and discovered the Messinants' dome."

Again, Rictook chose to halt the conversation to consider the advice, and his audience waited. When ready, his eyes fell upon Tiknock, a signal to continue.

"Most of all, Your Excellency, let us not forget that the humans found a nonfunctioning dome and repaired it," Tiknock said. "Although, it's likely it was more a matter of tinkering with what they considered was a derelict site and thinking that their machinations would conceivably have produced no response. By the dome's recording, we can see that they were taken completely unaware by their actions, which activated the dome."

Tacticnok chafed under the snickers from the advisors, who were probably replaying the images of the humans trapped in the dome. She felt they had no sympathy for their plight.

"So, Your Excellency, I ask myself the same question as did Master Pickcit: What value can the humans offer us today as opposed to what they might offer us in the future? If left to their own devices, it might take the humans hundreds of annuals to mature to a significant level of technology. But, by then, might they develop technology superior to ours? And, at that future time, will they wish an alliance with us when we failed to offer them assistance?"

Tacticnok had patiently limited her comments to the moments when she felt compelled to share her opinions, while Jaktook had maintained silence, although she could see he burned to enter the conversation. She reclined on her pallet, waiting for her father's permission to speak, knowing he would approve of her holding her counsel until it was her turn.

When Tacticnok's father turned his eyes on her, she felt a sense of great relief. The advisors' opinions balanced the decision on a blade's edge, and she intended to tip it in the humans' favor.

"The opinions of His Excellency's advisors speak of danger or offer a divided opinion as to whether to engage the humans now or later," Tacticnok said. "These opinions view these new aliens from the positions of military entanglement, economic opportunity, or technological exchange. I haven't any additional words to add to these learned statements, but there's one factor that hasn't been discussed, and it's the most important one."

Tacticnok had everyone's attention. She could imagine the advisors racking their brains to consider what she intimated.

"The humans are wrestling with a planet that we destroyed," Tacticnok continued. She quickly raised a hand to forestall the masters' retorts. "Yes, I know that it was the Gasnarians, whose treachery led to the final encounter at Gasnar and our disruption of their planet's surface. But, the Gasnarians are gone and probably died out not long after their home world's atmosphere was polluted."

Tacticnok sat up on her pallet. It was a sign of the intense emotion that she felt. "The humans are there now. Do we not owe them recompense for what was done to their world and the struggles that they've had to suffer? It will cost us little to help them recover their planet, and it will probably take many annuals to do so. If we're successful in this project, what will the humans think of us? Will we not have won their respect? And, will that not lead to their desire for an alliance with us, when their society blooms economically and technologically?"

Tacticnok gazed at the masters, and her eyes settled on her father, as she said. "A simple gesture that can reap a great reward in the future."

Jaktook eased down on his pallet. Everything he'd wanted to say, Tacticnok had expressed simply and elegantly. His admiration for the royal daughter had increased immensely over the course of the dome's investigation and during the encounter with the humans.

"Thank you for your thoughts, my trusted advisors and my daughter," Rictook said. "I'll consider your opinions and render my judgment soon. Good day."

With that, the group rose, dipped their heads, and departed. As they walked into the ornate reception hall, Masters Pickcit and Tiknock signaled Tacticnok and Jaktook to slow. Roknick either didn't notice or didn't care and quickly walked out of sight.

"If we might have a word in private, Your Highness, with you and your associate," Tiknock requested.

Tacticnok nodded and swept an arm toward a private lift off the reception hall, which would take them to her apartments. Once the foursome was comfortable in Tacticnok's outer salon, the apartment's administrator and a servant hurried to offer refreshments to the party.

"Master Pickcit and I would like to hear your thoughts on how we can best help the humans," Tiknock said, opening the discussion.

"Isn't this conversation a little premature, Master Tiknock?" Tacticnok asked.

"We don't believe so, Your Highness," Pickcit replied. "His Excellency's decision is a foregone conclusion."

When Tacticnok frowned, Tiknock added, "Understand, Your Highness, that we've been advising His Excellency for many annuals. His views on various subjects are well known to us, and, decidedly, they're in favor of long-range planning, especially when it comes to alliances that favor Na-Tikkook's economic growth."

"Your father was swayed by our opinions, even though we couched them in both positive and negative lights," Pickcit explained. "And, your statements as to what was owed the humans, Your Highness, sealed the deal."

"Oh, yes, indeed," Tiknock enthused. "His Excellency has made up his mind. The humans will get their aid. He simply wishes to appear as if he's giving this important decision its due consideration."

The master advisors flashed their teeth at the revelation of the political environment that operated at Na-Tikkook's highest level.

"I, for one, am thrilled to hear this," Jaktook said, lightly clapping his hands and accepting the masters' analysis of His Excellency's decision as a foregone conclusion.

"It'll be fascinating to see this proven out," Tacticnok replied, a little dubious about the masters' certainty. She did credit their long-time service as advisors, as opposed to her own short stint as an active participant in royal decision-making. "Assuming you're correct, how might we advise you?" she asked.

"An action of this sort must not be taken unilaterally. That is to say, it must not be considered solely in the light of a scientific venture," Tiknock said. "Let's take the issue of cooperation first. We're concerned by the teams' statements about the three Pyrean leaders. We possess too little information to guide us here."

"How can we get you more information?" Tacticnok asked.

"In that regard, Your Highness," Pickcit replied, "recognize that the science aspect of this venture will require some time to develop. In the meantime, events will be transpiring on Pyre. We've understood that you left the impression with Jessie Cinders that you'll return, if and when the tools are readied."

"You want us to return before then," Jaktook interjected.

"Yes, my bright young friend," Tiknock replied. "And not once but often."

"We return and make casual calls to the *Belle*, updating Captain Harbour as to our progress," Jaktook said to Tacticnok. In his excitement, he nearly grasped her hand. *You need to get hold of yourself, Jaktook,* he mentally admonished himself. *You're a dome administrator, and she's a member of royalty.*

"And in turn, Captain Harbour might tend to relay what events have transpired on Pyre," Tacticnok replied. "An admirable idea, Masters Tiknock and Pickcit."

The two advisors tipped their heads in acknowledgment of the praise. For two days prior to the evening's meeting with His Excellency, they'd strategized the presentation of their opinions so as not to antagonize Master Roknick, while leading His Excellency in the direction they favored. Alliances with other races had reached economic plateaus. The infusion of fresh opportunity from such an intrepid race as the humans was an opportunity not to be missed.

In addition, the masters had high hopes for His Excellency's daughter. They saw her as Na-Tikkook's developing leader, and they wanted to actively support her desire to help the humans. Nurturing a first contact with a new race would elevate her in the eyes of the Jatouche.

"What else do you need?" Jaktook asked.

"When you visit the Triton dome and make your calls, Your Highness," Pickcit said, "it's important to involve Jessie Cinders in your conversations with Captain Harbour. We see him as a central figure in Pyrean society, even if he has no status as a leader."

"Undoubtedly," Tiknock agreed, "Early data analysis from the dome, which Kractik recovered, indicates that the number of ships operating in system are relatively few. That Jessie Cinders owns three is quite telling."

"I thought Jessie Cinders' statement that we would only meet his associates at Triton to be illuminating," Jaktook added.

"Yes," Pickcit replied. "It affirms that he's an intrepid explorer, a human willing to take risks to achieve gains. We'll need humans like that on our side, if the Pyreans are encouraged to accept our help."

"Jessie Cinders' personal affections for Captain Harbour will also be of help to us," Tacticnok stated. "He and she shared the same opinion about the possibility of our aid."

"And Jessie Cinders enjoys the strong support of his associates, as evidenced by the actions seen in the dome's earliest recording," Tiknock added. "All in all, Jessie Cinders might not be a leader, but we surmise that his opinion will carry weight with Pyrean citizens."

"And let us apologize for our humor at the humans' tribulations, Your Highness," Pickcit hurried to say, "Its purpose was to prevent Master Roknick from perceiving our true intentions. We know it was rude, and you were annoyed by it."

"Apologies accepted, Masters," Tacticnok replied, and she turned to stare at Jaktook, whose furrowed brow indicated that he had no idea what she was requesting of him, although the advisors did.

"And we would be grateful for your forgiveness too, Jaktook," Pickcit said, with equanimity. There was no doubt in the advisors' minds of the point Tacticnok was making. She saw Jaktook as an integral part of her team and wanted him treated as such.

"Of course, you have it, Masters," Jaktook replied quickly. He glanced at Tacticnok to ensure that was what she desired, and she nodded authoritatively.

The masters wished the couple a good afternoon and left. The administrator judiciously closed off the doors to the salon, allowing Her Highness privacy.

Jaktook was painfully, yet excitingly, aware that he was alone with the royal daughter. The memory of her hand brushing his in the lift returned to him, and the fur on his arms rose slightly.

"Jaktook, you look as if you're ready to dash for the door," Tacticnok laughed. "You may relax. I'll ask your permission first if I wish to bite you."

"My apology, Your High —" Jaktook managed to say before a royal finger, raised in the air, silenced him.

"Triton rules apply, Jaktook, when we're alone," Tacticnok said.

A smile crept across Jaktook's lips. "I much enjoyed Triton rules, and I look forward to returning there with you."

"There," Tacticnok said, reclining on her pallet. "That wasn't so hard now, was it?"

Jaktook grinned in reply and lay down on his pallet.

"Now, let's talk about when we should return to Triton, what we should try to accomplish, and how we might gain more information about these other two leaders," Tacticnok said.

* * * *

Masters Tiknock and Pickcit congratulated themselves on two successful meetings.

"I think we were especially brilliant today," Pickcit said.

"I would credit His Excellency," Tiknock replied. "I believe he will do what is best for Na-Tikkook."

"I agree. I was referring to outmaneuvering Master Roknick," Pickcit replied. "The reports from Jittak were especially harsh and condemning of the humans. You'd think he was describing the Colony, when he was speaking about Aurelia, Captain Harbour, and the other empaths."

Tiknock eyed his lifelong friend and said, "I'm sure you noticed His Excellency's interest in hearing how Aurelia's emanations felt."

"Indeed, I did," Pickcit replied. "And, I'm grateful he asked. It would have signaled Roknick of our leanings if one of us had expressed interest in the phenomenon."

"Do you wish to experience it?" Tiknock asked, nudging his friend.

"From Aurelia, no," Pickcit replied firmly. Then, with a grin, he added, "But from Captain Harbour, yes!"

The two masters laughed uproariously, as they summoned their ride.

Rictook announced his decision, which, as the masters anticipated, signaled a go-ahead. His Excellency's command initiated days of analysis and planning. The dome's records and Jaktook's scope recordings revealed the extent of the damage to Pyre's surface. Scientists and engineers had an annual's worth of data. It provided them with a means of calculating the amount of heat remaining under the surface, which was created from the weapon's energy, and the density of particulate matter in the atmosphere.

The challenge for the scientists and engineers would be to design a device that could be manufactured, in a significant part, by the humans. That approach would limit the amount of material that would need to be transported through the Q-gate.

The device would have to accomplish multiple jobs. It would need to be able to draw heat into itself from a broad area, eliminating the need to deploy a great number of the constructions. It would need to transform that heat into a form of energy that could be ejected into space, without harming stations or ship traffic or heating the atmosphere. And finally, some of that heat would be required to power the device to do such things as filter the atmosphere at a tremendous rate, compact the particulate matter, and spit it out in inert form.

The two masters rubbed their hands gleefully at the thought of the task. They hadn't been so enthused about a new challenge of this magnitude in a long time.

-23-
What If

Knowing JOS tracking would report to the commandant when the *Annie* left Triton orbit and Emerson would tell Lise Panoy immediately, Harbour decided not to wait until Jessie joined her at Emperion before she broadcast her newest message. She chuckled to herself, imagining the commandant and the governor's reactions.

"Will you want to share the imagery from the dome that was seen on Captain Cinders' last comm?" Dingles asked Harbour.

"You mean the part where our spacers are surrounded by short, furry Jatouche?" Harbour asked. "You bet I do."

"Don't you think we might be scaring the topsiders and downsiders?" Dingles riposted.

"Dingles, ask yourself: How do you get an entire population to accept a monumental change in perspective?" Harbour said.

"I have no idea, Captain. How do you do that?" Dingles asked, feeling he was out of his depth in this conversation.

"I haven't the faintest idea, Dingles," Harbour replied, with a wry smile. "My intention is to continue throwing messages at Pyreans and see what sort of reactions they generate. Maybe that way we can figure out how to nudge them in the direction we want."

"Not exactly what you'd consider a tried-and-true technique," Dingles commented.

"Think of it this way," Harbour replied. "If the image of peaceful aliens surrounding our spacers scares our citizens silly, what are they going to think if we tell them the aliens are ready to venture among them and help restore the planet?"

"I see what you mean, Captain. It might be better to frighten them a little at a time instead of all at once."

"That's the spirit, Dingles," Harbour replied, slapping him on the shoulder and sending some emotional lift his way before she headed to her next appointment.

Dingles turned and made for the bridge. On the way, the thought crossed his mind that some time, during the last year, his captain had eclipsed his ability to advise her on greater matters.

* * * *

"I presume you listened to that woman's broadcast and watched the vid," Lise said to Emerson, her temper barely under control.

"I did," Emerson replied. He was mentally and emotionally prepared for Lise's call the moment he heard the announcement of Harbour's impending broadcast. It occurred to him that no amount of monthly stipend from the governor was worth going under with her. This shift in his perspective stemmed from the current moods of stationers that he perceived, as he walked around the station.

"It's time to stop trying to delicately handle the problem," Lise demanded. "I want you to arrest Jessie Cinders, when he next docks on a JOS terminal arm."

"I presume you have a charge in mind," Emerson said, enjoying throwing Lise's words back at her.

Lise stared hard-eyed at her comm unit, as if doing so would transfer her frustration to Emerson. "What part of Harbour's broadcast didn't you understand, Emerson? She said these fuzzy aliens are considering whether to help us reclaim the planet."

"A lot of people think that might be a good thing, Lise. Every stationer knows the JOS is running out of room, and constructing another station will be incredibly expensive," Emerson replied.

"Well, I'm glad the topsiders think that the help of these aliens is a good thing," Lise said sweetly, but Emerson could hear the poison in her words. "Did the thought not cross your topsiders' little minds that the aliens might be lying? Their offer to repair our planet might be just an excuse to repair Pyre and take it for themselves. I suggest you and every stationer stop being so naïve, Emerson, and start thinking about how to keep Pyre out of the hands of these aliens."

Emerson had to admit that he had been so focused on outmaneuvering Lise that he hadn't considered the possibility that the aliens might be as duplicitous as the governor. Then again, it was Jessie Cinders and Harbour who appeared to have adopted them, and, although they were pains in his backside, he knew that they weren't people who could easily be fooled by others, even aliens. He was left with a difficult choice: Cut the governor loose and risk being outed by her or risk the ire of every spacer and a good many stationers by arresting Jessie Cinders.

"I'll take your suggestion under advisement, Governor, and inform you of my decision," Emerson replied in a formal tone. "After all, there's no hurry. The *Annie* has only recently departed Triton for Emperion, and I expect those ships to be there for many months. In the circumstances, it would be foolish to communicate our intentions beforehand. Good day, to you, Governor."

Lise was tempted to toss her comm unit across the room, but she had done it so often lately that she stayed her hand.

"It appears that our control of the commandant is slipping," Rufus said. He was seated on the couch with Idrian.

To relieve her anger, Lise got up from her chair and walked to the room's rear window to stare at the lush garden. She didn't know why the view of flowering trees and plants calmed her, since she rarely walked through the expansive greenery.

"Ever since we discovered the monitoring software on my comm device, the tension between him and me has been on the rise," Lise replied. "I'm beginning to wonder if it wasn't Emerson's doing."

"That would indicate a third player," Idrian suggested.

"A third player or players on the station, who have access to the comm servers," Rufus added.

"Yes, it does, doesn't it?" Lise said, rounding to gaze at the two family heads. "And I have an idea of who that might be. Major Finian was the key figure in the arrest of Markos Andropov. It's quite likely that he's become aware of our liaison with the governor."

"That could be extremely dangerous for us, Lise," Idrian said, with concern.

"Not necessarily," Rufus objected. "If the major had something significant, he'd have presented it to the Review Board."

"Which means he's either guessing or he's obtained his information illegally," Lise surmised, taking her seat again.

"Either way, he should probably be dealt with, sooner than later," Rufus suggested.

"That's entirely premature, Rufus," Idrian countered. "We think there's a third player. Lise thinks it might be Major Finian. We think that he's guessing or obtained illegal evidence. That's a thin chain of presumptions. In addition, you might consider that the major has shared his knowledge with others."

"Idrian is correct, Rufus," Lise replied. "There's too much that's unknown in order for us to take action. However, if what we surmise is true, it means our communications with Emerson or topsiders, in general, are in jeopardy."

The shocked expressions on Rufus and Idrian's faces disgusted Lise. She wanted to sneer at them and decry their weak minds.

"We have to communicate on a daily basis with stationers, Lise," Idrian objected. "What are we going to do, if security is monitoring us?"

Lise stuffed her indignation back in its box. "Simple, Idrian. Keep your calls clean. If you have something manipulative to communicate, have someone else make the call. Or, I don't know, send them a printed message if you can't trust anyone to do it for you. Get inventive. It's not my place to help you figure out how to get around security's surreptitious surveillance of us."

"This subject aside, Lise, what are we going to do about the aliens?" Rufus asked. After the meeting, he intended to take Idrian to task for displaying weakness to Lise.

"I've been thinking about that," Lise replied. "The commandant does have a point, even if he made it obliquely. We have time. The aliens might not come through on their offer. Even if they do, any equipment they intend to introduce has to come through the domes. That will give us an opportunity to negotiate with the topsiders under what circumstances they're allowed to do this. There's no way we're opening up this planet to the likes of stationers and spacers."

* * * *

Jessie arrived at Emperion, transferred from the *Annie* to the *Spryte*. Immediately, the *Annie*'s crew joined the rotation of spacers responsible for moving the slush, much to the relief of those who had been hard at work for weeks to best the past trip's production rate.

Harbour was disappointed that Jessie didn't visit the *Belle* after arriving and found an opportunity to talk to Ituau in the cantina one evening.

"Getting some much-needed rest?" Harbour asked, as she came up from behind Ituau.

The other spacers who stood at the tall, drinks table with Ituau glanced at Harbour. They were looking for a sign as to whether the captain wanted a private conversation, and Harbour signaled them to stay.

However, Ituau wasn't fooled by Harbour's casual approach and knew exactly what the captain wanted to know.

"If I knew being captain required so much work, I think I wouldn't have been so excited to accept the appointment," Ituau quipped and downed the last of her drink.

A resident, who was earning extra coin as a server, passed by, and Harbour caught her attention. "Another round for these thirsty spacers on the captain's account," she said.

The spacers who'd been nursing their drinks finished them off in a hurry in anticipation of the free ones.

"I would imagine Captain Cinders wouldn't have that much to do after the way you've kept the crew busy, Ituau," Harbour suggested.

"Good thing the captain is back," Nate said. "Ituau was trying to work us to death."

"You'd think you don't like the prospects of a pile of coin," Ituau riposted.

"Can't spend it if I'm dead, Ituau," Nate shot back, and the spacers chuckled about the exchange.

"Captain has been a bit irritable after he returned from Triton," Buttons, an aging spacer, commented.

"That's nothing much," Nate said. "Just too many questions."

"What do you mean too many questions?" Harbour asked.

The spacers glanced toward Ituau, as if it were her place to discuss the captain's business in an open forum.

"You know how it is, Captain," Ituau said. "Spacers are a practical bunch. Once they heard there was the prospect of aliens coming to help recover the planet, they started discussing what it would take to facilitate the project. You know, the details of transport, design, manufacture, and every other little bit of calculation."

"And?" Harbour prompted.

"We didn't come with many answers, Captain," Buttons continued, since it appeared that Ituau had given them permission to talk. "So, naturally, we asked —"

"Captain Cinders," Harbour finished, laughing.

"Yes, Ma'am," Buttons agreed, grinning self-consciously and fingering one of the larger metal buttons festooned on his vest.

"And did your captain provide you with the answers you sought?" Harbour asked. She was enjoying the moment with the *Spryte*'s crew. They were like her spacers, open and forthright. *Why can't most people be like these individuals?* Harbour thought.

"I think that's what's bothering the captain," Nate offered. "Too many questions and not enough answers."

"There's still the possibility that the aliens aren't coming back," Kasey suggested.

"Don't think so, Kasey," Harbour said, and the crew's casualness disappeared, as they focused on her.

"You know something, Captain?" Ituau asked.

"I might not know Captain Cinders as well as the lot of you do, but I do know one thing about him," Harbour replied. "He's an excellent judge of character." The crew nodded their agreement, and Harbour added, "His judgment might apply equally well to aliens. Captain Cinders believes they're coming back, which means we should start thinking like that. To that end, keep working on your questions."

"Captain," Ituau said, touching her fingers to her brow, as Harbour smiled at them and walked away.

"That was odd," Nate said to the group, after Harbour was out of earshot. "I had the feeling that she wanted to talk about something else."

"She did," Ituau said. The other spacers waited for her to say more. Instead, she took a deep pull on her drink, and they moved on to other topics of conversation. Ituau spared a glance for Harbour, as she exited through the cantina's hatch, her figure momentarily outlined by the corridor's brighter lights.

"Dingles, you busy?" Harbour called on her comm unit.

Dingles wiped his hands. He was in the kitchen with Nadine, making a late-night snack. The two of them had discussed several times the question of his full-time availability to Harbour. As Nadine had put it, "The woman has too much on her shoulders as it is. She needs all the help we can provide her," and Dingles had wholeheartedly agreed.

"You want to join us, Captain? Nadine's making a green, and I'm fixing something edible," Dingles replied.

Harbour could hear Nadine's laughter, and her heart warmed at the thought that two of her favorite people had found each other. Before Harbour could reply, she heard Nadine say, "If it's not a private conversation, Captain. Come on over, put your feet up, and relax with us."

"See you two in five minutes," Harbour replied and closed her device. She could use a green, as she was in the habit of spreading emotional support wherever she went. By the end of a day, her body demanded the nutrients contained in an empath's green. But, more than that this evening, the austere formality of the captain's quarters had no appeal for her. She'd spent her life in a small cabin aboard the JOS and then later aboard the *Belle*. Cramped quarters were familiar to her, and some time with good friends appealed to her.

Minutes later, Harbour tapped twice on Nadine's cabin door and entered.

Nadine, who had heard Harbour's relief at the invitation, met her at the door, handed her a green, and waved her toward a seat in the corner of the small salon.

"My chair. You rescued it," Harbour exclaimed.

"It was a young couple with a baby who got your cabin," Dingles said. "They didn't have any use for such a ratty, old thing."

"Hush, you old fool," Nadine said, lovingly swatting Dingles' arm. "Don't listen to him, Captain. He didn't give the couple a choice. He grabbed some crew and hauled it over here straightaway. It's been waiting for you."

Tears glistened in Harbour's eyes, and Nadine hushed her. "You're probably draining much-needed minerals, Captain," she said, hugging Harbour and sending all the comfort she could muster.

"What did you want to talk about, Captain?" Dingles asked. He received a sharp glance from Nadine for redirecting the conversation, but he ignored it.

"This is a *what if* conversation, Dingles," Harbour said, pausing to drain half of her green, before she settled into her old reading chair.

"What if what?" Dingles asked, claiming a seat beside Nadine on the couch.

"What if the Jatouche return to help us with the planet?" Harbour replied.

"I don't follow you, Captain. What specifically are you asking me?"

"That's just it, Dingles. I'm asking about everything. What do we need to do to help them ... to enable them?" Harbour asked. She finished her green, and Nadine silently stood, took her glass, and proceeded to prepare her a second one.

"I can provide some of the bits and pieces, Captain, but I certainly can't perceive the overall strategy and most of the parts," Dingles replied.

"And that's why I'm here," Harbour replied enthusiastically, which confounded Dingles and Nadine, who peered at her lover from the kitchenette.

"Do greens have negative side effects that I'm not aware of?" Dingles quipped. His tone indicated that there was a serious element to his question.

"You're missing the point, Dingles," Harbour replied, sitting on the edge of her chair. "I don't have the pieces either. But, wouldn't we appear a little foolish if the Jatouche showed up someday, and we hadn't given this any thought."

"Ah," Dingles said on a slow exhalation of breath. "We need a council."

"Yes," Harbour replied triumphantly.

"There would be the problems of transport, depending what the Jatouche brought," Dingles said, staring at the deck and thinking out loud. "With the gate, they could have a mountain of material stacked on the other side and we wouldn't know it. Then there's the question of the number of individuals coming. They'll need long-term accommodations."

Nadine handed Harbour her second green, and the two women smiled at each other, as Dingles continued to enumerate the obstacles, as he saw them. When the first mate wound down, he'd listed some thirty or more major considerations.

"Which brings me to my next question, Dingles," Harbour said, relaxing deep in her old reading chair with her green cradled in both hands. "Who sits on the council?"

"And that's the real question, isn't it, Captain?" Dingles asked.

Harbour smiled and said, "Ituau shared with me that Captain Cinders was being inundated by spacers' questions about the *what ifs* when the Jatouche return."

"And Captain Cinders was trying to puzzle out the answers himself," Dingles finished. "Sounds like the captain."

"We need a list of those subjects that you mentioned, and I need to know who you'd recommend to cover them," Harbour replied.

"Captain, I'm good at what I do, but I can't foresee all the obstacles in the way of something as big as this project," Dingles objected. "Oh, I get it," Dingles suddenly said. "My first task is to contact the strategic thinkers and have them help me create a list."

When Harbour nodded, Dingles continued. "Those people, who are the most help, will be part of the council. Then the rest of the members would be those capable of solving the problems or, at least, would be able to detail the challenges."

"There you go, Dingles," Harbour replied, gulping down the last of her green. "Three steps: the strategic thinkers, the incremental steps to consider, and the problem solvers."

"How soon do you need this?" Dingles asked, as Harbour stood, stretched, and hugged Nadine.

"As I see it, we need to convene the council, thrash out the obstacles, and design solutions to surmount them before the Jatouche return," Harbour replied.

"But, we don't know when the Jatouche will return," Dingles objected.

Harbour paused at the cabin's door, her hand poised to open it. "Right you are, Dingles," she said, winked, and left.

Dingles stared, open-mouthed, at Nadine.

"Don't look at me," Nadine replied. "You're the one who said a year ago that you were excited by the prospect of sailing again and under such a good woman as Harbour."

While Dingles was trying to think of a retort, Nadine handed him his comm unit and sat on the couch with hers. "Let's get started. Walk me through those considerations that you enumerated for Harbour. We'll start with those, and that will direct us toward the strategic thinkers who can amplify or edit our list."

Dingles smiled at Nadine. She was a no-nonsense, practical person with a good heart, and that suited him just fine. He leaned over, kissed her temple, and started to reiterate his points.

The Council

"You're commanded to attend a dinner at eighteen hundred this evening with Captain Harbour before the council meeting tomorrow," Nate said, as Jessie entered the *Spryte*'s bridge. "The message came in while you were downside, Captain."

"I'm commanded, am I?" Jessie replied, lifting an eyebrow.

"Ituau said I need to learn to read between the lines when females speak," Nate replied, frowning. "She makes it sound simple, but it's not so easy. Captain Harbour was polite and all, but, when I offered to connect her to you, she said, 'Deliver the message, Nate.' So, I'm translating that as you better be there, Captain."

"You're not as bad at reading between the lines as you think, Nate," Jessie said, laughing and slapping his second mate on the shoulder.

Jessie checked the chronometer on his comm unit. He would have to hurry through a shower, change, and catch a shuttle if he didn't want to be late for dinner. As he hustled to his cabin, the reasons for his failure to visit the *Belle* since his return from Triton rolled through him. If he was honest with himself, they weren't reasons, they were emotions, and they were complex. That's what bothered him. He liked things simple — work, business, and relationships, in short, life. Trouble was, Harbour was anything but simple.

Jessie's shuttle delivered him to the *Belle* in time to shuck his vac suit, walk to the captain's quarters, and arrive a few minutes early. He stepped through the door, with a smile on his face, which quickly faded. Leonard Hastings and Yohlin Erring were chatting with Harbour, drinks in their hands.

"Captain Cinders, please join us," Harbour called out.

Leonard and Yohlin could tell by Jessie's expression that their presence was unexpected, and they weren't sure what to make of that.

Jessie was confounded by his own reactions. *You ignore Harbour for weeks, and, when she invites you to dinner, you're disappointed that she's not alone,* he thought.

Yasmin handed Jessie a drink, and he swallowed half of it.

"Everyone, please take a seat," Harbour invited. "We'll serve dinner in a few minutes, after we speak." When the captains had settled around the table, Harbour continued. "Tomorrow we initiate the council, which you've participated in organizing. What I want to talk about tonight, which we will keep to ourselves while we're in council, are the political ramifications of helping the Jatouche."

Harbour looked across the table at Jessie. He interpreted her glance, as asking permission to share what the two of them knew. Jessie agreed, but he chose to be the one to tell them.

"What Harbour is referring to is that any aid from the Jatouche will be complicated by the close liaison of the commandant and the governor," Jessie explained.

"How close?" Leonard asked.

This time, Jessie regarded Harbour. Others were involved, and it was a question of whether to reveal their identities. Harbour chose to protect them, as she said, "We've sources that know that the governor has the commandant on a monthly stipend. It's a considerable amount of coin."

Yohlin whispered a string of expletives, and Harbour didn't know if she should be shocked or take notes.

"Yes, well, what this means," Harbour continued, "is that we can expect the families to embrace the concept of repairing the planet and making the land arable only if they can reap a huge reward for their cooperation.

"How far do you think Lise will push it?" Leonard asked.

"My thought is that Lise Panoy would like to be president of Pyre," Harbour replied.

"You mean of the planet?" Yohlin asked in surprise.

"Lise is thinking much bigger than that," Jessie said. "Based on what we've heard, she's probably trying to find a way to be the leader of all Pyre — planet, stations, ships — in short, the entire system."

"In that case, I would anticipate the governor pushing hard to be the primary, if not the only, contact of the Jatouche," Leonard said.

Jessie pointed a finger at Leonard, underlining the accuracy of the captain's remark.

"Wait, if the two of you have this information, why doesn't the Review Board have Emerson up on charges?" Yohlin asked. When Jessie and Harbour hesitated, Yohlin rightly guessed, "Because the evidence is illegally obtained."

Harbour tipped her head in agreement.

"Well, isn't this a useless ore analysis," Yohlin commented. "The commandant and the governor are allied against topsiders and spacers, and we can't do anything about it."

"I wouldn't say that," Jessie replied. "Because we know of their alliance, we can anticipate their actions."

"I would imagine that informing us of their liaison isn't the only reason for this opportunity to have a wonderful dinner," Leonard said to Harbour, leaving his question unstated.

"It isn't," Harbour replied. "No one knows what the Jatouche will supply. The council's purpose is to entertain conjectures, as to what they will bring, and imagine the steps necessary to implement them. The purpose of this small group is to anticipate the political ramifications. One of the primary items on the list created by you is the difficulty of transporting overly large items downside via the El and through the domes."

"And that's when the governor and the family heads will seize their opportunity," Jessie interjected. "They'll be negotiating every step we intend to take, with the ultimate goal of expanding their power."

"And security's actions will be hampered by the commandant," Yohlin supplied. The disgust was evident on her face.

"So, now you know what you should be considering, while the council meets and plans," Harbour said. "It's time to eat," she added, sending a small measure of pleasure with her words. She touched an icon on her comm device, and Yasmin, Nadine, and two other empaths swept into the salon, pushing two carts loaded with the dinners.

For the next hour and a half, the captains spoke on various subjects from slush to the aliens. Occasionally, Harbour caught Jessie gazing at her, while he sipped on his drink. She couldn't help opening her gates and trying to sense his emotions. Unfortunately, they were subtle and mixed, which did little to help her understand what he was thinking.

When dinner finished, Birdie, who was becoming known as the eternal owl for her habit of staying up all hours, led the captains to their overnight quarters.

On the walk to Jessie's cabin, he recalled the first time he'd stayed aboard the *Belle*. The next morning, he was lost, attempting to find his way to the bridge. Thankfully, he was rescued by Aurelia and Sasha. His second meeting with Sasha was as memorable as the first. But, then, every meeting with Aurelia's powerful younger sister tended to be a memorable event.

* * * *

Early the next morning, a flash of blue light caught the *Belle*'s third-watch comm operator's eye. The crew member snatched his comm unit and made an urgent call.

"Dingles, aliens arriving," the comm operator said.

Dingles jumped out of bed, grabbed his comm unit, and called Harbour. When she answered his call, he could hear the shower running. He repeated the comm operator's message, and his call was cut off.

Harbour shut off the shower, grabbed a towel, and briefly wiped down. With wet hair, she slid on a set of skins and deck boots and ran for the bridge.

Dingles had the presence of mind to wake Jessie before he finished dressing and made for the bridge.

Harbour arrived in time to see four Jatouche on the bridge monitor that relayed the image from the *Spryte*'s array. The comm operator, who had already grabbed an ear wig for translation from the case Jessie had been given, handed one to Harbour.

On the bridge monitor, the crew watched Kractik, Tacticnok, Jaktook, and Jittak approach the console. Kractik was tapping at a panel, and, moments later, the image of Tacticnok appeared on a comm monitor.

"I would converse with Captain Harbour and Jessie Cinders," the Jatouche leader said.

Harbour decided it was time to set the record straight about Jessie. She replied, "Welcome back, Your Highness. If you'll allow me some time, I'll contact Captain Cinders and add him to our call."

"Thank you, Captain Harbour," Tacticnok replied.

"Owner of three ships *and* ship's captain," Jaktook whispered to Tacticnok.

"A most modest human," Tacticnok replied quietly. "We were favored to meet him first."

Jessie hurried onto the bridge, taking in who was present and the Jatouche on the comm monitor.

"Hello, Your Highness," Jessie said, adjusting the ear wig.

"It's good to hear your voice, Captain Cinders," Tacticnok replied. "I presume it's appropriate to use your title."

"As it is to use yours," Jessie replied.

"Yes," Tacticnok replied thoughtfully. "It makes one wish for the simpler times of our first meeting."

"What brings you back so quickly, Tacticnok?" Harbour asked. She was worried that the Jatouche were far ahead of her people's preparations.

"We wished to keep you apprised of significant developments, Captain Harbour. His Excellency Rictook has approved my request to assist you in recovering your planet."

"That's wonderful news, Tacticnok," Jessie replied. "Please thank your father for us. We appreciate his generosity."

"And for me?" Tacticnok asked.

Jessie paused to consider how to reply to Tacticnok, and Harbour chose to rescue him, when she said, "Tacticnok, I'm sure your skills, as a female, played a significant role in convincing His Excellency to heed your request."

Tacticnok flashed her teeth in reply. *Why do females understand relationships so much quicker?* she thought.

"Captains, my second announcement is that our scientists are confident that they've designed a device that will accomplish the processes necessary to pull heat from the surface and clean the atmosphere," Tacticnok said.

"Also excellent news," Jessie replied. "Do you have a timeline for completion of your device?"

"Your question is premature, Captain," Jaktook replied. "The engineers have a task in front of them to build and test some of the components. The Jatouche have never created such a device."

"Are they confident that they can?" Harbour asked.

"They're Jatouche," Tacticnok replied.

Harbour and Jessie glanced at each other. Neither chose to address the subject further.

"We'll need your services, in many respects," Jaktook said. "They'll include transport, use of your production facilities, and delivery of the device to the planet's surface. We'll build one unit to deploy and then more when we're assured it's functioning as intended."

"Captain Harbour has formed a council, which, incidentally, meets for the first time today," Jessie said. "The council will discuss the elements we need to put in place to assist you."

Tacticnok stared silently out of the bridge monitor, and the bridge personnel could see Jaktook whispering in her ear.

"Your actions, Captain Harbour, are most propitious," Tacticnok said. "Have the rulers been informed of our offer?"

"Yes," Harbour replied quickly and with emphasis.

The bridge crew, who had hurriedly grabbed ear wigs from the case when Harbour received hers, glanced from Harbour to Jessie, wondering why the Jatouche were referring to rulers.

"And how did they receive the announcement?" Jaktook asked, pursuing the subject.

"They haven't replied to our broadcast," Jessie temporized. He glanced guiltily at Harbour.

"We would appreciate more information about these two rulers," Tacticnok said.

Recognizing the topic couldn't be evaded, Jessie replied, "Commandant Emerson Strattleford is head of security, which is responsible for the application of the laws within the stations and any ships that are docked. Governor Lise Panoy is the head of the families who have control of the domes on the planet."

"How is it, Captain Harbour, your ship doesn't fall under the auspices of one of these rulers?" Jaktook asked.

"This is the colony ship, which brought humans to this system," Harbour replied. "It's too large to dock at either station. In that regard it never falls under the commandant's purview. Any ship underway is under the command of the captain."

"My scope's recording indicates that one of your stations, by its heat signatures, is used for manufacturing. We'll need the services of this platform. Will the ruler, Commandant Emerson Strattleford, allow the use of his station for our purposes?" Jaktook asked.

"We've waited to negotiate the terms of use until we knew that the Jatouche would be able to help us," Jessie replied.

By now, the bridge crew was more intent on watching the captains than the comm monitor, which displayed the furry aliens.

"Do you expect any difficulties in securing these permissions, Captains Harbour and Cinders?" Tacticnok asked. She received a firm no from each of them. "We'll return with another update, when we've more to report," Tacticnok added, and signaled Kractik to end the call.

Jessie kept his ear wig, but Harbour and the bridge crew returned theirs to the case. The crew stared expectantly at Harbour, but Dingles demanded, "We've operations underway. Slush is being transferred. Who's monitoring that?" That galvanized the crew to swivel around and attend their panels.

Harbour glanced at Jessie and tipped her head toward the captain's quarters, and he turned and preceded her through the bridge hatch.

"What do you think it means that the Jatouche are asking so many questions about our political structure?" Harbour asked, when she closed the cabin door to her salon.

"I know that I confused them trying to differentiate you from the commandant and the governor," Jessie replied. "With a single ruler, Tacticnok's father, they must find our fractionized leadership difficult to understand."

"I'm interested to see how you begin negotiations with the commandant, Jessie," Harbour said, with a quizzical lift of her eyebrows.

"Yeah, me too," Jessie said.

* * * *

After morning meal, the council convened in a small amphitheater that had been constructed, with the surplus of coin that flowed into the *Belle*'s general fund after the delivery of the second load of slush to the YIPS.

Jessie's captains and first mates were joined by a collection of engineers from every ship. Harbour and Jessie sat at a small desk on the amphitheater's stage.

When the invitees were assembled, Harbour stood and said, "Well, it's been two hours since the Jatouche called to tell us they'll be coming. I imagine, given that inordinate amount of time, all of you have managed to hear that by now." Her comment produced a round of laughter from the audience. Most of them had heard the news within minutes of the call.

"This council's purpose was to consider the means by which we'd support the Jatouche, if they came," Harbour continued. "Now that's no longer conjecture; we've got our work cut out for us. The Jatouche don't know what we can do, and we don't know exactly what they're bringing or what they expect from us."

Ituau raised her hand, Harbour recognized her, and the first mate asked, "Isn't there a means by which we can exchange more information?"

"From what we've learned at the dome, first contacts are supposed to take place over time," Jessie said, rising to answer the questions. "The only reason that this one is proceeding so quickly is that Her Highness Tacticnok and Jaktook were visibly shaken by the extent of damage caused to the planet during the Jatouche fight with the Gasnarians. They're working quickly to help us, and I think it's to prove to us that they're worth knowing."

"Toward what end?" an engineer asked.

"Good question," Harbour replied. "Perhaps Tacticnok took a liking to a tall, male alien."

The spacers and engineers chuckled at the thought of Tacticnok staring at Jessie with adoring eyes. The glance that Jessie gave Harbour definitely wasn't the admiring type.

"Seriously," Jessie said, calming the group. "The Jatouche are sailing this ship, and we need to act like good crew. They'll inform us of our tasks. The council's purpose is to anticipate the roles we might be asked to play so that we don't take months to deliver each step."

A *Belle* engineer raised her hand, and Jessie pointed to her. "We should consider transport first," she said. "It's important to give the Jatouche credit for their technical knowledge. Everything about them points to a superior race, and they've observed much about us already. You can figure they've seen our limitations and are taking steps to work with them."

"And how does this affect transport?" Harbour asked, happy to have the discussion started.

"I suspect the device the Jatouche is going to build will be huge," the engineer replied. "It won't fit through the gate. That means they'll bring the critical components, and we'll be required to manufacture the more common and larger items."

The engineer sat in the front row and had a good view of Harbour's furrowed brow. "Apologies, Captain. What I'm trying to say is that the Jatouche will need to transport a significant number of parts and individuals, engineers and techs. I don't see Captain Cinder's ships accommodating the needs of the Jatouche too well."

"Meaning the *Belle* should be considered the primary transport, when the Jatouche are ready," Harbour said, her frown clearing and nodding appreciatively to the engineer. "Anything else?" Harbour asked.

"Yes, Captain, best work to prepare the YIPS personnel. They're going to freak when the Jatouche swarm the station." The woman's comment elicited a rather disjointed response. Some laughed; others didn't. Those who didn't were wondering what they would do when they came face-to-face with the aliens.

"I can't disagree with the suggestion about transport," Jessie said, "which means the *Belle* will have to be ready to abandon Emperion, when the Jatouche arrive."

The assembly members continued to discuss the problems, as they saw it. One of the significant obstacles they envisioned was interrupting the YIPS manufacturing schedule. Additionally, the interruption might require modification of the YIPS smelting furnaces and metal forming lines to create the parts the Jatouche required for their device. That would take time and cost coin.

The question of coin was an issue brought up by Leonard Hastings, when he said, "The Jatouche must cover a majority of the planet, with their devices, tagging the greatest hot spots. It's going to take a good number of them. But, we haven't considered the cost of these devices. Considering we have a capitalist system, somebody will have to provide the coin to pay the YIPS for the production of these devices."

Another sticking question, as the assembly saw it, was how the pieces would be transported downside, through the dome, and reassembled on the surface. Spacers had worked in difficult conditions before, but the target areas on Pyre's surface, where the devices would be planted, were extremely dangerous.

No one mentioned the governor's reaction to the Jatouche arriving downside and traipsing through the domes. Most presumed that those tasks could be accomplished by humans.

The council adjourned at midday meal, with various jobs meted out to assess the issues and report back to the group. Harbour took the opportunity to invite the captains to dine with her in her quarters.

"It appears that every piece of the practical part of the puzzle, which falls in our lap is surmountable," Leonard said. Some captains paced the salon, while others found a comfortable chair and waited for the meal to be served.

"That leaves the YIPS, the stationers, the commandant, the downsiders, and the lovely governor to deal with," Yohlin countered.

"Yohlin has a good point," Harbour said. "We can make all the preparations we want to get the Jatouche to the YIPS, but, after that, control gets flimsy. We haven't the leverage to get the YIPS to do our bidding against the commandant and the governor's wishes."

Jessie sat for a few moments in a chair and got up to pour himself a cup of water. He drained the cup and sat down, his elbows planted on his knees and his hands propping his chin. "You're right, we don't," he finally said. "But then, we aren't the only ones who could benefit from a healed planet."

"True, stationers would love to have the opportunity to have more than a tiny cabin," Leonard agreed.

"And a nice garden, where they could grow fruit for themselves," Yohlin said, wondering what delectable items from the hydroponic gardens would be served for the midday meal.

"And spacers," Jessie added.

"Which is our leverage on the YIPS," Harbour said excitedly. "If spacers were behind us, the YIPS could face a shortage of slush and ore, if management didn't cooperate. And wealthy stationers would be thinking of their investments and the opportunities of opening the planet."

"That would get us from transport through manufacturing," Leonard said. "After that, we'd still have to deal with the governor and the families."

"If there were enough impetus from stationers and spacers, the governor would be forced to deal," Jessie said, pouring himself another cup of water. "We might not like the deal she offers, but we'll have to wait and see what she puts on the table."

"Then, I think the answer is to use Tacticnok's updates and our broadcasts to build a visual of Pyre's future with the help of the Jatouche," Harbour said. "We'll have to appeal to our people on multiple levels, including economic opportunities, an inhabitable planet, and an alliance with an advanced race."

The other three captains might have argued with Harbour's points, but their minds felt the enthusiasm and hope she emanated.

-25-
Recruitment

While the *Belle* and the *Pearl* filled their tanks with slush at Emperion, the Jatouche made several return trips to Triton. The bridge crew dutifully recorded each exchange. They were the fuel for Harbour's broadcasts to Pyre, and she spent hours preparing announcements to amplify the exchange that would be sent systemwide to influence citizens' opinions.

The Jatouche's initial updates were general, in nature, but as technical questions were asked of Tacticnok, she brought scientists and engineers to provide the answers.

The *Belle*'s broadcasts developed a dual nature. On the one hand, the engineers' technical explanations laid the foundation of Jatouche capabilities and indicated the feasibility of their plans. Harbour's words sought to convince the citizenry, topsiders, spacers, and downsiders, of the value of cooperating with the aliens.

There were only two locations capable of systemwide communication that could reach every citizen, regardless of where they abided — station, ship, or downside. The *Belle* was one; the JOS was the other. Every broadcast that Harbour issued was followed by a rebuttal by Commandant Strattleford, who controlled the JOS Pyre-wide comm, and his diatribe was carefully crafted by Governor Panoy. It became a war of words and images for the minds of humans.

The governor and the commandant's underlying message intended to foster doubt as to the aliens' real motive. Incidentally, in the commandant's broadcast, the word Jatouche was never mentioned. They were referred to as the aliens or the interlopers. The explanation for why the aliens wanted to help Pyre was that they coveted the planet for themselves.

Harbour's reply to the commandant's argument was that the Jatouche had incredible technical prowess. They'd defeated the Gasnarians, the aliens who originally inhabited Pyre, and were a technically superior race to humans. If they wanted Pyre, they could easily take it and repair it without human help.

The other contested issue was the manufacturing cost of the device's parts, which humans would be responsible for providing. Unfortunately, no one had any idea what those costs would be, but that didn't stop the commandant from harping on the subject. Emerson's broadcasts contained statements that spoke to exaggerated amounts of coin that would be required to pay the YIPS.

"Who's going to proffer the coin for this extravagant experiment?" the commandant asked. "Contributors could empty their accounts, hoping to see the planet recover, only to witness years from now the failure of this grand scheme."

Deliberately left unstated by the commandant was the subject of the JOS funds. The majority of these funds accumulated from the YIPS profits and a significant portion from the rentals of the station's cabins, shops, sleepovers, and cantinas. The commandant had administrative control over these operational accounts, which were used to maintain the JOS and the YIPS. However, capital expenditures, such as for additional terminal arms, required approval from station residents.

Harbour didn't have a solid rebuttal to the commandant's message about funding. There were no facts about the device or its manufacturing costs to present. All she could do was ask the question: What's it worth to have an ecologically viable planet?

* * * *

Downside, topside, and aboard ships, there was only one general topic of conversation that occupied people. It comprised the subjects of aliens, the experiment, and the possibility of success. Participating in the conversations were skeptics and believers, the uncommitted, the fearful, and the courageous. There were dialogs, arguments, and brawls.

However, the domes and station's elite were holding serious discussions. That there were incredible financial risks was obvious, but there were also enormous potential rewards.

In the elite Starlight cantina, a discussion went like this: "Do we want a referendum to release the JOS funds to pay for the devices?" asked Hans Riesling.

"I think the question is: Do we want the JOS and, by extension, the commandant to have control of the planet along with the governor, or do we want to be the donors and, thereby, the land owners?" retorted Trent Pederson.

"That depends on the ultimate cost and how many people we can interest in investing with us," Oster Simian added.

"How's the final bill for this project going to be determined in advance?" Hans asked. "Are we going to ask the aliens to estimate the cost? And what are they going to say: 'Oh, yes, it will cost 20 million whatevers,' to which we'll have no equivalent?"

"Captain Harbour said there will be an initial test deployment of the vehicle," Oster said. "If we haven't formed a consortium by then to underwrite the costs, we'll be missing the launch of this ship."

"That brings up a question of mine," said Dottie Franks, who had been listening to the conversation. She was the only woman in the discussion. "Do we know that we can trust what Captain Harbour is saying? The commandant disagrees with her on every point."

The three men stared silently at the woman.

"What?" Dottie asked.

"Never used an empath, have you?" Trent asked.

"No, never," Dottie replied.

"Trained empaths aren't wired to lie," Oster said, "and Harbour's their leader."

"And you shouldn't even waste your breath, asking people to believe what the commandant is saying," Hans supplied.

The men returned to their drinks, ruminating on their exchange. Dottie decided to remain silent and learn. Her husband had been a mining captain and ship owner, who had done well by them. But an accident in the inner belt had cost him and several crew their lives. She'd collected the life insurance and sold the ship, making her a wealthy woman. When young, her primary asset had been her beauty. Now, faced with decades of living and no useful skills, she knew that she had to invest her money, and the prospects of the alien work had intrigued her.

Trent finished his drink and signaled an attendant, swirling his finger to indicate another round. The female patron flashed him a generous smile and adjusted her position in the chair to better display her curves.

"Suppose we form a consortium to invest in this project, whether it's in tandem with JOS funds or not, what's in it for the investors?" Hans asked.

"Good question," Oster acknowledged. "It's the same up here as in the domes. You lease your place and downside you even lease your land. It would be a tough sell to topsiders and downsiders that the consortium would own portions of the planet."

"Then there's the question of return on our investment," Hans said. "The when and the how, most important."

Dottie realized one of the most significant differences between her and the men, besides gender. They were well on in age, and she was barely in her thirties. The men were wondering if they would see a return on their investment within their lifetimes or whether their children would reap the rewards. Whereas, she had time to see the benefits fall to her. She had visions of becoming a land owner and operating some sort of industry on her property. Her imagination was fueled by thoughts of wandering through a garden filled with fruit trees.

"That's what makes the timing of this venture so critical," Hans stressed again. "After the first device is installed, the data will reveal the effectiveness of each unit. We've got to be aboard before then."

"Doesn't this mean that the amount of invested coin will determine the number of devices that can be installed and the rate at which the planet can be reclaimed?" Dottie asked. She was beginning to understand the complexity facing the investors.

Oster hoisted his fresh drink to her, complimenting her on the question.

"It absolutely does," Trent replied. "Imagine the consequences if the data reveals that a huge number of devices are necessary and it will take, say, a hundred years to recover the planet."

"Investment will dry up quickly," Trent commented, "which means it will fall to the JOS to pick up the tab, providing the stationers vote for it, and I can't see them failing to give the initial go ahead."

Dottie discovered that the men met at the Starlight three times a week, on the same days, and at the same hour. She intended to be early for the next meeting and offer the first round of drinks. There was much more to be learned from these savvy investors.

* * * *

Mining ships in the inner belt kept JOS time. It made it easier for communication and for the crews' cyclical periods, when the vessels returned to the stations.

Late in the evening, it was usually an opportunity for captains to chat with one another. Lately, it was on the same topics as everyone else.

"You have to know that this is going to come down to a fight about who gets the land," Orlando Davos said.

Paul Kirsch asked, "Do you think it will be a sort of social arrangement, where Pyre owns the planet and the land is leased?"

"That's the fight I think that's coming," Orlando replied. "Do you think the families are going to like that sort of arrangement?"

"It might come down to the coin," Portia Deloitte interjected. "As in, who has it and who's willing to risk it?"

"You can bet that this kind of conversation is going on all over the stations and the domes," Orlando said.

"Yeah, those with coin are trying to figure out how to cut up the planet for themselves," Portia opined.

"I hear you presenting and lamenting the problems, but I don't hear any suggestions," Paul said. His comment produced dead comms, and he waited for a response.

"Okay, I'm waiting to hear yours," Portia finally said.

"I'm talking to two ship owners, right?" Paul asked rhetorically. "And all three of us have crews that total more than fifty. Add all the spacers together, and you might not have a huge number, but look what we do."

"He's got a point," Orlando admitted. "We might not have the numbers, but we have leverage. We can influence the decision."

"And another point," Paul added. "It's not the inner belt miners against the station and dome's wealthy. We'd be throwing in with Captains Cinders and Harbour."

"Now that would make a difference," Portia said. "We'd be allied with the two captains who deliver the vast majority of the slush and have met the aliens."

"So how do we do this?" Orlando asked.

"We start selling the idea to the other owner-captains," Paul replied. "We foster a common purpose before the aliens arrive with the makings of their device. You can bet those with coin will be ready with their proposals. We've got to be ready to back the one we like or be ready to reject them all, if none of them suits us."

* * * *

Rufus and Idrian sat in comfortable chairs, facing each other, in the nicely decorated office, located on the third story of Idrian's home.

"Do you believe her?" Idrian asked.

"I believe that Lise is working to further her own interests," Rufus replied. "If her plans need our support, then we'll be included."

"The plans she has discussed with us speak to bargaining for an expansion of dome space to allow the movement of the alien devices through the domes," Idrian replied. "That doesn't sound like Lise. She usually thinks much more strategically."

"Which is why I don't think we're hearing everything she's thinking," Rufus replied.

"So, what's our move?" Idrian asked.

"Which ones of the family heads might like to work with us to ensure that Lise doesn't become the exclusive title holder of newly recovered land or, worse, become the planet's governor?" Rufus asked.

"If you state the proposition in the latter manner, we can probably get most of them to work with us," Idrian replied, grinning. "But, of course, that begs the question of who replaces Lise, if we're successful in removing her."

"I've given that some thought," Rufus replied. "The Andropovs held the title of governor since the inception of the domes. Now, in the course of two or three years, we might see two replacements. That's too much instability."

"You think it might lead to the family heads getting ideas about becoming the next governor?" Idrian asked.

"That's exactly what I'm thinking," Rufus replied. "What if we formed a council? Every family head could have a vote, the majority rules. That way, there's no governorship to fight over."

"I like it," Idrian replied, "and for more than one reason. If we've formed a council, even without Lise's cooperation, think of the buying power we could amass, which we could use to get in on the planet's recovery."

Rufus and Idrian grinned at each other. Family heads had typically acted in opposition to one another, which the Andropovs had fostered in their efforts to hold sway over the domes. Now, there was the opportunity for the family heads to evolve into something bigger and more powerful.

The men hoisted their drinks to each other and began planning who they would contact first and what they would say.

26

Emerson

JOS tracking updated Emerson Strattleford. The *Spryte* was hours from docking at the JOS. The *Annie* and the *Pearl* were headed for the YIPS, and the *Belle* was more than a day behind Cinders' ships.

Emerson marched to Major Finian's office after arriving at security administration. "Major, the *Spryte* will be docking soon. You're to arrest Captain Cinders."

It wasn't necessary for Liam Finian to act surprised. Lieutenant Higgins and he knew that the governor and commandant had discussed the possibility, but Liam expected to get some warning. Picking up his comm device, he scrolled for active warrants.

"Don't bother," Emerson announced. "I haven't completed Cinders' charge sheet. New information has come to my attention this morning."

"Perhaps we should wait until we have a warrant," Liam suggested.

"Major, you have your orders. I don't wish to see the *Spryte* dock and launch before I can complete my investigation. We can hold Captain Cinders for seventy-two hours without a warrant."

Under normal circumstances, Liam would have pressed the issue, but where it concerned Captains Cinders and Harbour, it was anything but standard procedures.

"Understood, Commandant," Liam replied evenly. When Emerson left, Liam hustled out of his office, exited security administration, and sought a quiet place in the inner corridors.

"Captain Stamerson, we have a problem," Liam said, when his call was accepted. "The commandant has ordered me to arrest Captain Cinders."

"On what charges?" Henry exclaimed. "He's submitted nothing to the Review Board."

"He says that he's still completing his investigation. Says he has new information."

"Highly unlikely," Henry commented. "What do you intend to do, Liam?"

"Warn Cinders, of course," Liam replied.

"I'd like to hear his thoughts," Henry said.

"Hold one, and I'll connect us," Liam said. It occurred to him that he should add Harbour.

"Go ahead, Major," Jessie said, when Harbour was online.

"I've orders from the commandant to arrest you, Captain Cinders, when you dock the *Spryte*," Liam said.

"On what charges?" Harbour asked indignantly.

"Emerson says he's working on that," Liam replied. "Henry and I don't think the charges will ever be filed. I think he intends to hold Jessie for the maximum seventy-two hours."

"For what purpose?" Harbour demanded.

"It's probably an attempt to discredit Jessie," Henry replied. "He's the one who has spoken with the Jatouche and encouraged them to help Pyre. That's frightened Lise Panoy. She wants to smear Jessie's reputation in order to put her in a stronger negotiating position."

"Jessie, you can hold the *Spryte* off from the JOS and transfer to the *Belle* when we make the YIPS," Harbour volunteered. From Jessie, there was silence, which boded nothing good, as far as Harbour was concerned.

"Liam, will you be doing the honors?" Jessie asked.

"That's my intention. I thought it would be safer that way," Liam replied.

Jessie barely replied with, "Agreed," when Harbour burst out with, "Jessie, what are you thinking?"

"I'm doing what you wanted, Harbour," Jessie replied. Before Harbour could object, he hurried on. "You wanted to jostle the people's thinking. They have to be experiencing mixed emotions. The Jatouche are frightening them, but the prospect of recovering the planet is exciting them, at least according to the captains who've spoken to me. That has to be muddling their thinking."

"Understood, Jessie, but how does getting arrested help the situation?" Harbour asked.

Henry and Liam independently thought to help with the explanation, but common sense intervened. Harbour wasn't in the mood to hear from anyone but Jessie. In that regard, both men were happy they weren't in her company.

"Emerson is going to look like a fool for arresting me and preferring no charges against me," Jessie replied, "and he can only hold me for seventy-two hours."

"What if he does create a charge sheet and applies for a warrant?" Harbour objected.

"I can assure you, Harbour," Henry replied, happy to provide a calming influence, "Emerson won't get a warrant from the Review Board, not with what we know about his intrigue with Lise Panoy."

"Liam, make the arrest public and a little noisy," Jessie said.

"Will do," Liam replied and ended the conference call.

Immediately, Harbour called the *Spryte* and asked for Jessie.

"There's time to reconsider this," Harbour said.

"You're not worried about me, are you?" Jessie teased.

"I've just broken in a good business partner. If this arrest goes bottoms up, I'll have to negotiate a new contract with your captains. But, I guess that can't be helped."

Jessie laughed, but the words had stung a mite. *It's my own fault,* he thought. *Keep her at arm's length but hope for endearing words. That makes you a fool, Jessie Cinders.*

Jessie ended the comm with Harbour and told Ituau what would happen after they docked.

"Hmm," Ituau had replied. "I get to be acting captain again. I'm getting used to the promotion."

After docking at the JOS, the *Spryte* received a warning from the terminal arm manager that security was on its way.

Jessie stepped off the gangway ramp and was met by Liam and Sergeants Lindstrom and Rodriguez.

Liam announced in an officious and loud voice that Jessie was under arrest by order of Commandant Strattleford. Spacers and stationers, who were passing by, froze to watch the proceedings. Jessie, sounding outraged, demanded to know the charges. In a similar voice, Liam announced that the commandant would prefer the charges later.

Spacers on the arm, as well as the *Spryte*'s crew, grumbled at the unorthodox procedure. Arresting a captain of Jessie Cinders' standing, without the due process of procuring a warrant, angered them, and they closed in on the small group.

"Stand down," Jessie ordered. "Major Finian is following orders, as he should. My issue is with the commandant," Jessie added in a loud voice and marched off down the terminal arm with security in tow.

With Jessie's arrest, Emerson was feeling extremely satisfied. That was until Stamerson walked into his office a few hours later.

"I've issued no warrant for Captain Cinders. Why is he in holding?" Henry demanded.

"I'm formulating the charge sheets now, Captain. I'll have them to you before the seventy-two-hour holding period runs out," Emerson replied with equanimity.

"Well, what is he suspected of doing?" Henry asked.

"I'm not at liberty to say, right now, Captain," Emerson replied, enjoying his superior position in this gambit.

"This is most irregular, Commandant Strattleford," Henry replied with heat. "See that you don't hold Captain Cinders for the full seventy-two hours and fail to charge him. The Review Board will take a dim view of your actions, in that case."

Henry didn't wait for a reply. He executed the most indignant exit he could manage, waiting until he had turned a couple of corners before he allowed a smile to curve his lips.

Emerson diligently worked on creating a charge sheet. He knew his statements were broad, poorly defined, and, in most cases, purely dubious, but he was working in uncharted territory. They were all related to the aliens: inspecting an alien site and consequently activating it, communicating with the aliens without authorization, and endangering Pyrean society.

Emerson worked late and was leaving for the day, when he passed Major Finian's office. Inside were the major, Higgins, Lindstrom, and, unimaginably, Jessie Cinders. They were engaged in playing some sort of game on their comm devices.

"What's this?" Emerson demanded.

"Felon Search," Liam replied brightly. "Newest release of the game. We can accommodate another player if you'd like to join us, Commandant."

"I'm asking why the prisoner is here," Emerson pressed.

"I was invited," Jessie replied good-naturedly.

"You're under arrest," Emerson screeched.

"And so he is, Commandant," Liam replied. "I've two other security officers with me to ensure that I'm not overpowered by Captain Cinders, if he tries to escape. I feel quite secure with our numbers."

Emerson knew he could order Cinders to be placed in a cell, but the insubordinate gleams that shone in the officers' eyes worried him. Without another word, he spun on his heels and made for the exit.

Early the next morning, Emerson was wondering how he could counter the ease with which his officers were treating Cinders, when he received an anxious call from Evan Pendleton.

"There's a major problem brewing here, Commandant," Evan said hastily.

You've no idea, Emerson thought, reminded of the conversation with Liam Finian last night.

"I've four mining ships full of ore sitting off the YIPS. The owner-captains are refusing to dock," Evan hurried to say.

"Why?" Emerson asked.

"They say it's a protest, Commandant."

"A protest against what? Prices?"

"The say it's a protest against you, Sir, for locking up Captain Cinders."

"Let them sit out there, Pendleton. It's their coin to waste."

"But, Commandant, it's the *Pearl* and the *Belle* too. The YIPS has a good stockpile of ore, but we need the slush."

"How many days can you hold out, Pendleton?"

"A few weeks, Commandant, but what if Captains Harbour and Hastings decide to wait until the slush runs dry before they dock? At that point, they can set any price for their cargo, and, unless we want to have production come to a halt, we'll have to accept it."

"Let me think on this, Pendleton. I'll get back to you," Emerson replied, before ending the call.

Emerson sat at his kitchen table, his morning meal unfinished and his caf chilling, while he considered his reversal of fortune. It angered him that he couldn't enjoy the pleasure of Jessie Cinders' arrest for the full three days. He picked up his comm device, and his finger touched a stored number.

"Any other bright ideas, Lise?" Emerson asked, without introduction. "Your idea of arresting Cinders has backfired. We have mining ships withholding delivery to the YIPS."

"So?" Lise shot back.

"That includes the *Belle* and the *Annie*, which are carrying valuable loads of slush.

"Who organized the spacers?" Lise demanded.

"No idea," Emerson replied. "It could have been the owner-captains or it might have been Harbour and Cinders. Those two are getting quite politically minded. I'm going to have to release Cinders before this gets out of hand."

"Emerson, you're going to look foolish and weak in the eyes of spacers and stationers, if you don't charge Cinders," Lise warned.

"I know that, Lise," Emerson replied sharply. "I've had Stamerson in my office demanding to know the charges. I can tell you that the Review Board isn't going to approve my charge sheet."

"You should try, Emerson," Lise said, entreating the commandant in a softer voice.

"Lise, I've spent an entire day trying to write something substantive. I'd throw an officer out of my office, if he or she brought me the dribble I've composed. At this point, I don't need to make a greater fool of myself.

And, Lise, thank you for your excellent suggestion," Emerson added, before he abruptly cut the comm call.

Emerson cleaned up his plate and cup before hurrying to security administration. He was intent on releasing Cinders, as soon as possible.

"Free Captain Cinders, Major," Emerson said, stopping by Liam's office. "I've changed my mind. There'll be no charges filed."

"Certainly, Commandant," Liam replied. "He's with Sergeants Lindstrom and Rodriguez in their office, if you wish to tell him yourself."

"Why is he there? Playing more games?" Emerson asked.

"Not during work hours, Commandant," Liam replied in mock surprise. "Captain Cinders thought it would be a good idea if the JOS could pick up the signal from the Triton monitoring array, which overlooks the dome. I thought we should broadcast the comings and goings of the Jatouche, in real time so to speak, to the stations and possibly downside. It's too bad it will only be visuals, although we couldn't understand them even if we could hear them."

"And you didn't think to run this past me?" Emerson asked, his indignation showing.

"I tried, Commandant," Liam replied. "I stopped by your office, yesterday, but you were on the comm to the governor."

Emerson blanched at the thought that he hadn't closed his door for the call with Lise, and he wondered what the major might have overheard. "Tell Cinders he's released and get him out of security," Emerson said before he hurried to his office.

Liam eased out of his chair, a smile on his face as wide as the one Henry wore yesterday, when he left the commandant's office.

"How's it going?" Liam asked, when he entered the sergeants' office. The threesome were crowded around a monitor, and Cecilia was furiously working on entering code into her comm device.

"Almost have it," Miguel replied. He pointed to something on the monitor, and Cecilia grunted in reply and tapped on her device a few more times.

"Ha!" the three declared straightening up and pointing at the monitor.

Liam came around the desk and eyed the image. Considering the optics of the equipment and the distance it was transmitting, it was a fairly clean image.

"Well done, team," Liam congratulated. "By the way, Captain, you're officially released."

"Nuts," Jessie replied. "I was looking forward to getting some of my coin back from Miguel when we played Felon Search this evening."

"And here I was anticipating taking more of your coin," Miguel said, adding a grin.

"Major, a moment, if you please?" Jessie asked, indicating they should step into the corridor. "This is a gift, Liam," Jessie said, when they were alone. He handed Liam the small ear wig. "You can listen to the Jatouche yourself or put it next to a comm device to use its speakers in a group."

Liam frowned at the tiny unit before carefully pocketing it. "Thanks, I think," he said.

Jessie chuckled and said, "It's a translation device. You'll hear the Jatouche speaking in our language."

"Oh, for the love of Pyre," Liam hissed. He pulled the ear wig out and examined it. "That capability is in this little thing? It makes you believe that the Jatouche have the technology to successfully recover the planet."

"I don't think it'll happen anytime soon, but I do think it'll eventually happen," Jessie replied, clapping a hand on Liam's shoulder. He went with Liam to collect his personal things and then made his way out of security.

Once in the main corridor, Jessie opened his comm device and called Ituau. "I'm out," he said. "Let the captains know."

"A piece of news for you, Captain," Ituau replied. "We weren't the only ones objecting to your treatment. Four ore ship captains refused to unload."

Jessie chuckled at the thought of independent-minded captains choosing to take a protest stance.

"What's that I hear?" Ituau asked.

"I'm walking through the main concourse, and, apparently, I've become a popular individual. You're hearing applause," Jessie replied. His waves were brief, and he walked faster to hide his embarrassment. "Let

Evan Pendleton know I'm out. He can communicate that to the ore captains, if they haven't heard already."

Jeremy, the *Spryte* navigator, caught Ituau's eye and pointed at his board.

"The ore ships are moving toward the YIPS, Captain," Ituau announced. "Rumor mill beat your message. How was incarceration?"

"Actually, restful," Jessie replied. "The major endeavored to ensure I was well fed and entertained. His people, Lieutenant Higgins and Sergeants Lindstrom and Rodriguez, are solid individuals. If they were spacers, I'd hire them in a minute."

"Should I call Captain Harbour or will you do that, Captain?" Ituau asked.

In an earlier time, Jessie would have growled and told Ituau to make the call as directed. That was then; this was now. "I'll make that call," he replied.

"Understood, Captain," Ituau said, and Jessie could hear the approval in her voice.

"I'm out," Jessie repeated to Harbour, when he connected with her.

"Oh, for the love of Pyre, I've wasted all this time," Harbour lamented.

"Doing what?" Jessie asked.

"I was drafting a new agreement with your captains or whoever got your company. Having learned a thing or two, I was intent on making the deal a bit sweeter for the *Belle*.

"So, you don't think our arrangement is fair?" Jessie asked, while he called for a capsule to his ship's terminal arm. He was confused as to whether Harbour was serious.

"The previous deal has its perks, but, with a new owner, those perks would have disappeared," Harbour replied.

Harbour's roundabout compliment penetrated Jessie's mind, while he strapped into the cap and focused on what she was saying.

"I never considered myself a perk," Jessie replied. The young female spacer across from Jessie gave him a bright smile.

"A perk, Jessie, such as the one I'm referring to, is in the mind of the beholder or admirer, in this case. Dinner tomorrow night? We'll be stationary by then."

"I'll catch a shuttle. Eighteen hundred hours?" Jessie replied.

"Perfect," Harbour said and ended the call.

Jessie's steps along the terminal arm were quick. His front deck shoe barely had time to adhere before he slipped the rear foot. It amazed any passersby that the captain could walk that quickly without losing traction.

27

Come Collect Us

The Jatouche appeared again on the monitors of the *Belle* and at JOS security. The colony ship's bridge crew rushed for ear wigs, and Dingles signaled Harbour.

"We're ready, Captain Harbour," Tacticnok announced, when her call was answered.

"That's wonderful news, Your Highness," Harbour replied. "Our ships are stationed at Pyre. Within days, we can be sailing for Triton."

"Who will come for us?" Jaktook asked.

"Captain Cinders will be aboard one of his ships and will be the first to meet with you," Harbour replied.

"Most appropriate," Jaktook whispered to Tacticnok.

"I'll follow in the *Belle*, although our sailing time will be days longer than Captain Cinders' ship," Harbour said. "The Jatouche will be hosted aboard my ship."

"We're honored to be offered accommodations aboard the Pyreans' great ship," Tacticnok replied. "Please inform Captain Cinders that we'll begin transiting equipment in ten of your human days and stacking the cases in the main corridor. We presume his shuttles can land aboard your ship."

"They can, Tacticnok," Harbour replied.

"Then the first elements of the process are in place," Tacticnok said. "We'll discover the next challenges when we arrive at your manufacturing station."

"We call it the Yellen-Inglehart Processing Station or YIPS, for short," Harbour said. "I look forward to meeting you and your team, Tacticnok."

"Until then, Captain," Tacticnok replied and ended the comm.

"The leader of the empaths is coming," Jaktook said quietly to Tacticnok. "Does it make you excited or nervous?"

Tacticnok glanced toward Jittak, who seemed to have adopted a permanent scowl. She'd tried to have him replaced but ran into objections from Master Pickcit. The advisor successfully argued that a replacement, at this late date, would not possess the experience gained from contact time with the humans that was necessary to ensure Her Highness' safety.

Who is going to keep me safe from the errors created by Jittak's inconsiderate actions? Tacticnok had asked herself, when her father delivered his decision.

"Some of us are excited," Tacticnok replied. Swinging her eyes toward Jittak, she added, "And some of us are nervous."

Harbour called the *Spryte*, requesting Jessie. It was a few minutes before he answered Ituau's hail.

"Our guests appeared and announced that they're ready to begin operations," Harbour said.

"Sorry, I was in the shower," Jessie replied.

Harbour quickly updated Jessie on the conversation.

"Good timing," Jessie said.

The *Belle* and the *Pearl* had been emptied days ago and resupply was underway.

"I'll send the *Spryte*, under Ituau, and the *Pearl* to Emperion," Jessie said. "We can keep some coin flowing, while this operation is underway. Tomorrow, I'll launch the *Annie* for Triton. How soon can you follow with the *Belle*?"

Harbour glanced at Dingles, and he signaled two days. She scowled but accepted his judgment. "My trusty first mate says we need two more days to complete preparations. As soon as we're ready, I'll follow you," Harbour replied.

"Once I reach Triton, I'll work on communicating with the Jatouche about their equipment and transport," Jessie mused.

"Why the *Annie*?" Harbour asked. "Is that due to the personnel aboard?"

"Partly," Jessie replied, "I want the Jatouche to see familiar faces, but mostly I need the vehicles aboard the *Annie* to transport the equipment from the dome to the shuttles."

"Understood, Jessie."

"See you there, Harbour," Jessie said, ending the call.

Harbour hadn't put her comm unit down before she received a call from Birdie.

"Evan Pendleton for you, Captain," Birdie said.

When Harbour said hello, Evan said excitedly, "The JOS broadcast just showed the Jatouche appearing at Triton. What did they have to say?"

Harbour smiled to herself at the thought that the JOS was transmitting the signal from the Triton array. Obviously, Jessie had worked with Major Finian's people, while he was under arrest. It was so like the man to be detained and still make progress with his plans.

"They say that they're ready to proceed," Harbour replied.

"May I inquire as to who's going to Triton?" Evan ventured.

Harbour hesitated, but it was Evan Pendleton asking and YIPS tracking would reveal their courses soon after launching, so she relented. "Jessie is sailing aboard the *Annie*, first thing in the morning. I'm taking the *Belle* there later."

"Wonderful news, Captain," Evan said with obvious relief.

The YIPS manager's response was a new one for Harbour, and it eased her concern over Evan's call.

"Captain, I've been thinking about what the Jatouche might be bringing us. You know, alien stuff and such. Well, I suspect they'll need us to make alien metals and equipment, things we're not set up to do."

"Understood," Harbour said, encouraging Evan to continue.

"You're intending to haul the aliens here, aren't you, Captain?" Evan asked.

"Yes," Harbour replied.

"It seems to me, Captain, that you're not making the best of your return trip. That is unless your people can read alien schematics, understand their metallurgy, and parse out their exotic fabrication techniques. But, of course, you can't. Captain, what I'm trying to say is that I have the perfect person to accompany you. She's an extraordinary metallurgist and fabrication engineer. She can be working with the Jatouche, while you're en route back here."

"Good suggestion, Evan," Harbour replied. "Have her transfer to the *Belle* within the next two days"

"There's just one small problem, Captain," Evan said, wincing.

"Yes?" Harbour said slowly, drawing out the word.

"Nine years ago, Olivia Harden and her husband were working on the YIPS. They were together when an overhead pipe burst. He was killed and she was disfigured. Since then, Olivia's lived on the YIPS."

"What are you saying, Evan? Olivia has never left, never visited the JOS?"

"Since the accident, never, Captain. Those who work here at the YIPS accept who she is and how she appears. She prefers that and chooses not to subject herself to the stares of JOS stationers."

"Medical couldn't repair her disfigurement?" Harbour inquired.

"They tried, and they did make some improvements, but it's her face, you see. They couldn't do much with the amount of tissue that was lost."

"Are you sure that Olivia wants to come with us?" Harbour asked.

"To tell the truth, Captain, I haven't broached the subject with her. She loves engineering challenges, and I think she would jump at the chance, if she could feel safe aboard the *Belle*."

Harbour wondered about the dilemma. The opportunity to thrash out the challenges facing human fabrication of Jatouche equipment before arriving at the YIPS would be invaluable.

"Stand by, Evan, I'll be sending someone to meet with Olivia and you."

"Understood, Captain," Evan replied, ending the call.

Harbour stared at her comm unit. If Olivia needed calming when she faced new people, then she needed the right empaths at her side. "Lindsey," Harbour said, after connecting to the older woman, "meet with me immediately in my quarters. You'll be making a short trip to the YIPS. In the meantime, think about another empath who you'd wish to accompany you."

It gave Harbour a thrill to think her dear friend and mentor, the previous Harbour, was well enough to leave the *Belle* to take on an important task. Young Sasha, Aurelia's sister, had put her incredible power to use, playing the game of protecting the older empaths who suffered from the inability to block the emotions of others. The more the game was played and the harder the other empaths pushed to break through Sasha's protective veil, the more the older empaths regained their ability to block.

Harbour enjoyed watching Lindsey walk self-confidently through her cabin door. The elder empath had no fear of a challenge.

"And I'm going to the YIPS to do what?" Lindsey asked, without preamble.

"According to Evan Pendleton, the best engineer and metallurgist we have, Olivia Harden, resides there."

"She resides on the YIPS permanently?" Lindsey asked.

"She's a woman who's severely disfigured and prefers the relative solitude of the YIPS over the JOS."

"Oh, for the love of Pyre," Lindsey replied. "I take it that we're supposed to coax this engineer to travel with us."

"And you need to accomplish that in two days," Harbour added. "Who do you want to take with you?"

"Up until you shared the problem with me, I was going to invite Yasmin."

"And now?" Harbour asked.

"Only one choice now ... Sasha," Lindsey replied.

Harbour kept her expression neutral and clamped down hard on her emotions. "Do you think that's wise, Lindsey?" she asked.

"You want this woman aboard?" Lindsey retorted, her eyes challenging Harbour.

"I think we need this woman aboard. We'll have a load of Jatouche with us for the return trip. A few of them have met a few of us. Once they're aboard the *Belle* that's going to change, in a big way. It would be smart to have their scientists, engineers, techs, and what-have-you engaged in communicating with one of our best engineers. At least they'd be speaking the same language, of a sort."

"Then the best empath for me to take is Sasha. From what you've told me, Olivia will need to be shocked out of her complacency. I can't think of a better person to do that than Sasha."

"That's true," Harbour admitted, a smile quirking the corner of her mouth.

"I take it that's your approval?" Lindsey asked, pointing a finger at Harbour's face.

"I wouldn't call it wholehearted approval, but go before I change my mind," Harbour replied.

Lindsey gave her ex-pupil a hug, twirled around, and made a fast exit.

As the cabin door closed behind Lindsey, Harbour sent a quick wish to the stars.

* * * *

Lindsey and Sasha rode the *Belle*'s shuttle to the JOS. Then they transferred between terminal arms to catch the next station transfer shuttle to the YIPS. The effort allowed Sasha to experience much more of Pyre than she had after first riding the El from downside, a year and a half ago. She was in the growth spurt of her early teenage years and quickly maturing under Lindsey's tutelage. At least, her power control was maturing. In conversation, Sasha was still as blunt and direct as a plasma engine's exhaust.

Evan Pendleton met the two women at the YIPS arrival terminal arm and escorted them to his office, where Olivia was waiting.

"Does Olivia know why we're here?" Lindsey asked Evan.

"No, she doesn't," Evan replied, a little sheepishly.

Lindsey schooled her face, but Sasha scowled at Evan, who was taken aback by the lithe teenager's disapproval.

"You're the young lady who was freed from the governor's house, aren't you?" Evan asked, hoping to engage the girl in conversation.

"Yes, and I've a low tolerance for weak men," Sasha fired back.

"Sasha," Lindsey said, scowling mildly and working to keep a smile off her face.

When Evan entered the office, the two empaths heard him announce in an upbeat voice, "There you are, Olivia. Sorry to keep you waiting. I've two guests who are anxious to meet you."

Olivia, who had been slouched in a chair, rose quickly, twisting nearly around to present the right side of her face to the strangers.

"The woman is Lindsey, and the girl is Sasha," Evan said brightly.

Lindsey smiled genially at Olivia and eased open her gate. She detected intense anxiety and humiliation from the woman.

Sasha, on the other hand, chose to walk around to Olivia's left side to see what she was hiding. "Wow," the teenager said, examining Olivia's ruined face and scalp, "that must have hurt."

Olivia might have recoiled in horror at the comment, but she was mentally bathed in sympathy and concern.

"It did," Olivia managed to say before adding, "You're an empath."

"And you're an engineer; and Captain Harbour wants you," Sasha replied.

"Why does Captain Harbour want me?" Olivia asked, intrigued by the turn in the conversation.

"To meet the aliens. Don't you want to meet them? I do," Sasha declared.

"It's not that easy for me," Olivia replied in a maternal tone.

"Why, because of your face?" Sasha demanded. "So, it's broken. We're all broken," she added, twirling her fingers at the three women. "You on the outside, Lindsey in her mind, and me here," Sasha added, pointing to her heart.

"That's true," Lindsey said. "Life has been challenging for all of us."

"You don't have to worry about your face, Olivia. I'll make sure everyone around you is nice to you."

"Sasha," Lindsey cautioned.

"She always says that when I boast too much," Sasha said, acting a bit admonished. It was a game the two empaths played. Sasha would talk about her prowess, in no uncertain terms, and Lindsey would let her know not to broadcast it. The truth was that Sasha wasn't bragging, and Lindsey knew it. Normals would be terrified to realize the extent of Sasha's power, which was still growing.

Olivia turned toward Lindsey, who had her first look at what the woman hid. It took a great deal of self-restraint to maintain a pleasant expression. She eased her gate wider and sent a strong wave of comfort.

"You're an empath too," Olivia acknowledged, closing her eyes and bathing in the dual nature of what she received.

"Yes, I am," Lindsey acknowledged. "We're here to take you to meet the Jatouche. According to Evan, you're the best engineer we have, and our alien friends will need your expertise to help them interface their designs and equipment with our human technology. Aren't you interested in resurrecting Pyre?"

Olivia looked forlornly at Lindsey out of her one serviceable eye. Pain showed through it. Captain Harbour and Evan were offering her the engineering opportunity of a lifetime, and fear, despite the assurance she was receiving from the empaths, kept her rooted in place.

"Come with us, Olivia," Sasha said, taking the woman's hand. "It'll be all right."

In a relaxed dream state, Olivia, holding the teenager's hand, left Evan's office.

Sasha led Olivia back to the transfer shuttle, determined to never release the engineer's hand until Olivia was safely ensconced in her own cabin aboard the *Belle*.

Lindsey whispered to Evan, "Take me to her cabin. I'll pack Olivia's things. You can help me cart them to the shuttle. Oh, and Evan, there'll only be three passengers for the transfer shuttle. You're flying us directly to the *Belle*, and I want no cabin crew — pilot and copilot only."

"I can't authorize that expense," Evan protested, as he watched Olivia and Sasha round the gravity wheel and disappear from sight.

"Then, Evan, I tell you what. I'm chartering the transfer shuttle. Charge it to the *Belle*'s general fund."

Evan stared in shock at the expense Lindsey was assuming, but the empath nudged him to get moving. "Time's a wasting, Evan," she said.

-28-
Load Up

With the *Annie* holding station above Triton, the crew hustled to set up the processes to manage the transport of the Jatouche equipment. The first shuttle to land dropped off the shelter, the search rover, and the shelter crew. The second shuttle delivered another rover and the surveyor. The latter piece of equipment, with its telescoping arm, would be handy for lifting heavy crates and loading them into the second rover, the rear seats of which had been removed.

Jessie rode the surveyor to the dome with Belinda in the driver's seat. The remainder of the dome investigation crew rode in the rover. Inside the dome's entrance, Jessie was struck by the extensive number of crates that were stacked alongside the main corridor. The Jatouche left a narrow aisle to allow passage.

"It's going to take more than a few shuttle trips," Belinda said, eyeing the mammoth amount of equipment.

"I'm thinking we load the *Annie* with the equipment," Jessie replied. "It'll make it easier to transfer all of it to the YIPS. When we're done with that, we'll wait for the *Belle*, then load the Jatouche on the colony ship."

Jessie and the crew edged past the mountain of boxes. They hadn't reached the ramp to the deck level before Tacticnok, followed by Jaktook and Jittak, came bounding down.

"Captain Cinders, we begin," Tacticnok said excitedly.

"We begin," Jessie echoed. He wished he knew the proper means of expressing his profound relief for Tacticnok's generosity, but she beat him to it.

Extending her hand to Jessie, Tacticnok said, "It's good to be allies."

"It's good to have friends," Jessie replied, accepting Tacticnok's hand, as the royal daughter flashed her teeth in agreement.

Jessie explained his plan about the equipment and personnel to Tacticnok and Jaktook, and the Jatouche accepted his ideas.

The Jatouche worked to transfer the crates into the dome's airlock. Alternately, the Pyreans would close the inner door, open the outer, and load up the rover with as much gear as it could carry. When it was obvious to the Jatouche that the humans couldn't empty the airlock as fast as they could load it, they donned their vac suits. They made it their responsibility to transfer their equipment from the corridor, through the airlock, and stack it on Triton's dusty surface.

A halt was called after a long day, and Jessie and his crew retired to the shelter, primarily to charge their air tanks and comms. After a quick meal, everyone, except for the night watch crew, was fast asleep, including Aurelia.

The Jatouche did the same thing. Jaktook commented to Tacticnok that every muscle in his body ached to which Tacticnok replied, "I think we'd better get used to it. Humans don't possess the assistance equipment we do. It looks like they depend on physical labor."

"Perhaps, when we're aboard the great ship, there'll be more individuals to help with the work," Jaktook managed to say, as he drifted off to sleep.

The next day, the Jatouche finished transferring the entirety of their equipment outside the dome's airlock. The pile was enormous.

"The humans brought one carryall," Jittak said with disgust, referring to the rover. "It will take forever to transfer our equipment to their shuttles."

Tacticnok eyed the distance to the landing site and made a decision. "Each box has four handles. In this gravity, four individuals can carry a single crate to the shuttle. I suggest you get started, Jittak."

The military leader looked as if he'd been slapped. "Aren't we doing enough of the humans' work for them?" he snarled, forgetting he was speaking to a royal member.

"This won't be for the humans," Tacticnok replied. "It'll be for me. After you spend the day carrying equipment to their shuttle, you should be so tired that I won't have to hear your griping. Get moving or I'll send you back for failing to heed my orders."

Jittak's jaw snapped shut. Courtesy overtook his anger, and he ducked his head in obeisance.

Jaktook regarded the anger evident in Tacticnok's face.

"Too harsh?" Tacticnok asked, when she saw Jaktook's expression.

"Did Jittak deserve it? I think so, but there might be a way to take the sting out of your rebuke," Jaktook replied.

"I could use the advice," Tacticnok replied.

"Are you ready to carry a crate?" Jaktook asked, his eyes challenging her.

Tacticnok flashed her teeth in reply and gestured two engineers toward her. While Jittak was organizing others, Tacticnok, Jaktook, and the two engineers picked up a box and in synchronized steps bounded off toward the shuttle.

Jittak faced a backlash of grumbling for his directive that the Jatouche must carry the gear to the human's shuttle. It ceased immediately when they saw the royal daughter leading the way.

Riding in the rover on a return trip, Jessie was passed by Tacticnok and the other Jatouche, who were carrying a case.

"Looks like we're being shown up for being wimps," Belinda said.

Jessie grunted in affirmation. When they reached the stack of crates, Jessie examined the handles. Each had the ability to convert to an interlock. He pulled a box down from the top of a stack and laid another beside it. When he fiddled with the handle, a Jatouche hurried over, pulled and twisted the handle to convert it to the interlock. Jessie transformed his handle and tapped the small alien's arm in appreciation.

"We load the rover first," Jessie announced over the general comm channel. "Belinda and Aurelia, you drive it back to the shuttle and pick up four crew members. The rest of us are going to carry some crates."

"I can help with that," Aurelia said.

"Newbie," Belinda chastised. "If you've never synch-bounced, I don't recommend trying it for the first time with three other people, much less with the captain."

No one uttered another word, and Belinda and Aurelia worked on loading the rover with the help of some Jatouche.

Jessie directed his three crew members to hook together two crates by their long sides. He signaled that they would carry the load by grasping the four outer handles.

"Four of us are going to carry two crates, Captain?" Hamoi asked.

"Have you noticed the rapidity with which the Jatouche are changing tanks?" Jessie asked.

"Now that you mention it, Captain, they're doing it often," Tully replied. "I would have thought they had more efficient technology than us."

"It's not a question of efficiency," Darrin replied. "The Jatouche are breathing hard and sucking down their air."

"Darrin's right," Jessie added. "I don't think they're used to this level of work, but they're stuck with our limited tech. I think the least we can do is work as hard as them. So, if you three are done jabbering, I suggest you grab a handle and show these wonderful individuals how much you appreciate their help restoring our planet."

With their longer strides and stronger bodies, Jessie and his crew managed to catch Tacticnok about 50 meters before the Jatouche made the shuttle, and Jessie called to his people to fall in line behind them.

Jaktook's helmet had signaled the advance of something behind him, and he'd twisted his neck to see the humans fast approaching. A sigh escaped his lips when the humans failed to pass them.

"Why the sigh, Jaktook?" Tacticnok asked, on a private channel.

"The humans were coming so fast, carrying two crates between four of them, that I anticipated they might bound overtop of us. I wanted to see that."

"Did you think how that would appear to Jittak?" Tacticnok warned.

"My apologies. You're right. He fears the humans enough for their empaths. If they displayed great strength, he would fear them more," Jaktook replied.

* * * *

While the *Belle* and the *Annie* were outbound to Triton, Harbour held regular comm calls with Tacticnok. During her second call, Harbour requested a favor of Kractik.

"Kractik, can you open a permanent vid connection to the *Belle?*" Harbour asked.

"With certainty, Captain Harbour," Kractik replied. After a few taps on her panel, she said, "It's done, Captain. I've provided you with a dome-wide view."

Dingles substituted the bridge monitor view of Jessie's array for Kractik's broadcast. On Harbour's orders, Birdie relayed the signal throughout the colony ship and directed the transmission Pyre-wide. Aboard stations and ships and downside, people quickly abandoned security's display of the array for the sharp, dome view provided by the Jatouche.

However, excitement soon dwindled and boredom set in. There was nothing to watch for days, except for the same group of aliens coming and going via the gate or disappearing down a ramp. Then, with days to go before the *Annie* made station above Triton, the gate transited stacks of crates and many additional aliens followed.

Pyreans again tuned into Harbour's channel, as they called it. Whatever they expected, it wasn't the continual stream of gear and aliens that they witnessed. The platform would be cleared for several minutes. Then the bright blue light would extend from the base and meld with the dome, signaling the arrival of more equipment and individuals. After two days of witnessing the process over and over again, the Pyreans tuned their comm devices and monitors to other entertainment channels.

As one stationer put it, "Once you've seen four little aliens carrying a crate, there's no reason to watch it repeat interminably."

The downsiders mirrored the topsiders in their opinions of the dome's view. Excitement peaked, dwindled, rekindled, and then dwindled again.

Under cover of a birthday party for a six-year-old daughter, the formative domes' council met for the first time. The pretense was perfect, because it was widely known that the governor disdained children's celebrations. She had no partner and no children.

While the entertainers and servants kept the children's attention, Rufus and Idrian retired upstairs with six family heads, whom they had convinced to listen to their idea.

Rufus carefully laid out the concept of a council usurping the role of the dome's governorship. When he finished, Dorelyn, who was the matriarch of the powerful Gaylan clan, was the first to speak up.

"Your concept is clear, Rufus," Dorelyn said. "What you haven't provided us is the reason this would be valuable. The families have controlled the domes since the beginning. Our businesses and our personal lives have been good. Why change that?"

"And what will happen to the domes if the Jatouche are successful in recovering this planet?" Idrian asked.

"Who knows that they will be successful or how long it will take?" Dorelyn returned.

"And, what about our governor, who has no heir? What will happen when she dies or when security arrests her?" Rufus proposed. "Are the family heads ready to democratically select a new governor or will it be a power struggle, with lives being sacrificed?"

There were uneasy glances between the family heads. They may have been there to hear the proposal, but it didn't mean they trusted one another.

"There are many reasons why forming a council will be in the families' favor," Idrian said. "Smooth transitions of power by electing a Council Leader to speak to or negotiate with the topsiders. All our business interests can be represented. Most important, we'll be in control of where and how the Jatouche set up their experiment."

Idrian's last statement caused a deathly pall to sweep over the group.

"Come, come," Rufus urged. "There's no reason to deny what we all know. For centuries, our enemies have been dumped outside the airlocks.

Possibly the bodies were buried and possibly they were left on the surface, the ash soon covering them."

"And you think the council would do a better job of directing the aliens where to set up their experiment than the governor?" Dorelyn asked.

"Where are your bodies buried, Dorelyn?" Rufus asked. "Or yours, or yours, or yours," he continued, going around the room. "The governor only knows where hers are laid, not ours."

"And ask yourselves, friends, what will the topsiders do when they discover what we've been doing with our enemies?" Idrian added.

"You can see that it's critical that the aliens and the topsiders take their experiment far away from the domes along a path that keeps them from discovering our secrets. I think a council will have more political leverage making that request than a governor," Rufus said.

Idrian and Rufus watched Dorelyn, who was the de facto leader of the five family heads, turn to the others and slowly nod her agreement with the proposal. What remained to do was convince the remaining family heads of the idea and determine a means of instigating a political coup against Lise Panoy.

At the same moment as the discussion took place at Dorelyn's home, Lise was observing the scene from the Triton dome and consulting with Jordie MacKiernan, her security chief.

"It looks like the grand experiment is going to happen," Jordie commented, watching the activity on the dome's deck.

"Looks like it," Lise commented absentmindedly.

"What do you think the odds will be of them manufacturing and delivering a device to the surface?" Jordie asked.

"That's impossible to judge, Jordie, but my guess is that they'll be successful. We're talking about aliens who are comfortable transiting between worlds on a beam of light. They're probably pretty certain it's going to work."

"Do you want them stopped?" Jordie asked.

"No, that's not the right approach," Lise replied, staring out her office's rear window. "There's too much chance of things going wrong if humans or aliens are killed. I suspect the *Annie* and the *Belle* will be making for the

YIPS when they leave Triton. In the end, our adversaries aren't the aliens. It's who we'll face in the negotiations over access to the new land once the alien devices make significant progress."

"Harbour and Cinders," Jordie supplied.

"And that's who we need to embarrass," Lise said, turning from the window. "Jordie, work up some scenarios for me to review that you're sure you can put into operation at a moment's notice. At their core, they need to put Harbour and Cinders' people at odds with the aliens."

"Suspicion, anger, distrust," Jordie listed.

"Exactly. Get to work on it, Jordie. You've probably got several weeks before we execute one of your plans," Lise replied.

Introductions

After boarding the *Belle*, Olivia was left to her own devices and was content with the arrangement. Unfortunately, her tiny kitchenette's food stock ran out after three days.

As opposed to Olivia's preferences to remain isolated, Sasha wanted to pull the engineer out of her cabin on day one, but Lindsey had cautioned patience.

Harbour was anxious to talk to Olivia too, but she heeded Lindsey's advice.

On the morning of the fourth day, with Olivia staring at an empty cooler, Lindsey knocked on the engineer's cabin door.

"You haven't by any chance brought me food, have you?" Olivia called out.

"No, but we'll take you to some," Lindsey replied, shouting through the door. "It's going to be a morning meal with the captain."

When Lindsey and Sasha didn't hear a response, Sasha said, in her high-pitched youthful voice, "It's going to be you and three empaths. How hard can that be, Olivia?"

The women heard some movement, and then the cabin door slowly opened. Olivia stood there in her skins and deck shoes, with a scarf laid over her head and tied underneath her chin.

Sasha offered her hand, and Olivia quickly took it, welcoming the reassurance that filled her mind. Sasha's emanations were like a beam that swept through everyone in front of them. Spacers, empaths, and residents happily smiled and greeted the women. Olivia was tempted to return the pleasantries, but her face would twist in a frightening grimace if she tried to smile.

At the captain's quarters, Harbour met the three women at the door and invited them inside. The table was already set for four, and there was no one else in sight, much to Olivia's relief.

Harbour felt Sasha's heavy broadcast. She subtly hand signaled Lindsey to shut down, having detected some of Lindsey's efforts.

Rather than argue with Sasha in front of Olivia, Harbour decided to demonstrate a capability known only to empaths. She focused on the teenager, targeting Sasha's gate. Slowly and incrementally, Harbour closed the portal through which the young woman was broadcasting.

Sasha perceived it was Harbour's power that attenuated her broadcast. Being the willful individual that she was, she fought it but not with malice. Sasha was curious more than anything. She wanted to test her strength against Harbour. When her gate closed, despite her best efforts, she smiled. To the teenager, it meant there were more talents to explore and more power to accumulate.

In the meantime, Harbour approached Olivia until she stood directly in front of the woman. There were no more broadcasts from the empaths, and Harbour witnessed anxiety creep across Olivia's face.

"I'm told you're the best fabrication engineer and metallurgist we have," Harbour said gently.

Olivia stood transfixed, as the captain reached out, untied her scarf, and carefully removed it from her head.

"Are you?" Harbour asked, when the engineer failed to reply. "Because that's what I need ... the best. That's what Pyre needs."

Olivia stared back at the captain's cool gray eyes, which seemed to demand an answer and a truthful one at that. "I'm not a boastful woman, Captain," Olivia finally said. "But I've been told that so many times by my peers that I have accepted it as so."

"Good," Harbour replied. She turned toward the table, saying, "Let's eat. I'm starved, and, while we enjoy this food, let's talk about what I hope you can accomplish with the Jatouche."

When Olivia chose to take a seat at the far end of the table, Harbour pulled out a chair next to her, and said, "Please, Olivia, sit near me so we can talk."

To Olivia's horror, the chair Harbour indicated would place her ruined side toward the captain. Eating in company was one of the most embarrassing moments for her to manage. Food had a way of escaping from the left side of her mouth, where the ungainly lips had no muscle control or nerves.

Harbour locked eyes with Olivia again, when the engineer hesitated to take the seat she offered. "You're a brilliant engineer with a disfigured face, Olivia," Harbour said, her voice quiet but firm, "but, at least you're thought of as human, a normal. You're dining with three women who are empaths and aren't even considered that. It's time you put aside your fears. All of us, for better or worse, are what we are. The question is: Are we making the best of who we are?"

"Remember that you said that, Captain," Olivia replied, with the first touch of mettle in her voice that Lindsey and Sasha had heard, "when food spills from my mouth onto your plate."

Harbour laughed, waved a hand to Olivia to join her, and said, "I'll appreciate that you were considerate enough to chew the food for me. Now come and sit."

Olivia forgot to cover her mouth, when she grinned at Harbour's incredulous response. The camaraderie of the three women emboldened her. It helped her focus on the conversation and not her face.

Harbour outlined the basic plan of transporting the Jatouche aboard the *Belle*, while their equipment rode in the bays of the *Annie*.

"That will facilitate the transfer of the equipment to the YIPS, but also allow the Jatouche to enjoy the comforts of this ship," Olivia supplied.

Harbour was to note that Olivia would do that frequently. The engineer's mind processed thoughts so quickly that she was able to jump ahead of a speaker and see the pros and cons of what was being said to her. It was the one thing that Harbour most wanted to determine about the woman, exactly how flexible was her mind. After all, Olivia would be working with advanced alien technology, not to mention the aliens themselves.

When Harbour wound down, she enjoyed her meal, preferring to let Olivia eat in peace and allowing her to cogitate on what she'd been told.

Olivia finished eating, pushed her plate away, and steepled her hands, allowing the fingertips to touch the tip of her chin. "Biggest challenge, Captain, will be the language barrier," Olivia said.

Harbour held out her hand, and Olivia gazed at the small device resting there.

"Some sort of ear comm?" Olivia asked. When Harbour grinned at her, she exclaimed, "No! A translation device," and snatched it out of Harbour's hand, holding it up to examine it. "Any other goodies?" she asked.

"Afraid that's it," Harbour said. "Understand that we've had limited access to the Jatouche language. These ear wigs hold early communication versions. I believe we'll get updates from the Jatouche."

"But they'll primarily be based on first contact conversations," Olivia pointed out.

"Unfortunately, yes. You can imagine that Captain Cinders and his crew didn't have engineering and metallurgy dialogs as priorities," Harbour said.

Olivia's laughter about Harbour's comment erupted as a strangled snort. Unfortunately, it loosed a small amount of spittle flying from the corner of her mouth to land on Harbour's empty plate.

Harbour leveled her gray eyes into Olivia's wide ones and said, "Did I misunderstand you or were we only going to share food in this manner?"

Sasha's raucous laughter rocketed around the salon. Seated across from Olivia, the teenager's reaction was devoid of accusation or recrimination. It was simply a response to an incredibly funny and quite human moment. Moreover, it allowed Olivia to relax and join in the laughter about the awkward moment and Harbour's jest.

"Just testing the parameters, Captain. It's something all engineers do, as a matter of habit," Olivia allowed, using a cloth to wipe her mouth.

"Yes, well, to return to our discussion," Harbour said, smiling. "You'll have the Jatouche aboard for weeks, with their scientists, engineers, and techs at your beck and call. While you work at understanding what they have, what they need from us, and how this device will be deployed, I need you to keep some things in mind."

"Such as," Olivia queried.

"The Jatouche will have the opportunity to observe us in detail over the course of this project. It's possible that they'll want to leave engineers and techs behind to monitor the device," Harbour started to explain.

"But we won't be learning anything about their home world or civilization unless I ask the right questions," Olivia finished. "I take it you wish me to be a social scout. Learn about them, their customs, their home world, and so forth."

"It would be good to know about their gates too," Lindsey offered. "Triton has one. How many do the Jatouche have? Where do they go?"

"What's the relationships they have with other races?" Olivia supplied, and Lindsey nodded in agreement.

"I have a thought," Sasha announced.

The three adult women turned to regard the teenager. "This is something Aurelia said to me. One of the Jatouche didn't like her. Actually, what she said was, 'I detected animosity from him.'"

"Who was that?" Harbour asked.

"Jittak," Sasha replied.

"Did she know why?" Lindsey asked.

"Oh, yes!" Sasha replied, eager to take part in the adult discussion. "It was when the Jatouche discovered Aurelia was an empath. She demonstrated just a little of her power to Tacticnok, and Jittak wasn't happy to learn that the Jatouche are highly susceptible to an empath's sending. Aurelia said she detected plenty of pleasant reactions and one that was cold, hard anger. She said it came from Jittak."

"Who is he?" Olivia asked. "And please don't tell me he's the lead engineer."

"Captain Cinders thinks he's a military officer who was assigned to protect Tacticnok, who, if you haven't heard, is a royal member of Jatouche," Harbour explained.

"I heard her spoken of as Her Highness Tacticnok. Are you saying she's like a princess?" Olivia exclaimed.

"Rictook, her father, rules the Jatouche, and Tacticnok is his heir, or so I understand," Harbour replied.

"Is this a good thing or a bad thing that she's running this project?" Olivia asked.

"According to Captain Cinders, the plan to rehabilitate the planet wouldn't have happened without her efforts. I think it's an excellent thing that she's in charge," Harbour said.

"Anything else you want me to investigate?" Olivia asked. "We have plenty of time yet before we reach Triton and even afterwards to work on this."

Harbour regarded Lindsey, her mentor, across the table. Cool gray eyes regarded green ones.

"Come to think of, I have a big one," Lindsey said, leaning back in her chair to consider how to phrase her thoughts. "From what I've learned from our captain, the Jatouche are attempting to repair Pyre because of a fight with a race called the Gasnarians, during which they somehow damaged the planet. All well and good, if they can repair the problem, but is that it?"

"You mean, do the Jatouche fix Pyre and go home because we're a primitive lot in their eyes and they have no need for us?" Olivia asked.

"That's precisely what I mean," Lindsey replied, "which makes it important to find out what, as a society, they do need. Maybe we don't have it now, but, if we knew what it was, maybe we can work on creating something they need."

"Did anyone think that it's who we are that the Jatouche might want?" Sasha asked.

"What do you mean, Sasha?" Harbour replied.

"Well, we're human. We're different from them. We might be valuable to them just because of that. And we've got empaths. They might value our services," Sasha replied.

The adult women paused to consider Sasha's statements. Harbour admitted to herself that she hadn't thought of a relationship with the Jatouche from that point of view and made a mental note to speak with Jessie about it.

* * * *

The Jatouche's equipment was loaded on the *Annie* long before the *Belle* made Triton. Afterwards, much of Tacticnok's support staff journeyed home through the gate. The contingent who remained consisted of the eight original team members and a collection of scientists, engineers, and techs, totaling thirteen more individuals.

Once the *Belle* arrived, it was recommended to Harbour by Dingles and Danny that the colony ship's last shuttle wasn't to be risked in a moon landing. It fell to the *Annie's* shuttle to transfer the twenty-one Jatouche to the colony ship.

Harbour and a select few individuals waited anxiously in the corridor outside a bay for the *Annie's* shuttle to dock and the bay to pressurize. Through the viewplate in the airlock, they watched three human figures bound down the gangway. One came through the airlock, and the other two waited on the bay's side.

In the corridor, Jessie popped off his helmet.

"Who's with you?" Harbour asked, tipping her head toward the two individuals standing in the bay.

"Belinda and Rules," Jessie replied.

"Problem?" Harbour asked Jessie, gazing behind him and expecting to see the Jatouche trooping down the shuttle's gangway.

"Our guests will need a few moments to collect themselves," Jessie replied, stripping out of his vac suit.

"We can help with their personal gear," Harbour replied. "There's no need for our guests to cart it off the shuttle."

"That's not it," Jessie replied. "They're going to need time to compose themselves. I would guess Jatouche transports are a great deal more sophisticated than ours, meaning a lot smoother. I think if you shaved the fur off our alien friends' hands, you'd have seen white knuckles on every one of them during the flight until we hit zero gravity. I witnessed a lot of terrified eyes and gritted teeth.

Jessie tried to keep a sincere expression on his face, but a lift of an eyebrow and a twitch of a smile gave him away.

The humans waited in the corridor for several minutes before the aliens walked down the ramp, one by one. They were none too steady on their legs. But, as they crossed the deck, they pulled themselves together, and, with Belinda's help, the first eight of them filled the airlock and came through.

Those individuals with Harbour took the suits from the Jatouche and stored them.

"Your Highness, welcome aboard the *Belle*," Harbour said, as graciously as she could manage.

"Your offered courtesy of both my title and the hospitalities of this ship are much appreciated, Captain Harbour," Tacticnok replied. She introduced Jaktook, Jittak, Jakkock, and Kractik.

In turn, Harbour introduced Lindsey, Nadine, and Dingles.

"Perhaps, you'd like to rest and freshen up after your trip," Harbour suggested, as Belinda and Aurelia continued to bring groups of Jatouche through the airlock.

"That would be appreciated," Tacticnok replied.

"Afterwards, I'd like to introduce your technical individuals to a few of our preeminent engineers, who will be working with you," Harbour said.

Several of the Jatouche, who were busy removing their suits, chittered excitedly among themselves, but Harbour didn't receive a translation. *They must have comms control with their ear wigs,* she thought, noticing every Jatouche wore one.

"Afterwards, if you'd like, Your Highness, you can dine with Captain Cinders and me to discuss the project," Harbour offered.

"We've brought sufficient rations to last many cycles, Captain, in case your dietary habits don't agree with us," Tacticnok said.

"We consume fruits, vegetables, and other plant-based products, as well as cultured protein," Harbour replied.

"Excellent," Tacticnok replied excitedly. "We're omnivorous but don't consume the flesh of animals." Listening to a great deal of chatter from behind her, Tacticnok flashed her teeth at Harbour. "My team is pleased to hear that they won't be depending on Messinant paste to get through the many cycles we'll need to deploy the first device."

"If you and your Jatouche will follow Nadine and Lindsey, they'll take you to your cabins," Harbour said, directing the way down the corridor. "After you have some time to refresh yourselves, we'll collect you for the meetings. In the meantime, we'll have your gear removed from the shuttle and brought to you."

"Again, Captain, your courtesy is appreciated," Tacticnok said. "I can see why Captain Cinders admires you," she added, flashing her teeth, as her eyes sought Jessie's reactions. As she suspected, he was surprised by her comment. *Admire her from afar, do you, Jessie Cinders?* Tacticnok thought.

Jakkock stopped briefly in front of Harbour and handed her a small case. "More ear wigs with the latest translation iteration, Captain."

"Thank you, Jakkock," Harbour replied, accepting the silvery case. "We'll collect our first lot and return them to you for an update."

"No need, Captain," Jakkock said, patting a case he carried. "Your first group of ear wigs will be updated soon after I've found my lodging."

Harbour, Dingles, Jessie, Belinda, and Aurelia stood aside, as the Jatouche streamed past them. Each of the aliens tipped a head, as they passed Harbour.

After the Jatouche disappeared, Harbour signaled to everyone to remove their ear wigs and cup them tightly in their hands.

"Did everyone notice that some of the Jatouche chatted together, but we didn't hear translations?" Harbour asked quietly.

"Comm control over their ear wigs," Jessie replied. "I wonder if we have that capability."

"Or if we'll be led to think we've got control, when they'll always be on," Dingles replied.

"Either the voice of reason or paranoia," Jessie murmured.

"Only time will tell," Belinda added.

"Which means, for now, be careful what you say, when anyone in the group has an ear wig," Jessie said.

"Dingles, for now, don't distribute these freely," Harbour ordered, handing off the case to him. "They're to be given out for meetings and collected afterwards. The exceptions are the five of us, along with Olivia, Pete, and Bryan."

"Understood, Captain," Dingles replied.

"One last thing," Harbour said. "I understand the nod to a captain, when the Jatouche passed me, but why the gleams in their eyes?"

Aurelia giggled, and Belinda said, "The Jatouche spread the word about the effect Aurelia's sending had on them. Apparently, it was more potent than we understood. To the Jatouche, Captain, you're royalty ... the empaths' leader. Every one of them is probably hoping for a taste of your power."

"Not all of them," Jessie said, with a sour expression.

"Yes, Jittak. I noticed he didn't seem to appreciate my presence," Harbour replied. "Dingles, a cabin for our two spacers. I'll see to Captain Cinders myself."

"Aurelia, Belinda," Dingles said, turning around, bending his arms, and offering them to the two women. They laughed, hooked an arm, and sauntered down the corridor with him.

"Dingles has sure changed," Jessie said, shaking his head at the view of the three bantering spacers walking away.

"Love of a good woman will do that to a man," Harbour said, watching Jessie closely for his reaction.

"Even if the woman is an empath?" Jessie asked, returning Harbour's gaze.

"Especially if the woman is an empath," Harbour replied. "Shall we?" she said, sweeping her arm in the same direction that the Jatouche and the three spacers had taken.

-30-
Engineers

The Jatouche were surprised to discover they were allotted a cabin for every two team members, except for Tacticnok. They had expected dormitory accommodations.

As they were led to their cabins, most of the Jatouche became quickly disoriented by the warren-like corridors and decks. Soon, a few of them were utterly lost.

"Not to worry, Your Highness, I've had Kractik tracking our every move." Jittak whispered, with his ear wig output off.

Tacticnok had just commented to her two human hosts about the vastness of the *Belle*. She glanced toward Kractik, whose embarrassed expression revealed her unhappiness following Jittak's request.

"With this information, Your Highness," Jittak continued, "I can return us to the bay, at any time."

Tacticnok switched off her ear wig output and asked, "What then, Jittak?"

"I've stored weapons in our personal carryalls, which the humans are unloading. If necessary, we can force them to return us to the dome and journey back to Na-Tikkook."

Tacticnok swallowed her anger, and, instead of replying, she walked quickly ahead to join the human females. Jaktook stared silently at Jittak, as he passed the officer to catch up with Tacticnok.

The Jatouche were shown their cabins and its features, and they were able to relax in the accommodations. Once refreshed, Jaktook returned to Tacticnok's cabin and tapped softly on the door.

"No need to state your reason for being here," Tacticnok said, after she invited Jaktook to join her. "Jittak is growing more paranoid every day."

"It's the presence of so many empaths that's frightening him," Jaktook replied.

The pair of Jatouche reclined on pallets to speak further, appreciating that their hosts had made an effort to provide their preferred manner of relaxation.

"Have you felt any of the empaths' power since we've been aboard?" Tacticnok asked.

"None, and I think that it might be scarce," Jaktook replied.

"Why?" Tacticnok asked.

"If Captains Cinders and Harbour were Jatouche, what role in our society do you think they would occupy?" Jaktook asked.

Jaktook's question was why Tacticnok valued his advice. He helped her think of the greater issues, when the smaller ones fought to occupy her mind.

"I'm unsure of where to place Captain Cinders, but Captain Harbour would probably occupy the exalted position of emissary to a partner race," Tacticnok replied.

Jaktook flashed his teeth and nodded in appreciation, and Tacticnok was warmed by his admiration.

"My judgments are the same," Jaktook said. "Captain Cinders' team evidenced surprise after witnessing our reaction to Aurelia's sending. Surely this event must have been shared between captains and their associates, which is why we've felt none since arriving."

"I've lost your train of thought, Jaktook. What is it you saw in the dome that I missed?"

"I've spent much of my time carefully observing Captain Cinders. Before Aurelia demonstrated her talent to us, he spoke with her and gestured. Since that time, I've learned the hand motion he signaled to her before she performed for you. It indicated his desire that she exhibit a low level of power," Jaktook explained, imitating Jessie's descending, open palm movement.

"And?" Tacticnok prompted.

"The expression on every humans' face after Aurelia shared her power, despite curtailing it, was one of surprise. I believe that humans aren't nearly as susceptible to empaths as we are."

"Perhaps Jittak has a right to be worried," Tacticnok mused.

"Each race has the ability of using some sort of method to enforce its will on others, Tacticnok. What's the difference between an energy weapon, a stinging tentacle, and a mental sending?"

"For one thing, the energy weapon is the most destructive," Tacticnok quipped.

"Something we haven't asked and should is: Why are the empaths here on this great ship?" Jaktook said.

"You're right, Jaktook. Captain Cinders said that Captain Harbour was the empaths' leader. She's responsible for protecting them, implying they're all here. What we felt from Aurelia should certainly be valuable to the mental health of other humans. Why aren't the empaths spread throughout Pyrean emplacements to help the citizenry?"

"Now you see the conundrum that Jittak, for his fear, doesn't perceive," Jaktook said. "Two rulers and one leader, and it's the leader who protects humans, whom we perceive as invaluable to their society, but she must huddle here on this ship."

"It leads one to believe that there is more turmoil in human civilization than the captains want us to know," Tacticnok acknowledged.

"Yet, I don't believe the captains are the primary concern. Based on our cordial reception and treatment, I think it's the two rulers, whom we must learn more about. And, we must be prepared. The answers to our questions might not be to our liking."

Tacticnok and Jaktook continued to chat until a soft knock at the door indicated that the empaths had returned to collect them. The two Jatouche joined the other team members, who waited in the corridor, and then the group was led to an expansive meeting room. There were no pallets, and the Jatouche chose to stand.

In the meantime, Harbour had gathered Dingles, Jessie, Belinda, Aurelia, Olivia, Bryan Forshaw, and Pete Jennings. The captain walked through the meeting room's double doors, with her people in tow. Each human wore an updated ear wig.

Jessie was happy to follow in Harbour's wake. She appeared to be running the social aspects of the operation, and he had to admit that he hadn't considered much more than the necessary physical processes.

Harbour began the meeting by introducing the *Belle*'s technical team members — Olivia Harden, Bryan Forshaw, and Pete Jennings — who would be working with the Jatouche.

Without a word, Tacticnok approached the three humans, who stood in a row beside the captain. She reached out a hand toward Bryan's prosthetic, and he extended it toward her. Tacticnok lightly gripped it and turned it slowly left then right. Next, she stood in front of Pete and regarded the heavy burn scarring that was visible on his hands and neck. Finally, she tried to regard Olivia's face, but the engineer turned the ruined side away.

Tacticnok stepped back and said, "I assume these aren't decorations?" The choked laughter she received caused her to say, "I assumed not. Then, when this project is over, we'll have to do something about all this," and she twirled a finger at the humans' tortured bodies. "Come. Let me introduce you to those who will lead our technical people."

"Don't let the gray hairs fool you," Tacticnok said, indicating a Jatouche whose frail stature indicated advanced age. "Gatnack is one of our preeminent metallurgists. He'll be invaluable in helping you combine your base minerals to produce the components we need."

Gatnack tipped his head just the slightest, as if he dropped it any farther, he would have difficulty lifting it. "I'm honored to be here and help a young race establish a firm foothold on its planet."

"And, this is a male progeny of Gatnack's youngest female progeny," Tacticnok said, moving on to a Jatouche who was as young as Gatnack was old. "Drigtik is a marvelous fabrication engineer. Truly gifted, for one so youthful, he'll manage the final assembly of the device and its activation."

"I too am delighted to be here," Drigtik said.

The leaders and the nontechnical people stood back and let the scientists, engineers, and techs mingle. It wasn't long before Olivia plugged her comm unit into the room's wide display monitor and images of the YIPS appeared.

The Jatouche dug in their hip packs and pulled small devices to capture the images on the monitor. Discussions shot back and forth, as the two races, Pyreans and Jatouche, oriented themselves to the experiences and qualities of the other.

When Harbour felt the technical sorts had been given enough time to forget that they were two different species, having become absorbed in the common language of science, she lightly clapped her hands. Heads came up in response, and she asked, "Is anyone hungry?" Harbour received a chorus of assents and called out, "If my people would be so good as to lead our guests to the meal room that's been designated for them, staff are waiting to serve them."

Pyreans and Jatouche filed out and excited conversations could be heard down the corridor.

Harbour leaned over to Tacticnok, and said, "Captain Cinders and I wish your company for a meal."

"Excellent," Tacticnok replied. "Jaktook will be joining us." Tacticnok nodded toward her side, when Jaktook meant to follow the group out the door. Jittak attempted to join her, but Tacticnok motioned for him to follow the others. None of the senior people missed the frown and the lift of lip exhibited by Jittak.

Harbour led the foursome out of the room and turned in the opposite direction taken by the group.

"An incredible ship," Tacticnok commented. "One could be lost and probably starve to death before being found."

"That's how I felt the first time I was here," Jessie replied, grinning. "It was Aurelia and her sister who found me and led me to the captain's quarters."

"You were unfamiliar with the layout of your great ship?" Jaktook asked.

"Most Pyreans are," Jessie replied.

"Fascinating," Tacticnok. "This will be a subject for us to explore during our meal."

The group was quiet until they reached Harbour's quarters, where Lindsey, Nadine, and Yasmin were waiting to serve a meal. Gone were the central table and chairs. In their place were four makeshift platforms that stood a meter off the deck. Comfortable pallets, with decorative covers, were laid on top of the platforms. Two more platforms and pallets rested against the bulkheads. In front of each platform sat a small end table on which food and drink could rest.

"Please, make yourself comfortable, Your Highness," Harbour said, with a swing of her arm in the direction of the platforms.

Yasmin had worked with Makana, the artist, to create six different coverlets for the pallets. The women felt they represented different moods, and they were curious to see which of them the Jatouche chose.

Tacticnok and Jaktook unhesitatingly chose the most peaceful of the patterns. Immediately, they reclined, with contented expressions on their faces.

Harbour indicated a strong, masculine-patterned pallet for Jessie and lay down on the remaining pallet. The empaths, who were prepared to serve fruit juice, noticed that Jessie was sitting upright on his pallet rather than reclining, and they hid their smiles.

Tacticnok eyed the brilliantly edged container set before her. She picked it up and held it to the light, fascinated by the display of colors refracted and reflected by the sharp edges. "Marvelous," she said.

"We call it crystal," Harbour explained.

When Tacticnok set her cup down, Lindsey filled it with fruit juice. A frown formed on Tacticnok's forehead, but quickly disappeared when Lindsey added a clear tube by which she could drink. "Most considerate," Tacticnok acknowledged.

Jaktook sipped his fruit juice through his glass straw, and his face lit. "An incredible mix of fruits," he said.

"We grow them in our hydroponic gardens," Harbour replied. "You'll have the chance to tour the ship during the weeks that it will take to reach the YIPS."

"Which will give us much-needed time to get to know each other better, Captain," Tacticnok said, sipping on her drink, and savoring every mouthful.

Conversation ceased while the meal was served and enjoyed, not the least by Jessie. This was his first fresh meal in more than a month, and he suffered a twinge of regret for his crew, who were sailing aboard the *Annie*.

After the dishes were cleared, Lindsey offered a brandy to Tacticnok, who sniffed at the small glass and shook her head. Only Jessie chose to partake of the amber liquid, and Nadine left the bottle next to his glass before the empaths slipped out.

"Why are empaths only aboard this ship, Captain Harbour?" Tacticnok asked.

Right to the point, Harbour thought. "First, let us dispense with titles, in this group, if you don't mind?"

"Fitting," Tacticnok replied.

"In general, Pyreans are frightened by empaths. They worry an empath might manipulate their emotions to their advantage."

"Can this be done?" Tacticnok asked.

"The more powerful an empath, the more easily it can be done," Harbour allowed. She wanted to sit up, but thought maintaining her reclining position would indicate she was comfortable with the conversation. A glance at Jessie caught him finishing his first brandy quickly.

"Have you ever thought this, Jessie?" Jaktook asked. He felt uncomfortable speaking to the human without using his earned title.

"All my life," Jessie admitted, "until I met Aurelia. She changed my mind about empaths."

"How?" Jaktook asked.

"An empath has power that most humans don't," Jessie replied. "Aurelia made me realize it's not the power that should be feared, but the person who wields it. Aurelia is a gentle person, who does what she can to help others. Can she hurt someone with her power? Yes, she can."

"How would you compare your power, Harbour, to Aurelia's power?" Tacticnok asked.

"An empath's power can't be measured in any scientific manner, at least with any form of testing we possess. Only in specific circumstances can comparisons occasionally be made," Harbour replied.

Tacticnok and Jaktook witnessed the nervous glance that Harbour sent Jessie's way. His head was bowed, and he was holding his empty brandy glass in both hands, slowly rubbing it between them.

"I can see that this subject is making the two of you uncomfortable," Tacticnok said. "Let us speak no more of it." By that she meant, she wouldn't talk to Harbour about it when Jessie was present, but she had every intent of exploring the subject further with Harbour.

"Tell us about these two rulers of yours," Jaktook asked. "Why do you distrust them, and what challenges will they represent to us?"

Jessie broke out in laughter. He waved a hand in apology to the Jatouche and regarded Harbour. "Remember, it was your idea to invite them to dinner," he said, in fine humor.

Harbour stared at the expectant faces of the Jatouche and worked to organize her thoughts. "Rather than try to answer your questions, which is essentially the history of Pyre," she said, "let me tell you the story of the *Honora Belle*."

Harbour related the hopes of a dying Earth, and the people who sent their colonists to the stars. She spoke of the *Belle's* troubles, which shortened its journey and brought it to the present system. And, she described the orders given the ship's captain to set in motion the processes to create the new society.

"If I understand what you're saying, you believe these two rulers have usurped your rightful place," Jaktook surmised.

"Only as far as it was the captain's responsibility to ensure that democratic elections were held," Harbour replied.

"Explain this process that wasn't followed," Tacticnok requested.

"Humans, for the most part, believe in a democracy," Jessie said. "In this form of society, everyone is equal and has the same rights, which can't be taken away. When it comes to those who lead, humans vote to choose them. Individuals with the most votes are the leader for a specified length of time."

The Jatouche stared at each other, their jaws slightly open. Jaktook turned to Jessie and asked, "And does this work?"

"When it's done fairly and without guile, it works well," Jessie replied. "But those conditions aren't always present."

Tacticnok prepared to ask another question but halted when she spotted Jessie's upraised hand.

"We have questions," Jessie said. "In the dome's lower level, it was made clear to me that the Messinants built the dome, the gates, and uplifted the Jatouche. Where are the Messinants now?"

"No one, by that I mean, no alliance race, having discovered a dome, has ever been in the presence of Messinants," Jaktook replied.

"Do you even know what they looked like?" Harbour asked.

"Oh, yes," Tacticnok replied. "We found their images in the consoles. They don't give one the impression of intellect. They're easily the height of humans, but powerfully built. They're furred, and their faces are a mix of characteristics. Overall, I would say their most unsettling features are their eyes, dark and knowing. They appear to peer into your mind, seeking your thoughts.

"What do you know about them?" Jessie asked.

"What we know is what we surmise by comparing our ancient stories with those of the other races," Jaktook said. "We believe that the Messinants worked on a concept of mutualism. When they viewed their uplifting of a species as successful, they'd build a dome and a Q-gate to link the developing species to another planet that held a second species also in ascendancy."

"Why do you think they built the gates away from the planets?" Harbour asked.

"To improve the odds of their concept being successful," Jaktook replied. "The Messinants didn't wait for developing races to achieve sophisticated cultures. After satisfactory levels of sentience and language were achieved, they stopped visiting the race. Their work would either end in failure or success."

"What do you mean by failure?" Jessie asked.

"The species would collapse into war, starvation, or disease," Tacticnok replied.

"We think that the Messinants calculated that if a species achieved space travel, they were likely to be ready to meet others," Jaktook continued. "A dome was preprogrammed with the DNA of every species that was developing, which allowed that race to access the dome's entrance."

"But our DNA accessed the Triton dome, and our people never found a gate," Jessie objected.

Jaktook spread his hands in apology. "You would have to ask the Messinants how and why they did that, Jessie Cinders."

"Continue with your point about mutualism," Harbour urged.

"Having gained access to a dome, a race must possess the curiosity, patience, and technical skills to discover the secrets held in the console," Jaktook said. "Once the mysteries of the console and platform were unlocked, a species could send four to twelve of their number through a gate, depending on their size."

"But nothing much larger," Jessie pointed out.

"Exactly," Jaktook agreed. "The platforms were meant to allow individuals to journey to other worlds but not ships. One of two things would happen to those first intrepid passengers, who took passage to a quantum-linked dome. They would either find another race waiting for them or they wouldn't."

"What if the second dome was destroyed?" Jessie asked.

"Then passage wouldn't be enabled by the console," Tacticnok replied. "These circumstances existed when your dome's power supply was truncated."

When Jessie nodded in understanding, Jaktook continued. "If there were no one to greet them, the passengers would activate the console and return home. They had little choice."

"So, mutualism was predicated on two species achieving a technical level of society that could manage space travel sufficiently to discover their domes. Then, when one or both of them could unlock the gate's operation, they were able to meet," Jessie summarized

"Yes," Tacticnok agreed.

"How has this worked out?" Harbour asked.

"Much like your democracy," Tacticnok replied, "not always successfully."

"We believe that the Messinants were mesmerized by intelligence, but their logic held a flaw," Jaktook explained. "They equated greater intelligence with a superior race. Unfortunately, uplifting a species did not mean its darker nature was eliminated."

"You're implying that some of the Messinants' projects resulted in dangerous species, possessing intelligence and aggressive natures," Jessie said, his eyes staring hard into those of Tacticnok. "Worse, the Messinants weren't around to correct their mistakes."

"This is true," Tacticnok replied.

"You've mentioned other races several times, Tacticnok. You must have Q-gates that go to other worlds, correct?" Jessie asked.

Jessie's question created momentary consternation for Tacticnok and Jaktook. Based on the expression on Jaktook's face, Jessie surmised that he was deferring to Tacticnok, as if answering were a royal decision. When the silence extended, Harbour said, "It looks like it's been our turn to make you uncomfortable, which wasn't our intention."

However, Jessie wasn't so willing to let the question go unanswered. "Putting aside the number of gates, could you tell me how the Jatouche are faring among the other races? Are you technically superior? Do you dominate them?"

Tacticnok hesitated again, and Harbour sat up to focus her eyes on Tacticnok. "I would be interested to hear your answer, Your Highness."

Tacticnok could have hoped for her father's advice. This was one of the crucial moments of first contact that required a senior emissary's experience. The thought occurred to her that she'd done well, so far, and much of that success was predicated on forthrightness with the humans. She decided it was no time to change her ways.

"The Jatouche are known for producing sophisticated technical devices and medical solutions," Tacticnok replied. "But ..."

"But what?" Harbour pressed, but Tacticnok seemed incapable of answering. It appeared to Harbour as if Tacticnok was embarrassed to answer.

"If I might?" Jaktook gently requested of Tacticnok, and she assented.

"Earlier, we explained about the Messinants choosing to uplift a variety of species," Jaktook said. "We don't know why the Messinants chose us over the numerous creatures that inhabit our world. But, one thing is clear. We weren't the most aggressive species on our planet, and we certainly aren't among the races we've met or heard about."

"Is that why your fight with the Gasnarians was difficult?" Jessie asked.

"We didn't even have weapons in the beginning," Jaktook offered. "It took time to design, test, and manufacture them. We owe a great deal to the sacrifice of many of our species, who resisted the initial onslaught of the Gasnarians. Without their efforts, we would be a captive race."

"I'm sorry for the pain that you've suffered," Harbour said softly. "It must have taken a great deal of courage to come back to this place to see who fixed the dome."

"Credit goes to Her Highness," Jaktook said proudly. "And once the images of you were seen in the dome, Tacticnok pushed for the opportunity to meet you."

"Sounds as if the Jatouche could use a friendly ally," Jessie said, and the Jatouche flashed their teeth at him.

"Perhaps, we should call an end to the meal," Harbour said, rising.

"Most appropriate timing," Tacticnok replied.

Harbour called Dingles to lead the Jatouche back to their cabins.

-31-
Line Three

The *Annie* made the YIPS ahead of the *Belle*, and, after docking on a terminal arm, the crew began unloading the crates provided by the Jatouche. YIPS cargo crew floated the equipment onto sleds, strapped it down, and made their way along the lower level of the arm toward the axis. From there, they would head toward the station's far structure, where the melding, pouring, fabricating, and assembly would take place.

"Is any of this stuff dangerous?" Evan asked Yohlin, during a call.

"Evan," Yohlin replied, with a bit of exasperation. "What I can tell you is that this stuff is alien, which means I've no clue as to whether it's dangerous or not. But, the Jatouche sent it through a gate. Our people and the aliens trooped these crates across Triton, shot it into orbit aboard a shuttle, and I carted it here over a period of weeks. If it were going to go boom, it would have probably gone up already."

"I'm just being careful," Evan replied.

"You're being paranoid, Evan," Yohlin retorted. "The stuff we make is probably ten times, if not a hundred times, more dangerous than theirs. Remember, in their eyes, we're the primitives."

Days later, Danny maneuvered the *Belle* into a stationary position off the YIPS. Transport to and from the YIPS for the captains' ships would require either the YIPS, *Belle*, or *Annie*'s shuttles. Unfortunately, Evan made it clear to Harbour that he couldn't put one of the YIPS shuttles at her disposal.

Tacticnok was anxious to get started, but Harbour and Jessie arranged an important meeting with the Jatouche leader, who brought Jaktook and Jittak with her.

"Tacticnok, we wish to inform you of two arrangements," Harbour said. "The first is that within the YIPS there isn't gravity, except in the wheel. We've taken the liberty of procuring deck shoes for you and your team members. You'll need to wear them, at all times, to adhere to the decks."

"You managed to find these items that would fit our feet?" Jaktook asked in surprise.

"Actually, they've been made for human children, but they should work," Jessie replied. "One of our artisans took the liberty of comparing them to your footwear."

Tacticnok accepted the concept with a tip of her head, and asked, "And the other item?"

"We wish to assign two humans to accompany each of your team members, when they leave this ship," Harbour replied.

"That's unnecessary, Captain," Jaktook replied. "We've brought a large case of ear wigs and can distribute them to any new humans we meet to facilitate communication."

"What Captain Harbour is indicating, Your Highness," Jessie said, "is that we expect every member of your team to be accompanied, at all times, by two of our people. Our people owe allegiance to us and will have your well-being in mind, first and foremost."

"You expect trouble from the humans aboard this station," Jittak accused.

"We don't expect trouble," Harbour replied, careful to keep her power under wraps. "The conditions aboard the YIPS can be dangerous. The Jatouche will be unfamiliar with its operations. It's better to have our people with yours so that they are kept safe."

"A wise precaution, Captains," Tacticnok, "I thank you for your consideration of my team."

Tacticnok's pronouncement effectively ended the protestation that Jittak was about to voice. However, as the three Jatouche left the captain's quarters, Jittak vowed to further his plan to arm his three soldiers with the weapons he'd snuck aboard the colony ship. As per his orders from Master Roknick, he was prepared to endanger the formative first steps with potential allies in order to protect Her Highness.

"Dingles," Harbour called over her comm unit, when she was alone with Jessie.

"Here, Captain," Dingles responded.

"Tacticnok accepted the escorts. Danny and you have responsibility for the head counts. And, I want that count by name, the Jatouche and the humans, who are escorting them. Am I understood?"

"Clear, Captain," Dingles acknowledged, ending the call.

Danny, who overheard the exchange, said to Dingles, "Sounds like a captain more every day."

"And acts like one too," Dingles agreed. "To translate her message: Don't you dare fail to return to the *Belle*, at the end of the day, without accounting for every one of our guests."

"In that case, I've an idea," Danny said. "Instead of just names. We take vids and names each day of who gets off the *Belle*. That way I can confirm by vids that all the Jatouche have been retrieved. If not, I'll know which personnel to contact to determine the whereabouts of their Jatouche."

"I like it," Dingles replied. "Let's get the *Annie* shuttle pilots on the comm and share the idea. More than likely some of the *Annie*'s crew will be aboard the *Belle* and assigned to escort the Jatouche."

Dingles and Danny's plan worked well. An *Annie* pilot volunteered the idea of naming the teams, which added a shorthand to the tracking process.

The YIPS received its first alien visitors, and Evan soon found himself surrounded by Jatouche and human engineers and techs. After an overview presentation by Olivia, Evan threw up his hands in exasperation.

"This isn't some quick assembly process," Evan cried. "You're talking about taking over line three for, what, weeks?"

"Gatnack and Drigtik estimate seven to eight weeks," Olivia replied.

"You're usurping a quarter of this station's production output for two months," Evan objected. "Who's going to pay for the loss in income? Without someone offering compensation, including the priority fee, I can't approve that."

"Who could approve it? The commandant?" Olivia asked.

"That's who, and I can tell you he won't do it," Evan replied.

"Why not?" Olivia asked. "This is for the good of the planet."

"Olivia, this is an experiment with alien technology. You're hoping it works. The commandant isn't going to risk JOS coin on a hope." Evan held out his hands in apology.

"What's your estimate of the cost, Evan?" Olivia asked.

Evan pulled up his production schedule, which extended out several months. He isolated line three, highlighted the schedule for the next two months, and jumped to the billing summary. "It comes to eleven point three million in coin to give you priority control of the line for eight weeks."

Gatnack and Drigtik witnessed Olivia and the humans deflate. The Jatouche chittered among themselves, without the humans receiving translations. They'd followed the conversation on their ear wigs.

"I've no idea of the value that the manager is quoting, but, by our humans' reactions, it's substantial," Drigtik said.

"It's a shame that we have no financial arrangement with this race. It's probably a paltry amount to us," Gatnack replied.

"Is this the end of our work?" Drigtik asked Gatnack.

"Patience, Drigtik. We're about to witness our humans encountering their first considerable obstacle. We'll discover the extent of their persistence and ingenuity."

"I think I prefer our way," Drigtik replied. "One individual, our ruler, says yes or no. Then we do or we don't."

Buck up, Olivia mentally scolded herself. *You're an engineer, not a businesswoman.* Olivia snatched up her comm unit and made a call.

"Go ahead, Olivia," Harbour replied, placing her device on the table between Jessie and her. The captains had spent the day traveling together, anticipating just this sort of issue.

"Problem number one, Captain. The first of many, I presume," Olivia replied. "Evan advises us that to take over line three for two months, we'll need to compensate the YIPS for the loss in production."

"Olivia, Captain Cinders here. What's Evan asking for?"

"Eleven point three million in coin, Captain, to jump to the head of the production schedule," Olivia replied.

Harbour looked at Jessie in shock. "Wait one or two," she said to Olivia, and put the comm unit on mute. "That amount would drain the *Belle*'s general fund, and I'd still be a million short."

"If we split the amount, I'd be short for operating capital, especially if anything happened to one of my ships," Jessie replied.

Olivia heard Pete muttering. Reacting to what he said, she signaled the line for attention and received Harbour's acknowledgment. She said, "Captain, Pete was grumbling about the exorbitant cost and, in doing so, he gave me an idea."

Harbour whispered to Jessie, "That's Pete. Good ideas wrapped in a complaint," and Jessie grinned at her.

"We've got to consider that we'll be producing lightweight metals, with greater malleability, which will yield higher tensile strength," Olivia explained.

"Aren't malleability and tensile strength characteristics a contradiction in metals, Olivia?" Jessie asked.

"Bryan here, Captains. The Jatouche process is multiple stage, like ours: pouring, cooling, rolling or shaping, and then hardening. According to Gatnack and Drigtik, we're expecting a tremendous improvement over our materials."

"A faster production process too," Pete added.

"Olivia, any reason that line three couldn't be left in its final state when you're finished?" Harbour asked.

A grin crossed Olivia's face, which twisted its shape, but she didn't care. She understood Harbour's question. "Absolutely not, Captain, and I don't see a reason why the other lines couldn't be converted to be more efficient and produce better products." She stared at Evan, as she spoke into her comm unit. "Now, I wonder who'll hold the rights to these processes."

"Olivia, proceed with your plans," Jessie replied. "Tell Evan that Captains Cinders and Harbour are committed to delivering the required amount of coin. He should contact customers to notify them of new delivery times for their orders."

"Any questions, Evan, or do you want to argue personally with the captains?" Olivia asked. She felt vindicated by her decision to refer the problem to them.

Gatnack shared something with the Jatouche, and they tittered. When Olivia frowned at him, Gatnack said, "We'd be interested in seeing Evan Pendleton confront Captain Harbour, the leader of the empaths. The event should be enlightening."

Olivia and the humans had to laugh at that one. The only one not sharing in the moment was Evan.

"Well, Evan?" Olivia persisted.

"You have the line for eight weeks," Evan agreed.

"It would seem our humans are highly motivated, Gatnack," Drigtik admitted privately.

"Okay, I'm all ears," Harbour said to Jessie, after Olivia ended the call.

"It seems to me that we have an opportunity to involve Pyrean citizens in this operation," Jessie replied.

"You expect Pyre to raise the coin?" Harbour asked in surprise.

"Why not? This planet belongs to everyone," Jessie objected.

"That wasn't what I meant," Harbour said. "I'm doubting that the citizens would contribute anywhere near enough coin to meet the YIPS requirement."

"Let's say they don't," Jessie argued, "but they do come up with a quarter or half of the amount. Then you and I are that much better off if we have to make up the rest."

"I can't argue with that logic. Is it broadcast time?" Harbour asked.

"Absolutely," Jessie replied. "Just give me a few minutes first." He hurried into Harbour's study to use her monitor, activating his comm device as he ran.

"What are you planning to do?" Harbour asked, running after Jessie.

"I'm opening up a new account to accept deposits," Jessie replied. He hesitated and saw Harbour's narrowed eyes. "I don't want to broadcast an account number. It's too hard to remember. I need a name."

Harbour smiled. "Pyrean Green," she said.

"Perfect," Jessie replied, grinning.

Harbour stood close behind Jessie, watching him work. She'd been reaching to rest her hands on his shoulders and barely caught herself in time.

"That's smart thinking," Harbour said, when she saw Jessie give Major Finian and Captain Stamerson full account access. "Keeps everything air tight."

"Ready," Jessie announced, when the account setup was confirmed.

"Birdie, open a Pyre-wide broadcast," Harbour called over her comm unit.

Birdie tapped her comm panel. She'd programmed a subroutine for the operation and placed its icon among the panel's top routines. When the app signaled it was running, Birdie linked to Harbour's comm device.

Harbour could hear Birdie's announcement. She was alerting Pyreans of Harbour's upcoming message. When Birdie finished, Harbour said, "This is Captain Harbour. Captain Cinders and I've just learned that to make use of the YIPS facilities for two months to produce the first Jatouche device, and defer the station's scheduled production runs, we're expected to pay twelve million in coin."

Jessie frowned at Harbour and she amended her statement. "Actually, it's eleven point three million, but I'm adding seven hundred thousand for contingencies. Any unused amounts we collect will go toward rehabilitating retired or injured spacers."

Harbour caught Jessie's grin out of the corner of her eye, and she felt redeemed. She'd intended the extra to add to the coffers of Jessie's company and the *Belle*. In hindsight, that appeared a little greedy.

"What we've learned from our engineers is that the YIPS will be producing superior metals with the Jatouche techniques. So, the question is this: Are you willing to contribute to the recovery of the planet and enable the YIPS to manufacture better metallurgic products?"

"Here's our idea," Jessie interjected. "We've opened an account under the name Pyrean Green and given Captain Stamerson and Major Finian full access. If you're interested in what the Jatouche can do for us, make a contribution. In this way, you can have a hand in saving Pyre."

"What's a green planet worth to you?" Harbour asked. She waited a moment, and then said, "Captains Harbour and Cinders out."

Liam, who was in his office, heard the announcement and ducked his head into his hands. He knew Emerson was nearby in security administration, and he mentally counted the seconds, expecting the commandant to walk through the door within minutes. He wasn't disappointed. The count was two minutes, thirteen seconds.

"Why did you set up that account with the captains?" Emerson screeched.

"I didn't know anything about it," Liam said, leveling a calm gaze at Emerson.

"And you expect me to believe that?" Emerson accused.

Liam bit back his anger. "It's the truth, Commandant, whether you believe it or not."

The blood rushed to Emerson's face. He whirled around in an exhibition of righteous indignation and marched out of sight.

Liam exhaled a long sigh. He was getting tired of dealing with the commandant's tirades. He got up from his desk and walked around to where the sergeants sat. Miguel was out, but Cecilia was present.

"Did you hear the latest announcement from the *Belle*?" Liam asked Cecilia.

"Major, I think every Pyrean has a programmed alert on their comm unit to alert them of a *Belle* message. No one's missing them," Cecilia replied.

"I take that as a yes," Liam shot back, regretting his harsh tone.

"Problems, Major?" Cecilia asked gently, her motherly instincts coming to play.

"My interactions with the commandant are getting increasingly rancorous. I might have to lock one of us up to prevent a physical altercation," Liam replied, easing his stance and running a hand through his short hair.

"I wouldn't worry, Major, I think you can take him," Cecilia replied, with a wink. The major's laughter was the reaction she was hoping to induce. "What do you need, Sir?" Cecilia asked.

"I want you to stream an image of the account that Captain Harbour mentioned, Pyrean Green," Liam requested. He scrolled through his comm unit and tapped a few times. "You've received a viewer's access level."

"What? I can't get to the coin?" Cecilia asked, with a pout.

"Enough, you," Liam replied sternly, but he couldn't maintain a straight face, and it spread into a grin.

Cecilia's smile faded, as she asked, "Do you think it'll work ... the captains' plan to raise the funds?"

"I haven't a clue, Sergeant," Liam replied. "Right now, I want transparency. I want all of Pyre to see the incremental deposits and the accumulated amount until the account is emptied by transferring it to the YIPS or the spacers' rehabilitation fund."

"Yes, Sir," Cecilia acknowledged. When Liam exited the office, she accessed the account. To her surprise, Pyrean Green was already several thousand in coin richer. She smiled to herself and transferred fifty in coin from her personal account, feeling quite satisfied. Afterwards, she opened a channel on security's servers, added the account view, and sent a Pyrean-wide message about the Pyrean Green channel.

Liam received Cecilia's note that the account was online, and he opened his comm unit to access the channel. He too was taken aback to see the account was growing in small increments even while he watched it. Smiling, he accessed his personal account and contributed two hundred in coin to the attempt to resurrect Pyre. *I wonder how much you're going to contribute, Commandant,* Liam thought.

Emerson dropped into his desk chair with a thud. The control he thought he possessed seemed to be slowly leaking through his fingers. It was obvious that his staff, from the major to the sergeants, no longer worried about keeping their positions. Major Finian and Lieutenant Higgins seemed to be the worst of the lot, and Emerson suspected they held knowledge that could hurt him. The thought made his blood run cold.

Emerson picked up his comm unit and tapped a stored number.

"Have you heard about Harbour's YIPS account?" Emerson asked Lise.

"Everyone has heard about Pyrean Green," Lise replied with disgust. "The good news is that there's nothing but small deposits. Even though there's already thousands of them, they don't total more than two hundred and fifty thousand. The captains don't stand a chance of raising the necessary funds, at this rate. If they're forced to use their own coin, it might empty their reserves."

"I don't think that last part is true, Lise," Emerson replied. "Those two captains have delivered three huge loads of slush to the YIPS. I think they have the coin between them."

"If they have the funds, then why the charade?" Lise asked, upset at having her good mood smothered.

"That's obvious, Lise," Emerson said. "This is an opportunity for them to galvanize Pyreans into a common cause."

"It must be those documents," Lise retorted in anger. "I'm sure Harbour's found them, and, if Cinders is in league with her, then he knows about the documents too. That's the reason the two of them are trying to foment a rebellion."

"Uh-oh," Emerson muttered.

"What?" Lise asked.

"Get to your monitor and look at the account," Emerson replied.

Lise hurried to her desk, linked her comm unit, activated the monitor, and selected the icon she'd programmed. The first thing that caught her eye was the account balance. For hours, it had crawled slowly and incessantly upward. Now, it was jumping, even as she watched. She scrolled down the list of recent deposits. They no longer averaged fifty or so units, but seven hundred or more.

"They still have a long way to go," Lise said, trying to sound positive.

"Let's hope so," Emerson said, ending the call.

-32-
Pyrean Green

Idrian and Rufus were following the growth spurt in the Pyrean Green account, along with every other downsider, during their spare moments. Within the first day, the account passed its first million mark, and deposits weren't slowing.

"What are you suggesting?" Rufus asked, when Idrian arranged a conference call with Dorelyn.

"Rufus, this is the perfect opportunity for the council to make a private but significant gesture. Later, we can claim that it showed the council's intent to undertake a new direction in dome government."

"You want the council to make a major contribution to the Harbour-Cinder account but not claim any credit now?" Rufus asked incredulously.

"Not now," Idrian said.

"I like it," Dorelyn replied. "The transactions are anonymous, except to security, but they're required to get the Review Board's consent. Lise will never know unless Emerson has his people do some snooping off the books."

"If this alien experiment succeeds, the council has to be seen as having backed it," Idrian argued. "We can give permission to have security verify our claim that we were major contributors to the effort. It would be a huge validation of our group."

"How much were you thinking?" Rufus asked.

"There are eight family heads on the council now," Idrian replied. "I was thinking we should donate at least fifty thousand each."

"I could afford that," Rufus replied.

"You can afford much more," Dorelyn shot back. "Fifty thousand is too little."

"What are you thinking?" Rufus queried, with trepidation. He wasn't risk-averse, but he'd always insisted on generous returns for his risky investments.

"The fund is over one million," Dorelyn explained. "If we contribute a paltry four hundred thousand, it will evidence our support, but it won't make an impact in the minds of Pyreans."

"She's right, Rufus," Idrian added. "I say we need to more than double the account balance."

There was silence on the call, and Rufus was about to object, when Dorelyn said, "Two hundred thousand apiece. Let's do it."

The council agreed, despite Rufus' efforts to persuade them to accept a lesser amount. Dorelyn and Idrian organized the transfer of funds from the members to a new account that was kept private. That allowed it to be identified by a number only and not a name.

When the council's private account held the entire 1.6 million in coin, Idrian transferred the funds to the Pyrean Green account.

Shock rippled throughout Pyre, when monitors and comm units displayed the doubling of the YIPS account. The rumor mills worked overtime discussing who might be capable of contributing such an extravagant amount of coin.

While the uproar over the major depositor continued, Dorelyn called Idrian. "I must confess, Idrian, your idea was a brilliant strategic maneuver. Are you angling for the Council Leader's position?"

"More than anything, Dorelyn, I'm interested in seeing the council replace Lise Panoy and bring a stable governing body to the dome," Idrian replied. "My fear is that the family heads might be caught sitting on the sidelines, when the planet recovers and is opened to settlement.

* * * *

In the Starlight cantina, the regular meeting of the four wealthy patrons, three men and one woman, was on again. In the past two months, they'd become a fixture in the establishment. An attendant made nice tips, ensuring their favorite table with lounge seats, situated next to a view panel, was always saved for them.

As far as the four patrons knew, none of them had made a contribution to the YIPS account, and it had become a major topic of their discussions. The primarily voiced concern was that there didn't seem to be a means of generating a return on their investment.

"Here's something to think about," Hans Riesling said. "Suppose one way or another, the captains raise the funds and the alien device is successful ... confirmed by data, of course?" He left the question hanging in the air.

"If things come to fruition, as you suggest, the question on everyone's lips will be: Did you contribute?" Trent Pederson replied.

"You could always say that you did," Oster Simian quipped.

"What if security releases the names of the contributors?" Dottie Franks asked.

"Why would they do that?" Oster objected.

"I don't know that they would," the female patron replied. "I'm just asking *what if.*"

"I think it might be time to stop playing it safe," Trent said. "The situation has ventured far past the question of investment and return. It's become a political position, and the citizens will want to know who stood on which side."

"Meaning?" Oster asked.

"Meaning, I'd like my children or grandchildren to enjoy a green planet. What about you?" Trent asked, turning to gaze at Hans, who'd proposed the supposition.

"If you're asking me," Hans replied, "I contributed about three hours ago."

"I realize this might be an indelicate question," Dottie said. "But could you give us some sort of indication as to the amount of coin you contributed?"

"You want to know what it took to salve my conscience, is that it?" Hans asked.

"If you could," Dottie replied.

"I transferred a third of my liquid assets," Hans replied. He leaned back in his seat, sipping on his drink and enjoying the shocked expressions on his fellow patrons' faces.

"What is this? You trying to establish a legacy or something?" Oster asked.

"We won't live forever," Hans replied. "My grandfather was a miner who struck it rich. He died in an accident on an asteroid four years later. My father took my grandfather's legacy and grew it through investing in shipping. He never stepped once into space. I've inherited the wealth of these men. Giving up a third of my coin won't hurt the tremendous assets my children will receive. But, I want to give them more than coin, I want to give them a future. You have to ask yourself: Are you living for yourselves and just for today? Or do you want to play a part in something more significant, something that benefits generations to come?"

* * * *

It had been four days since Harbour and Jessie started the Pyrean Green fund. It was no longer an idle hope. Instead, it had surpassed eight million, and deposits continued to roll in, small and large.

Much to Lise Panoy's chagrin, Jordie and others were reporting to her that downsiders were contributing to the fund. Two contingents were forming. The first was a fad created by the sons and daughters of the wealthy. They were hurrying to be considered part of a unique clique — one that showed they could thumb their noses at the governor and the status quo.

The other group had no uniform definition. Small to moderate amounts were attributed to them. The reports indicated they came from cooks, house attendants, gardeners, technicians, cargo crew, and sundry other professions. No names accompanied the messages delivered via security's informants. Either there were none available, which Lise doubted, or they chose not to share them.

The latter condition bothered Lise. She could sense her absolute control of the domes slipping away. Staring out her office's rear-facing window, Lise calmed her anger and thought through the changes that had affected the domes. She'd considered the removal of Markos Andropov as an opening for her and thought the governorship would continue on as it had done under him and his family throughout the centuries.

Now, Lise realized that the removal of Markos had stirred downsiders' emotions. Typically, the governor relied on a divisive message, pitting downsiders against topsiders. But, the aliens presented a new reality, and the separation of Pyre's stations and domes no longer mattered. There were greater considerations.

The other thought uppermost in Lise's mind was the 1.6-million-coin contribution to the Pyrean Green fund. It irked her that none of her sources had uncovered the origin of those funds. It occurred to her that a conglomerate of stationers might have been responsible for the largesse. Having had that thought, she berated herself. Moments ago, she'd been considering the changes evident in the domes' citizens. Putting the two ideas together, it struck her that the families might have been the source of the funds.

Having made the leap, Lise continued to stare out the window, letting the greenery soothe her mind, while she reviewed the families one by one. In her mind, she put them in one of two groups, those she considered too timid to rebel and those who would want the governorship. What she failed to do was consider the possibility that the major contribution heralded a greater level of cooperation among the family heads than the domes had ever seen.

The question Lise proposed to herself was what to do next. Events were headed in a direction that excluded her, and she needed to find a means of upsetting the trends. Lise returned to her desk, picked up her comm unit, and called her head of security.

"I think it's time to disrupt the progress at the YIPS," Lise said, when Jordie sat on the other side of her desk.

"Are you still adamant that there are to be no deaths?" Jordie asked.

"A death doesn't serve us," Lise replied. "Besides, it's too risky. It would take some sort of explosion to resemble an accident, wouldn't it?"

Jordie nodded his head, and Lise grumped in reply.

Drumming her fingernails, Lise asked, "What are our options?"

"We know little about the aliens. Our agents can't get close to them," Jordie replied.

"Why not?" Lise asked.

"Many reasons," Jordie replied. "First, Harbour and Cinders' people use ear wigs to understand them."

"Can't one be stolen?" Lise asked, interrupting.

Jordie shook his head, explaining, "The aliens are on the YIPS for the day shift, and then they're collected and returned to the *Belle.*"

"The aliens could lose an ear wig, if they're jostled," Lise suggested.

Again, Jordie shook his head, which he could see was annoying Lise. "From our agents' observations, the alien ear wigs might have comm control. Sometimes they jabber on, and Pyreans don't know what they're saying."

"Okay, you were telling me why our agents can't get close," Lise reminded Jordie.

"The captains have tasked their people as minders. Two human spacers, engineers, or techs are with each alien, at all times. Harbour and Cinders must have been heavy-handed when they gave out the orders, because the minders get off the shuttles with their aliens and stay with them throughout the day. Occasionally the ratio varies a bit when the Jatouche are in meetings, but, before they break up, the minders are back with them. At the end of the day, the aliens are escorted to the shuttle and returned to the *Belle.*"

"Really?" Lise asked, and Jordie was happy to be able to nod in agreement on this one. "This might work to our advantage. Suppose you were to target a threesome. Whom would you choose?"

"The minders and the aliens sometimes switch up, depending on the meetings they need to attend," Jordie replied. "If we were to try to target a particular human and alien pair, it would be difficult."

"Put that aside," Lise ordered. "Who's the weak link, the one individual who's indispensable to the operations?"

"That would be a YIPS engineer by the name of Olivia Harden," Jordie replied. "She's the key figure coordinating among the aliens and the human engineers and the techs."

"That's who we target," Lise said, a satisfied smile on her face.

"And what are we trying to achieve?" Jordie asked. "Injury to her that might take a while to heal? Or are we trying to sow a little discontent between the aliens and our people?"

"I like the latter idea," Lise replied. "You say there's always a threesome."

"Yes, sometimes six or nine, walking as a group," Jordie replied.

"Whom does Olivia accompany?" Lise asked.

"She's usually with one or the other of two aliens. We don't know them by name, but the agents know them by sight. One appears to be quite aged, and the other is young. They must be of singular importance, because I'm told Olivia is often seen in their company."

"Perfect, we target Olivia, and, odds are, we'll get a key alien," Lise said. By now, she was smiling. It was a fierce expression that made Jordie uncomfortable.

"Did you have something in mind, Governor?" Jordie asked.

"Oh, yes," Lise replied, her smile widening into a savage grin.

-33-
Excess Energy

A YIPS conference room was festooned with monitors, displaying line three and various parts of the Jatouche's device. Crowded around the central table were Olivia, Gatnack, Drigtik, Bryan, Pete, and many other individuals.

Gatnack held everyone's attention, as he expounded on the transformations that line three would undergo to produce the metals that were needed.

As a propulsion engineer, Bryan was studying the temperature levels that would be maintained throughout the processes. He made some quick calculations and passed his comm unit over to Olivia, nudging her arm, since he was approaching her from her left side.

"This is going to create a long-term problem," Olivia said. "We've got the gases to drive production for the two months, but the YIPS can't keep line three operational indefinitely after we convert it nor can they afford to convert the other lines."

"Is there a problem, Olivia?" Gatnack asked.

"It's the temperatures for your metals, Gatnack," Olivia replied. "The YIPS is an old facility, built soon after the arrival of the *Belle*. It burns gases to drive the furnaces. It's not the most efficient of processes."

"Why wouldn't you want to use the output of our intravertor to drive your lines?" Drigtik asked.

"Wait," Pete exclaimed. "What's the intravertor putting out? I thought it was radiating the heat as coherent light, a laser beam."

"That's an option," Drigtik replied.

When Gatnack saw the humans stare at Drigtik and him expectantly, he laid out the other options available to the Jatouche's intravertor.

"You're describing microwaves," Pete said, when he heard one of Gatnack's explanations.

The Jatouche were unfamiliar with the term, but quickly shared it among themselves, adding the term microwave to their vocabulary.

"If we used microwaves, we'd need a receiver on the YIPS," Bryan noted.

"That can be assembled and coupled to your energy systems," Drigtik supplied.

"What about the atmosphere, Drigtik?" Olivia asked. "Won't it interfere with your transmission, spreading, and diffusing its energy?"

"Initially, much of the intravertor's energy will be lost," Drigtik acknowledged. "This will happen despite our tuning of the frequency and the beam's focusing through the barrel. However, it should be enough to help drive line three."

Olivia, Pete, and Bryan stared in surprise at one another.

"When other intravertors are planted near the first one, it'll assist in opening a hole in the atmosphere and will greatly increase the energy focused on this station's receiver," Gatnack said. "At some point, multiple intravertors will deliver more energy than can be absorbed by the receiver. Then, future intravertors can be fitted with different output options, such as coherent light."

"Gatnack, you speak as if your intravertor is guaranteed to work," Pete said.

Olivia winced at Pete's statement and was pleased to see by the furrows on Jatouche brows that his comment hadn't translated.

"Gatnack," Olivia quickly said, "Pete would like to understand your level of confidence in the intravertor functioning as designed."

Gatnack cocked his head in confusion, but Drigtik flashed his teeth and said, "Please understand, we aren't experimenting with the intravertor. Several models were built on Na-Tikkook and rigorously tested. Scientists examined the data and chose the best design. Three more of these units were created and tested on the harsh conditions of an ice moon. If Pete's word *guaranteed* is asking for our assurance that the intravertor will work as designed, then you have our *guaranteed*."

The humans in the room laughed and smiled, and Jatouche teeth were bared in appreciation.

"It looks like we're no longer playing with an experimental unit," Olivia announced to her people. "The Pyrean Green account reached its goal. I say we get busy, build this intravertor, and start saving Pyre."

A rousing cheer went up from the humans. The Jatouche were momentarily taken aback, but Drigtik yipped and his teammates joined in the noise.

The news of the intravertor's thorough testing buoyed the Pyreans, and they bent to the first steps with a will, preparing line three.

Olivia left the meeting, while the engineers and techs dove into their work. She headed for Evan's office. After first hearing of the need for the receiver, she'd considered calling the captains to request additional funds, but decided against it. Instead, she was going to imitate their style and be inventive.

In Evan's office, Olivia laid out the concept in detail to Evan.

"Think of it, Evan," Olivia said in summary, "microwave transmission from the planet's heat represents a huge, long-term benefit for the YIPS. Eventually, there'll be no need for gases to drive line three. As more intravertors are deployed, all the lines can reap the free energy, while the planet cools."

"What about when the intravertors can no longer drive the lines?" Evan asked.

"You mean in twenty or fifty years, Evan?" Olivia retorted. "Or do you think the Jatouche can heal the planet overnight? And another thing, how much coin will you save not burning gas to drive the furnaces and power the lines? Maybe the coin savings will go toward constructing a new and better production station."

What Olivia was proposing dawned on Evan, but his next question indicated he hadn't understood where she was headed. "Do you know how much additional coin you'll have to raise to build the receiver?" he asked.

This was the reaction Olivia thought she'd receive, when she was traversing the axis on the way to Evan's office.

"It doesn't matter what it costs, Evan, we're not going to expend a single coin. You are," Olivia said defiantly.

"You know that's the commandant's call," Evan replied, voicing his usual objection.

"And here's what you're going to tell Emerson Strattleford," Olivia said, leaning toward Evan, despite her urgent desire to turn her face aside. "You're going to tell him that he'll be a hero to Pyreans for making a bold choice to invest in Jatouche technology."

"And if he doesn't buy it?" Evan asked.

"Then I guess it'll be time for the captains to make a broadcast about the tremendous opportunity the commandant was presented but let slip though his fingers," Olivia replied, her face twisting in a grimace.

Evan was wondering where the retiring, withdrawn engineer he'd worked with for years had gone. *It must be some effect of working with the aliens,* he thought.

* * * *

Olivia caught the day's last shuttle, ferrying the Jatouche from the YIPS to the *Belle*. She'd boarded in the company of Gatnack and Belinda but chose to sit by herself. She was enjoying a sense of accomplishment, a deep, rich feeling that overshadowed her ever-present fear of facing people.

As the hatch was sealed, Aurelia slid into the seat next to her. "I'm not here to chat or disturb you, Olivia," Aurelia said. "I thought I'd get a little closer and enjoy the glow."

Aurelia sat on Olivia's left, with a full view of the crippled side of the engineer's face. "Drink your fill, Aurelia," Olivia said, leaning her head into the seat back, "there's enough for two."

Aboard the *Belle*, when Olivia passed through the bay's airlock, she was met by Harbour and Jessie.

"We received a message from Commandant Strattleford about you," Jessie said sternly.

"Oh," Olivia replied in surprise, her earlier elation fading.

"Yes, the commandant said he doesn't like being threatened by engineers, of all people," Harbour said.

"That it?" Olivia asked, perplexed that the commandant hadn't said anything more.

"One more thing," Jessie supplied. "He said he would pay for the microwave receiver, providing we mentioned that in our next broadcast."

When Olivia heaved a sigh of relief, Harbour extended a hand, "Well done, engineer."

Olivia delivered her crooked grin, shaking Harbour and then Jessie's hands, who said, "Welcome to the fight, Olivia."

"I believe this calls for a drink," Harbour suggested.

"The cantina," Jessie chorused and extended his arms to both women.

When Olivia hesitated, never having stepped into the *Belle*'s popular spot, Harbour said, "It works like this, engineer," and she hooked her arm into Jessie's. "Among spacers, we call it latching on."

With both captains staring expectantly at her, Olivia succumbed and added her arm.

"Off we go," Jessie said gallantly.

Minutes later, the threesome walked through the hatch of the *Belle*'s cantina. It was crowded. What shocked Olivia was to see the Jatouche present. The cantina was fitted with stand-up tables to prevent the spacers and residents from spending too much time in the place. Scattered around the tables were half-meter high, short benches, which the Jatouche stood on to speak eye-to-eye with humans.

Harbour noticed the aghast expression on Olivia's face and said, "The Jatouche found this place on their second night aboard the *Belle*. A bunch of them tried the alcoholic drinks and spat them out, but they love the fruit juices."

Harbour raised an arm high in the air, and Dingles, who had seen her entry, bellowed for quiet. A bartender cut the music, and the cantina quieted.

"Thanks to the ingenuity of the Jatouche," Harbour said, "the YIPS will receive energy from the intravertors, drastically cutting costs over time. Yes, this means that there will be a reduced demand for slush but not immediately. My announcement tonight is that the YIPS must have a microwave receiver to enjoy this abundant and free energy. I'm here to tell you the commandant has agreed to pay for its construction."

There was a moment of silence, as Pyrean faces frowned suspiciously at the commandant's largesse.

"Of course," Harbour continued, "the commandant was nudged to make the right decision by the arm twisting of our own Olivia Harden."

A cheer went up from the humans, and the Jatouche, recognizing a moment of celebration, joined in with howls and yips.

Jessie grasped Olivia's hand and hauled it upward, and the cantina's joyful noise got louder. As spacers, empaths, residents, and Jatouche surged forward to congratulate Olivia, patting her on the back and offering to buy her a drink, Harbour and Jessie stepped backward. Olivia was fully engulfed by well-wishers, when the captains slipped out the hatch.

"Would you like a private drink?" Harbour asked.

"I could use one," Jessie replied.

Once in the captain's quarters, Harbour and Jessie carried their brandies into the study. They sat side by side on the comfortable, padded couch, with their deck boots off and their feet up. The crystal cups were cradled and warmed in their hands, and their heads rested against the couch's top curve.

"Looks like we're going to do this," Harbour said, feeling deeply satisfied by their success.

"Maybe," Jessie said quietly.

"Why so pessimistic?" Harbour asked.

"You don't think repairing the planet isn't going to frighten the governor and the family heads?" Jessie posited.

"They have their domes," Harbour replied, lifting her head to stare at Jessie. "Why should they object?"

"You say that because you aren't a power-hungry individual desperate to hold on to your position," Jessie replied. "What if the *Belle* residents wanted to hold a captaincy vote tomorrow?"

Harbour considered the question, and her eyebrow quirked up in acceptance, as she admitted, "I'd organize it."

"And if you lost?" Jessie asked.

"I'd do what I could to support the new captain," Harbour replied.

Jessie mumbled something, and Harbour said, "Sorry, didn't hear what you said."

"You're rare," Jessie repeated.

"You say it like I'm an oddity. I think I've had enough of being considered an outcast," Harbour replied, tension creeping into her voice.

"My comment wasn't meant in a negative fashion, Harbour." Jessie replied quietly. He regretted that most things that came out of his mouth sounded the same, like orders to crew. *Maybe I need to join Nate and get some training from Ituau,* Jessie thought.

"What do you think the family heads or governor might try to do?" Harbour asked, redirecting the conversation.

"I don't know. That's what worries me. The governor has been entirely too quiet about this project," Jessie replied.

"You were detained by security," Harbour pointed out.

"True, but I wasn't charged. That was Lise testing the commandant's power, and it came up short," Jessie replied, chuckling at the memory of Emerson finding him in various security offices, enjoying himself.

"Maybe she's waiting until we request access through the domes?" Harbour proposed.

Jessie replied with "hmm," tipped back his crystal glass, finished his drink, and sat up. "Time for me to go," he added, slipping on his deck shoes.

Harbour set her drink on the arm of the couch and followed Jessie to the cabin's door.

Jessie felt the brandy warming his senses, and Harbour's face beckoned him.

"I was wondering if I might have another," Jessie asked.

"Another what?" Harbour asked, her voice thick with emotion, as she leaned close to Jessie.

Rather than reply, Jessie leaned over and kissed Harbour. Unlike the many dispassionate kisses he'd shared with downtime women and coin-kitties over the years, this one had feeling, and he reveled in it.

When Jessie finally pulled away, Harbour smiled at him. She'd felt the genuine waves of pleasure rolling off him, while he kissed her. For Harbour, a powerful empath, it was a moment that had been a long time coming.

"Night," Jessie said, smiling in return.

"Night," Harbour whispered, and Jessie slipped out the door.

It wasn't until Jessie was many meters down the corridor that he realized his elation, during the kiss, was his own. He'd received nothing from Harbour except the warmth and taste of her lips. For a moment, he was pleased about that. Then, in the next second, he wondered if that was fair, asking Harbour, an empath, to shut down her natural reactions because he was a normal. The conflicting thoughts evaporated much of his residual pleasure.

* * * *

The next morning two events took place.

The first was another broadcast by Harbour and Jessie. They communicated the news that the intravertor, as the Jatouche called their device, wasn't as experimental as Pyreans had supposed. In addition, they happily stated that the intravertor would be able to supply some amount of energy to the YIPS via microwaves and stressed that it would take multiple devices to power the entire station.

"Credit should be given to Commandant Strattleford for volunteering JOS coin to fund the cost of the microwave receiver that will be built on the YIPS," Harbour said.

"Although, it should be recognized that this was an elementary decision, one a child could make," Jessie interjected. "For the investment capital of three-quarters of a million in coin, the YIPS will be able to eventually save a couple of million a year in slush purchase per manufacturing line. This will grow to well over ten million annually, when the entire station is powered by the planet's output."

Emerson, who had been listening to the broadcast, threw his half-finished meal plate in the direction of the kitchenette. Fuming, he picked up his comm unit, but he couldn't think of anyone to call who could help him. Feeling completely impotent, he sat staring at his device, wondering why life was treating him so cruelly.

The second event marked the arrival of the *Pearl* and the *Spryte* at the YIPS from Emperion. The *Pearl* docked, and crew began unloading the tanks of slush. The *Spryte* also docked, requiring Jessie to add the docking fees for that ship to those of the *Annie*.

Captain Hastings and Ituau caught an *Annie* shuttle from the YIPS with Captain Erring to meet with Harbour and Jessie.

When the group was settled around the table, Harbour opened the discussion by saying, "We have two assignments for the new crews. Line three is undergoing a heavy overhaul to make the Jatouche metal and fabricate the parts for the intravertors. With your people, we have the numbers to run this part of the project around the clock. You know your people and can choose the engineers and the techs who will best serve these functions. You'll work with Olivia Harden, the YIPS engineer in charge of the Jatouche, to coordinate assignments."

Leonard and Ituau cast quick glances toward Jessie, who seemed content to let Harbour lead the conversation.

"The second task is just as important as the first," Harbour continued. "We need minders for the Jatouche. The rule is that a single Jatouche will always be in the company of two humans. This isn't a suggestion; it's an order."

Yohlin had experienced this subtle shift between Harbour and Jessie, but Leonard and Ituau hadn't. When the pair glanced at Jessie again, he said. "Let me be clear. The Jatouche efforts eclipse most organizational structures we're comfortable with, our ships, my company, the stations, even the domes ... everything. As far as this entire alien thing is concerned, Harbour is our leader. So, listen up, and follow orders."

Jessie received crisp nods from Leonard and Ituau, who turned attentive faces toward Harbour.

"Dingles coordinates the exits from the *Belle* for every Jatouche," Harbour said. "Danny handles all shuttle receptions at the YIPS. No Jatouche exits a shuttle to step foot on the station without his or her two minders, and the Jatouche return at the end of a work day the same way."

"What if the Jatouche have a meeting or something that keeps them late?" Leonard asked.

"The minders must coordinate with Danny for any extension past first shift's hours, but these will be limited in length to two hours. No exceptions," Harbour replied evenly and held Leonard's gaze.

"Yes, Ma'am," Leonard replied. "Permission through Danny, max two hours for the Jatouche, and no exceptions after that."

"There might be a small problem with assignments," Ituau said. "The *Belle* and the *Annie's* crews have had an opportunity to become accustomed to the Jatouche. From reports I've received, some spacers aren't relishing rubbing shoulders with them."

Harbour eyed Leonard, who said, "Have to agree with that, unfortunately. I know they're a little odd looking, but they're here to save our planet. To me, that should go a long way toward tolerating anything about them."

Yohlin started laughing. When she had everyone's attention, she looked at Leonard and Ituau and said, "You two should warn your crews that if they have any issues with the Jatouche, they'll have to forgo the *Belle's* cantina. Our alien friends love the place, the fruit juice drinks and the camaraderie."

Leonard and Ituau gazed around the table only to see faces smiling and heads nodding.

"What a difference a couple of months can make," Ituau commented softly.

Harbour picked up her comm unit. Her request was brief. "Dingles, a senior empath, who's still aboard, to the captain's quarters."

A few minutes later, Yasmin came through the door. She had an acerbic quip readied for Harbour, but it died in her throat when she saw who was gathered at the table. "Captain," was all she said.

"Yasmin, you're now in charge of sorting out the crews of the *Pearl* and the *Spryte* into those who are comfortable with the Jatouche and those who aren't," Harbour ordered.

"I'd have to assign an empath to accompany every Jatouche," Yasmin replied. "Should they be one of the two minders or a third?"

"Make them a third," Harbour replied.

"And what happens when an empath discovers someone is displaying negative feelings toward a Jatouche?" Yasmin asked.

"They're to report that to you, and you'll communicate it to the appropriate captain. We'll take the necessary actions," Harbour replied. "I need this in place immediately. Thank you, Yasmin."

After Yasmin left, Ituau asked, "What happens to crew who aren't qualified to work on line three and who an empath disqualifies from minding the Jatouche?"

"So far that hasn't come up," Jessie said. "I would suggest you inform your crews that their employment is at risk if you can't find work for them on this project. We need all hands on deck, not lying around in their bunks."

Soon afterwards, Leonard, Yohlin, and Ituau were dismissed and made their way down to the shuttle bay deck.

"Is it my imagination," Leonard asked, "or does Harbour act more like a captain, if not a commandant, each time we see her?"

"Growing into the job," Ituau commented.

"Yes, but the question is: Which job?" Yohlin added.

"Ambassador," Ituau replied. "Isn't that what they call the person who interfaces with foreign entities?"

-34-
Jordie's Agent

David Yersh finished his meal, such as was available aboard the YIPS. He was a tech, responsible for monitoring temperatures and flow of the output of line two. He'd have loved to have been part of the line three project but didn't qualify. The information he could have gained from the Jatouche would have been invaluable to Jordie MacKiernan, his benefactor.

YIPS personnel were unaware of David's double life. His simple existence aboard the YIPS belied the comforts he enjoyed on the JOS. David's JOS cabin was in the expected, cheaper corridor, but it was crowded with items only senior engineers and techs could afford.

David was an ambitious young man, whose limited skills and training would never allow him to rise much higher until he invested more effort in his future. But David was impatient and the thought of toiling for years in an effort to improve his abilities and, therefore, his station made him sick.

In order to relax for the evening, David was about to pull out his private cache of vids, when his comm unit blinked. He picked it up and studied the bizarre message. To anyone who might have looked over his shoulder when he received such an odd text, David could have laughed and said, "My little nephew is playing with his mom's device again." They would have shared a laugh, and David could have gone about his business, no one the wiser and no one aware that he had no nephew.

Among the message's scrambled letters and notes were simple codes, which David studied. He was directed on his next rotation to the JOS to meet with a contact at a store on a specific date and time. David deleted the message and dug out the memory stick that contained his vids. He was ecstatic and in the mood for one his favorites. An assignment from Jordie MacKiernan loomed, and that meant more coin in his account.

It was three days before David rotated back to the JOS. That evening he was excited and unable to concentrate on a vid. Instead he spent some coin entertaining himself at a cantina. He bought drinks for two young coin-kitties, but, when he refused their invitations for the evening, they quickly deserted him.

Early the next morning, David gulped down a morning meal, dressed in a simple pair of skins, and made his way to the Latched On. As a source of spacer supplies, David frequented the place, which provided a good cover for his meeting. He browsed and picked up a few small, sundry items, most of which he did need.

"I noticed you favor the gloves with the pads on both sides," David's contact said. As usual, it was a stranger, as David never met the same contact twice.

"Protects the back of my hands if they slip off a tool and strike metal. The engineers don't like them because they're not flexible enough, but, then again, they do the thinking and techs, like me, do the grunting," David replied.

The stranger laughed and picked up a pair of gloves. "What do you think of these?" he asked, holding them up for David to examine. Cradled in the center of the gloves was the stranger's comm unit. He had closed shoulders with David to prevent the display of his device from being observed by others.

David glanced at the display and quickly memorized the information, which comprised a date, a time, a name, and a number. "A good pair for the price," David commented, which signaled the stranger to withdraw his device. The information was quickly deleted.

"Thanks for your advice," the stranger said and moved along the display shelves.

David spent a few more minutes to browse, repeating the information continuously. He wasn't allowed to write anything down, ever. After he'd been recruited, his first contact had laid down the rules for communication in no uncertain terms. After every instruction, the stranger had ended it saying, "without exception." The repeated admonishment might have become boring, except the deadened eyes of the contact had frightened David, and he carefully committed the rules to memory.

"Find what you needed, David?" Gabriel, the Latched On store owner, asked genially. David was a good customer, and Gabriel presumed he was a highly paid specialty tech on the YIPS.

"I'm good," David replied with a bright smile.

It would be two more days before David retrieved his package. On the appointed day, he spent some time perusing some shops near the El terminal arm. With a quarter hour to go, David queued for a cap to transit to the arm. He joined a group of passengers headed downside, arriving on the arm and walking down the ramp. But, rather than following them to take a seat on the upper level of the El, he turned toward the cargo pickup area.

A cargo inspector waited on a customer, and David took note of the name on the coveralls. It didn't match. He stood to the side, opening his comm unit, and studied the device to appear as if he were engrossed in it.

Cargo inspectors came and went, helping customers. Eventually, an inspector took a customer's request, as another inspector came from the cargo storage area. The name matched and David stepped forward.

"I've a package to retrieve," David announced. "BL7102."

The eyes on the youthful cargo inspector, which had been glazed with boredom, suddenly sharpened. "What was the code?" he asked. When David repeated the number, the cargo inspector nodded and ducked through the doors into the storage area.

The inspector accessed his locator unit, which was attached to his coveralls, tapping in the code. The row, shelf, and cubbyhole location came back, and he quickly retrieved the package. He pulled a small tool from a pocket and turned the package over. Next to a seal along an edge was a smear of dark ink. He made a short slit along the seal, reached inside, and pulled out a small canister, only 6 centimeters long. After slipping the canister into his coveralls, he sealed the package again.

At the scanning station, the inspector laid the package on the conveyor belt and walked alongside while the machine examined its contents. When the scanner flashed green, the inspector picked up the package at the end of the belt.

"Here you are," the inspector said to David. As he handed the package across, he slipped the small cylinder to David, who palmed it.

"Thanks," David replied, with a cheery smile. He waited until he was queued with the arriving passengers to transit into the station before he transferred the small object in his hand into a pouch at his waist.

In his cabin, David opened the package. This was one of the perks of working for Jordie MacKiernan that he loved. There was a set of three beautifully decorative pillows for his couch. It amazed David that each gift was something he could use. It never dawned on him that his cabin was regularly investigated by his contacts.

David placed the pillows on the couch, admired them, and then stepped into his kitchenette to retrieve a small spray unit marked oil. He pulled out the object he'd been handed and examined it. It was a pressurized canister. Standing over the tiny sink, David turned the canister slowly in his hand, while he sprayed it with the solution disguised in the oil sprayer. When he finished, it took several minutes before the coating on the canister developed.

There was an image of a woman's face and the word *gas*. David recognized the face. It belonged to Olivia Harden. To David, it didn't matter who was on the canister. He washed the cylinder over the sink, and the coating, with its image, slid off, and spun down the drain.

Immediately, David jumped on his couch and activated his comm device. Accessing his account, he gave a whoop of joy. The deposit was more than usual. It was an indication of the importance of this job. The best part was that these funds were only the first half.

David leaned into his new pillows, placed his hands behind his head, and planned how he'd deliver the gas. This was how he earned his substantial coin payments. He had to design the job and execute it successfully. Usually, there was a number next to the image, which marked the date by when the deed was to be completed. There was none on this canister, which meant he could take his time.

* * * *

"We've got a problem," Pete said quietly to Olivia and Bryan.

It was late in the evening. Their Jatouche were aboard the *Belle*, but the Pyrean engineers, after depositing their alien friends on the shuttle, had decided to work late. The pourings had begun, metal fabrication was underway, and the Jatouche were spending the days uncrating the sophisticated parts they'd brought.

"What's wrong?" Olivia asked.

"I've been studying the final assembly," Pete replied, "looking for how this device could be broken down for shipment."

"And?" Bryan prompted.

The problem suddenly dawned on Pete. "You two have never shipped anything downside, have you?" he asked. When he received blank stares, he said, "You have several choke points: shuttle bay doors, cargo gangways, El cargo bay, and the domes' airlocks. I can't see how the pieces of this thing are going to fit through those restrictive spots."

"I'm sure ..." Bryan started to say, but stopped when he realized his mistake. The Jatouche wouldn't be aware of the problems either. "Oh, for the love of Pyre," he moaned. "Don't tell me we're going to make an alien intravertor and we're not going to be able to use it because we can't get it to the surface?"

"Do you want to wait until tomorrow or find out tonight?" Olivia asked.

"Danny's been standing by at the shuttle for us," Pete proffered.

"Let's go," Olivia said, gathering her comm unit and shutting down the monitors.

The three engineers were the only people aboard for the return to the *Belle*. After they cleared the airlock, Olivia called Dingles. "I'm looking for Gatnack or Drigtik," she said. "Do you know if they've turned in for the night?"

"This early? Never," Dingles replied. "They're with us now at the cantina. Problem?"

"I hope not, Dingles." Olivia said. "How about the captains?"

"Captain Cinders is here; Captain Harbour is touring one of the hydroponic gardens. What do you need?" Dingles asked.

"I would love to have all of them together, and we need several monitors," Olivia replied, as the three engineers hurried up from the lower decks.

"Make for the bridge, Olivia," Dingles said. "I'll arrange it."

Olivia, Pete, and Bryan were ready on the bridge by the time the Jatouche, captains, and Dingles arrived. They'd loaded the 3-D models of the intravertor's various subsections on the display monitors.

Gatnack and Drigtik arrived in jovial moods, the captains wore frowns, and Dingles effused calmness.

"What's the issue?" Harbour asked Olivia.

"We don't know that there is one, Captain, but it was too great a question to wait until the morning," Olivia replied. "Pete, why don't you walk us through it?"

Pete carefully detailed how the intravertor's massive length and size, 40 meters and 28 tons, would be assembled on the YIPS. "Once everything tests out, we would disassemble it into these structural components. However, these are the limitations of cargo transport downside."

The monitor flicked through a series of frame shots with notations of widths, heights, depths, and angles at the choke points that Pete had enumerated to Olivia. "The upshot of all this," Pete summarized, "is that not a single one of these subsections can get from the YIPS to the planet's surface. The Jatouche will have to break their subsections into smaller components, reassemble them on the surface, and run their tests again."

The Pyrean engineers turned frustrated expressions on the Jatouche, who were busy chittering to each other, the translation application offline. Finally, they turned to the human engineers and flashed their teeth.

"Your conundrum, as you see it, Pete, was precisely represented," Gatnack said, after restarting his ear wig communications. "Well done."

For the humans, there was no doubt that the Jatouche were enjoying themselves.

"Does it occur to anyone that we're being laughed at?" Pete inquired, with a hint of rancor.

"Apologies," Drigtik said, holding up his small hands. "There are such great differences in our technology that we've failed to take into account the possibility that you wouldn't understand the intravertor's deployment. We'll assemble it outside of the YIPS on a carrier bed."

"A carrier bed?" Olivia queried. "For what reason?"

Jessie twigged to it first and started laughing. His guffaws were so loud and hard that the humans started smiling, unsure of the reason, especially since the Jatouche had joined Jessie.

"Time to educate the rest of us, Captain," Harbour demanded.

Jessie took a deep breath, letting it out and wiping the tears from the corners of her eyes. "The carrier bed is attached to a ship or shuttle and holds the device. This enables it to be dropped to the planet. Somehow, it flies to the surface and embeds itself." Jessie was staring at the Jatouche, his expression asking for confirmation, and they were bobbing their heads in affirmation.

"How is that possible?" Bryan asked.

Gatnack launched into an explanation, asking Pete to display certain components of the monitors to elaborate his comments.

"But you don't have retro rockets to slow the descent," Bryan objected.

Gatnack requested the second stage area on the screen. Unfortunately, it was displayed as fully assembled so he resorted to gestures. He portrayed himself as the intravertor, dropping to the surface. Then, he spread his arms out at about 30 degrees away from his body and began to spin. At his advanced age, he was soon dizzy, and Drigtik steadied him, when he stopped.

"Vanes," Bryan shouted. "You're using high-speed vanes to slow the descent."

"You're correct, Bryan," Gatnack acknowledged.

The Pyreans were chuckling about the misunderstanding, except for the captains, who were busy staring quietly at each other.

"Captain?" Dingles queried.

Harbour didn't want to have a discussion with Jessie in front of the group gathered on the bridge, and she searched for a way of making her request clear without explaining too much. Jessie beat her to it, when he said, "There is a significant advantage to keeping this discovery quiet for as long as possible."

More than one individual thought to question it, but Harbour said firmly, "agreed." As she spoke, she eyed Dingles, who replied, "Aye, aye, Captain."

Gatnack and Drigtik glanced at each other. Then Gatnack, determined to add their agreement, said, "Aye, aye, Captain."

"Thank you, everyone," Harbour said, smiling at the assembly. She sent the mildest wave of appreciation before she caught Jessie's eye and tipped her head toward the captain's quarters.

The three Pyrean engineers left together, headed down two decks toward their cabins.

"What do you make of that order to keep the delivery mechanism a secret?" Bryan asked.

"Politics. Has to be," Pete replied.

"What do you mean?" Olivia asked.

"The intravertor was headed through the domes. That's what every one of us believed up until a few minutes ago," Pete replied. "Passage through the domes would have involved the governor and the family heads. For some reason, the captains want them to believe the intravertor is still headed that way."

Olivia and Bryan mulled that thought in their minds, while they made their way below.

Gatnack and Drigtik chose to return to the cantina and consume another fruit juice. Their translation software was off, allowing them to speak privately.

"Might there be other assumptions that we've made that the humans have misconstrued?" Drigtik asked.

"A good question, Drigtik. This revelation will necessitate that we be more instructive with Olivia," Gatnack replied. "Let's treat her as a junior engineer in training. At times, we might be too pedantic, but better that than assume she understands the intravertors' capabilities."

"On another subject, did you feel it?" Drigtik asked.

"It was too brief for my taste," Gatnack replied. "I could have bathed in it."

Drigtik chittered humorously in reply. "I think we should be deliberate in misleading the human engineers. Then, when there is confusion, we can clarify the issue in front of Captain Harbour."

"The dangerous foibles of youth," Gatnack replied, but he flashed his teeth in a broad grin.

* * * *

The next morning, Harbour finished her meal, an attendant clearing away the dishes, when she received a call from Dingles.

"Captain, Tacticnok is on the bridge, requesting an audience with you," Dingles said.

"Escort her here, Dingles," Harbour replied. She signaled the attendant to hurry and took a moment to check herself in the sleeping quarter's mirrored door.

"Your Highness," Harbour said in greeting, when Dingles arrived with Tacticnok.

"Captain," the Jatouche replied.

Harbour and Tacticnok waited until Dingles and the attendant left the room before dropping formalities.

"How can I assist you, Tacticnok?" Harbour asked.

"I would like to have a female-to-female discussion," Tacticnok replied.

"Oh," Harbour uttered. She regretted having replaced the raised pallets with the table and chairs, but a thought occurred to her. "Please, come into my study," Harbour added, indicating the doorway with a hand.

Inside the study, Harbour pulled down the two cushions from the couch and threw them on the floor. Tacticnok's small, sharp teeth were shown in appreciation.

Once the two females were comfortable, Tacticnok said, "I would learn more about empaths."

"Ask your questions," Harbour invited.

"How many more exist on the stations and on your planet?"

"Only children, who have yet to develop their powers, are found on the JOS, Tacticnok. To our knowledge, no empaths are presently in the domes."

"Then your empaths, here aboard the *Belle*, are but a small percentage of humans."

"An extremely small part," Harbour agreed.

"Are they disappearing?"

"No, the number is slowly rising, but it's the power they possess that's growing."

"Aurelia is young," Tacticnok commented

"Yes, and she's strong."

"As strong as you?" Tacticnok asked.

"One day, perhaps. Her power is still increasing."

"I'm told she has a younger sister, who is also powerful."

"Sasha, yes."

"As strong as you?"

"Again, perhaps one day," Harbour replied.

"I see no males who have these abilities," Tacticnok said.

"This phenomenon is peculiar to human females because of their genetic makeup," Harbour replied.

That piece of information seemed to resonate with Tacticnok, and, before the Jatouche could ask something else, Harbour asked, "Why the questions, Tacticnok?"

"Jittak fears your empaths. He's made this abundantly clear to Master Roknick," Tacticnok replied.

"I don't understand the word master, as you employ it," Harbour said.

Briefly, Tacticnok explained her father's advisors and the power they wielded. Then she continued their discussion, saying, "That empaths are exclusively female will carry weight in the upcoming arguments that I expect Master Roknick to make to His Excellency."

"Why should the subject of empaths be a source of discord?" Harbour asked.

"We're helping you recover your planet, Harbour," Tacticnok said, her yellow eyes locking with Harbour's grays. "Do you wish anything else from us?"

"Yes," Harbour replied, sitting up on her cushion. "I want Pyreans and Jatouche to become friends."

"This word friend is not used by the races," Tacticnok replied. "Among members of the alliance, we would refer to contracted relationships as allies."

"Then I want our two species to become close allies," Harbour insisted.

"And how do you think that will happen?" Tacticnok asked.

Harbour stared at the Jatouche, thinking furiously. Nothing came to mind, forcing her to admit her shortcomings.

"Tacticnok, you must understand that humans have been here for hundreds of years. In that time, we've had no contact with our own people on Earth, and we've had no contact with any other intelligent life forms until you arrived. We wouldn't have any idea how to develop an alliance."

"Then it's fortunate for you that we're friends," Tacticnok replied, grinning. "I'll help you take the first steps that will introduce Pyreans to the Jatouche."

"Thank you," Harbour replied, reaching out a hand that Tacticnok took in her small padded one.

"But be prepared, Harbour. The first steps are easy. They are there to demonstrate a willingness to listen to each other. Afterwards, negotiations will begin, and they can be arduous."

"I understand," Harbour replied.

"I wonder if you do," Tacticnok said. "I think you've not put together the reason for this conversation. Whom would you send to represent Pyre? Your commandant? Your governor?"

When Harbour bristled, Tacticnok chittered. "I thought not. Then whom?"

Harbour ran through the names of people she trusted. First and foremost among them were Jessie, Henry Stamerson, and Major Finian.

Again, Tacticnok displayed her humor at Harbour's struggle. "I would guess the one name that hasn't occurred to you, Harbour, is your own."

"Tacticnok, I was elected captain only a year and a half ago by our calendar. It will take me years to properly learn this job and its responsibilities."

"Perhaps this isn't the position you were meant to hold, Harbour."

Harbour opened her mouth to object, but Tacticnok cut her off with a wave of a hand. "But, then again, Harbour, you couldn't represent Pyreans anyway."

For a moment, Harbour was relieved. Then a bit of curiosity mixed with consternation flared. "And why not?"

"Well, for one, you're an empath."

Harbour drew breath to pronounce that concept foolish, when the entire thread of the discussion occurred to her: Jittak, Master Roknick, and human empaths. Rather than voice an objection, Harbour's cool eyes examined Tacticnok carefully. It hadn't been until this moment that Harbour understood how Tacticnok's life, as a royal daughter, had prepared her to envision futures and work toward them.

"And how would you resolve this dilemma, Tacticnok?" Harbour asked evenly.

"I'm pleased you asked," Tacticnok replied. "From our discussion, I gather you possess the greatest power among your empaths."

"Probably," Harbour replied. "It's not something we test against one another."

"Commendable," Tacticnok replied. "I wish to experience it."

"Why?" Harbour asked.

"That's simple. Jittak will argue that empaths must be barred from ever visiting Na-Tikkook. I must have experiences to present in rebuttal."

"Your argument won't work, Tacticnok. From what I've learned, the Jatouche are quite susceptible to our sending. Demonstrating my power would only prove Jittak's point."

Tacticnok waved her hand, indicating she thought otherwise, but Harbour wasn't finished. "And there's something that you might not have considered, Tacticnok. All emotions can be sent by an empath."

The royal daughter's eyes widened. "Any emotion?" she queried.

"Joy and hate, sympathy and anger, love and fear ... you understand?" When Tacticnok nodded, Harbour added, "And emotions can be sent with equal force if the empath feels them. Now, do you still want to experience a sending?"

Tacticnok swallowed in trepidation, but she quelled her fear. "Yes, I do, but, if you don't mind, select for me a gentle emotion."

Harbour smiled. She spun up her power, enveloping the appreciation she felt for Tacticnok's help. Holding back most of her strength, she opened the gate and let the emotion sweep over the little Jatouche.

Tacticnok's eyes fluttered, and a small moan escaped her mouth. She melted into the over-sized pillow and curled into a fetal position, rocking gently back and forth.

Harbour let Tacticnok experience the pleasure of her sending for a full two minutes before she eased off, as Aurelia had advised her to do with the Jatouche.

Tacticnok lay quiet, enjoying the emotional glow. Finally, her eyelids struggled open. She propped up on an elbow, and her bushy tail swept across her legs and lay still. "Perhaps, Jittak is right but for the wrong reason."

"How so?" Harbour asked.

"If human empaths were among us, your kind would be given whatever you want in order for us to continually enjoy this pleasure. Our society's industrial output might eventually grind to a halt," Tacticnok explained. "You wouldn't need to conquer our world, as Jittak proposes. We would hand it to you."

"There would be an easy fix for this problem," Harbour replied. "The empaths remain at Pyre."

"That's a possibility," Tacticnok offered. "But, I prefer you as the emissary to my world. We must find another way to surmount this challenge. Besides, did you not say that empaths are slowly growing in number and power? What then, when your kind is numerous and more powerful than you, will empaths wish to do? Are they to live on a single world, while other humans travel to distant places? Those who journey would return and share wondrous stories of their travels. What would empaths think then?"

"Your arguments are valid, Tacticnok," Harbour admitted. "And you think far into the future, which is something I've rarely done. I'll consider your words."

"That's all I can ask," Tacticnok replied. "Before I go, I wonder if you've thought what would happen to Captain Cinders if you were to spend much of your time at Na-Tikkook."

Tacticnok's comment caught Harbour off guard. She blinked twice. Moments before, her thoughts had spun, imagining various futures, most of which frightened her. Now Tacticnok had added another consideration that further complicated her thoughts. All she could do was laugh. It was long and hard, and she held up her hands in defeat.

"Tacticnok, you challenge me in so many ways that I can't begin to keep up with you," Harbour said. "How are you doing this?"

"Easily, Harbour. You work every day to manage this ship and this project. And, you're calculating the actions of these rulers that you see as dangerous to Pyre's development. I've the luxury of sitting back and watching all of this unfold. And, my father has taught me that a wise leader makes no decision until he or she has considered the impact on future generations."

With those final words, Tacticnok wished Harbour a good day and left.

-35-
Gas Attack

The YIPS was a massive construction. Its size prevented it from having the sort of engines necessary to maintain it in a low orbit, as was the JOS, which was tethered to the planet. Instead, it kept a geosynchronous orbit by holding the station farther out.

A huge gravity wheel — with administration, cabins, dining facilities, and communication antennas — was located at one end. A long, thin axis ran from the wheel to the far end where the furnaces were located. The axis had two levels: a personnel walk transport on the top and a cargo transport on the bottom. The lower section could move slush through compression lines or ore along an enclosed conveyor system.

Located along the axis were the terminal arms that reached out like the legs of a gigantic spider and allowed room for the docking of spacers' mining ships.

Aft of the axis, far away from the gravity wheel, were a series of sections where engineers and techs worked to fabricate and manufacture the equipment produced by the furnaces or the labs.

It was the axis that David identified as the optimum point of attack. It had taken him longer to determine the best location than he originally allowed. The challenge was that Olivia Harden kept an irregular schedule. Her meeting times shifted daily, and she inspected metal pourings and assemblies without notice. Worse, at the end of the day, the engineer didn't return to the gravity wheel but left for the *Belle*.

Another problem for David was that he didn't know what the cylinder contained, and that, in and of itself, was unusual. He considered the possibility of wearing a vac suit and releasing the cylinder's gas as he approached Olivia. But, he dismissed that approach for two reasons: the deadly eyes of his contact and the increased amount of coin. Both items were an indication of the danger the gas represented.

A complication of that particular scenario would come from residue that might cling to his vac suit, if he was too close. Minute amounts of the gas could contaminate him afterwards when his skin touched the vac suit. In order to prevent that, he would have to undergo a decon routine, and that would raise eyebrows, if anyone checked the log. If he chose to forgo decon, sniffers might pick up residue on his suit and condemn him.

When the phase was reached, where Jatouche equipment mated with the outer cases and parts built by the YIPS, David was provided with an opening. It became Olivia's habit to check on the progress of the assemblies, a few times a day, and her last inspection always fell at the day's end. The clincher for David was that Olivia took the same route from the assembly site to the shuttle.

David's shift ended hours before Olivia finished her day, which allowed him to watch and ensure that the engineer's habit was consistent. When he was confident that her routine was established, he examined the route, looking for the perfect opportunity.

Unfortunately, David saw no easy means of executing the attack without being present. Once Olivia left the assembly site, her path took her through the passenger level of the axis to a terminal arm that led to the docking gangway of the *Belle*'s shuttle. That route was finished in smooth walls, with gravity bars overhead.

The clean walls didn't afford David a place to hide the cylinder, with its accompanying trigger. In addition, he needed a means of timing the gas release. It would look odd for him to place the cylinder, loiter at the junction of the axis and a terminal arm in his vac suit, and wait for Olivia to pass. In the end, David decided that the attack must be delivered up close and timed with the engineer's passage through the axis.

On Olivia's last inspection for the day of the assembly site, her face twisted into a smile, as she patted Drigtik's furry arm. "Perfect fit," she declared, watching the techs successfully slide a piece of Jatouche technology into a housing manufactured by YIPS engineers. "As I would expect," Olivia quickly added.

Drigtik's teeth were shown at Olivia in appreciation of her compliment. "It's been a good day," Olivia declared. "Let's catch a shuttle."

"Fruit juice," Drigtik declared in anticipation.

"You're going to turn yellow and red if you keep drinking those concoctions," Pete said. "Oh, wait, you already are!"

"Is it true that alcohols consumed copiously destroy brain cells?" Drigtik innocently asked Olivia. Then he glanced up at Pete, examined him carefully, and said to Olivia, "Yes, I guess it's true," which set Olivia laughing, Drigtik chittering, and Pete grumbling, having been bested in the exchange.

Olivia, Pete, and Drigtik made their way out of the assembly clean rooms. As the threesome entered the passenger level of the axis, a vac-suited tech, identified by the suit color, entered the broad corridor ahead of them and preceded them down its length. Within a few moments, the tech turned down a terminal arm and disappeared from sight.

A few moments later, Hadley and Jensen exited an airlock along a YIPS terminal arm. They'd finished their shift, having been assigned to check airlock seals. As they entered the terminal arm, they passed a vac-suited tech with no name patch. The helmet was enclosed and the faceplate shielded, which made identification impossible. Nonetheless, the two techs raised a hand in passing, and the stranger did likewise.

Olivia and her friends reached the intersection where the tech had disappeared. Pete, who was nearest the corner noticed a small device peeking out at eye level. He was attracted to it by the hissing sound it issued. No sooner had he thought to mention it to the others than his nose, mouth, and lungs filled with a sweet-smelling gas.

After passing the unknown tech, Hadley and Jensen heard a soft hissing. They adopted emergency procedures that had been rehearsed since day one on the YIPS. Hands slapped down faceplates, and suits ordered to switch on air supplies. Yanking sealant and hard patches from their kits, the techs raced toward the sound, expecting to find a small puncture in the bulkhead, possibly created by the high-velocity strike of a speck of space dust.

Instead, when the techs reached the corner, they identified the source of the hissing as coming from a tiny cylinder. They also managed to frighten the threesome who faced them. Two humans and a Jatouche screamed in panic. One human picked up the furry alien, and the three fled down the passageway toward the aft end of the YIPS.

Hadley reached for the cylinder, which was about head high and pointed toward the axis walkway, as the hissing ceased.

"Whatever it was, it's empty now," Hadley said to Jensen.

"Admin, this is Jensen," the tech called over his suit comm. "Activate emergency procedures. Gas released at corner of axis upper level and terminal arm four."

"State status of personnel and type of gas released," the emergency officer replied.

"This is not a YIPS containment issue, admin," Jensen replied. "It's a deliberate attack. I believe an individual dressed as a tech planted a device designed to debilitate two humans and a Jatouche."

"State the nature of their injuries," the officer requested, while signaling Evan of the emergency.

"Unknown," Jensen replied. "The three of them freaked when they saw us and ran away screaming."

"Say again?" the officer asked.

"Admin, this is Hadley. I'm guessing, but it's likely this was plumerase gas."

The emergency protocol officer was about to respond, when Evan rushed into his office, cut the relayed signal to his comm unit, and leaned over the officer's comm panel.

"This is Evan Pendleton, are you positive it was plumerase gas?"

"Negative, Sir," Hadley replied. "The cylinder that released the gas is tiny, approximately six centimeters. It's designed to cover a small area. However, the reactions of both humans and a Jatouche were identical. I think they're suffering from hallucinations. They saw Jensen and me fully enclosed in vac suits. I can't begin to think of what imagery that generated in their minds under the influence of this nasty gas."

"Which only the downsiders can make," Evan muttered quietly to his security officer. "Hadley, Jensen, stay put and protect the device for investigation. We're shutting down that section and sending you emergency protocol staff."

To the officer, Evan said, "Get it done, and shut down all shuttle service. I don't want the perpetrator getting off the YIPS."

"What about arrivals?" the officer asked.

"No arrivals," Evan confirmed. "Except for those authorized by Captains Harbour or Cinders," he quickly added.

Why me? Evan mentally asked himself, as he picked up his comm device, stepped out of the officer's office, and pulled up his contacts. He selected the *Belle.*

"Call for you, Captain," the comm operator said.

Harbour set down her cup and accepted the call. She listened intently to Evan. Her only words to him were, "We're on our way." She wanted to scream in anger. If the gas were plumerase, it was a powerful hallucinogen, and there was no telling to what degree it affected the Jatouche. She forced her mind to focus, telling herself it was imperative to think. Thoughts occurred to her, as she raced to the bridge.

"Heads-up," Harbour declared, as she gained the bridge. "We have an emergency on the YIPS involving our people. There's been a gas attack, possibly plumerase. Comms, get me Danny."

"Danny here, Captain," was heard over the bridge speakers.

"Danny, who's unaccounted?" Harbour asked.

"I'm waiting for Olivia, Pete, and Drigtik, Captain. I was going to find them and remind them the two-hour curfew limit was nearly up, when the station announced emergency protocols. I thought it best to sit tight."

"Stay put, Danny," Harbour said and hand signaled comms to drop the call.

"Get me, the captains, Evan Pendleton, Dingles, Ituau, Nadine, Lindsey, and Yasmin," Harbour called out quickly, and the comm operator's hands flew over the panel.

Harbour paced, thinking furiously, while she waited for the connections. Jessie, Dingles, and Birdie, of all people, arrived on the bridge at a run.

"What?" Jessie asked, but Harbour waved him off.

"Ready, Captain," the comms operator said, when the conference was ready.

Harbour outlined what she knew from Evan, whom Danny confirmed were attacked, and the hallucinations the three were probably suffering.

"Where did they go?" Jessie asked.

"The techs who encountered them said they ran back the way they came, which would take them into the labs and assembly areas," Evan supplied.

Leonard's groans could be heard. "The largest and most convoluted section of the YIPS," he said. "They could be hiding anywhere. It'll take days to search it thoroughly."

"Captain Harbour, their fears," Lindsey volunteered.

"Yes, brilliant idea, Lindsey," Harbour said. "Listen up, everyone. Evan, you're to meet our shuttles and assign search quadrants to my teams, with YIPS personnel to direct them. Understood?"

"Absolutely, Captain," Evan replied, pleased not to be the focus of Harbour's anger.

"Lindsey, organize the empaths in pairs to search the areas that Evan defines. If his people interfere with reception, send them to the rear."

"Understood, Captain," Lindsey replied.

Evan wasn't sure what Harbour's order meant, but he wasn't about to question it.

"Captains Erring and Hastings, I need your shuttles over here to ferry the teams to the YIPS," Harbour said.

"Captain Harbour," Yohlin replied. "We shuttle spacers, who have vac suits. It's safer that way. Do these people have suits?"

"Oh, for the lover of Pyre," Harbour moaned. "Birdie, recall Danny."

"Aye, aye, Captain," Birdie snapped in reply and issued an emergency recall to Danny, which allowed him an express exit from YIPS terminal docking.

"Disregard my request, Captains," Harbour said.

"How can we help?" Leonard asked.

"Cinders here," Jessie said, "I want at least two crew members to accompany each pair of empaths. Get your crews to the YIPS and have them meet the *Belle*'s shuttle. If you didn't understand Captain Harbour's instructions to Lindsey, she's telling the empaths that if the emotions of any crew interfere with their sensing, those individuals are to be positioned to the team's rear, as far back as needed."

"What are the orders to our crew?" Yohlin asked.

"The empaths will locate our engineers by the tortured emotions they're emitting," Harbour said. "Have your crew take directions from the empaths. If the empaths can soothe the engineers, they're to standby. If they can't, they might need to restrain them."

"Be aware that restraining a distraught Jatouche will be dangerous," Tacticnok said from the bridge hatch. Jaktook stood behind her shoulder.

Harbour schooled her reaction. She'd hoped to speak to Tacticnok privately. Somehow, word had gotten around, and the Jatouche team leader had responded accordingly.

"This is Evan. That might not be the case. I spoke further with the techs who were present at the attack. They tell me that the male engineer, who we now know was Pete, snatched up Drigtik, and the Jatouche clung to him as the three of them ran off."

"That's valuable information," Tacticnok replied. "It means there is trust between them. Under these circumstances, I would not advise restraining anyone. Drigtik will attack if you seek to harm either human or him, and you don't want to find out what Jatouche teeth can do."

"Captain, Danny's on approach," Birdie warned.

"Lindsey, you better get started," Harbour said.

"Ahead of you, Captain," Lindsey replied. "Half of us are crammed in the airlock, waiting to board, and the other half are either in the corridor or arriving soon. We'll find them, Captain."

* * * *

Danny made several unauthorized and probably unsafe maneuvers to land aboard the *Belle*, collect the empaths, some of the *Belle*'s spacers, and return to the YIPS. Evan, YIPS personnel, and more spacers were waiting for them.

Once Evan got a count of the number of teams, which Lindsey had organized, he assigned sections.

"Each team has either four or five areas to search," Evan said, apologetically. "I didn't know there were so few of you."

"We're a rare breed," Nadine quipped, and the empaths laughed.

"Remember the advice we've been given," Lindsey said. "Locate them, communicate that location, approach them slowly, and don't add to their fear, under any circumstances. Let's go."

The empaths hurried down the terminal arm, and the YIPS personnel and spacers quickstepped to keep up with their assigned teams.

The search was underway by eighteen thirty hours, but the empaths were quickly daunted by the size of the YIPS. Slowing their search was the necessity to investigate spaces that had to be opened by the station personnel.

A young empath queried why it was necessary to search a locked section, and a YIPS person with her team replied, "Olivia Harden has access to just about every place on this station, except for Evan Pendleton's cabin. She's our senior and foremost engineer."

The youngest and weakest empaths gave out first. Exhausted and unable to manage their gates, they became unable to sense their surroundings effectively. Dejected, they returned to the shuttle, surprised to find Danny waiting with a supply of green. It had been Yasmin's idea. She'd called on the food preparation specialists, who had spun up several kilos of the drink and rushed a large container and cups to the bay before everyone boarded. Many were able to drink, nap, and return to the search within a couple of hours.

One of the empath teams was composed of Lindsey and Sasha. Nadine had smiled when Lindsey chose Sasha. Her thought was, *The perfect pairing of maturity and power. Just what the situation requires.*

Sasha's power ranged far around the team, more to the front than the rear, but it required the support members to stay far back. The YIPS senior personnel, a female tech, had to run forward, unlock an office, lab, or assembly zone, and hurry to the rear.

Lindsey held Sasha's hand and added her power to the young empath's. It enabled the pair to cover more area faster than any other team. They were deep into their fourth hour, when Lindsey felt her power waning, but Sasha was still going strong.

"Rest," Sasha whispered to Lindsey, gripping her elder's hand firmly, and Lindsey eased off on her sensing.

The search continued for nearly another hour. The team had just exited a set of labs and moved on to another area. Passing a small door, Sasha halted. "What's in here?" she asked the YIPS tech.

"It's a supply section for small calibration and measuring equipment. Hardly enough room to hide anyone," the tech replied.

"Give us access, but don't open the door and stand back," Sasha ordered.

Lindsey's sensing was so depleted that, effectively, she was mind blind to whatever Sasha was focused on.

Sasha gently placed her forehead against the door. She stood that way for so long that team members who had been nervous grew bored and sat on the deck or leaned against the bulkheads.

The YIPS tech walked a good distance away and called Evan. "Sir," the tech said, when she reached Evan, "I'm not sure what I'm seeing, being that I've never escorted empaths, but we stopped at a supply door, M-114."

"Go on," Evan urged.

"Well, Sir, the young empath, Sasha, is leaning against the door. She's been that way for about fifteen minutes."

"Just leaning against it?" Evan asked in confusion.

"Well, Sir, it's the way she's doing it. She's facing the door and her forehead is against it."

"Understood, stay put," Evan ordered. He called the YIPS personnel who were accompanying the other teams and gave them the section and corridor location.

Immediately, the teams converged on Lindsey and Sasha's location. By now, only the strongest empaths, along with a few rejuvenated youths, were able to continue the search.

When the empaths spotted Sasha, they bade the normals stand back. Then, slowly, they approached her, sought a portion of skin to touch, hand or neck, and added their power to hers. Sasha wasn't sensing; she was sending. With all her strength, Aurelia's powerful little sister was attempting to calm the three severely panicked individuals who cowered on the other side of the door.

When Aurelia arrived with Nadine, she eased through the group of empaths and cleared a few hands away from the side of Sasha's neck. She placed her forehead to the door and her temple against her sister's.

The other empaths felt an enormous boost of power, which was transmitted through the door. It was more than the simple sum of two empaths. It was the synergistic twining of two sisters who had been raised in close proximity, and it was a phenomenon all its own.

The ramping up of the empaths' powers produced a keening from inside the tiny room. It was marked by its need, its desire for help. The empaths were cutting through the hallucinations, calming the threesome, and the engineers were desperately clinging to the mental lifeline.

-36-
Standoff

Word came to Harbour from Evan that the engineers were located, and the empaths were attempting to calm them.

"I'm going to help," Harbour announced. "The empaths will be running low on power after all this time. They're facing exhaustion. Dingles, get me a shuttle."

"Only Captain Cinders' shuttles are available, Ma'am," Dingles said. It was a subtle means of reminding Harbour that mining shuttles required vac suits, and Harbour had yet to become qualified.

"The captain won't need one," Jittak said, easing through the bridge hatch, with his weapon focused on Harbour. His soldiers followed quickly behind him, and they spread out to cover the Pyreans. "If I feel anything from you, Captain Harbour," Jittak said, aiming his weapon at her, "I won't hesitate to shoot."

Jaktook growled and Jessie moved to protect Harbour.

"Don't," Harbour warned Jessie, which froze him in place.

Dingles and the other spacers took in the energy packs strapped on the soldiers' backs and the long, thin tubes that were held in their hands. All of them were thinking of the damage that firing an energy weapon inside a space-going vessel was going to create.

"You forget your station, Jittak," Tacticnok said sharply.

"On the contrary, Your Highness, I'm following orders," Jittak replied.

"Whose?" Tacticnok demanded. "Not my father's."

"I've no commands from His Excellency Rictook," Jittak replied. "But, I do have strict instructions from Master Roknick to take action if Jatouche are threatened."

"This is not a widespread threat, Jittak," Jaktook protested. "It's a focused attack on these engineers."

"Not on all the engineers," Harbour added. "I would say the target was Olivia Harden, and Drigtik and Pete were unfortunate casualties."

Jessie signed briefly to Dingles, but Jittak's weapon swung toward him.

"Captain, I'm highly qualified with beam armament," Jittak said coldly. "I can easily remove your hand if you continue to signal your crew. To your point, Captain Harbour," Jittak added, training his weapon on her. "The who and why of the attack are unimportant. This event proves humans can't be trusted. You'll indiscriminately harm Jatouche and Pyreans."

"Well, Jittak, you're holding the weapons," Harbour said, her voice hardening. "What is it you want?"

"We'll collect Drigtik, ensure all Jatouche are aboard, and this ship and one of Captain Cinders' ships will return to Triton," Jittak announced. "Then we'll depart and, hopefully, never return."

"You hope to commandeer this ship and hold it hostage for weeks until we reach Triton?" Jessie asked, in a derisive tone.

"What my soldiers and I'll do is hold you two captains hostage in the captain's quarters," Jittak announced, swinging his beam weapon between Jessie and Harbour.

"And if I don't wish to cooperate with your idiotic plan?" Tacticnok asked, as she stepped in front of Jittak. Her eyes blazed in anger, but she kept her control.

Jittak expertly slid to a new position to keep Harbour and Jessie in sight. "I have my orders, Your Highness. This action is for your protection."

While staring hard at Jittak, Tacticnok demanded in a strong voice, "Soldiers, attention."

The three soldiers made subtle movements to straighten, but they glanced nervously at Jittak and resumed guarding the Pyreans.

Jittak's lips curled, revealing his teeth.

"Soldiers, you're commanded by Her Highness Tacticnok to come to attention," Jaktook demanded. "Where is your loyalty to His Excellency Rictook?"

Mentioning the supreme leader was what it took to break Jittak's hold over his soldiers. Above everything, Jatouche were loyal to their ruler.

It was Tacticnok's turn to bare her teeth, and she did so with pleasure. "Soldiers, you're commanded to take Jittak into custody. He's to be taken to his cabin and kept there until I order differently. Food and water are to be brought to him. Am I understood?"

The soldiers delivered a resounding affirmation. It was obvious to the Pyreans that they were relieved to be removed from Jittak's authority.

Jittak realized he'd lost. He couldn't hold the ship by himself, not for the lengthy period it would take to reach Triton. Eventually, he would become drowsy and be mentally overpowered by Harbour. He lowered his beam weapon, and his soldiers stripped it from him. Without a word, he turned but was halted by Harbour's words.

"I'm captain of this ship," Harbour said in a voice hardened by barely controlled anger, "and I don't allow weapons aboard it. Do whatever is necessary to deactivate them and leave them here. You may have them back when you travel to Na-Tikkook."

When the soldiers hesitated, Tacticnok added, "You heard the captain. Or do you believe her authority is any different than that of our captains?"

The soldiers stripped off their packs. They briefly chittered among one another. Then, one of them pulled a part of the weapon's electronics package and silently held it up to Harbour. She nodded her agreement, and they yanked the component from the remainder of the weapons, grasped Jittak by the arms, and led him off the bridge.

There were audible and silent exhales of breaths.

"Dingles, find a safe place for these things," Harbour said disdainfully, sweeping a hand toward the weapons.

Dingles tasked other crew members, who picked up the packs and weapons, as if they would bite them. Later, Harbour would discover that the *Belle* lacked any sort of large vault in which Dingles could deposit the weaponry. So, he decided the safest place to store them was the captain's liquor larder.

"My apologies, Captains," Tacticnok said. "I had no idea Jittak would be so foolish. A complaint will be lodged with my father, when I return."

"We'll talk later, Tacticnok," Harbour said. "Know for now, that your apology is accepted, although it wasn't necessary. At the moment, I'm more interested in the welfare of our three engineers."

* * * *

Inside the supply room, the engineers huddled together in a tight bundle, Drigtik sandwiched between the two humans. The Jatouche's nails were dug desperately into Pete's coveralls. Sensations of comfort fought in their minds against the terror and horrible images generated by the plumerase gas.

Hour by hour, two things happened. The engineers' bodies slowly cleared the gas from their systems, and the empaths won the battle for their minds. The indications of success were the easing of the engineers' tightly bunched muscles, exemplified by the relaxation of Drigtik's fingers.

Fright and terrifying images had taken their toll. They were drained of energy, and exhaustion overcame them. Freed from their nightmares and lulled by the empaths, they fell asleep.

"Medical teams," Lindsey whispered to the nearest YIPS tech, when Yasmin gave her a thumbs up.

Most of the empaths, except for Aurelia and Sasha, ceased their sending. The sisters dialed down their power and kept a gentle stream of support flowing to ensure the engineers experienced pleasant dreams.

When the medical teams arrived with stretchers, Lindsey whispered to the sisters, "Step back now. Let the medics take them."

The engineers were lifted off the floor and carefully deposited on the stretchers. A medic pulled a syringe gun, but Aurelia blocked her arm.

"We need them receptive," Aurelia said, which confused the female medic, who regarded the sleeping forms. "In here," Aurelia added, tapping her temple.

"We're not to put them under," the medic told her teams.

"Lindsey, Sasha, stay with them. I need to talk to Captain Harbour," Aurelia said.

As the group hurried toward the *Belle*'s shuttle, Aurelia caught one of the YIPS personnel by the arm. "Patch me through YIPS admin to Captain Harbour."

When Belinda saw Aurelia stand back with the tech, she tapped Nate on the shoulder. "We stay with Rules," she said.

The tech called admin, and Evan Pendleton was alerted. Aurelia updated him on the retrieval of the three engineers and requested a comm transfer to the *Belle*.

"The *Belle*," Birdie announced, when she received the call from Evan.

"Birdie, this is Aurelia," the young empath replied without waiting for Evan to speak. "I need Captain Harbour."

"She's here, Aurelia," Birdie replied, and switched the call to bridge speakers at Harbour's signal.

Aurelia informed Harbour of the rescue of the engineers and their impending transfer by the medics to the *Belle*'s shuttle. Harbour waggled her hand at Birdie, as if it were flying, and Birdie contacted Danny to notify him of the incoming personnel.

"Captain, I had a thought," Aurelia said. "We found the engineers through our empathetic abilities. Could that work to find the attackers?"

"Whomever they are," Evan interrupted, "they're still on the YIPS. I shut down all shuttle flights, in and out, from the JOS, except for yours, Captain."

"Good thinking, Evan," Jessie interjected. "The question is whether this is a YIPS employee or an interloper."

"I'm sorry to say, I think he's a YIPS tech," Evan replied.

"What leads you to that conclusion, Evan, besides the type of vac suit the attacker was wearing?" Harbour asked.

"No vac suits have been reported stolen. It would be a rare thing in the first place because they're all fitted, as you know," Evan replied.

It was something Harbour didn't know, but she kept that piece of information to herself. "The attacker could have brought the vac suit with him or her," Harbour said, challenging Evan's logic.

"It's possible," Evan replied.

"Evan, what did the two techs, who were present at the attack, say about the way it went down?" Jessie asked.

"Wait one," Evan replied. A couple of minutes later, the emergency protocol chief joined the conversation.

"In answer to your question, Captain," the chief said, "Hadley and Jensen said that it was creepy how the job was done."

"Explain," Tacticnok requested, not understanding the term.

"It was the timing and the placement of the gas that was seemingly fluid," the chief replied, when he heard the translation in his ear. He'd been issued an ear wig to enable him to communicate with the Jatouche in case of problems. "The techs believed he had an extremely small window of time to set the device at the corridor corner and trigger the timer. The engineers must have been fewer than fifty or sixty paces behind the attacker."

"It's an employee," Jessie announced firmly. "Whoever it is, they know the YIPS intimately. They knew when and where they could release a small amount of gas and ensure they sprayed the target, which presumably was Olivia."

"Are all employees accounted for?" Harbour asked.

"Yes, that's one of the first things we do in an emergency situation," the chief replied.

Jessie had his hand on his chin deep in thought. As a company owner and captain, he had intimate knowledge of job assignments and rotation. The YIPS ran three shifts around the clock so the furnaces were never shut down.

"This employee was off during second shift," Jessie announced. "Otherwise they would have been reported, as missing duty. Any reports like that?"

"Two," the chief replied. "Both have been in medical for more than a day."

"This tech we're looking for could have been with the teams searching for the engineers," Evan volunteered.

"No, Sir," Aurelia replied. "The empaths would have noticed someone who was emitting emotions related to this attack."

"Unless they're a cold-blooded murderer," Jessie offered.

"No, Aurelia's right," Harbour said. "They would have been detected. Captain, you're suggesting the attacker might have been a psychopath or some such thing. If that were correct, he or she would have come across as an emotional blank, and that would have evinced an empath's concern."

For the normals on the line and within earshot that was a piece of news about empaths that none of them had known, and it took a moment to be absorbed.

"Evan, if the YIPS personnel, who are accompanying the empath teams, stay at the *Belle*'s shuttle, where will the rest of the techs be at this time?" Harbour asked.

"We're into our third shift, Captain," Evan replied. "Most techs will be on the wheel, asleep, or eating. The rest will be tending the furnaces and the pours. Third shift is our smallest employee group."

"Aurelia, I'll send the teams out to search for the attacker. Evan coordinate with the teams to direct them to the furnace and the wheel," Harbour ordered.

"Many of the techs will be asleep," Evan countered, "We'll have to get access to their cabins and wake them up."

"Probably not, Sir," Aurelia said. "The stronger empaths should be able to sense the emotional states without entering the cabin. If they're asleep, you'll only have to knock, and we'll know quickly what they're feeling."

"Captain, I'm headed to the wheel," Aurelia said.

"Chief, you need to ensure every empath team is prepared," Jessie said. "You don't know what this attacker will do, when he or she realizes they're discovered."

"Do you think they'll release more gas?" Evan asked with trepidation.

"I've no idea, and that's the problem," Jessie replied.

On Harbour's signal, Birdie cut the comm. Then she ordered contact with the shuttle and Danny.

"Danny, once the engineers are aboard, get them back here soonest," Harbour ordered. "Lindsey and Sasha are accompanying them. When Lindsey reaches the shuttle, I want to speak with her. The active empaths are going to be assigned to locations to search out the attacker."

"Captain, many of the younger or weaker empaths are spent," Danny replied. "You're only going to have five or six who can still do the job."

"Understood, Danny," Harbour replied.

"Wait one, Captain. The med teams are arriving."

A few minutes later, over the bridge speakers was heard, "This is Lindsey, Captain."

"Lindsey, you're going to search for the attacker," Harbour said. "Aurelia believes the individual will stand out emotionally in contrast to other techs."

"Clever girl," Lindsey commented.

"YIPS admin will direct those empaths teams, which are still viable, to search the furnace areas and the wheel. I want you to make sure any empaths who are drained return with Danny. I don't want to have one of our women shutting down."

Dingles and a few spacers glanced at one another. This was the third revelation about empaths in as many minutes.

"Understood, Captain," Lindsey replied, ending the call.

37

Celebration

David was overjoyed. Everything had gone as planned. He frequently eyed his comm device but stayed his hand. It was too early to check his account for the second payment. News would have to reach downside about the release of gas aboard the YIPS, which injured three engineers. He didn't know how detailed the announcement would be, whether it would mention the Jatouche or not, but he knew Jordie MacKiernan would recognize his handiwork.

To occupy his mind, he hooked a memory stick into his comm device and played a vid. He had time to play several, while emergency announcements were sent over the station and then quieted. He was curious about the type of gas released, but that information was never provided.

David, relaxing and celebrating his success in his cabin, was unaware that the empaths were searching for him. Nor was he aware that Evan was personally leading one of the strongest empaths, Aurelia, to search the wheel.

"This is the meal room, Aurelia," Evan said, stepping through the twin doors, as they slid open.

Aurelia walked into the room, her senses open. Evan started to follow, but Belinda laid a hand on his arm.

"She doesn't need any more interference from us," Belinda told Evan.

Men and women looked up from their food, as Aurelia circulated the room. Her reputation preceded her: a powerful empath, judged innocent by Captain Harbour, and still sought by JOS security. Fortunately for Aurelia, there were no legitimate security officers aboard to ensure the commandant's edict was executed.

"Nothing," Aurelia commented to Evan, when she finished perusing the room. "Curiosity, concerns, anxiety, and some fear, but nothing to warrant a second look," she added.

"We should check the tech cabins next," Evan volunteered. "The majority of them are off duty. At this time, that's where they'll be."

The group worked their way around the YIPS giant gravity wheel. Unlike a mining ship, there were four tubes of corridors — housing admin offices, cabins, meal rooms, vac suit rooms, and other structures — fused together inside the wheel.

At the first tech's cabin, Aurelia paused. She sensed the slightest of emotions. They were at the level of her sister's dream state.

"Knock, Evan," Aurelia requested.

"Yeah," came a hard growl from inside the cabin, after Evan firmly rapped on the cabin door.

"Evan Pendleton," the YIPS manager announced. "Due to the emergency, we're checking all cabins to be sure that we haven't lost anyone."

"Sorry, Sir, all good here," the voice announced.

Aurelia shook her head, and Evan said, "Good to hear. Back to sleep."

At the next door, Aurelia sensed an awake individual. By the emanations she received, she thought they belonged to a woman. The emergency chief's report indicated the attacker was most probably a man and likely a young individual, judging by the frame and the walk.

"No," Aurelia said, shaking her head.

Thus it went, cabin after cabin. Either Evan knocked to wake the occupant or Aurelia received something through the cabin's door of a tech already conscious.

At one cabin door, Aurelia sensed nothing. She frowned and opened her gate wider. Still nothing.

"Is someone supposed to be here?" Aurelia asked.

Belinda tapped the access panel next to the door, pointing to a row of lights. "Occupied," she said.

"Dead?" Nate asked, screwing up his face at the oddity of his own suggestion.

"Give them a moment," Evan said. "They could be in the facilities."

Sure enough, a few minutes later, the group could hear a woman humming loudly.

"No," Aurelia said, smiling to herself.

At the next door, Aurelia received a strong impression of excitement. She frowned, concentrating on some of the other subtler emotions. The celebratory joy was wrapped in the output of a powerful ego. The individual was luxuriating in a sense of superiority.

"This one is all wrong," Aurelia said. "You'd think he was a miner, who struck it rich."

"A fat payday of coin for a successful gas attack might produce the same result," Belinda commented.

"Who's in there?" Nate whispered.

Evan pulled up his comm unit, checked the cabin number, and said, "David Yersh, tech, been with us four years."

"Does he fit the profile? Young and about the right height?" Belinda asked.

"He does," Evan replied, after perusing the details of Evan's employment profile. "I'll call for reinforcements," Evan added, bringing his comm unit close to his face and stepping away from the door.

"Don't, Sir," Aurelia whispered softly. "There's something strange about this individual. I don't think he'll put up a struggle."

Evan and Nate stared at Aurelia in confusion.

"If you say so, Rules," Belinda said, using Aurelia's spacer name, which cued Nate to latch on. "Knock, Evan, and nicely invite David to a discussion. We're questioning every tech about their whereabouts at the time of the incident. Just routine."

Evan nodded his understanding and rapped on the door.

"Yeah?" came a young male voice.

"Evan Pendleton, David. Get your skins and boots on. We've got questions for the techs."

"Sure thing, Sir. Be right with you," David replied.

The group could distinguish movements within the cabin.

Aurelia strained her senses to detect any change in David's mood. "This man is as odd as they come," she said.

"How so?" Evan asked.

"No change in his emotional state after being told by the YIPS manager that he's about to be questioned," Aurelia replied.

"None?" Nate asked.

Aurelia shook her head and frowned.

"That's freaky," Belinda commented.

Minutes later, the door opened. A slender, dark-haired, young man stood in the doorway. "Ready, Sir," David said cheerily.

"Go with these people, David," Evan directed, "I've others to collect," he added, sticking to the line that the group had agreed to if a suspect was found.

"Lead on," David said to Nate, supposing he was the senior individual.

Nate gave David a congenial smile and started off toward a spoke that would take them from the wheel to the axis.

Belinda walked beside David, and Aurelia took the rear.

Several times, David glanced back at Aurelia. At one point, he began walking backward to stare at Aurelia. It was a good trick. Walking in reverse was a practiced art, when gravity was absent, such as in the axis, where they were.

"Don't I know you?" David asked Aurelia.

"We've never met," Aurelia commented dryly. She supposed David might be hitting on her. A month short of her eighteenth birthday, many young men had commented on her looks, when they tried to get close to her. Unfortunately for them, Aurelia had no desire to enter into any sort of relationship. After sixteen-plus years of confinement, ending in sexual assault, she was intent on embracing her freedom.

The thought that did bother Aurelia was the lack of a shift in David's emotional state. Not only had he not asked where they were going, but it seemed as if he didn't care.

When the group turned down a terminal arm, David finally had a question. "Shuttle ride to the JOS?" he asked.

"The *Belle*," Aurelia supplied, hoping for a reaction.

"Great," David replied. "I'd hoped to get a look at the colony ship one day. Will I get to meet Captain Harbour?"

"I'm sure that can be arranged," Belinda said.

David immediately put two and two together, turned around to Aurelia, snapped his fingers, and said, "I've got it. You're the girl who murdered Dimitri Belosov, the ex-governor's nephew."

"Self-defense, if you haven't heard," Aurelia replied with a little heat. "But, yes, that was me who ended him."

"Hmm," David replied, turning around. "Probably deserved it."

Belinda looked over her shoulder at Aurelia, her expression a confused query. David's reactions were surprising her too.

When they reached the *Belle*'s shuttle, Danny had already made the round trip to the colony ship to drop off the engineers and the first load of empath teams. David bound up the gangway. He ran into Danny on the other side of the shuttle's hatch. "David Yersh," he said, extending a hand to Danny.

"Danny Thompson," Harbour's pilot replied, accepting the hand.

"Sit anywhere?" David asked, seeing the shuttle was empty.

"Be our guest," Danny said, sweeping a hand toward the shuttle's bow.

"Great," David replied, hurrying forward.

Danny gave Belinda a bewildered look, and she replied, "Don't ask."

In the meantime, Evan called YIPS admin, requesting to speak to a senior empath involved in searching the YIPS aft end. His call was taken by Lindsey.

"Yes, Evan?" Lindsey answered.

"I need another empath team at the wheel," Evan requested.

"What's happened?" Lindsey asked, with trepidation. She feared that Aurelia might have pushed her powers too far.

"Aurelia thinks she has a suspect. She and some of Captain Cinders' spacers are escorting him to the *Belle*'s shuttle. I hope Danny's back by the time they get to the gangway."

"I've received word from the *Belle* that Danny's docked on the YIPS. How did Aurelia identify the suspect? Fear?"

"Negative," Evan replied. "She said it was the absence of expected emotions. She thought he was celebrating, and she was especially alarmed when David, the tech, didn't show any emotional change when he was told he was going to be interviewed."

"That would do it," Lindsey commented. "What else do you need searched?"

"Well, come to think of it, we checked the galley and most of the techs' cabins. There's only three left to examine. What's your status?"

"We've finished the search of the furnace and pour areas and found nothing suspicious. Our teams are headed to the terminal arm for our shuttle."

"Then, I believe that Aurelia probably has our culprit," Evan said.

"That's my thinking, Evan," Lindsey replied. "I'm returning to the shuttle with the others. We'll be in touch, Evan."

"Lindsey, before you go, I must remind you that David Yersh is a YIPS employee and, as such, is protected by JOS protocols, including rules of examination, the right to counsel, and informing security and the Review Board of his detainment.

"I'll pass along your message to Captain Harbour, Evan," Lindsey replied, ending the call.

Despite Evan's insistence on David's rights, he was fairly certain that he heard a tone of dismissal in Lindsey's voice. He hoped it was only because she might be exhausted from the search, which had lasted throughout the night and early morning hours. First shift was due to start in forty-five minutes.

Lindsey, the empath teams, and spacers separated ways from the YIPS personnel and proceeded down the terminal arm toward the *Belle*'s shuttle. They straggled aboard, exhausted, the empaths drained of their powers.

Danny and two attendants from the cantina handed out greens to the empaths and caf to the spacers. Everyone got a hot sandwich.

Lindsey walked toward the shuttle's bow, choosing to sit next to Aurelia and eye David Yersh, who faced her.

"Hi," David said to Lindsey, around a mouthful of sandwich.

"Hi, yourself," Lindsey answered, taking a bite of her own.

* * * *

Harbour received an image of David Yersh on her comm unit, which Danny had surreptitiously taken and forwarded to the *Belle*'s bridge control. She shared it with Jessie.

"Birdie, Evan, please," Harbour requested.

None of the individuals who had been on the bridge when Jittak and his soldiers tried to take control had left despite the late hour. Harbour thought to say something to Dingles, but he stood resolute, with his hands behind his back, as if he were a statue. The rest of the crew, including Jessie, held the same stiffened-spine positions. Even Tacticnok and Jaktook, who preferred the prone postures of their pallets, were still present. Over time, the pair had edged next to Harbour in a declaration of support.

"Evan have you conducted a search of David's property yet?" Harbour asked, when she reached the YIPS manager.

"I haven't received a warrant authorizing me to conduct such a search, Captain," Evan replied. This was the conversation Evan feared. Spacers took a dim view of anyone trying to harm their people. It looked like that applied to Harbour's people and aliens too.

"Extenuating circumstances, Evan," Jessie replied. "Consider the ramifications if David Yersh is the culprit, which one of the strongest empaths known to Pyreans believes is the truth."

"What do you mean?" Evan asked. He was hungry and tired and knew he wasn't thinking clearly.

"How many cylinders of gas do you think David brought aboard your station?" Jessie asked.

"And what if he accidentally released some of the gas on his suit or in his cabin?" Harbour added, catching on to Jessie's tactics.

"How long is the gas viable if it was in liquid form when it was spilt?" Jessie asked.

"I wouldn't want to be in your deck shoes, Evan, if there's further contamination, and you didn't take precautionary measures," Harbour said in a voice that evinced commiseration.

"All right, all right," Evan replied, annoyed by being pressured. "We'll search David's cabin for gas cylinders and the presence of a foreign gas. We'll do the same for his personnel locker and vac suit. But, I'm warning you, Captains. If we find anything else, no matter how much it might implicate David, it will not be reported. He has rights."

"Understood, Evan," Harbour replied in a conciliatory manner. "We'll be interested in the results of your search."

"Captain Harbour, we have a little more than thirty minutes before our shuttle unloads in the bay," Dingles said. I suggest it's an appropriate time for some food and drink."

"Fruit juice," Jaktook announced agreeably.

"Rotate the bridge crew, Dingles, including yourself. Food and rest for everyone," Harbour ordered. She fixed her eyes on Dingles to drive the point home.

"Aye, aye, Captain," Dingles responded.

The captains and the Jatouche retired to Harbour's quarters, and she ordered sandwiches, salads, fruit drinks, a caf for Jessie, and a green for her.

Tacticnok lounged on the study's couch pillow beside Jaktook, who lay on the other one. Harbour and Jessie sat on the floor to be polite, while everyone enjoyed their small meal.

"What's Drigtik's state?" Tacticnok asked.

"He and our people are still sleep. Empaths watch over them," Harbour said.

"And when they wake? What then?" Tacticnok asked.

"We don't know. None of us have ever seen the effects of this gas," Harbour replied.

"Then they might continue to suffer from the effects," Tacticnok surmised.

"Empaths will stay with them until they experience no more waking bad dreams," Harbour explained.

"It's not understandable why some of your kind fear you," Jaktook said. "You're capable of so much good."

"It's understandable, if you know their power can be used to achieve any effect," Tacticnok said. "The answer lies in the heart of the empath. It's good that they're all female. Less chance of danger."

The group's meals were barely finished when Harbour received a call from Dingles that Danny was on approach. Harbour, Jessie, Tacticnok, and Jaktook abandoned their dishes and made for the landing bay. They arrived in time to see Aurelia descend first with some spacers and hurry for the airlock.

"Captain," Aurelia said in a rush to Harbour, "you're going to have your hands full with this one. I've never sensed the like. All joy and brightness and little else."

"Odd," Harbour agreed.

"Is Sasha still with the engineers?" Aurelia asked, concern in her voice.

"Yes," Harbour admitted.

"That's too long," Aurelia said, adding, "Excuse me, Captain."

The group could hear Aurelia call Dingles and ask for the engineers' location, as she ran down the corridor.

Tacticnok glanced questioningly toward Harbour, who said, "Sasha is Aurelia's younger sister."

The royal daughter nodded in commiseration, adding, "Most understandable. And I find it informative that these two youthful sisters are the ones who located our engineers, helped them, and identified the one who's being brought here. As you indicated, Captain ... empaths are becoming stronger."

The last to exit the shuttle were Belinda and Nate with David Yersh between them. He appeared nothing like Harbour expected. His youthful good looks and sense of bon vivant indicated a carefree, young man.

When this last group cleared the airlock, Harbour introduced herself, extending a hand.

"Wow. I get to meet the famous Captain Harbour. This is a treat," David gushed.

"And I appreciate you taking the time to talk to us," Harbour replied. "Why don't we retire to the captain's quarters, where we'll be more comfortable?"

"That sounds great," David replied.

Harbour would have preferred to meet David alone, but Jessie was having none of it. To complicate matters, Tacticnok insisted that she observe the interaction. And lately, where Tacticnok went, Jaktook followed.

"Captain, this is a matter of observing the application of justice among your people," Tacticnok said, able to speak without David understanding her.

Neither Harbour nor Jessie knew what that meant, and they had images of everything from swift executions on the basis of mere suspicions to a means of reading an individual's thought, which would convict the accused.

On the way to Harbour's quarters, she received a call from Evan and motioned the others to go ahead.

"Captain, we searched David's cabin and found no other cylinders or any dangerous gas contamination," Evan said. "We also checked his personnel locker and his vac suit. Same results, nothing."

"And if I were to ask about his comm unit, Evan?" Harbour suggested.

"You know that we couldn't investigate that without a warrant, Captain," Evan replied. "However, it's a moot point. We never saw the device. I suspect David's got it on him. And, if he's the guilty party, then I would guess it's probably wiped by now."

"Thanks for the update, Evan," Harbour replied.

Evan meant to ask some questions of his own, but Harbour abruptly ended the call.

When Harbour reached her quarters, Jessie sat at the salon table's end, closest to the door. David sat on a long side, and the Jatouche stood against a bulkhead, silently observing.

"Pardon me, David, important call," Harbour said pleasantly and took a seat across from David.

"This is fantastic," David said. "My friends aren't going to believe that I got to see the captain's quarters of the *Belle*, much less meet with two of the most prominent Pyrean captains."

"Are your best friends on the YIPS or the JOS?" Harbour asked, starting with a simple question to build a rapport, while she measured David's emotions.

"They're on both," David replied.

"We're talking to techs who might have witnessed the event that took place," Harbour said.

"Can't help you much there, Captains. I finished my shift ... that's first shift, got a meal, took it to my cabin, and fell asleep soon afterwards. It was the emergency announcements that woke me. I'm not even sure what happened."

"Weren't you curious?" Jessie asked. "Stepped outside to see what's going on or called someone?"

"Those are against emergency protocols, Captain, and I'm a by-the-rules tech. It keeps me safe and employed." David smiled to demonstrate his preference to remain in the good graces of his questioners.

For the next half hour, Harbour and Jessie double-teamed David with questions and general conversation, but they were unable to evoke a single point on which they could trap him.

Abruptly, Harbour stood up and called Dingles. Apparently, the first mate was waiting outside her door. He was inside in seconds, which took everyone by surprise.

"Yes, Captain?" Dingles asked.

"Dingles, David has been most cooperative. Before we send him back to the YIPS, I think it's incumbent on us to show some appreciation. How about you take David to the cantina? His tab is on me."

"Sure, Captain, come on, Davey," Dingles said, throwing an arm around the young man's shoulder to guide him out the door.

"I've heard about the *Belle*'s cantina. This is going to be great!" the group heard David say, as he started down the corridor.

Harbour sent a quick text to Belinda and Nate. It read, "Join Dingles in the cantina. David's to have a good time, drink up, and sleep the day away in a cabin."

Suddenly a thought occurred to Harbour, and she moaned, "Oh, for the love of Pyre, it's the start of the day, the cantina's going to be empty."

Jessie laughed. "You haven't been around spacers long enough, Harbour. We kept crews out all night. They're in the cantina now, unless I miss my guess. And my captains will have given them the day off. Tired people are dangerous people aboard ship or station."

"Good," Harbour replied absentmindedly. She was tapping her comm unit against her chin, deep in thought.

"What did you discover?" Tacticnok asked, stepping away from the bulkhead.

"Nothing," Harbour replied.

"Explain," Tacticnok said.

"Aurelia was right. David doesn't evince the common range of emotions I would expect. There's certainly no guilt or remorse. If I were a medic and giving David a physical, it would be similar to not finding a heartbeat. If nothing else, he's entertaining."

"Like an insipid vid, where all the characters are unrealistically pleasant," Jessie grumped. While everyone was alone with their thoughts, Jessie snatched up his comm unit.

"Who're you calling?" Harbour asked.

"Major Finian," Jessie replied.

"A senior member of Pyre security, especially for the stations," Harbour explained to the Jatouche.

"I was waiting for this call, Captain," Liam answered promptly. "May I know who else is on the call?"

"Captain Harbour, Her Highness Tacticnok, and Jaktook," Jessie replied.

Liam quickly snatched the ear wig from his pocket and installed it before he said diplomatically, "Welcome to Pyre, Your Highness.'

"That's kind of you to say, Major Finian," Tacticnok replied.

There was a moment of sheer amazement for Liam, recognizing he was conversing with his first alien. "Captains, I'm guessing you're calling about the incident on the YIPS. Evan has updated me. Are your people okay?"

"That remains to be seen, Major," Harbour replied. "We're still waiting on that."

"Any information out of David Yersh?" Liam asked.

"Nothing," Harbour said with disgust. "My experience, as an empath, says he's our culprit, but there's nothing definitive in the way of proof or self-incrimination."

"Major, any way you can search David's quarters?" Jessie asked.

"I don't have probable cause for a warrant," Liam replied.

The group could hear that Liam wasn't happy about the circumstances.

Tacticnok stepped close to Jessie, and he lowered the comm unit to her level.

"Major, this is Tacticnok. One of my citizens has been attacked by one of yours. This constitutes a breach of first contact procedures, as defined by the alliance. I'm making a royal request that you take Captain Harbour's suspicions about this youth into consideration and conduct yourself accordingly."

There was silence on the line. The seconds ticked by. Then Liam said, "I've heard your request, Your Highness. Rest assured that we appreciate what the Jatouche are doing for Pyre, and your request will be assigned the importance it's due. I'll be in touch," Liam said and ended the call.

Tacticnok cocked her head, glanced at Harbour and then Jessie. "I'm used to more direct answers," she said.

"Your request was well phrased, Tacticnok," Jessie replied. "It gives the major the leverage he needs to get a warrant and begin the search."

38

Leverage

Liam checked Emerson's whereabouts. It was early morning, and the commandant hadn't arrived at security administration yet. Liam hurried to Devon's office, but the lieutenant wasn't in either. The next stop was the sergeants' office, and he was relieved to see Miguel Rodriguez and Cecilia Lindstrom at their desks.

"Morning, Sergeants," Liam said perfunctorily. "Pull up all the public information on David Yersh, a YIPS tech."

"What are we looking for?" Miguel, the senior sergeant, asked.

"Captain Harbour believes David is the mystery tech who gassed the three engineers," Liam replied.

"Why don't we get a warrant and deep dive into his life, Major?" Miguel asked.

"Harbour is relying on her empathetic abilities. Unfortunately, she failed to get David to admit to anything or even display something that would tell her that she was absolutely sure David was guilty."

"Just how are we supposed to get a warrant, Major?" Cecilia asked.

"Search first," Liam said, swinging a finger at their monitors. He lounged in a chair, while the sergeants ran through the public records.

Nearly a quarter of an hour later, Cecilia said, "I've got nothing. The boy looks clean."

"Same here, Major," Miguel added. "Nothing stands out. No trips downside. No expensive cabin in the upper rings."

"What now, Sir?" Cecilia asked.

"We request a warrant to search the cabin," Liam said.

"On what grounds?" Miguel asked.

"Sergeant Cecilia Lindstrom, I'm informing you that I have a credible source of intelligence that indicates that the perpetrator of the gas attack aboard the YIPS is one David Yersh," Liam announced in an official tone. "I'm concerned for the safety of the JOS citizenry that, if this proves out, the tech might have more of this dangerous gas in his JOS cabin. I'm requesting a warrant to search his cabin."

Cecilia glanced at Miguel, who stared back. She looked at Liam, who wore a hard expression.

"I'll request the warrant on the information that you've relayed to me, Major," Cecilia replied in the same manner. She stood up, grabbed her comm unit and cap, and marched out of the office.

Out of earshot of the major, Cecilia mumbled, "Why me?"

"Do you think she'll get it?" Miguel asked Liam.

"She has a better chance than you or me," Liam replied.

"Hmm," Miguel agreed. "Nice, motherly face ... level disposition, believable."

"Something like that," Liam replied, which had nothing to do with what he was thinking. Captain Henry Stamerson, head of the Review Board, and he had recently begun meeting frequently. Liam needed someone else to request the warrant. If Cecilia was denied, it gave him an excuse to rant at Henry. The captain should see through the ruse and realize that there were extenuating circumstances.

An hour later, Liam, Miguel, and Cecilia were on their way to David's cabin with a warrant on their comm units.

"Well done, Sergeant," Liam had said to Cecilia, when she presented him with the warrant.

"The captain was amazingly accommodating," Cecilia replied. "He didn't ask a single question."

"Imagine that," Liam replied, which prompted confused glances between the sergeants.

At the cabin door, Miguel entered the security override code into the access panel, and the door slid aside.

The team hadn't penetrated far into the cabin, when Cecilia moaned, "Oh, for the love of Pyre, why didn't I become a YIPS tech. Look at all this stuff."

"This wasn't purchased on David's stipend," Devon noted, picking up some of the electronics gear that was lying around.

"We have enough for a security deep dive warrant," Liam said. "I'll get this one," he replied to Cecilia's inquisitive glance.

When Miguel received a copy of the second warrant, he checked David's financial records. Interestingly, he found two accounts. *Odd for a tech,* Miguel thought. The first account looked normal: regular stipend deposits from the YIPS and the usual modest expenses. It was the second account that was the shock. Opened less than three years ago, the deposits were enormous for a tech and the expenditures were extravagant. His favorites seemed to be electronic gear, cantinas, and coin-kitties.

Cecilia accessed David's comm account via the security servers. "Clever boy," she whispered, when she discovered the history was empty. It was the prerogative of a comm unit user to clear the device and the server's history, not that security appreciated that ruling.

"So, what do we have?" Liam asked, when he stopped back into the sergeants' office. "Commandant wants an update on the YIPS incident."

"Odds are, Captain Harbour has the guilty party," Cecilia said. "He wiped his comm unit and server account."

"Trouble is that what we have is circumstantial, at best, Major," Miguel added. "Too much coin flowing into his account from multiple sources, whose accounts were opened and closed after each transaction."

"Our David Yersh is working for some high-level operators," Liam surmised.

"Downsiders," Miguel added.

"I'll talk to the commandant," Liam said. "In the meantime, I want the two of you searching security vid history. Find out the period when David was last on the JOS. Then track him. Get the monitoring team to assist you."

As Liam walked to Emerson's office, he made a quick call to Jessie and updated him on their findings.

* * * *

"What did Liam have to say?" Harbour asked, when she found out the major had called.

"His evidence is circumstantial, nothing directly ties David to the gas attack," Jessie reported. "In anticipation of being investigated, David wiped his comm unit and server account. Security discovered that David has a luxurious lifestyle, which he's careful to hide. He also has two accounts, and one of them shows a history of large deposits."

"Could Major Finian trace the sources of the deposits?" Harbour asked.

"Accounts were opened, coin deposited, entire amounts transferred to David's account, and then they were closed," Jessie replied.

"Then young David isn't as innocent as he pretends. He's been playing with some bad people," Harbour surmised.

"The major believes he's been working for downsiders," Jessie said.

Harbour loosed a strangled chuckle. "No doubt," she said, with disgust.

"The major requested we transfer David to JOS security immediately," Jessie said. He watched Harbour stare at the nicely decorated walls of her study and waited for her to speak.

"If David is handed over to security, we'll have lost the opportunity to find out anything of value from him," Harbour said thoughtfully, leaning against the front of her desk. "David will request counsel and go through the motions of a trial, and that will waste a great deal of time."

"What's the alternative?" Jessie asked. He watched Harbour's eyes lose their thoughtfulness and develop a gleam.

"I think David has enjoyed our hospitality long enough," Harbour said, with a grin. She picked up her comm unit and called Dingles.

"Dingles, wake David. Give him a cold shower to clear his head, and then bring him to the bridge's small conference room. Once he's there, stand in the room with a couple of hard-looking spacers. Give him the silent treatment. I'll get Tacticnok and join you after you've been there a while."

"Can I assume we have the guilty party, Captain?" Dingles asked.

"It would appear so, but we're about to find out conclusively," Harbour replied and ended the call.

Harbour's next call was to the bridge comm operator. She requested Tacticnok be located and brought to the captain's quarters. Over the course of the next three-quarters of an hour, Harbour discussed her plan with Tacticnok and Jessie. When everyone was satisfied with their roles, Harbour led them to the conference room.

"Captain, I'm glad to see you," David said, with relief. He started to rise, but a spacer shoved him into his seat. "See. This is what I mean," David added, spreading his arms in supplication. "I've been cooperative, and I don't understand why I'm receiving this treatment. I insist you return me to the YIPS."

"You've been a naughty boy, David," Harbour said, as she took a seat across the conference table from David.

"I don't know what you mean," David protested.

"Too late for the innocent act, David," Harbour said, fixing a cold gray-eyed stare on David. "Security's been in your cabin and found your stash of expensive toys. And, they've discovered your private account, the one with the large deposits and expenditures."

"It appears you've been well paid for your treacheries, David," Jessie added. He'd taken a stance behind Harbour's shoulder. "How many people have you betrayed, injured, or killed?"

"Being paid coin means nothing," David replied, with a smile. "You're trying to make me admit to something I didn't do."

"David, your story is so full of holes that you're bound to be convicted of multiple charges, and I can tell you that you're one individual I won't rescue for service to the *Belle*," Harbour ground out.

David's smile never waned. He was confident of his position and wanted everyone to know it. "If we're done here, then you'd better get a move on and turn me over to security."

"We would, David, but, see, there's this problem," Harbour replied, switching to a sweet tone. "Here, you're going to need this," she added, handing David a Jatouche ear wig, and he quickly inserted it.

"What problem?" David asked. For the first time, his bon vivant was missing.

"We know you gassed the engineers, David," Jessie said. "Your target was probably Olivia Harden."

"True," Harbour added, nodding. "But here's where you went wrong, David. You gassed two humans and a Jatouche." Harbour waved her hand toward Tacticnok, who'd stood just inside the door with Jaktook.

"You shouldn't have done that, David," Jessie warned, shaking his head in a lament.

"Yes, David, you see I've received a request from Her Highness. She demands you be punished by her father, the Jatouche ruler, for your attack on one of her subjects, not that I know how these aliens do that," Harbour said.

David glanced toward the Jatouche, who displayed their teeth and then abruptly snapped their jaws closed.

"You can't do that," David objected. "I'm a human; I have rights. You have to turn me over to security."

"Do I, David?" Harbour asked innocently. "And here I thought I was the captain of this ship, which isn't docked at a station. Captain Cinders, doesn't that make me the arbiter of justice aboard this vessel."

"It does, Captain," Jessie replied matter-of-factly.

"You see, David," Harbour said, with a sense of finality, "The Jatouche are my guests. They reside aboard the Belle, and, as such, they're my responsibility. Furthermore, the Jatouche have come here to fix our planet, and you come along and try to screw up our budding relationship with these helpful aliens. My choice seems clear. If I give you to our new friends, things will be back on track."

"Can we have him now, Captain?" Tacticnok asked, stepping forward and flashing her teeth.

"No, no," David yelled.

"Then give me something worthwhile," Harbour cried harshly, pounding a fist on the table. "Or the Jatouche will be the ones punishing you."

"I don't know any of their names," David blubbered. "They keep their contact brief, show me a target, indicate what to do, and that's it. I've got to figure out the rest, and there's no record of communications."

"That's not helping your case, David," Jessie said from behind Harbour.

"Honestly, they keep me in the dark," David insisted. That part of his story was true. David knew who was behind the coin. He also knew that if he ever gave up that name he was a dead man.

"You can have him, Tacticnok," Harbour said in disgust.

Tacticnok whistled, and the door opened to reveal six Jatouche. All of them wore hungry expressions.

"Wait, wait," David screamed. "I can tell you when we met."

"Talk," Harbour said, mettle in her voice.

David gave up the details of his last meeting with a contact at the Latched On, date, time, and location within the store.

"One meeting, that's it?" Harbour asked dubiously. "That's not enough." She glanced toward Tacticnok, who took a step forward.

"I can tell you how I got the gas cylinder," David said quickly, holding up his hands in protest to being handed over to the Jatouche.

"Keep talking," Harbour said.

David explained how the man he met gave him a date, time, package number, and contact name at El cargo. "I don't know how they get the cylinder through inspections."

During the interrogation, Harbour carefully monitored David's emotions. She detected the tiniest element of anxiety from him, but nothing significant. Her conclusion: David's display of fear was a performance. His intent was to be handed over to security and force the interview to restart.

"You're a clever young man," Harbour said, the façade of anger on her face replaced by an eerie calm. "You pretend well, but I'm unconvinced. We're offered a few underlings who've helped you, but no one of importance, and you hope that by sharing this meager information you'll be turned over to security."

David's expression of terror swiftly morphed into a gentle smile. "And I applaud your performance, Captain. You have no intention of turning me over to the Jatouche. It would destroy your reputation among the citizenry. And, yes, I'm expecting to be taken to JOS security. There, they'll begin their own interrogation, because everything I've said to you will be considered hearsay and inadmissible before a Review Board."

"You've been well schooled about the legal process," Jessie said, stepping from behind Harbour and laying his comm device on the table in front of Harbour. "Hasn't he, Major?" Jessie added.

"I would say so," Liam said, over the comm unit.

The smug smile fled from David's face. He frowned but quickly schooled his expression. "And you're a clever woman, Captain, but you've neglected two important points."

"I would appreciate you educating me, David," Harbour said graciously, leaning back in her chair.

"You've threatened me to pry information from me. And you've compounded your mistake by having security eavesdrop on our conversation, and they've failed to read me my rights," David announced defiantly.

"I think your first objection might be up to interpretation," Jessie said, smiling, "but you're welcome to contest it before the Review Board. However, I'd defer to the major's opinion on your last point."

"David, whoever taught you failed to educate you on the fine details of security regulations," Liam said. "At the time you shared your information, you weren't charged with any crimes, much less arrested. As such, there was no requirement for security to read you your rights. And, as to your first objection, no legal precedence exists. It would be up to the Review Board to determine whether an alien race's royal member had the legal right to claim your punishment for intentionally harming her citizen. All in all, David, I would say you're about ready to exit an airlock without a vac suit."

"Thank you, Major," Harbour said. "Danny will notify you when he's on approach to the JOS."

"Thank you, Captains and Your Highness Tacticnok, for your efforts today," Liam said and ended the call.

Dingles and the spacers led David out of the room. On the way to the bay, Dingles called Danny to ready the shuttle for a flight to the JOS.

When Danny heard who his passenger would be and what had transpired, he said, "We could save everyone a great deal of trouble, you know, Dingles. Accidents occasionally happen with airlocks."

"Understandable sentiment, Danny, but the captain has ordered him delivered to JOS security."

"It was just a thought, Dingles."

"And one I approve, Danny, but orders are orders."

In the conference room, after taking a moment to regard Harbour and Jessie, Tacticnok said, "This has been a most informative exercise. May I suppose we were successful?"

"Yes," Harbour replied. "David Yersh has incriminated himself and will face a trial in front of the Review Board."

"What is liable to happen to him?" Jaktook asked.

"More than likely, he'll be convicted of numerous charges and incarcerated," Jessie replied.

Jaktook chittered to Tacticnok, but the humans didn't receive a translation. In turn, Tacticnok asked Harbour a question, but the captain politely stared back at her. When Tacticnok didn't receive a reply, she presumed the translation app wasn't broadcasting, and she engaged Jaktook in conversation, with the ear wigs online.

Harbour let the Jatouche converse for a few minutes before she interrupted. "Now, you understand, Your Highness, how we feel when you converse in front of us with your ear wigs tuned to a private channel."

Jaktook's jaw snapped shut, and Tacticnok nodded her head serenely in understanding. "For our arrogance, I apologize, Captains. In the future, we will conduct personal conversations in private."

"Will we be able to control the ear wigs one day?" Jessie asked.

"When you are members of the alliance, many things will be open to you, Captain Cinders," Tacticnok replied.

-39-
Recoveries

Persistent fear lingered in the back of Drigtik's mind despite the pleasant sensations flowing through him. He'd dreamt of home and his mate, but there was an ever-present tendency to turn toward the dark only to revert and embrace the light. After enduring an interminably long period of tension, the embraceable dreams persisted longer, and the subversions dwindled.

Drigtik saw the cool, gray eyes of Captain Harbour. She leaned over him, and he struggled to differentiate dream from reality.

"Am I awake or is this another dream?" Drigtik asked.

Harbour laughed. "You're awake, Drigtik. Welcome back," she said.

The sound of their voices woke those lying on pallets, and Gatnack, Aurelia, Sasha, Olivia, and Pete struggled up and came to Drigtik's side.

"Gatnack's appearance, I understand," Drigtik said, after examining the faces above him. "But, I sincerely hope I don't look as poorly as the four of you, the captain excluded, of course."

"Olivia and Pete woke just hours ago," Harbour said, standing up and stepping back. "And, I attended you only for today. Credit for your mind's healing goes to Aurelia and Sasha."

"How long have we been unconscious?" Drigtik asked.

"It's been three days since Sasha located us," Olivia said.

"Such darkness," Drigtik said and his body shivered.

"We've been told the empaths kept us unconscious to prevent our struggles against the terrorizing hallucinations," Olivia said. "While we slept, they could more easily focus their powers on us."

"Here, young one, drink," Gatnack said, offering Drigtik water. "Once you've wet your throat, we've prepared juice for you."

"Yum," Pete said, with disgust and hoisting an empty juice glass. "I can't wait to get back to the cantina and have a hot sandwich and a real drink."

"That's because you're a disgusting human, Pete," Drigtik replied. He tried to display his teeth and indicate his humor, but he coughed and was forced to sip on his water tube.

"And you, you furry thing, have the sharpest nails I've ever felt," Pete replied.

"Apologies, Pete," Drigtik said. "I remember two humans in vac suits morphing into Crocians and coming for us. I was frozen in terror, but you snatched me up, and we ran. I was determined to hold on to you. I'm sure my legs would have failed me if my feet touched the deck."

"It's okay, Drigtik. Next time, you can carry me," Pete replied, with a grin.

"I will try, Pete, but I don't think we'll get too far," Drigtik replied, chittering his humor.

"Here, Drigtik," Gatnack said, passing him a glass of juice.

After a few grateful sips, Drigtik said, "Terror's grip had me for so long, I felt an annual had passed. Then this wonderful blanket of calm smothered the dark thoughts. I was sure that the ugly images would return, tearing through that coveted covering, but they never did. The pleasant sensations continued, and I was so tired that I welcomed oblivion."

"Sasha found the three of you, Drigtik," Aurelia explained. "She chose not to open the door of the utility room, where you hid, and frighten you. Instead, she transmitted her power through the door."

"You can send, with your mind, through a door?" Drigtik asked in surprise.

"Doors, walls, bulkheads —" Sasha started to enumerate.

"Sasha," Harbour said quietly, ending the teenager's listing. The teenager was sharing more information about empaths than she wanted the Jatouche to learn.

"I'm grateful for your attentions," Drigtik said, looking around. "For you, Olivia and Pete, who chose to keep me safe rather than abandon me;

for you, Sasha, who sought us out; and for you, Captain, who have accumulated truly wonderful beings in your orbit."

Before anyone could respond to Drigtik's generous words, Sasha blurted out, "What's a Crocian?"

"That's a discussion for another time," Gatnack said. He glanced toward Harbour, and the engineer's old eyes warned of a sensitive subject.

"Except for Gatnack, I think the rest of you should get some food and rest," Harbour said. "I'll keep Drigtik company for a while longer. Gatnack, please inform Her Highness that Drigtik is awake."

After Drigtik's supporters left, he finished his drink and dozed off. While he slept, Tacticnok quietly eased into the cabin.

"Gatnack shared your words, Captain," Tacticnok whispered. "He thought Drigtik was lucid and his thoughts ordered. I would hear your opinion."

Harbour closed her eyes and focused more of her power on Drigtik, searching for the darkness she had detected in the early hours of the morning, when she relieved two drained empathetic sisters.

"His body has been clear of the gas for more than a day, Tacticnok, and, at present, his mind shows no indication of dark dreams," Harbour reported. "We talked for a while before he fell asleep, and Drigtik was in good humor. Will he have bad dreams about the episode? I imagine he will. In time, those will fade."

"Humans seem incredibly contradictory. David Yersh and those who employed him frighten us. In contrast, you and your individuals give us hope for a lasting alliance. Many lengthy arguments will follow our return to Na-Tikkook," Tacticnok said, keeping her voice low.

"I would imagine the outcome wouldn't be in our favor," Harbour replied glumly. The insidiousness of the attack showed high disregard for the sanctity of life. David and those who hired him couldn't have known whether the gas would have permanently incapacitated a Jatouche.

"Don't be discouraged, Captain. You've many fine things to recommend you. Fruit juices, for one." Tacticnok replied. She covered her mouth to lessen the high-pitched chortle she released, and Harbour smiled at her, sharing some of the emotional relief she felt.

* * * *

"Are we covered?" Lise asked Jordie.

Jordie chose his answers carefully. It was evident that the governor was not only annoyed, she was dangerously annoyed. "JOS security hasn't reported any deaths. The plumerase gas didn't kill anyone. Reports from the YIPS are that the empaths attenuated the hallucinogenic effects after they found the engineers."

"What's our exposure with David Yersh, now that security has him?" Lise asked.

Jordie watched the fire blaze in Lise's eyes. He kept breathing calmly. "Minimal, Governor. I've used David for three years. I know what drives him. Since no one was killed, he'll receive a light sentence, and he'll do his time. He knows what will happen if he doesn't. When he's released, we'll bring him downside. Then, we can either employ him or make him disappear."

"And how did JOS security find him? Are you getting sloppy, Jordie?" Lise asked. She stood, with arms folded, which Jordie took as a bad sign.

"Security didn't find him, Governor. According to my sources, the empaths did. Specifically, it was Aurelia who located him. How? I've no idea," Jordie replied.

"I rue the day that Markos brought that dark-minded nephew of his, Dimitri, in contact with a powerful empath. Much of our standing has unraveled since that day," Lise said. She unfolded her arms and turned to stare out her garden-facing window, and Jordie breathed a quiet sigh of relief.

"Did David expose anyone?" Lise asked, without turning around.

"Two people, a longtime resident of the station, who we've used repeatedly in the past, and a new recruit in El cargo inspections," Jordie replied.

"I trust they've been dealt with accordingly," Lise demanded, turning around to face Jordie.

"Both of them suffered unfortunate accidents," Jordie replied, offering Lise a conspiratorial grin.

"A clean exit, Jordie. You've turned a potential catastrophe into a successful operation," Lise said, taking a seat behind her desk. "Dismissed," she added perfunctorily.

Jordie hadn't been so anxious to leave Lise's sight in a long time, but he took the time to wish Lise a good day and stride calmly from the office.

When Jordie left, Lise eyed the open doorway and considered the possible repercussions of the attack. Then she reviewed the risks, as she had judged them prior to issuing the go ahead, and the steps Jordie had taken to execute them. In the end, she judged that her decision to undertake the action was the key problem, and the ensuing events weren't Jordie's fault.

Lise experienced momentary relief. It was an unpleasant thought, thinking she would have to remove Jordie from service. Recruiting and training a new security chief was a daunting task, and Lise was relieved that it appeared unnecessary.

* * * *

Two days later, Lise attended a unique meeting of the family heads. It was singular in that she hadn't called the meeting, which had always been the exclusive purview of the governor.

When Lise arrived, she found eighteen family heads arrayed in two rows in front of her podium.

"Well, I'm here. Suppose someone tell me why," Lise demanded.

Dorelyn Gaylan rose, as a courtesy, and said, "Those you see here have formed a council. There are also other family heads who have promised loyalty to the council. Together we represent more than eighty percent of the domes' leaders."

"I'm impressed by the depth of your organization," Lise replied with disdain. "Would you care to state your purpose or do I have to guess?"

"It's simple," Rufus said, rising. "The era of governors is effectively at an end, except as a figurehead."

"And how do you propose to accomplish this?" Lise sneered. She was doing her best to throw the group emotionally off kilter but failing to do so, and that, more than anything, scared her.

"The council's membership represents the vast majority of enterprise within the domes," Idrian said, standing up between Rufus and Dorelyn. "You can either accept our terms or we can crush your businesses. If you choose the latter, you'll be destitute in less than a year."

"Commerce isn't the only way to conduct business," Lise threatened.

"Regarding that point, Lise, your security head and several key members of your security force have been relieved of duty ... permanently," Dorelyn said. "We will provide you with a new security chief and senior staff, who will report to the Council."

"This is a coup, and I won't tolerate it. I'll bring JOS security down on all your heads," Lise yelled in rage.

"We think not, Lise," Idrian replied calmly. We know that Jordie MacKiernan, on your orders, orchestrated the gas attack at the YIPS."

"That's an incredulous lie," Lise shot back.

"True, we can't prove it," Rufus said, "but the council members will swear to the Review Board that you told us of your plan. What do you think the Review Board will decide, under those circumstances?"

"Save it, Lise," Dorelyn said acrimoniously. "The concept of governor, as leader, is dead. The families no longer wish to place their fate in the hand of one individual who can make a dangerous misstep, as in the YIPS attack on the engineers."

"Well, I presume that someone will lead this council. Doesn't that amount to the same thing?" Lise riposted.

"The council is led by a triumvirate, who will begin with term lengths of one, two, and three years. At the end of their terms, the positions will rotate to other family heads according to seniority," Idrian explained.

"And who are these initial triumvirates that I must address for each and every decision?" Lise snarled.

"Dorelyn, Rufus, and me," Idrian said.

"Well, well, you're a surprise," Lise sneered. "Rufus, I understand. Dorelyn, I might have suspected, but you, Idrian, I wouldn't have guessed."

"It's not a matter of usurping your power, Lise, to be governor," Idrian said. "It's more a matter that the domes and Pyre itself have outgrown the need for the position. For the sake of continuity, we'll keep you in place until the council is ready to reveal itself."

"And if I choose to announce you first?" Lise asked. She gazed around at the stony faces that stared back at her. They were hard and unflinching. There wasn't a weak member among them. "I see. So be it," she said, accepting their conditions. "What's the council's first order of business?"

"The triumvirate and you, Lise, must meet with Captains Harbour and Cinders," Dorelyn replied. "We need to be part of this operation to restore the planet, not attempting to sabotage it, as you've tried to do."

-40-
Triumvirate

"Lise wants what?" Jessie yelled over his comm unit. He was at the YIPS assembly site for the intravertor, and the excessive noise compelled engineers, techs, and visitors to wear ear protection.

"Get to a place where you can hear me," Harbour replied loudly, hoping the bridge pickup transmitted her voice sufficiently.

Birdie grinned and checked the audio gain on the comm panel. It was at maximum.

"Better?" Jessie asked, when he enclosed himself in a nearby office.

"Much," Harbour replied. "I was saying that I've received a call from Lise Panoy. She wants to meet with you and me to discuss the Jatouche intravertor. She says it's time that negotiations begin in earnest."

"Does she?" Jessie queried. "Gassing our engineers didn't stop the project, so she plans to cut the domes in on the new land, which will be available once the planet is healed. Did she say anything else?"

"She did," Harbour replied. "And, now that I think about it, it was odd. She said that three other family heads would be attending with her."

"Who?" Jessie asked.

"Idrian Tuttle, Rufus Stewart, and Dorelyn Gaylan," Harbour replied. "I know the two men, but I've never met the woman."

"I've heard of her," Jessie said. "She's one of the tough, silent types. Now, why would Lise Panoy need to have three family heads on the calls with her?"

"Let me correct your assumption," Harbour said. "Lise Panoy wants to meet in person, aboard the JOS."

"This gets more and more interesting. Lise coming to us and bringing help," Jessie replied.

"I assume that by negotiations Lise means she intends to hold up the project coming through the domes until she has what she wants," Harbour said. "It sounds like the intravertor's deployment method is still unknown to her."

When Jessie didn't reply, Harbour glanced at Birdie, who indicated with a thumbs up that the comm link was active.

Finally, Jessie responded, saying, "It's the three family heads that's puzzling me. There's something odd about that."

"I think the more immediate question is: What are we going to do about Lise's offer?" Harbour asked.

"Why, I'm going to listen to the woman's proposal and try to figure out what the attendance of the other family heads mean," Jessie replied.

"You? Don't you mean we, Captain?" Harbour asked.

"What do you think will be the purpose of one or both of us attending the negotiations?" Jessie asked.

Harbour had to admit to herself that this was where Jessie excelled. He had spent a lifetime negotiating deals for the purchase of a new ship, contracts with the YIPS, and interviewing crew. "Okay, Captain, educate me," Harbour replied, wishing she'd made the call from the privacy of her quarters.

"To stall," Jessie simply replied. "I intend to draw the negotiations out for as long as I can."

"And buy the engineers time to get to the deployment stage," Harbour concluded.

"Exactly," Jessie replied. "Besides, Captain, the Jatouche, and by that I mean Tacticnok, trust you. You have to remain available to her."

"Understood," Harbour replied. "Shall I tell Lise that you're available?"

"Negative," Jessie replied. "Ask Lise for dates when she would like to begin negotiations and take your time choosing one."

Harbour grinned, "I understand. My schedule is incredibly impacted lately."

The bridge crew could hear Jessie's chuckle. "That's the idea," he said.

* * * *

Harbour managed to stall Lise and the family heads for nearly two weeks before the first negotiations meeting took place in a JOS security conference room. In addition to Lise and the three family heads, Emerson, Henry, and Liam were present. The fact that the major had been invited by the captains irked the commandant, especially since he had to persuade Lise to ensure he was included.

"Apologies for my lateness," Jessie said, hurrying to join the meeting. "Problems with the intravertor. Engineers are having to rethink some assembly issues."

"Understandable, Captain," Lise replied diplomatically. "I would presume mating alien technology with our own to be a daunting task. Do you expect it to delay the completion by a little or a long time?"

"Hard to say, right now," Jessie said, taking a seat on the other side of the table from the governor and the family heads. "They just discovered the issue, but I don't think it's going to be an easy fix based on the discussion I heard."

"Dorelyn Gaylan," a woman announced, extending her hand across the table to Jessie. "I believe I'm the only one who hasn't met you personally, Captain Cinders."

"Pleasure to meet you," Jessie replied, taking Dorelyn's hand.

"Forgive me," Lise said, "I thought the two of you had met."

So that's the game we're going to play, Dorelyn thought, giving Lise a polite smile.

These were the sort of conditions that had Jessie regretting Harbour's absence. He would love to have her whispering the emotional reactions of the family heads in his ear. When he thought of Harbour's breath in his ear, a tingling sensation threaded through him.

"Are we waiting for Captain Harbour?" Lise asked.

"No, we're not," Jessie replied. "She's playing arbiter for the Jatouche and Pyrean engineers."

"Fine," Lise said, exuding a touch of annoyance at the stumbling start to negotiations. "Let's begin. On the table is the division of land, if and when, the planet is healed."

Henry Stamerson coughed at Lise's presumption and took a swallow of his water. Even Emerson was taken aback by the boldness of the statement.

Jessie appeared unfazed and replied, "I believe that this idea of land sharing, as you've phrased it, is not within my purview to discuss. If that's the question on the table, I think negotiations are at an end."

"Perhaps, we should start with a lesser subject," Idrian said. "After you move the intravertor through the domes, how far out do you think you'll proceed before you plant and activate the device?"

"That's a difficult question, Idrian," Jessie replied. "While I don't have the safe operating distance for the intravertor, I can tell you that some of the limitations would be vac suit air, a shelter with tank-recharging capabilities, personnel rovers, and a mobile vehicle capable of carrying six tons ... at least, I think that's the smallest section, but I'll have to check on it."

Jessie watched the family heads lean back, contemplating what they'd heard.

"I take it none of you have any experience with space mining operations?" Henry asked the governor and the family heads. When he received blank expressions, he added, "Pyre's surface is, for the purposes of this discussion, a hostile place. It requires the transport and assembly of the intravertor to be treated similarly to a mining operation on a moon or asteroid. What Captain Cinders is asking you is: What portion of the installation equipment can the domes supply?"

The family heads glanced at Jessie, and he nodded his agreement.

"We don't have rovers and heavy transporters that will function on Pyre's surface," Rufus protested.

"Well, for certain, those types of vehicles won't fit in the cargo hold of the El. You'd have to dismantle them, cart the pieces through the dome, and reassemble them outside an airlock," Liam explained.

"Speaking of which, we'll need the dimensions of both interlock and exterior surface airlocks," Jessie said. He could see Idrian taking notes in his comm device and inwardly smiled. *I'm keeping them busy, Harbour,* he thought.

"I don't hear resolutions to these technical questions," Dorelyn said.

Jessie upgraded his estimation of the family leader. The woman had a keen mind and wasn't sidetracked by minutiae, but, then again, Jessie wasn't a novice at negotiations either.

"I haven't either," Jessie said, gazing at Lise.

"These must be tabled for later discussions," Lise replied, looking toward Idrian, who nodded as he entered a note in his device.

"I want to address a concern of mine," Rufus said, sidetracking the discussion. "Who will be in charge of the transport and assembly?"

Two things struck Jessie as interesting. The first was the tiny flicker of annoyance across the faces of Dorelyn and Idrian, when Rufus brought up this subject, and the second was it was an odd question.

"Generally, engineers and techs," Jessie replied, deciding to play dumb.

"That's not what I mean," Rufus replied firmly.

"Then I suggest that you phrase your questions in specific terms if you're looking for a more detailed response," Jessie said, locking eyes with Rufus.

"Will the Jatouche need to visit the domes?" Rufus asked.

"How else do you expect them to get to the surface?" Jessie replied. Within minutes of the meeting, he'd identified the weak link in the group. Idrian was thoughtful and detailed; Dorelyn was quiet but a dominant personality; Lise was Lise; but Rufus was hot-headed, opinionated, and xenophobic. The last word was a new one for Jessie. Harbour had taught it to him, when he'd struggled for a means of describing the individuals who might have paid David Yersh.

"Can't human engineers do the job?" Rufus asked.

Idrian leaned forward on the table to address Rufus, but Jessie waved him off. "The intravertor is a Jatouche device. Humans built the support structure: shells, ring connections, microwave receiver, and a bunch of other sundry items, but the exotic parts are all Jatouche. It will take Pyreans and Jatouche working together to make this successful. Now, if our furry friends make you nervous, I suggest you find a far dome to hide in while the important tasks get done."

Jessie had sat unnervingly still while he spoke, but his eyes were hard.

"Sirs," Henry said into the stillness that followed Jessie's comments, "we've a long way to go in these negotiations. I suggest you pace yourselves."

"Many of us don't share the opinions that have just been expressed," Dorelyn said, staring fixedly at Rufus before she turned to Jessie, "and we appreciate the support of these furry friends." She ended her statement with a suggestion of a smile.

Definitely a leader, Jessie thought of Dorelyn's remarks but *of who or what* were his questions.

Perhaps we can get an understanding of the dimensions of the overall device and the structural components," Idrian suggested.

"I can send you the details of those," Jessie replied. "As to the completed device, the intravertor will measure forty meters and weigh twenty-eight tons."

Jessie's words brought conversation to a halt. The only one who wasn't awe-struck was Henry, an ex-mining captain, who'd dealt with ships and equipment that size and larger.

"You're trying to cure a planet," Jessie added, into the silence. "You can't do it with something the size of an e-cart. And, while we're at it, you'd better get used to the idea that every intravertor we produce will accelerate the removal of heat from the surface."

"That's if it works," Rufus said, with disdain.

"Didn't the captain tell you to pace yourself?" Jessie asked. "Do you think aliens, who know how to operate a gate system and travel between worlds, wouldn't know how to build something like this intravertor?"

Rufus might have replied, except he caught the stares of the other three downsiders. They were none too happy with his clumsy attempts to push his opinions.

Communications on several minor subjects continued for another two hours before Emerson suggested they break for early meal.

A sudden thought occurred to Jessie and he announced, "I'll be dining at the Miner's Pit. I'll be happy to comp anyone who joins me, as an apology for my lateness to the meeting." As he suspected, only Liam and Henry accepted the offer.

Emerson was surprised that he was left to his own devices for midday meal. The governor and the family heads had closed ranks and excluded him.

On the way to the Pit, Henry eyed Jessie several times before he asked, "Is it my imagination or are you trying to be helpful one moment and antagonistic the next?" When Jessie grinned at him, Henry said, "I thought so."

"You're stalling, aren't you?" Liam asked.

"Yes, and I could use some help," Jessie replied.

During their meal, Jessie explained that he was prolonging the negotiations in order to give the governor and the family heads a reason to believe they were getting what they want. "I'm going to act like they're wearing me down," he said.

"For how long?" Liam asked.

"According to the engineers, we need another three or four weeks," Jessie replied.

"I don't know if my schedule can accommodate that much time," Liam said.

"Speaking of your schedule, have you located the two individuals who David identified?" Jessie asked.

"Oh, yes, within days of receiving David's details," Liam replied. "By a phenomenal coincidence, both men died from different accidents on the same day."

"Someone works quickly," Henry said, putting down his utensil and taking a drink, in hopes his appetite would rebound.

"Someone with a great deal of coin and a lot of contacts," Jessie added.

"What angers me," Liam commented, "is that the trails are so convoluted and grow cold so quickly that my teams can't tell if we're dealing with wealthy topsiders or downsiders."

"It could always be both," Henry offered.

"Back to your plan, Jessie," Liam said, "Even when you finish negotiations with the family heads about the transport of the intravertor, it doesn't settle the question of land distribution, which was Lise's opening statement today."

"I couldn't believe her brazenness," Henry said, shaking his head. "She wants to balance the deployment of a world-changing device against the domes' territorial growth."

"Lovely piece of work," Jessie agreed. "Too bad the joke is on her."

Jessie was smiling and it caused Henry and Liam to join him.

"Why are we grinning like fools?" Liam asked.

Jessie glanced around to ensure he wasn't overheard. Nonetheless, he leaned in, and the others did too.

"The intravertor gets delivered by ship or shuttle. It drops down through the atmosphere and embeds itself in the ground," Jessie whispered.

"It doesn't go through the domes?" Liam asked incredulously.

"Nope," Jessie said, his grin widening.

There was a moment of silence before the three men erupted in laughter that drew the stares of every spacer in the Pit.

Maggie stopped by their table, saying, "Two captains and a major having a good time, and you're not even drinking. You celebrating?"

"You have no idea," Jessie replied, with a wink.

"Humph, I've seen that look before," Maggie replied. "Now, I don't want to know," she added, as she hurried away to greet new customers.

* * * *

The meal at the Starlight among the family heads was less cordial than Jessie's. When Lise took the opportunity to visit the facilities, Dorelyn leaned toward Rufus and said, "I'm rethinking my decision to accept you as a member of the council's triumvirate."

"Too late," Rufus shot back.

"Actually not," Idrian commented quietly. "If you'd read the charter carefully, Rufus, you would have noted an article that said: If two members of the triumvirate believe the third member is not acting in the best interest of the council, they may petition the council to have that member removed for just cause."

"So now you're taking her side," Rufus accused.

"No, I'm taking the council's side, Rufus," Idrian replied. "We've known each other a long time, and I value your friendship, but you're letting your personal animus toward aliens and this project blind you to the greater prize."

"Let me phrase it more bluntly, Rufus," Dorelyn said. "Stop fighting with Cinders. As the council's representatives, we've two goals. The first is to get Cinders and Harbour to cooperate with us in the deployment of the intravertor. We want those two captains singing our praises when the negotiations are over."

"And Dorelyn means the three of us, not Lise, when she refers to our praises," Idrian added. "That's our second goal. We're trying to minimize Lise's participation. The other side of the table must perceive her as a limited player in the negotiations."

"Understood," Rufus said sullenly. "Just don't ask me to apologize to Cinders."

"Absolutely not," Idrian said. "It's one thing to irritate the man; it's another to appear weak to him."

When Lise returned to the group, the triumvirate quieted. "Talking about me?" Lise quipped. Without missing a beat, she sat at the table and said, "I think it's obvious by the lack of progress in these early discussions that certain people possess the wrong attributes to successfully negotiate a good deal for the domes. I suggest the three of you leave this to me. After all, I believe I understand Jessie Cinders better than any of you."

"I was wondering, Lise," Idrian said, "Who do you think Harbour and Cinders suppose is responsible for the attack on the engineers?"

"It doesn't matter, neither she nor anyone else has a clue about who's the guilty party," Lise replied.

"Is that because Jordie tied up every loose end for you?" Dorelyn asked.

"Maybe it was better that Harbour was too busy to attend this meeting," Rufus said.

"I was thinking the same thing," Idrian interjected. "If the captain were sitting across from us, I'm sure she'd bring up an embarrassing subject, like the attack, just to read us."

"And I would have loved to have asked her," Dorelyn started to say before she switched to a sweet entreating voice, "Captain Harbour, did you detect anything unusual when you accused us of trying to destroy Jatouche–Pyrean relations?" Then Dorelyn's voice hardened, while she continued. "What do you think she would have said, Lise?"

"The three of you are tiring," Lise replied in a huff. "You're welcome to continue your banter. Me, I'm starving and ordering."

Dorelyn winked at Rufus. It was an uncharacteristic gesture for her, but she was intent on complimenting Rufus on his recovery. They wanted to constantly challenge Lise and demonstrate the strength of the triumvirate.

When meals were finished, dishes were cleared away, and drinks drained, Lise made to stand, intending to leave the group.

"A word more before you leave, Lise," Dorelyn said. She relished the brief flash of irritation that swept across Lise's face. "You stated that you knew Captain Cinders better than any of us. I wonder what you made of his comments during the meeting."

Lise felt this was a perfect opening to demonstrate her superior knowledge, and she lectured the threesome on the finer points of the meeting's discussion.

When Lise finished her recitation, her expression was smug. "I'm sure the council can afford the coin to pay for this meal," she said, rising and sauntering away.

Rufus whispered a few expletives in Lise's wake, careful that he wasn't overheard.

"What was the purpose of your question, Dorelyn?" Idrian asked.

"To see if Lise knew what she was talking about. She doesn't," Dorelyn replied.

"Could you elaborate?" Idrian asked.

"The only time Cinders showed true anger was when Rufus displayed his xenophobia," Dorelyn explained. She held up a hand to interrupt

Rufus' denial. "Other than that, Cinders was playing with Rufus, allowing his comments to derail the conversation."

"Why?" Idrian asked.

"I don't know, and Lise doesn't even perceive it. I never liked Markos, but he was a lot smarter governor than this one," Dorelyn said, staring at the doors through which Lise had exited the cantina.

-41-
Drigtik

After a few days of rest and several tests by the empaths, during the engineers' waking and sleeping periods, the engineers were pronounced fit to return to work.

Drigtik had adopted a certain swagger that was noticed by Pyreans and Jatouche. He didn't laud over his peers. He was simply proud of what he was privileged to experience, which definitely weren't the horrible dreams. As he said to Olivia, "As much as that gas spun nightmarish images for hours, it was the wonder of being enveloped by the empaths afterwards that was true bliss. While I might have wished for another reason to have received their gifts, enduring the darkness was worth it."

"I can't argue with you," Olivia had replied. "The empaths freed me from my phobia about leaving the YIPS. Every step of the way, they made certain that I didn't pay a price for my decision to accompany them to meet you. Personally, it was the best decision I've made in many years, and the empaths made it happen."

Pete overheard their comments and added his own, "They've helped me with my anger over my *decorations*," he said, using Tacticnok's word and lifting his hands to display the scars that extended over much of his arms and upper torso.

It was the stories brought back to Na-Tikkook by the Jatouche who had experienced Aurelia's power, during the first encounter with Pyreans, that had driven the desires of others of their kind to experience the empaths' wondrous emanations. That Drigtik was fortunate enough to experience days of the empaths' ministrations had given the engineer an elevated status among the Jatouche.

Tacticnok kept to herself the revelation that she'd experienced a private session with Harbour. On the one hand, she wondered how her father and advisors would react to empaths visiting the Jatouche home world. Assuredly there would be criticism for her treatment of Jittak, but she was prepared for that discussion. If she were given the opportunity to nominate the emissary from the Pyreans to her father's court, there was only one choice for her. It was Captain Harbour, one of the most powerful empaths.

* * * *

Drigtik was in his element during the assembly phase, urging the techs of both races on and double-checking the success of the interlinking process, as the device grew in size. Finally, assembly was taking place in a huge bay that had been previously used for metal ingot delivery. Its bay doors were large enough to accomplish the launch of the device in its completed form.

Harbour had deliberately tried to stay out of the way of the engineers during the initial phases, but curiosity drove her to take an inspection tour, and Tacticnok accompanied her.

When the two leaders entered the assembly bay, work came to a halt. Drigtik ordered them back to work and hurried over to attend the two females.

"Your Highness," Drigtik said, dipping his head in obeisance. "Captain Harbour," he added, his eyes glowing in admiration.

"I think some of my father's subjects are ready to abandon their home world, if they can inhabit the *Belle*," Tacticnok commented.

Drigtik was only momentarily thrown off balance by Tacticnok's statement. His enthusiasm for the near-successful completion of the intravertor was his primary emotional driver. "How can I be of assistance?" he asked.

"I need a beginner's summary of the intravertor," Harbour said. "I want to know how it will accomplish its job."

"That'll be my pleasure, Captain," Drigtik replied and led them over to the massive construction.

The device rested on its launch sled. The engineering teams had begun final assembly, starting from the aft end, and the structure was three-quarters complete, already measuring about 30 meters.

Harbour was awed by the enormous size of the intravertor and stood staring at its length, which had yet to reach the end of the sled.

"Impressive, isn't it?" Olivia asked proudly, choosing to stand beside Harbour. Pete and Bryan were behind her.

"That's hardly the word for it," Harbour said, watching teams maneuver another section overhead to add to the assembly. Harbour took the opportunity to lay a hand over Olivia's.

"I'm fine, Captain," Olivia said softly, feeling the slightest of power from Harbour.

"Just checking," Harbour replied, with a smile.

"I'm not sure that I've fully recovered," Drigtik offered, hoping for the same treatment.

Tacticnok chittered a rebuke, but Harbour laughed, gripped his hand, and sent a small touch of warmth his way.

Drigtik flashed his teeth in appreciation and waved them toward the aft end of the intravertor. As they walked in that direction, Harbour laid a hand on Pete's neck, seeking the darkness. Much to her relief, Pete exhibited the most positive emotional balance she'd ever felt from him. When Harbour retrieved her hand, Pete sent her a grateful smile.

"This first section," Drigtik said, pointing to the aft end of the device, "contains the thermal-seeking tendrils."

"What?" Harbour queried.

"Tendrils are coiled inside this subsection, Captain," Olivia explained. "When the intravertor embeds itself in the surface, these tendrils are released. They're a metal hybrid that can be directed."

"How?" Harbour asked.

"Forward of this section is a Jatouche generator," Bryan explained. "It activates the tendrils and temporarily supplies their energy, which enables the tendrils to spread out beneath the surface. The way they're formed makes them bend toward heat as they're uncoiled, much the way plants grow toward light. Once they're fully extended, the energy flow is reversed.

Instead of the generator supplying, it receives. As long as there's heat, the generator is driven by the tendrils."

Harbour shook her head in disbelief.

"As I said, Captain, incredible technology," Olivia admitted, in commiseration.

Harbour glanced toward Drigtik, and the engineer took it as a signal to continue.

"When our generator's energy flow is produced by the planet's heat, the intravertor will be active and require none of its internal energy source. Every function of the intravertor will be operable," Drigtik explained. "This section above the generator contains the vanes, which have a dual purpose. In their first form, they will ensure the intravertor descends upright and at a predetermined descent speed. After deployment, the blade angles and their spin direction will be reversed."

"That's when the intravertor starts pulling in Pyre's air," Harbour said. It was one of the functions that Harbour was most keen to understand.

"Yes," Pete said, "the air is filtered, removing the dust and noxious gases. Those items will concentrate in the next forward section."

"That will be a great deal of material. Where do those materials go?" Harbour asked.

"In the section that Pete is explaining," Gatnack said, "the particulate matter and gases are heated and fused together, creating pellets. Those pellets will be spun out at a great distance from the intravertor."

"You're speaking of the need for a huge amount of energy: driving the generator, spinning the vanes, fusing the atmospheric contaminants, and spitting them out," Harbour summarized. "Will that use up the entire amount of energy provided by the tendrils?"

"You're concerned about the excess energy that we intend to transmit as microwave energy to this station, Captain?" Drigtik asked.

"Yes," Harbour replied.

"This is the primary variable, Captain," Drigtik continued. "Initially, the first intravertor deployed will consume the majority of the tendril energy, if not all of it, while cleaning the atmosphere. As more intravertors are built and launched, the atmosphere will clear and more energy will be available to focus on the YIPS receiver."

"Most of this depends on the rate at which we produce intravertors," Olivia said.

"Can we make a device by ourselves?" Harbour asked.

"No, Captain," Olivia replied. "We can fabricate the shells, the vanes, and many other parts, and we can deliver the intravertor to the surface. However, the tendrils, generator, filtering system, fuser, and microwave transmitter are Jatouche components."

Harbour glanced down at Tacticnok, who replied, "To be discussed, Captain."

"Between us?" Harbour asked.

"With His Excellency Rictook," Tacticnok said.

"Shall I continue, Captain?" Drigtik asked.

"I've learned what I needed," Harbour replied. "I'm proud of your cooperative efforts to produce this first device."

When Harbour and Tacticnok left, Drigtik eyed Olivia and asked, "Was my presentation not to the captain's liking?"

"It wasn't that, Drigtik," Olivia said, laying a comforting hand on Drigtik's shoulder. "The captain is thinking about the future. One intravertor doesn't do us much good."

"But it will prove the feasibility of the process," Drigtik objected.

"And what if we can't get components from you or we can't raise the coin to produce more shells even if you do send us components?" Olivia asked.

"Taking incremental steps, which prove successful, is how greater goals are reached," Gatnack intoned. "We are engineers; we build the tools. Captain Harbour and Her Highness Tacticnok are leaders and must have our successes to create a future alliance. Come, it's time to return to work."

Harbour and Tacticnok hadn't yet made the shuttle when she received a call from Olivia.

"Captain, I think you need to return to the assembly site. We've a major problem," Olivia said.

"Coming," Harbour replied.

"Do humans enjoy walking so much that they refuse to install personnel movers to allow you to ride?" Tacticnok asked, as she hurried to keep up with Harbour.

"It's a matter of priorities, Tacticnok," Harbour replied, slowing. "We've been desperate to produce ships, expand the domes, add terminal arms to both stations, and repair what wears down. There hasn't been the coin or the opportunity to produce some of the comforts I imagine the Jatouche enjoy."

Harbour and Tacticnok caught the five engineers in a heated discussion. They weren't yelling at one another, but, they were jabbing at images on a wide monitor, as if they were intending to poke holes in it, and earnestly arguing the pros and cons of the vessels displayed.

"You called?" Harbour asked from behind the engineers, who weren't aware of her approach.

Olivia glanced at her comrades. None of them seemed inclined to reply. She took a deep breath and said, "We lack the right vehicle to launch the intravertor."

"Which one do we need? Is it a matter of coin to hire a captain and his ship?" Harbour asked.

"None of our ships can handle the job," Bryan admitted, before he examined his deck boots.

Harbour and Tacticnok's mouths hung open for a moment before closing.

"Olivia, how did we get this far without realizing that problem?" Harbour asked.

"None of the engineers, neither ours nor theirs, have ever designed a ship or flown them, Captain. It wasn't until we talked to various captains that we realized the problem," Olivia admitted.

"Which is what?" Harbour prompted.

"The task is multifold, Captain," Bryan explained. "First, the ship has to penetrate deep enough into the atmosphere to launch the intravertor and allow gravity to take over. This can't be done in a flyby pattern, as if the ship were orbiting the planet at near escape velocity. According to the

Jatouche, the ship maintains a stationary position when releasing the device."

"And mining ships haven't the ability to lift out of a stationary atmospheric position," Harbour said, realizing the problem."

"The other choices were mining shuttles," Pete added, "but they're too small to handle the device. The sled attachments need another five to eight meters in ship length, depending on the model that you're considering. The only vessel that has the length is the *Belle*'s shuttle, but it's too old. It could never handle the stress of the flight."

The dejected faces of Olivia, Pete, Bryan, Gatnack, and Drigtik stared at Harbour, and her mind raced to find an answer. It was inconceivable that they could get the project this close to completion and be unable to deliver the device to the surface. Suddenly, Harbour smiled, pulled out her comm, and made a call.

"Danny," Harbour said, when she reached the pilot, "how long before the *Belle*'s new shuttle will be delivered?"

"It's been ready, Captain, about three weeks ago," Danny replied. "I'm supposed to take it through its test flights, but I've been too busy with daily transport between the *Belle* and the YIPS. Once I approve the shuttle, they'll want final payment."

"Hold one, Danny," Harbour said, and made a second call.

"Ituau, here, Captain," the first mate answered.

"Ituau, I need pilots to sub for Danny, pilots who can handle the *Belle*'s ancient, over-sized shuttle," Harbour requested. "Do you have them?"

"We've got excellent shuttle pilots, Captain," Ituau replied. "If they're given a couple of days training with Danny to check out the ship, they should be fine. I take it you're only asking for transport between the *Belle* and the YIPS."

"Affirmative," Harbour replied.

"No problem, Captain. When do you want this done?" Ituau asked.

"It's a priority request, Ituau," Harbour said.

"Understood, Captain. I'll communicate with the other captains. The pilots will meet Danny at whatever dock he's occupying and begin training immediately. Is there an emergency?" Ituau asked, hoping that wasn't the case.

"No, Ituau," Harbour said. "We're looking for the right vehicle to launch the intravertor, and it might be sitting, docked at the JOS, ready for us to test.

"Understood, Captain," Ituau replied. "Safe flights for the tests. We'll take care of this end," she added, ending the call.

Harbour scrolled through her comm unit, searching for the imagery and specifications on the *Belle's* new shuttle. When she found them, she handed her device to Olivia. "Will this do it?" Harbour asked anxiously.

Olivia knelt on her knees, as did Pete and Bryan, while Gatnack and Drigtik crowded around. The effortless way the engineers had adapted to the height differences made her smile before her concerns returned.

The conversation among the engineers went back and forth, as they examined the specifications and discussed attachment positions. Most important, they examined the ship's thrust capability and maneuvering performance in low orbit and within the atmosphere.

The engineers deliberated for so long that Tacticnok felt compelled to remind them of who waited. "Engineers, I believe you weren't asked to draft a performance evaluation of this ship. The captain is asking for an initial opinion. Is there a possibility of this shuttle being capable of performing the task?"

"Yes, Your Highness, there is," Drigtik replied sheepishly.

"Engineers," Tacticnok said, raising her arms in supplication. "You have your answer, Captain," she added.

Harbour held out her hand for her comm unit, and Olivia reluctantly returned it. "Danny?" she asked.

"Here, Captain," the pilot replied, around a mouthful of hot sandwich.

"Ituau is gathering pilots to relieve you. Give them the training they need in cooperation with our backup pilot. Don't scrimp on that. Warn the engineering company to prepare our new shuttle for test flights. When you're ready to hand over the daily transfer flights, get over to the JOS, and test that ship out."

"Understood, Captain," Danny replied enthusiastically.

"And, Danny, take with you one of the best of Captain Cinder's pilots, who you'll be training. He or she will be your copilot," Harbour ordered.

There was a pause on the comm, and Harbour could imagine the thoughts going through Danny's mind. He hadn't flown with a copilot for years.

"What's up, Captain, if I might ask?" Danny eventually replied.

"Looks like our new shuttle might be just the vehicle we need to deliver the intravertor to the planet," Harbour said.

Of all possible reactions, Harbour didn't expect to hear Danny chuckle.

"I knew that was how the intravertor was going to be delivered, when I saw that sled and the components being assembled," Danny said.

"That's not common knowledge, Danny," Harbour warned. "Don't spread it around, especially on the JOS."

"Understood, Captain," Danny replied. "It might be helpful to tell Olivia to send me the specs on that device, how they intend to attach the sled, and what sort of maneuver is required to release it."

"I'll get the engineers on it," Harbour replied and closed the call.

"You heard?" Harbour asked Olivia.

"I'll send them to Danny," Olivia said.

"And afterwards," Harbour said, focusing intently on each face, "the five of you are responsible for taking Danny into your confidence for every element of the final operation. He's to know everything you know about the attachment process, the specs of this device, and its deployment."

Harbour was worried about Danny's end of the operation. Focusing on her concerns created a lapse in control and caused her power to leak.

Immediately, the engineers who faced her were nodding to her requests, frowns evident. Belatedly, Harbour shut down her gate. "Apologies," she said.

"None needed, Captain," Bryan said. "The error was ours, and we'll ensure that Danny and his copilot are well informed."

Harbour nodded her approval and walked away with Tacticnok.

"So that is what other types of sharing feel like," Tacticnok said.

"It was a mistake on my part, Tacticnok," Harbour said, as they entered a corridor. "I overreacted. I've known Danny for years. He's been diligent in caring for me, and he's done a marvelous job keeping the *Belle*'s last original shuttle flying."

"It was an instructive moment," Tacticnok replied. "It made me feel the way I do in the presence of my father, when he makes an official pronouncement. I was ready to stand with the engineers and agree to anything you wanted." Tacticnok displayed her teeth to indicate her sympathy for Harbour's reaction, but Harbour's face wore worry lines.

"All creatures capable of thought will make mistakes, Captain," Tacticnok said. "My father has told me many times that the aftermath of a mistake is the more critical time. It requires an apology, followed by forgiveness of one's self, and then actions to prevent the same mistake from occurring again."

-42-
Danny

Docked at the YIPS, Danny's pilot chair was leaned back, and he was taking a nap before the next return flight to the *Belle*.

"Permission to come aboard," Danny heard a female voice call. He sat upright and called back, "Come aboard, I'm in the pilot's cabin."

Danny leveraged out of his chair onto his prosthetic legs and stumped back to meet his guest. Instead of one individual, Danny met three.

"Reporting for flight training, Danny. I'm Claudia Manning, a *Spryte* shuttle pilot," the woman who'd called out said, and extended her hand.

Danny shook the pilot's calloused hand, as Claudia added, "These two excuses for spacers are from the *Annie* and the *Pearl*."

Claudia introduced the other two pilots, but Danny had trouble focusing on her words. Claudia had the typical spacer buzz-cut hair. Hers was blonde and topped a lightly lined face. It was the warmth in the green eyes and the quirky smile that captured Danny's attention. She was what men would call a handsome woman, who wore her forty-plus years well.

"Ready when you are, Danny," Claudia said, when she completed the introductions and Danny continued to stare at her.

"Yeah, sure, sorry," Danny sputtered. "This way," he said, waving them forward.

The *Annie* pilot started to tease Claudia about her new partner until he caught sight of Danny's prosthetics, and the comment died in his mouth. *There are too many of us with those,* he thought.

Danny indicated the copilot seat to Claudia, and the other two pilots stood behind them, while Danny explained the system layouts and controls.

About five minutes into Danny's explanations, the *Pearl* pilot, who stood behind Danny, said, "I thought this was going to be an hour's orientation and then we would be flying this ship. How old is this thing?"

"From construction date, probably five hundred-plus years," Danny replied. "I'm guessing that it was the last ship to be unpacked after the original colonists lost the *Belle*'s other shuttles setting up the first domes. If you're asking how long it's been operational, I've no idea."

"Everything you're showing us are manual operations," the *Annie* pilot exclaimed. "Is anything on this ship automated?"

Danny thought for a moment, as if the list might be lengthy, then he looked back at the *Annie*'s pilot and said, "Nope."

Claudia's laughter bubbled out, and Danny grinned at her.

"How long do we have you for training, Danny?" Claudia asked.

"The captain said to make sure you were comfortable before I handed this ship over to you," Danny replied. "The good news is that you'll have the *Belle*'s backup pilot beside you."

"Then why isn't he or she flying this ship?" the *Pearl*'s pilot asked.

"You see these," Danny said, indicating his prosthetics. "They're nothing to what Isley's wearing. He's a great pilot, but this old girl challenges his prosthetics. He'll be sitting copilot on every flight and guiding you."

"Okay, I feel a lot better," the *Annie*'s pilot said.

"One more thing before I continue," Danny said, "One of you will be going with me to sit copilot and test the *Belle*'s new shuttle."

"If you're looking for the best shuttle pilot, that's a done deal," the *Pearl* pilot said. "It's Claudia."

"Without a doubt," the other male pilot agreed.

"Looks like you'll be stuck with me," Claudia added, throwing a quick smile at Danny.

"We'll see," Danny replied laconically, covering the thumping of his heart and his suddenly dry mouth.

After three days of training, the new pilots met Isley. He was a snow white-haired man, with two prosthetic arms, who'd also lost the right eye.

In addition, he walked with a heavy limp from a BRC operation that didn't take.

"You're probably happy I'm not sitting first position," Isley quipped, holding up his arms. "Well, if you screw up, I'll become your pilot, so keep that in mind." He looked at Danny and said, "I understand you're getting the best of these children. Which ones am I left to babysit?"

Each of the men raised a hand, and Isley growled, "Well, get your butts forward, and let's see what you've learned."

When Isley and the other two pilots disappeared into the forward cabin, Claudia looked at Danny and grinned. "You might have warned them about Isley."

"That's just Isley's style. He's making sure he has their attention," Danny replied.

"Well, he sure had mine," Claudia replied. "I've got my duffel at the rear. Are you packed to catch the next shuttle to the JOS?"

"Absolutely," Danny replied.

The pilots walked the terminal arm, their duffels over their backs. They were headed toward the axis to make their way down a second arm, which held the YIPS shuttle dock. For the first time in a long while, Danny wished to have his legs back. He thought he'd gotten used to having lost them, and Harbour's constant attention had done wonders for his acceptance. But struggling to keep up with Claudia made him feel inadequate, once again.

Claudia noticed Danny's hurried and uncertain gait. She stopped, faced him, and said, "Danny, this isn't going to work. We're headed to the JOS to fly a brand-new shuttle design. Something larger and more powerful than I've ever had my hands on. You and I have to form a team, and team members talk to each other. Like now, you should have told me to slow up."

"Understood," Danny replied quietly. He glanced around to ensure no one was within earshot. "There's something you should know. The reason that we're in a hurry to test this shuttle is because it's urgently needed."

"For what?" Claudia asked, checking left and right like Danny had done.

"The Jatouche intravertor is nearly ready, and the captain is hoping this ship can deliver the device to the surface," Danny replied.

"Wait one, Danny. Please tell me that we're not going to try to land on Pyre," Claudia said alarmed.

"No, not that," Danny replied quickly. "But we have to enter the atmosphere, achieve a stationary position, launch it, and then climb out."

"Oh, is that all?" Claudia asked, with mock relief. "Was this shuttle designed to do that?"

"Nope, but we're hoping it can," Danny replied. "It's an involved story, but the important point is that this information is for you and me only. Copy?"

"Aye, latched on," Claudia replied.

"We'd better get going if we want to catch the shuttle," Danny said, shouldering his duffel. "And, by the way, don't walk so fast."

Claudia's laughter warmed Danny, and concerns about his prosthetics were temporarily forgotten.

* * * *

Danny and Claudia met for a morning meal. They'd enjoyed some upscale cabins for the night, which Harbour had booked for them.

"Nicest accommodations I've ever had," Claudia said, as they enjoyed their food. "By the way, I meant to ask you who designed this shuttle."

"The architect's name is —" Danny started to say.

"No, no, I didn't mean that," Claudia interrupted. "I want to know who created the wish list that the architect followed. Whose baby is this?"

"I guess that's me," Danny replied, after taking a sip of his caf. "The captain said to be sure to get what I wanted."

"I'd love Captain Cinders to give me that sort of permission," Claudia opined. "How long have you known Captain Harbour?"

"I was a jockey pilot at the YIPS, when I lost my legs," Danny said, his eyes staring out, remembering events of the past. "I'd gotten my prosthetics and was laying up in a cheap, inward cabin, feeling sorry for myself. There was a rap on the door, and I told them to go away. Then I heard this woman's voice ask, 'Then you don't want the job?'"

Danny chuckled at the memories that flooded back, and Claudia prompted, "Go on. Don't leave me guessing."

"I was determined to shame this idiot at the door who didn't know I'd lost my legs," Danny continued. "I was wearing shorts and a T-shirt when I answered the door. I hit the door panel and could have smacked myself upside the head."

"Are you telling me Harbour was standing there?" Claudia asked.

"All one hundred percent of her in her filigreed skins," Danny affirmed.

"She does make an impressive sight, that woman," Claudia agreed. Her eyes tracked Danny's carefully for his response.

"That's true, but my thought, at that moment, was how stupid I must have looked," Danny replied. "So, I'm standing there, embarrassed beyond belief, and she says, 'How about you get dressed, and we get some food, while I talk about my offer.' But you know what I remember most clearly?"

"What?" Claudia queried.

"From the moment I opened the door, Captain Harbour never looked at my prosthetics. She stared into my eyes," Danny replied.

"Dreamy like?" Claudia teased, imitating the expression.

"Not hardly," Danny objected. "The captain has those gray eyes that tend to throw you off. When she looked at me, it was like she was challenging me, like she was saying, 'I dare you to get off your butt and prove yourself.'"

"Wow," Claudia murmured. "How did Harbour become the latest empath leader? I've understood from Ituau that the title is passed on."

"It is. Captain Harbour was once Celia O'Riley. I've been told that she arrived at the *Belle* as one unhappy child."

"Did she lose her parents?" Claudia asked.

"No, they gave her up. They couldn't handle her," Danny replied.

"Because of her power?"

"Yeah, the captain learned, as a young child, to manipulate the people around her. She was capable of using her gifts, without being detected, even before she reached puberty."

"Scary," Claudia commented, "a child who could manipulate adults to get what she wanted. What happened after she got aboard the *Belle?*"

"From what I've heard, it was touch and go for the first few years. Apparently, she was a handful."

"So, what brought her around?" Claudia asked.

"At that time, the Harbour was Lindsey Jabrook; she and the other empaths did the trick," Danny explained. "According to Yasmin, you can be a willful, powerful, empathetic child, but once surrounded by a host of empaths, you eventually succumb. Over the years, Celia mellowed and took her place among the empaths. Once she was fully trained, she became the *Belle*'s biggest coin earner. One out of three individuals I transported to the *Belle* were there to see her. Lindsey kept upping her price, and they kept coming."

"Why? Why not go to a less-expensive empath?" Claudia asked.

"According to Lindsey, the captain's ministrations lasted longer than others and, underneath her tough exterior, she's a kindhearted person. She did right by her clients to the best of her ability."

"Have you ever seen Captains Cinders and Harbour together?" Claudia asked, switching subjects.

"Yeah, it's a strange dance, isn't it?" Danny replied.

"Wonder what they're waiting for?" Claudia asked.

"I'd say they have more important things on their minds than each other," Danny replied.

"So, you don't think anything will happen?" Claudia pushed.

"Don't know, it might and it might not," Danny said, finishing his caf. "One thing for sure, I'm glad those two met. Pyre has needed a pair like that for too long. Come on. Let's go check out this new girl."

Danny and Claudia made their way to one of the older terminal arms that was reserved for delivery of new ships to owners. It charged the least amount of coin for docking services. New ships took time to complete, and the JOS wanted to help the new owners get their vessels into service, when they would represent much more income for the station.

Waiting outside the shuttle's gangway were the architect, the two chief construction engineers, and a fourth individual who Danny didn't know.

After introductions, Danny learned that the fourth person was the pilot, who would familiarize them with the controls.

"How much flight time has the shuttle had?" Danny asked.

"None," the architect replied. "We conducted engine and control system tests at the YIPS. When the hull was finished, sealed, and the engines installed, we shipped everything over here to end the exorbitant assembly charges from the YIPS. It was cheaper to dock the hull here and complete the interior."

"We've run checks on everything, multiple times," an engineer said. "The engines, of course, at the YIPS, and the electronics here at the JOS."

"Let's see what you have," Danny said, turning and heading up the gangway.

"I'm sure that Captain Harbour will be pleased with what we've constructed," the other engineer said.

"If you make me happy, the captain will be," Danny replied firmly.

"Yes, indeed," the architect said to placate Danny.

"Shades of Isley," Claudia whispered to Danny, as she walked up the gangway.

Once Danny and Claudia entered the shuttle's main aisle, they came to a halt. The interior was a complete contrast to the utilitarian nature of mining shuttles and the ancient ship that Danny piloted. The interior was pristine and well lit. The seats were nicely padded and unmarred, awaiting their first passengers.

"I feel like we should have bought new skins to board this beauty," Claudia remarked.

"First impressions?" the architect asked anxiously from behind Danny.

"Pretty interior," Danny replied. "I hope she flies as well as she looks."

Danny and Claudia made their way forward, both of them casually touching the top of the seats to enjoy the coverings' texture. They were speechless in the pilot's cabin but for different reasons. Claudia was enjoying the updated panels, which resembled the array available on the bridge of a new mining ship. Danny was taken aback by the amount of automation that had replaced his outmoded, manual system.

Rather than display intimidation, Danny said gruffly, "Let's get to work. Pilot, walk us through the systems, and I mean from passenger loading and dock release through to arrival at a terminal arm. We can work on power, maneuverability, and emergency procedures next."

The architect and engineers quietly disappeared, while the three pilots got to work. It was Claudia who reminded the men when it was time for midday meal and that she expected to be fed. Unfortunately, her expectations of a nice meal were dashed when the men selected a standup eatery near the terminal arm's exit into the station.

For days, the three pilots went through training exercises, without engine power, letting the terminal arm's energy supply run their systems. One morning, when Danny felt ready, he slid his comm ear wig into place, strapped in, and contacted terminal arm management. Without a word, Claudia followed suit. The training pilot hurriedly occupied a third seat in the pilot's cabin.

The terminal manager wished Danny a safe flight. After days of training, Danny was beginning to enjoy much of the automation. With the touch of an icon on a panel located between Claudia and him, the hatch slid closed and the icon turned green, indicating a seal.

When the terminal manager indicated the gangway was clear and the crew had released services, Claudia said, "Generator online. All systems go."

Danny replied, "Employing jets," and gently directed the shuttle away from the arm, reversed orientation, and dropped away from the station.

"Smooth," Claudia commented, "I love the way the computer calculates velocity and measures the attitude jets' gas output."

"There's always manual, when emergency conditions call for it," the training pilot noted.

"Engines spinning up," Claudia called out, when the shuttle was clear of the JOS. She smiled at Danny and asked, "Where do you want to go for our first trip?"

"Circle the *Belle*," Danny replied. "Captain deserves to get a good look at her new shuttle."

"Appropriate," Claudia replied. "Should I program the flight?"

"Yes, I want to ensure that these automated functions will perform adequately," Danny replied.

Claudia hid her grin. Danny had never stopped playing Isley's role. She had to admit it kept the training pilot on his toes. He was working hard to please Danny.

"Full circle before returning to the JOS?" Claudia asked.

"I like that," Danny replied. "Program acceleration at fifty percent power. Invert before the *Belle* to slow us as we circle, and then invert us again for the return."

Claudia rapidly punched in commands to the navigation console. Danny was still becoming accustomed to the shuttle's automation, and he was doubly glad that he had chosen Claudia as his copilot. She was a whiz on the panels. What might have taken Danny minutes to puzzle through, she could do in seconds.

"Course programmed," Claudia said, when she finished.

"Execute," Danny replied and watched Claudia touch off an icon that she'd placed on the surface to run the program.

Danny felt the shuttle accelerate smoothly, and he leaned back in his, oh-so-comfortable pilot's chair. "I could get used to this," Danny said, eyeing Claudia settling into her chair.

"Which part?" Claudia asked, giving Danny a cheeky smile.

"*Belle* shuttle two, calling home base," Danny sent over the comm system, ignoring Claudia's tease.

"This is Birdie, at the *Belle*'s comm. You enjoying your new toy, Danny?"

Danny smiled to himself, allowing Claudia to reply first. "You bet he is, Birdie. Looks like a kid playing freefall for the first time."

"You have my sympathies, Claudia, having to sit second to that grump," Birdie said.

"Yeah, but flying this beauty makes up for a lot of it," Claudia quipped.

"If you two women are done gabbing, I'm requesting the captain," Danny said tartly.

Claudia glanced Danny's way and saw he was still smiling.

"She's aboard, wait one," Birdie said.

"Hello, Danny," Harbour said, after gaining the bridge.

"Captain, our new shuttle is on her maiden flight. I'm bringing her past the *Belle* in a flyby. Thought you might want to take a look at what your coin bought."

"Thoughtful of you, Danny," Harbour replied. "When you're done with your flyby, I want you to communicate with Olivia at the YIPS. She's been anxious to get a close look at the shuttle's undercarriage."

"Will do, Captain," Danny said quickly, not wanting Harbour to say anything that the training pilot, who was on the ship's comm, shouldn't hear.

-43-
Intravertor

Danny offered an excuse to the training pilot, as to why he was returning him to the JOS before he made the flight to the YIPS.

"I know these engineers," Danny told him. "They're going to pour over this shuttle for days, but you can ride with us if you don't mind hanging out at the YIPS."

"I'd rather not," the training pilot replied. "But, if I'm not aboard and you're flying her, the company will consider the shuttle as accepted. Are you willing to sign off on delivery?"

"Affirmative," Danny replied.

When they dropped the training pilot at the JOS, Danny called Harbour. "Captain, we had a company representative aboard, when you were talking to us. To get rid of him, I had to accept the shuttle. The final payment is due."

"Not a problem, Danny. You happy?" Harbour asked.

"I'm happy," Danny said, breaking into a smile.

"Then I'm good," Harbour replied.

"We're on our way to the YIPS, Captain," said Danny. "I'll let Olivia know. Shuttle out."

"Wow," Claudia exclaimed, staring at Danny, as if seeing him in a new light. "You weren't kidding when you said Captain Harbour told you to get what you wanted in the shuttle design."

Claudia had programmed their flight to the YIPS. It allowed Danny to lean back in his chair and return Claudia's gaze. "I'm not much for storytelling or outright prevarication. What you see is pretty much what you get."

Once they made the YIPS, Danny allowed the engineers several hours to examine the undercarriage, which they did by remote, while the shuttle was docked at a terminal arm. During that time, Danny and Claudia booked cabins, knowing they might be local for a while.

The next few weeks became a push and pull between Danny and Olivia. She wanted the engineers to have more time to study the shuttle, attach the hooks for the sled, and run tests on the shuttle. In contrast, Danny wanted the maximum time with the shuttle to discover its power, maneuverability, and control systems. Neither of them ended up with what they wanted, but compromises became the norm for the weeks thanks to Claudia's efforts as chief negotiator.

The time arrived when Danny was satisfied with the ship's capabilities, and Olivia announced to Harbour that they were ready to launch the intravertor.

Harbour, Tacticnok, and Jaktook made the flight to the YIPS for the momentous moment.

Danny brought the shuttle around to the assembly bay. The engines were shut down, and he maneuvered with attitude jets. The bay doors were open, and the pilots could see the engineers and techs in vac suits, highlighted in the bay's lights.

"Position stable," Claudia reported, when the distance from the YIPS held.

"Keep an eye on that, Claudia," Danny said, "The YIPS occasionally fires its jets to maintain position and doesn't announce it to anyone, except to the pilots on approach or launching from an arm. I don't think it's been shared with YIPS management that we're back here, loading this device."

Two jockey sleds were used to nudge the intravertor and its sled out of the bay toward the shuttle.

Claudia used a central panel to display an external vid of the device. "Why does it look bigger now?" she asked.

"Because, now we have to carry it, not the YIPS," Danny replied. He was staring at the same image as Claudia, and he had a sinking feeling about the mission.

"You know, it'd be a shame to make a successful drop of the intravertor and not make it out of the atmosphere, especially since she's brand new," Danny said.

"Don't talk like that, Danny," Claudia fired back. "We're going to make it work. Besides, you owe me a drink at the cantina, and I aim to collect."

"I owe you a drink?" Danny asked. "How do you figure?"

"Because I want you to buy me one," Claudia said, smiling invitingly for him.

"Oh," Danny replied. "Good a reason as any, I guess"

"That's the charmer I've come to know," Claudia said, laughing.

Harbour and Tacticnok were standing in an adjacent office, watching the proceedings behind the room's blast windows. Jaktook chose to don a vac suit and record the event from the vantage point of the bay doors overlooking the operation.

"You know Drigtik is upset with you," Tacticnok said to Harbour.

"I know," said Harbour.

"Drigtik believes that it's unwise that an engineer of his caliber isn't aboard the shuttle for this crucial test," added Tacticnok.

"And I understand," Harbour replied. "However, this is a dangerous flight, and the last thing I need is a member of your race being killed trying to help us, when it can be prevented. If anyone is to die, it must be humans only."

"And that's why you'd make a great emissary, Captain," Tacticnok said, staring up at Harbour. "You see that the way to forge an alliance must be taken carefully. Let us hope that there is no concern for any of our citizens."

The engineers received an acknowledgment from the shuttle. A ship's panel reported solid linkage with the sled and signaled connection to the intravertor's generator. Olivia turned to Harbour and gave her a thumbs up. In turn, Harbour sent a short message to Jessie, who was in another interminably boring negotiations meeting.

Throughout the recent weeks, Jessie had all but caved to the demands of the family heads. He allowed their constant pressures to appear to be winning. It was with extraordinary relief when he pulled up his comm unit and read: *Charades are over. Tune into our broadcast.*

"Major, can we get the *Belle*'s broadcast in this room?" Jessie asked, interrupting Idrian.

"Assuredly," Liam replied. He jumped up from the table, happy to stretch his legs, swung a wall monitor toward the group, and set it to display the requested channel.

Due to the colony ship's proximity to the station, the broadcast contained both vid and audio.

Around the negotiations table was heard, "This is Captain Harbour. We're at the YIPS, watching the final moments of the intravertor's loading under the *Belle*'s new shuttle. By an unplanned, yet marvelous, coincidence, this recently tested ship is the only Pyrean vessel capable of delivering the intravertor to the surface. The mission requires the shuttle to drop tail first into the atmosphere, release the intravertor, and climb out again. Unfortunately, it's not known if the shuttle, which is piloted by Danny Thompson and copiloted by Claudia Manning, will be able to complete the maneuver successfully."

Pics of Danny and Claudia appeared on monitors across Pyre, and everywhere spacers cheered the courage and incredible roles being played by two of their own in the attempt to resurrect the planet.

During Harbour's broadcast, Lise stared at Jessie in anger, and he refused to acknowledge her. From behind Jessie, he heard a polite snicker from Henry, and, in front of him, Liam was trembling, as he tried to control his laughter, which itched to burst from him.

Lise mumbled several expletives under her breath, and Idrian and Rufus appeared to be in shock at the unexpected turn of events. The only one who seemed to be unperturbed was Dorelyn. Out of the corner of Jessie's eye, he caught her watching him.

Harbour managed her commentary via her comm unit, bouncing it through the YIPS to the *Belle*. On the bridge of the colony ship, Birdie was enjoying herself. On the fly, she spliced together imagery from various views provided by Jaktook, the bay techs, the sled jockeys, and the shuttle for the broadcast.

"Once the shuttle is underway," Harbour continued. "We'll have a long-range vid pickup trained on the ship until we lose sight of it in the atmosphere. Throughout the mission, we'll have the audio pickup from the pilot's cabin. We're awaiting the outcome of this incredible event and hoping for the safe return of our people."

Across Pyre, those who were able were glued to monitors to watch and wait.

In the negotiations room, Lise stood in a huff, slapping the back of her chair. Hate for Jessie poured from her eyes. She was on the verge of saying something, when she suddenly spun around and marched out of the room.

Idrian and Rufus glanced toward Dorelyn, who nodded toward the door. As the men exited, Dorelyn gave Jessie the merest of smiles. "It's been a pleasure watching you work, Captain," Dorelyn said. "I'm looking forward to the next time we cross paths." Her smile grew brighter, but her eyes denied that it was meant to be taken as friendly. She nodded to Henry and Liam and then followed the others out of the room.

Emerson had no intention of being left alone in the room with those arrayed against him. He hurried to follow Dorelyn out the door.

"Is it my imagination," Henry asked, "or did Dorelyn Gaylan just threaten you, Jessie?"

"That's a whole different kind of family head," Liam added. "A type we haven't seen before."

"Agreed," Jessie said. "I wonder if there are others like her."

Birdie picked up the image of the shuttle, as it rounded the YIPS. She focused the long-range vid on it. For the Pyreans, it was their first look at the tremendous size of the device, which the engineers had built. The intravertor and sled appeared too great a mass for the sleek, new shuttle. If the ship were to descend into the atmosphere, gravity might drag it to its death.

A foolish patron in the Starlight went so far as to offer to take bets that the shuttle wouldn't make its return trip. Two patrons left his table, and an attendant pretended to be bumped and spilled a drink in his lap.

On Harbour's cue, Birdie cut to the shuttle's audio feed. Audiences were treated to long silences and short statements as Danny and Claudia constantly checked and rechecked their systems. Then quiet reigned for nearly three hours. Work in the domes, stations, and aboard ships ground to a halt, while people listened intently for the next sounds.

Eventually, Claudia broke the silence, saying, "Inversion point in two minutes."

"Confirmed," Danny said. "Standby for rotation."

"Countdown's on the panel," said Claudia.

Danny watched the readout run down to zero. His finger hovered over a single icon on his panel. It was programmed to smoothly flip the shuttle end over end. Danny missed flying by the joystick, as he did the old shuttle. However, under these circumstances, with gravity at play and a heavy load attached to the undercarriage, he was happy to let the engineers' programming fly the ship.

At zero, Danny touched the icon. "Turning over," he announced.

Claudia monitored their change in trajectory. When the shuttle finished its rotation, she said, "Inversion complete. We're on course."

On monitors, Pyreans and Jatouche watched the image of the shuttle fade as it entered the thickened atmosphere.

Once again, Harbour's voice was added over the broadcast. "Let me explain the reason the shuttle must drop far into the atmosphere. The intravertor has a swath of vanes, which spin around the device's middle at high speed. They serve two major functions. The first is to ensure the intravertor descends in a vertical position. To make this happen, the shuttle must drop the device, while standing on its tail. This allows the intravertor time to deploy the vanes before it begins to tumble. Once the vanes are in motion, they will keep the intravertor in a vertical orientation. The vanes won't halt the descent of the intravertor. They're programmed to allow the intravertor to strike the ground with enough force to penetrate several meters."

When Harbour ended her explanation, there was no word from the pilot's cabin. The audience strained their ears. Then the distinct sound of a kiss was heard and a voice said, "That's in case we don't make it back."

"Shut down engines," Danny said.

"Engines offline," Claudia reported.

"Prepare the intravertor," Danny ordered.

Claudia tapped an icon on her primary panel. It set in motion a series of events. The intravertor's generator came online, and system checks were run by the device's computer. Claudia's icon turned from red to green, and she reported, "All systems go. Intravertor ready to deploy."

"Release the device," Danny ordered. His voice was steady, but the pitch was little higher. The shuttle continued to drop toward the surface, accelerating from the increasing pull of gravity and the engines offline.

"Intravertor away," Claudia said. Her voice showed stress too.

The sled mechanism launched the intravertor past the aft end of the shuttle to enable it to clear the shuttle's engines when they fired. To ensure there was clearance, Danny used up some precious seconds, crabbing the shuttle sideways with his attitude jets.

"The intravertor is clear," Claudia announced, a little loudly.

Danny called out, "Firing engines. Pushing them to one hundred percent."

Everywhere, Pyreans and Jatouche were frozen, waiting for the next report. When it came, it wasn't good news.

"We're decelerating, but still descending," Claudia reported. She was monitoring their program, which reported their altitude in comparison to a red, no-return line on a graph.

There was a short silence. Then Claudia called out, "Danny, we've got two point three minutes to end our descent before we'll be too deep in the atmosphere to climb out."

"Paranoia is a beautiful thing," Danny mumbled to himself. Then loudly, he called out, "Lose the sled. Fire the bolts."

It had been Danny's idea to ensure that the shuttle could shed the weight of the sled, if necessary. The engineers said that their calculations proved that it wouldn't be necessary and that Danny was worrying for no reason. However, Danny persisted in his request, while the engineers stood firm.

It took Harbour to resolve the argument, which she did by saying, "Danny, the engineers are convinced of their science. So, I suggest Claudia and you sit out the flight and let them deliver the device." She gazed over the line of engineers, adding, "Which two of you are volunteering?" When no one stepped forward, she said, "Then, since it's the butts of Danny and Claudia on the line, I suggest you stop arguing and heed the pilots' request."

"Sled's away," Claudia reported. "Descent is slowing. Approaching point of no return in one and a half minutes."

"Pushing engines to one hundred ten percent," Danny said, the strain evident in his voice.

"Engine temperatures rising, but holding within constraints," Claudia said, keeping a close eye on the panel's readout. Part of her mind was screaming that it was a ridiculous thing to do, but she couldn't help herself. In that moment, that was her duty, and her years of experience were grounding her.

The audiences held their collective breaths. Many had set their comm units to follow the shuttle's countdown. They shared their readouts with others, when the time passed and continued to grow. Over the monitors, they heard Danny murmuring to the shuttle, as if it was his lover. He was urging her to climb, whispering endearing words to her.

Claudia's excited voice broke into the clear. "Zero descent speed." Moments later, she added, "We're accelerating."

Humans and aliens cheered, clapped, hugged, and slapped backs. Noisiest of all were the spacers in the Miner's Pit.

"One hundred knots and still accelerating," Claudia announced, after a while.

"Powering back to ninety percent," Danny replied. The relief in his voice was obvious. "We're coming home, Captain," he added and reached out a hand to Claudia, who grabbed it and held it tightly.

Audiences were unable to turn away from the broadcast. They waited for confirmation of two events. The first of which came when the *Belle*'s long-range vid picked up the shuttle, as a speck, breaking though the atmospheric haze.

In an unusual display for human and alien, Harbour rested an arm across Tacticnok's shoulders, and the shorter alien encircled the captain's waist with her arm.

During the shuttle's venture to the planet and into the atmosphere, the YIPS assembly bay was sealed, and the crew had stripped off their suits. Drigtik witnessed the leaders' embrace and nudged Gatnack, who turned to observe it.

Gatnack responded, "Relationships are made in this way, my young engineer. Trials that test bonds prove an alliance's strength."

Harbour picked up the broadcast's narration, which audiences were hoping she would do. "Our shuttle has safely returned to space but will probably need an overhaul after that flight. Next on the broadcast are the key engineers responsible for the deployment of this device. There were tens of engineers and techs working on it, at any one time. But the primary responsibilities fell to two of our new friends, Gatnack and Drigtik."

The Jatouche engineers perked up at the mention of their names, which they heard through the broadcasting monitor. Further enthralling them was the appearance of their images.

"In addition," Harbour continued, "three human engineers, Olivia Harden, Bryan Forshaw, and Pete Jennings, were the primary administrators for the YIPS personnel."

Olivia held her breath when her image appeared. It was taken from the healthy side of her face. Then she turned forward, and the image held for a moment before it changed to that of Pete and Bryan. Olivia chuckled. She realized she was too proud of their achievement to care about her appearance.

"Olivia, over to you," Harbour said.

"Thank you, Captain," Olivia replied.

Birdie had managed the audio switching without missing a beat. "I love this," the bridge crew heard her say.

"We're receiving signals from the intravertor, which indicates its status," Olivia explained, and Birdie picked up the vid imagery from Pete's comm unit, which was focused on the engineers' panels. "Power for the intravertor is supplied by a Jatouche generator. We know that the vanes are deployed and revolving at an incredible speed. The device's descent is slowing, and it appears the intravertor will reach a safe implant speed. It's designed to strike the ground and bury itself a few meters deep. Then metal tendrils, located in the lowest section, will extend."

While the engineers waited for touchdown, Olivia explained the mechanisms by which the intravertor would operate. It was obvious to Pyreans that humans might have supplied the shuttle and some parts of the device, but the ingenious working of this incredible invention belonged to the Jatouche.

"Impact," Olivia reported, interrupting her running lecture. "Wait one. We have a signal. It's strong. The tendrils have been activated and are deploying."

Everyone was forced to wait for the next phase to be reported. Three hours later, Olivia came online, saying, "The tendrils are fully deployed. They've located numerous hot pockets within the surface. The generator is now being driven by this heat. Phase three is complete."

This time there was only a slight delay before Olivia announced, "The vanes have rotated and are fixed in their new orientation."

Each of Olivia's next reports were spaced a few minutes apart: "They're revolving again. Rotation has reached programmed rpm. The filter is reporting intake of gases and particulate matter. It will take a little while before we see output. According to the Jatouche, the intravertor struck one of the planet's greater hotspots, which is promising."

An hour and a half later, Olivia was online, once again. "The infuser has been activated. It's solidifying the particulate matter and selected, unwanted gases into pellets. These pellets should ... yes, the pellets are flying. They're flying!"

Olivia's jubilant celebration echoed out of monitors around Pyre. When she could regain control, she said in a gasping breath, "For the planet, that's the final phase of the intravertor. It's operating successfully. We're now moving to the panel that displays the signals from the YIPS microwave receiver. The Jatouche anticipated that the odds were slim that the intravertor would find a hot enough surface pocket to generate sufficient excess energy to transmit a microwave signal through the atmosphere. Sorry, everyone, but we're waiting again."

It wasn't long before Olivia said, "There it is, weak but constant. With one intravertor planted in the right place, the YIPS will be receiving about four percent of the power it needs to run line three. If you care to invest in the planet's resurrection, I suggest you donate more coin to the Pyrean Green account. We're going to need more intravertors unless everyone wants to wait a lot more generations for this happen."

-44-
Heroes

Knowing Danny would return to the *Belle*, Harbour, Tacticnok, and Jaktook hurried to catch a ride on the next flight of the colony ship's old shuttle from the YIPS.

When the *Belle* loomed in Danny's slender, forward view window, he heaved a sigh of relief.

"The first time I saw this ship," Danny said, "I was in Harbour's care. She'd rescued me from a dark place, and I was feeling hopeful once again. Seeing this old girl now brings back memories. For a moment there, in Pyre's atmosphere, when we passed the engineer's no return estimate, I thought I'd never see her again."

"I never had much thought for this ship one way or the other," Claudia replied. "My life has always been the stations and mining ships. When the captains teamed up, it seemed to open a whole new world. What spacer wouldn't enjoy visiting a cantina and a having a nice cabin for a sleepover, while working at Emperion? But, after today, my life will never be the same, and I'll always think of this ship as home, whether I'm working here or not."

"You will be, Claudia. I'm not stupid enough to think I can fly this shuttle by myself. The captains just have to approve your transfer, if you want the job," Danny said.

"Oh, for the love of Pyre, are you kidding? Of course, I want the job," Claudia declared. "Wait! Are we going to be making more intravertor drops?"

"What do you think?" Danny asked.

"I think I've some more suggestions for the engineers," Claudia retorted.

"Me too," Danny agreed, chuckling. He guided the shuttle into one of the colony ship's bays. Once air pressure was normal, Danny and Claudia trooped down the gangway. They could see faces peering at them through the airlock windows, but the pilots kept them waiting. They walked slowly around the shuttle pointing to hull areas and discussing the damage. The pristine hull coat was scoured, as if the shuttle had seen years of rough service. When they were done, they exited the bay through the airlock.

Danny managed to say, "Captain, sorry, I dinged up our new shuttle," before Harbour threw her arms around him and smothered him with a wave of joy that embarrassed Danny.

"I never managed to put that expression on his face," Claudia quipped. However, when Harbour gave her the same treatment, Claudia's expression turned goofy, and she said, "Okay. That was almost worth risking my life to feel."

"Congratulations. We're extremely proud of you," Harbour said, continuing to share her feelings of admiration. "I think you have a welcome party waiting for you in the cantina."

"Perfect," Claudia chimed. "Danny, you can buy me that drink you owe me."

Along the corridor, the pilots were congratulated by spacers, empaths, and residents. The gauntlet of empaths was an incredible experience for them. They were inundated by shades of supportive emotions, flooding through them.

"I feel drunk already," Claudia said to Danny after they cleared the line of well-wishers.

"It's a heady experience," Danny agreed, the grin so wide on his face that it was starting to hurt.

The pilots entered the cantina to a heroes' welcome. They were greeted in an assortment of ways and urged toward the bar. Spacers hoisted Danny and Claudia up to sit them atop the bar. Drinks were pressed in their hands, and, when Danny pulled his comm unit to pay, he was booed.

"You two are drinking for free this evening," Ituau yelled over the din. "Put your device away, Danny."

Claudia leaned over to project her voice into Danny's ear. "This doesn't get you off the hook," she said. "You still owe me one."

Dingles' whistle broke over the noise, and the cantina quieted. "Our esteemed first mate has a question," he said. He flourished his hand toward Ituau.

In a loud voice so the entire cantina could hear, Ituau said, "We were wondering which one of you kissed the other. My bet is on Claudia, but others think Danny did it."

Claudia raised a hand, ducking her head in embarrassment. A chorus of laughter and jeers accompanied her admission.

"In all fairness, I thought we were going to die," Claudia shouted back. "Besides, I had to find some way to buck my pilot up. He looked like he was going to fold under the pressure."

When the crowd guffawed and booed Claudia, she relented. "Okay, it might have been for other reasons," she admitted, grinning, and the crowd cheered and stomped their approval of that answer.

While the festivities were underway in the cantina, Harbour strolled slowly through the *Belle*'s corridors with Tacticnok. There were many hints shared by the royal daughter that gave Harbour an idea of the worlds to which the Jatouche had journeyed, but there had never been a solid overview.

"Tacticnok, are the members of the alliance equal?"

"By the charter that each race has acknowledged, we are, but some are more equal than others," Tacticnok replied cryptically.

Harbour's impression, given to her by the expression on Tacticnok's face, was that the Jatouche were far from foremost in the alliance.

"Then, let me ask you this, Tacticnok: Are all the sentient races, which the Jatouche have met, members of the alliance?"

"We wish it were so, Captain, but the Messinants, in their hubris, made mistakes, egregious mistakes. More than one alliance member has to contend with unwelcome visitors who've learned to operate their end of the gate pair."

"Do the Jatouche —" Harbour began, but the question died at Tacticnok's upraised hands.

The small alien faced the captain. "I've said more than my father would have permitted had he known. This information is for you and your confidant."

"Confidant?" Harbour asked.

"Every leader must have one, Harbour, to whom they can confide and who can provide honest counsel. I would imagine yours in Captain Cinders."

Before Harbour could reply, Tacticnok flashed her teeth and said in a joyous voice, "Come now. I would visit the cantina and witness the celebrations. Fruit juice!"

* * * *

"You're saying there's no monitoring necessary?" Olivia asked Drigtik, seeking to clarify his statement.

"Not of our device, Olivia," Drigtik replied.

"It's not like we could do anything about it, if there were a problem," Bryan riposted.

"What if it fell over and the microwave beam hit a dome?" Pete asked.

"The intravertor has a stabilizer sensor," Drigtik explained. "If it tilts more than a few degrees, the microwave transmission will shut down. If the device falls over, it will cease operating, before it touches the surface."

"You've thought of a lot," Olivia admitted.

Gatnack, who wasn't one for wasting words, said, "The Jatouche build well."

"Then that's it. Time to pack up your team and your gear," Olivia said, a sudden sadness clenching her chest.

"Yes, we'll be ready soon, Olivia. Will you join Pete and Bryan to journey with us to the gate? Gatnack and I would wish it," Drigtik asked.

"I'd love to accompany you to Triton," Olivia replied. "I'll talk to Evan Pendleton for some time off and request passage with Captain Harbour."

"Not necessary, Olivia," Gatnack replied. "Both have given their permission. Come. Let's see you packed." He ambled off, and Drigtik raised his furry eyebrows at Olivia.

"You've been busy," Olivia said.

"Efficiency. It's an engineer's watch word, Olivia. Let's not keep old Gatnack waiting. You know how he gets."

It took less than a day for the Jatouche to recover their equipment from the YIPS. It was carried in the belly of the old shuttle, which could more easily accommodate the remaining crates. There were quite a few less than had been carried on the journey from Triton. Much of the containers' contents was now on the surface of Pyre, sucking up heat, spitting out fused pellets of pollutants, and shooting excess energy to the YIPS.

When the Jatouche and Pyrean personnel were ready to transfer to the *Belle*, Danny and Claudia, whose transfer was approved, did the honors via the new shuttle.

Gatnack was the first to climb aboard. He took in the new interior and nodded in appreciation. "This transport I heartily approve," he said.

"Will it be able to land on Triton?" Drigtik asked.

"According to Danny, it's prepared to do just that," Bryan replied.

"Here I was lamenting the loss of our home world's comforts, and Pyreans are beginning to provide upgrades. Should we stay, Gatnack?" Drigtik asked.

"I've had enough excitement for a few annuals, my young engineer. I'm anxious for home," Gatnack replied.

When the elderly engineer settled into one of the shuttle's plush seats with a heavy sigh, Olivia and Drigtik exchanged concerned glances. The effort of the last few months had cost Gatnack a great deal.

* * * *

While the engineers, the techs, and the spacers made the transfers to the *Belle* and Jessie readied his ships, Harbour and Tacticnok shared a celebratory dinner in the captain's quarters. The conversation was light, while they were being served. When the plates and glasses were removed, Harbour accepted a brandy, and Tacticnok relished her favorite fruit juice concoction. They adjourned to the study, where Harbour threw the twin couch seats on the floor.

"I've meant to ask you, Tacticnok, your race is called the Jatouche, but none of your names are similar to this word. How did you come to be called this?" Harbour asked, slipping off her deck boots and stretching out on the pallet. She was enjoying this method of conversation. The postures tended to eliminate a discussion's more aggressive actions, such as hand waving, fist thumping, or arm motions, in general.

"It wasn't our choice, Harbour. Jatouche is a Messinant word. It's what they called us. From early times, before records were kept, ancestors handed down stories of Messinants' visits to our planets. It's been told they observed us over the course of many generations."

"Did they assist you, in any way?" Harbour asked.

"Not that the stories said. They merely watched us develop," replied Tacticnok in a desultory fashion.

"You don't sound as if you admire them," Harbour said, carefully observing Tacticnok for her reaction. She was tempted to read the royal daughter, but realized she'd have no basis from which to compare what she sensed.

"Why should we?" Tacticnok said with heat. "We've come to understand that the Messinants were involved in some grand scheme of genetic tinkering. They spent eons playing with the creatures of many worlds to see how effectively they could introduce intelligence and speech. Then they stood back to monitor their experiments."

"Do you have any idea why the Messinants did this?" Harbour asked.

"Races have postulated more theories than you could imagine, Harbour," Tacticnok replied. "The most popular is that the Messinants lived enormously long lives. Therefore, they didn't procreate frequently. In which case, they needed a larger number of sentient individuals to do their bidding."

"Is that a theory that you subscribe to, Tacticnok?" asked Harbour.

The royal daughter merely cocked her head to the side and back, as if to say it made no difference to her. Then she pulled on her glass straw for another sip of her juice.

Something Tacticnok had said earlier to her about unwanted guests coming through the gates caused Harbour to have a dark thought and decided to give it voice. "It makes you wonder how many of their experiments produced negative results."

"You needn't wonder," Tacticnok cackled. "There have been a sufficient number to antagonize many of us."

Harbour waited for Tacticnok to say more, but she didn't. "Where do you think the Messinants went, when they left?" she asked.

"This is unknown, Harbour. None of the races we've met have seen them for more annuals than can be counted. It's assumed that, at some point, they grew tired of their scheme and left the experiments to their fates."

"How do the Jatouche and the other races feel about that?"

"How do humans feel about Pyre and their existence here?" Tacticnok rejoined.

It was Harbour's turn to offer a limited reply. She said, "It is what it is, and we've got to make the best of it."

"Just so," Tacticnok replied. Her straw made a sucking sound, as the drink was finished. There was a slightly disgusted expression on the little alien's face, and Harbour was unsure whether that was from the empty juice glass or her opinion of the Messinants' desertion of the races they uplifted.

* * * *

On the evening before the ships sailed, Jessie visited with Harbour aboard the *Belle*.

"Looks like we're back in the slush business," Jessie said, enjoying his brandy with his feet comfortably resting on a stool in the captain's study.

"Only four percent of the energy supply for a single line," Harbour lamented. "I guess that's something, but I was hoping for a little more."

"That's for one intravertor, at the present time," Jessie replied. "Plant some more, clear the air a bit, and you'll improve transmission."

"That's easy to say," Harbour rejoined, sitting in a chair facing Jessie, "except more intravertors means more Jatouche equipment."

"You've requested more, haven't you?" Jessie asked.

"Where do you come up with these sorts of questions, Jessie?" Harbour asked, aghast. "You expect me to go up to Tacticnok and say, 'Thanks for your help. Your fantastical experiment worked. When can we expect the next shipment?'"

Jessie delivered a cross between a grimace and a shrug, and Harbour laughed at the absurdity of his question and his response.

"Listen, my confidant —" Harbour started.

"Your what?" Jessie interjected.

"Oh, yes, Tacticnok said every leader must have a confidant, and, according to her, you're mine," Harbour replied tartly. "Now, as I started to say, I think we've developed the wrong impression of the Jatouche."

"How so?" Jessie asked, suddenly attentive to Harbour's words.

"My impression has been of this superior race, with advanced technology, who's engaged in some incredible alliance and whose members are connected via a series of gates," Harbour summarized.

"Agreed," Jessie replied. "What's your pic now?"

"I think the characterizations of the technology and the gates are accurate, but not the alliance."

"Oh, interesting," Jessie said, sitting up.

"Bits and pieces of things Tacticnok and Jaktook have said, during the time they've been with us, have me thinking," Harbour replied. "The most interesting comment she said recently was that there's little respect for the Messinants."

"From the alliance?" Jessie asked.

"I don't know about that, but certainly from the Jatouche. She's said the Messinants have made some big mistakes."

"Mistakes? When? How?" Jessie asked.

"We were discussing the alliance and its membership, and Tacticnok said many of the races had to deal with unwelcome guests. She implied that some of the uplifted species, who aren't members of the alliance, still attempt to use the gates."

"I wonder if it's a matter of poor visitation manners or something a lot worse," Jessie mused.

"It got me thinking about the alliance in terms of Pyre," Harbour said.

"You mean our political mess?" Jessie asked.

"Exactly. Who says that technology makes everything better?"

"It improves the quality of life," Jessie argued.

Harbour nodded her agreement and said. "And yet, does it make for better relationships or does it just embolden the powerful?"

"Good question. Did Tacticnok say anything else?"

"Yes, I was asking about the alliance members and if they were equal. My intent was to discover whether we would be junior members or some sort of lesser category if we were to join. Tacticnok replied that all members are supposedly equal by approval of a charter, but that some members are more equal than others. And here's the important part, Jessie. I got the feeling that the Jatouche are not one of the highly regarded members."

"With their technology?" Jessie asked, incredulous at the concept. "That's frightening."

"I wonder if it's not a matter of who has the greater technology, Jessie, and I've been trying to see us through the eyes of the Jatouche." Harbour said, sitting up too. "Ask yourself why the Jatouche came here, Jessie, besides checking out to see if the Gasnarians repaired the gate."

"You mean when they didn't appear to get anything out of it?" Jessie replied. "I was too focused on the operation and keeping the governor and family heads at bay while we reached the endpoint, I guess."

"By the way, well done there," Harbour said, hoisting her crystal glass to Jessie. "You'll have to tell me about those meetings when you get an opportunity. But, back on the subject of the Jatouche. Did they get nothing out of this entire process?" she asked.

"Not much more than our goodwill," Jessie replied. He made the comment offhand, but when Harbour's eyebrows went up, he considered what he'd said. "Ah, I see where you're going. There's this big alliance with various degrees of equality, and the Jatouche don't have a big piece of it. They find us ... this backward race ... and hope to develop allies."

"I think that's a simplistic description, Jessie," Harbour said, sitting back in her chair and taking a sip on her brandy.

Jessie was intrigued. It was obvious that Harbour had been mulling over these subjects for a while and was earnestly trying to assimilate the elements into a cohesive image.

"Educate me," Jessie requested, hoping to help Harbour coalesce her thoughts by speaking them out loud.

"If you were a race among many, who didn't hold an equal level of respect from some of the others, what options are open to you?" Harbour asked.

"Fight for your rights, invent a superior technology, discover resources that everyone covets, or ..." Jessie froze in midsentence.

"What? What're you thinking?" Harbour queried.

"I was going to say or find a powerful ally, but that's not us," Jessie replied.

"Maybe because you're thinking like a man," Harbour teased.

"Ouch," Jessie replied, smiling at the jest. "What's the female's point of view, if I might deign to be annotated with such a rare gift?" When Harbour frowned at his choice of words, Jessie said, "I heard that in a vid and always wanted to use it in conversation."

Harbour laughed, and then her face took on a serious countenance. "Remember, that Tacticnok spoke of an emissary visiting her world, when she was describing the first steps toward alliance membership."

"And it was a female who visited us," Jessie said, lightly smacking his forehead.

"Yes, and a royal member at that," Harbour added. "We have to ask ourselves why she would see us as valuable allies."

"My impression is that the Jatouche are a gentle race," Jessie replied, his brain kicked in gear by Harbour's musings. "They would see us surviving and slowly progressing under extremely difficult circumstances. Wait ... Jaktook once said that he wondered if the Jatouche would have survived on Pyre under similar conditions."

"Now, put that together with the concerns of Tacticnok, Jaktook, and, especially, Jittak, as to whether humans could be trusted," Harbour added. "In addition, Tacticnok and Jaktook wanted to make certain that we were the leaders who could make the decisions necessary to ensure the implementation of their intravertor."

"I think that last part was our test," Jessie posited.

"I'd agree," Harbour replied. "It came when the Jatouche learned our language from you and your crew via the console's programmed queries, which had to be Messinants' filtering for potential interspecies relationships."

"And we passed," Jessie said with pride.

"Then Aurelia slipped and things changed," Harbour said, shaking her head at serendipity.

"Are you thinking they changed for the worst?" asked Jessie.

"Oh, no, at least not for Tacticnok," Harbour hurriedly replied. "For Jittak, yes, I'm afraid, and I wonder what he'll tell his superiors."

"Especially after that stunt he pulled on the bridge," Jessie added. He thought to summarize their train of thought by saying, "So Tacticnok sees qualities in humans that she admires ... our perseverance, our lovable personalities." Jessie couldn't help throwing that in, and he grinned at Harbour's wince, which was followed by her lips curving in a tiny smile. "And your empaths," he finished. "So where do we go from here?"

"As far as we're concerned, nowhere," Harbour said. "According to Tacticnok, the next step is on their side, and it involves His Excellency Rictook."

"Hmm, going to be an interesting presentation of counterviews between Tacticnok and Jittak's superiors," Jessie posited.

"You know, it's all rather anticlimactic," Harbour said, finishing her brandy, and twirling the crystal glass to see the reflections from the overhead lights. "I mean, one moment we're meeting aliens, creating a marvelous device, and taking the first step to rescue our planet, and, the next moment we're back to slinging slush."

"Well, let me offer you a pragmatic way to look at this," Jessie offered, finishing his drink. "Despite what we raised to cover the YIPS costs, how's your general fund doing? Because my company account is low."

"Mine too," Harbour replied. "Paying for YIPS cabins, laying out stipends, purchasing the shuttle, and now overhauling it has emptied it of a great deal of coin."

"So, we sling slush," Jessie said.

"Ready when you are, Captain," Harbour replied. "You taking your ships directly to Emperion?"

"I think we can fill the *Pearl* before you arrive and send that ship on to the YIPS. We can probably do that several more times before your ship's full, especially since our crews are accomplished at the process. Any concerns about handling the return of the Jatouche?"

"If you'd asked me that two years ago, I'd have wondered if you'd lost your mind, making me the responsible party."

"Lot's happened in two years," Jessie agreed. He stood, walked to the study's door, reached for the latch, but Harbour's hand held it shut.

"I'd like my kiss here," Harbour said, in a husky voice. "It'll be a long dry period until Emperion," she added, with a little smile.

"And I'd like one with a taste of your emotions," Jessie replied.

Harbour's face was close to Jessie's, but she pulled back to study his eyes. Thoughts warred in her head. She desperately wanted to oblige Jessie's request but felt it was too early in their relationship. "Not yet, Jessie. Maybe someday," Harbour replied.

"I'll leave the timing in your hands, Harbour. You're the expert," Jessie said, leaning across the short space to kiss her.

-45-
Decorations

During the trip to Triton, the weeks passed comfortably for the individuals aboard the *Belle*. It wasn't uncommon to see a Pyrean teasing a Jatouche, and the furry alien giving as good as he or she got. The camaraderie that had developed between the races, over the months, would have seemed extraordinary to most outside observers, but the reality was that spacers, engineers, and techs, of both races, were results-oriented individuals. Together, they'd accomplished something wondrous, and they were immersed in a great sense of satisfaction.

A few days out from the moon, Tacticnok requested a private meeting with Harbour, and they adjourned to the study and their usual arrangement of pallets made from the couch seats.

"There's something important to discuss with you, Harbour," Tacticnok said. "I apologize for the lateness of this request. I had hoped to make this offer myself, sometime in the future, but I've been implored to do this now. Gatnack and Drigtik wish to invite Olivia, Pete, and Bryan to return to our home world with us."

Harbour fought to keep her composure, and she worked to order her thoughts. "Why would your engineers want my people to journey with you?"

"Gatnack and Drigtik want to offer your engineers the opportunity to remove ... um, to remove their decorations."

"To what extent can this be accomplished?" Harbour asked.

"Completely, Harbour."

Harbour stared in amazement at Tacticnok, who raised an open, facedown hand, inviting understanding.

"Harbour, this is what the Jatouche are known for among the races. Many journey via the gates to see our medical specialists and repair all manner of injury and infirmities to their bodies."

Harbour thought of the many spacers and stationers who suffered from severe debilities and could benefit from such services. A sudden thought occurred to Harbour, and she said, "We'd have no means of compensating you."

"This time, it isn't necessary, Harbour. In the future, I believe that we'll find an equitable means of exchange between our races."

"In an alliance," Harbour whispered.

"It's my hope," Tacticnok replied, her eyes glowing with promise.

"Well, I appreciate you sharing Gatnack and Drigtik's request, Tacticnok, but the decision to journey with you belongs to those individuals who would be making the trip."

Harbour received Tacticnok's slightly annoyed gaze, and she reacted by asking, "Is this emissary training?"

Tacticnok displayed her teeth at Harbour's quick uptake.

Harbour thought through the ramifications of the Jatouche engineers' offer. The opportunity for the human engineers to see and report on the Jatouche home world was invaluable, and these three engineers would be excellent observers. And, if the Jatouche could return these three individuals with their bodies fully restored, she could think of no better reward for them. Finally, three engineers healed of limb, skin, and eye would go a long way toward convincing Pyreans of the value of entering into negotiations with the Jatouche.

"I approve, Tacticnok," Harbour said, when her considerations were complete. "Will you or your engineers make the offer?"

Once again, Harbour received Tacticnok's squint.

"Right," Harbour quickly replied, "I'll speak to them."

"An excellent idea, Captain," Tacticnok replied, which met with Harbour's laughter.

* * * *

Olivia, Pete, and Bryan sat around the captain's table with Harbour. The engineers had polished off a beautifully prepared dinner and were enjoying various offerings from the captain's private cellar.

"This was a wonderful meal, Captain," Olivia said. "Is this the part where we receive the bad news?"

"Yeah, I don't ever remember a beautiful ... I mean, a captain ... buying me a nice dinner and serving me whatever's this stuff," Pete said hoisting his glass.

"It's called port," Harbour replied.

"Why would they name this stuff *left*?" Pete asked.

"Never mind, Pete. Enjoy," Harbour replied with a smile. "I've brought you here to hear Tacticnok's offer. She's requesting that you be allowed to travel with the Jatouche when they return to their home world."

The engineers chose to talk at once, and Harbour silenced them with an upraised hand. "Let me finish," she said. "You're invited in order to remove your decorations, as Tacticnok has referred to them."

"All of them?" Bryan asked, raising his prosthetic arm.

"According to Tacticnok, limb, skin, and eye can be replaced," Harbour replied.

"With what?" Olivia asked. "Something mechanical?"

"No, Olivia. According to Tacticnok, the Jatouche are known for their medical skills. You'll receive your own regenerated tissue. I didn't get into detail with her, and you're welcome to ask her for more information before you make your decisions. I wanted you to know that I've approved of your journeying with them."

Harbour searched the engineers' faces. They'd glanced briefly at one another before they sat silently with their thoughts.

It was Bryan who broke the silence. "And here I've grown so fond of these two substitutes for limbs," he said, banging the table and kicking the chair leg with his two prosthetics.

"Yeah, I agree," Olivia echoed. "I don't know how I'd operate with stereo vision, once again."

"You two have no idea of my complication," Pete said seriously. "Women wailed when they lost their handsome Pete. It's going to be a shock to them when he appears again."

There was the briefest moment of open-jawed stares at Pete by the other engineers before they broke into hilarious laughter. Harbour curtailed her smile. She'd sensed that Pete was partly serious. It struck her how much psychological damage had been done through the loss of appearances and mobility.

"Do you think they can do it ... what Tacticnok said?" Olivia asked, her hand touching the horrendous scars on the left side of her face.

"You people should know that, although it was Tacticnok who came to me with the offer, it was Gatnack and Drigtik who proposed and pushed for the idea. They want to help you," Harbour explained.

Olivia, Pete, and Bryan visibly brightened. The strong bonds between the engineers of the two races were obvious.

"How do you feel about it, Captain, other than having approved of our going?" Bryan asked.

Harbour opened her senses a little wider. Bryan was one of her earliest rescues from security detention. He would want to know where she stood on the issue, in more ways than one. She could feel his hope and anxiety mixing together.

"Do I think the Jatouche can deliver? Yes," Harbour replied. "It's the royal daughter, who has driven this operation to rescue our planet and who is supporting the offer. I think she will do right by you. But, and this is a big but," Harbour added, grinning before her expression turned serious, "Do I think the Jatouche want something from us? The answer to that is also yes. You traveling to the Jatouche home world represents wonderful personal opportunities for you, but it's also a chance to help Pyre. We need to learn about the Jatouche and the worlds they meet. You could provide us with incredibly valuable information."

"Well, boys, feel like becoming medical experiments on the off chance we can get healed?" Olivia asked.

"I'm in," Pete said.

"Can't be much worse than these," Bryan said, laying his good hand on the prosthetic.

Harbour wanted to urge them to talk to Tacticnok before they made up their minds, but the hopes and joy flooding out of them wouldn't be diminished by any details that the royal daughter might offer them.

* * * *

The *Belle* kept a stationary position high above the Triton dome. Danny and Claudia ferried engineers, techs, and crates down to the dome.

Spacers accompanied the Jatouche on every trip. There were no surface transports, and more hands made lighter work of hauling the remaining equipment from the shuttle to the dome.

Of mild interest to everyone was that Jittak and his minders, the three soldiers, took the first passenger trip downside, and Danny reported they had immediately exited the ship on touchdown. Even the Jatouche chittered among themselves when Jittak and the soldiers marched off toward the dome without carrying a single item. Their personal gear and weapons would be delivered to the dome on a later shuttle run.

Kractik was also on the first flight to the surface. Unlike Jittak and his soldiers, a female Jatouche tech and she grabbed a crate and attempted to carry it between them. Two human techs had their own crate and followed them out of the cargo bay. When the Jatouche faltered, the Pyreans stacked their crate on top of the Jatouche crate and trekked onward.

"We wouldn't want you to be late, sending Jittak home," one Pyrean tech quipped to the Jatouche, who long since had adjusted their suit comm systems to receive the humans' comms.

"Jittak can wait, as far as I'm concerned," Kractik rejoined.

"You misunderstand, Kractik," the second human tech said. "This isn't for Jittak's benefit. Everyone is anxious to see Jittak go."

The Jatouche cackled at the idea that they shared a common dislike for the military officer.

"Jittak is not representative of our military," Kractik said, walking briskly to keep up with the humans, despite their load of two crates. "He's a xenophobe and detests the idea of another alliance with our race."

"What's a xenophobe?" a Pyrean asked.

"Someone who doesn't like aliens," Kractik replied.

The humans chuckled on hearing the explanation. "Good thing there's none of those around," the other Pyrean shot back, and the four techs shared a great joke.

The last passenger shuttle trip carried Tacticnok, Jaktook, Jakkock, the last of the engineers, a few spacers, and, of all people, Harbour, who had arrived at the *Belle*'s bay in her vac suit.

Spacers stared at their captain. Several searched for a way to explain to Harbour that simply possessing a suit didn't mean she could be allowed on the surface.

"Don't get yourselves in a twist, spacers," Dingles growled. "The captain's qualified. I handled the training and tests myself, and her ratings are entered in the ship's log."

When the *Belle* delivered the latest load of slush to the YIPS and eliminated Emerson's ridiculous quarantine edicts, Harbour had enlisted Dingles' help. The first mate was handed a pair of Harbour's skins and deck shoes for measurements and they were sent to the JOS.

Gabriel, at the Latched On, heard the request for a vac suit to match the skins. He held them up and examined the curves. "Yours, Dingles?" he inquired, with a twinkle in his eye.

"Captain Harbour needs an outfitting," Dingles replied, emphasizing the requestor's name.

"Happy to oblige that woman," Gabriel replied. "Basic, advanced, or something in between."

"Basic but high quality," Dingles replied. "This is for safety's sake when transferring between ships, riding passenger in a mining shuttle or —"

"Visiting a dome." Gabriel finished.

When Gabriel delivered the vac suit, Dingles was requested by Harbour to keep the training secret. He chose an empty bay, stored the gear there, and they met late in the evening. Dingles' rating allowed him to train and test newbies and surface explorers.

Dingles was surprised that Harbour, who had never donned a vac suit, turned out to be an extremely quick learner. Then it occurred to him that he didn't need to reprimand her, when she did something wrong. The captain was reading him and correcting the error before he could voice his thought.

The last load of passengers hurried onto the shuttle, and Danny and Claudia lifted off when the bay was cleared. Many aboard felt a deep ache in their chests at the coming separation.

"Danny reported that Jittak was aboard the first flight to the surface and made for the dome immediately," Harbour said to Tacticnok, who sat next to her.

"This isn't a race, Harbour," Tacticnok replied. "My father will wait to hear all sides. And, if Jittak knew my father better, he'd not be so quick to report before His Excellency's daughter." Tacticnok had flashed her teeth, and Harbour laughed.

"I've a great deal to learn to become politically wise," Harbour said.

"Most of it is experience, Captain. You already carry inside what is most important to your people. Their best interests reside in your mind and heart."

In the dome, most engineers, all techs, and all crates had been transported. The last to climb on the platform were Tacticnok, Jaktook, Jakkock, and the five engineers, who'd done the most to deploy the intravertor. Kractik glanced toward Tacticnok, who twitched two fingers. Then she looked toward Harbour, who nodded. Kractik activated the platform on a short delay and hurried to join the others.

Harbour stared at Olivia, who raised her hand in a goodbye wave. Then the platform fired, and the blue light obscured them. Seconds later they were gone. Harbour looked at the empty platform, a mix of emotions swirling through her.

Finally, Dingles, who wasn't about to let his new trainee out of his sight on her first vac suit foray, touched Harbour's shoulder. "Time to go, Captain," he said. "I'm sure we'll see them again soon."

Harbour couldn't tell whether Dingles spoke of the three human engineers or the Jatouche. It didn't matter. She missed them all.

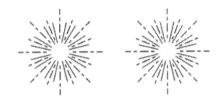

— The Pyreans will return in *Jatouche*. —

Glossary

Colony Ship (*Honora Belle*)

Beatrice "Birdie" Andrews – Comm operator on the *Belle*

Bryan Forshaw – Propulsion engineer on the *Belle*

Celia O'Riley – Former name of the current Harbour

Danny Thompson – Pilot of the *Belle* and its shuttle

Darby – Engineer and biologist

Dingles – Nickname for Mitch Bassiter, first mate on the *Belle*

Harbour – Protector of the empaths, captain of the *Belle*, originally known as Celia O'Riley

Helena Garmenti – Kidnapped by the governor, mother of Aurelia and Sasha

Isley – Backup shuttle pilot

Lindsey Jabrook – Previous Harbour

Makana – Artisan who decorated Harbour's skins

Michael "Monty" Montpellier – Retired spacer on the *Belle*

Mitch "Dingles" Bassiter – First mate on the *Belle*

Nadine – Older empath

Pete Jennings – Engineer and ex-spacer

Sasha Garmenti – Younger daughter of Helena, Aurelia's sister

Yasmin – Harbour's closest friend, empath

Downsiders (Domes)

Dimitri Belosov –The former governor's dead nephew

Dorelyn Gaylan – Matriarch of Gaylan clan

Giorgio Sestos – Former governor's head of security, in jail

Idrian Tuttle – Dome family head

Jordie MacKiernan – Chief of security for Lise Panoy

Lise Panoy –Governor of Pyre's domes

Markos Andropov – Former governor of Pyre's domes, in jail

Rufus Stewart – Dome family head

Stevens – Security member for Lise Panoy

Tinder – Lise Panoy's comm tech

Jatouche

Drigtik (drig-tick) – Fabrication engineer, grandson of Gatnack

Gatnack (gat-knack) – Elderly scientist at Pyre

Gitnock (git-knock) – Scientist who proposed space travel by colony ships

Jakkock (jack-cock) – Linguist

Jaktook (jack-took) – Dome senior administrator

Jatouche (jaw-toosh) – Alien race

Jittak (jit-tack) – Military leader

Kiprick (kip-rick) – Dome supervisor

Kractik (crack-tick) – Tech and relief console operator

Pickcit (pick-sit) – Master Economist

Pinnick (pin-nick) – Tech at the Gasnar dome

Rictook – Jatouche ruler, His Excellency

Roknick – Master Strategist

Tacticnok (tack-tick-nock) – Daughter in the royal family, Her Highness

Tiknock – Master Scientist

Spacers

Aurelia Garmenti – Eldest daughter of Helena, also known as Rules

Belinda Kilmer –Second mate on the *Marianne*

Buttons – Aging spacer aboard the *Spryte*

Claudia Manning – *Spryte*'s shuttle pilot, copilot of the *Belle*'s new shuttle

Corbin Rose – Former captain of the *Marianne* and the *Unruly Pearl*, bequeathed his ships to Jessie Cinders

Darrin "Nose" Fitzgibbon – First mate on the *Marianne*

Hamoi – Assay tech on the *Marianne*

Ituau Tulafono – First mate aboard the *Spryte*

Jeremy – Navigator aboard the *Spryte*

Jessie Cinders – Owner of a mining company, captain of the *Spryte*

Kasey – Tech aboard the *Spryte*

Leonard Hastings – Captain of the *Pearl*

Nate Mikado – Second mate aboard the *Spryte*

Orlando Davos – Captain and owner of a mining ship

Paul Kirsch – Captain and owner of a mining ship
Portia Deloitte – Captain and owner of a mining ship
Rules –Nickname for Aurelia Garmenti
Tully – Survey engineer on the *Marianne*
Yohlin Erring – Captain of the *Marianne*

Stationers or Topsiders (the JOS and the YIPS)

Cecilia Lindstrom – Sergeant in station security
David Yersh – Jordie MacKiernan's agent on the YIPS
Devon Higgins – Lieutenant in station security
Dorsey – Security major before Liam Finian, dead
Dottie Franks – Starlight cantina patron and investor
Emerson Strattleford – Commandant of the JOS
Evan Pendleton – YIPS manager
Gabriel – Latched On store owner
Hadley – Tech
Hans Riesling – Starlight cantina patron and investor
Henry Stamerson – Head of the Review Board, retired mining captain
Jensen – Tech
Jorge Olas – Forensics specialist in security
Liam Finian – Major in station security
Lily Tormelli – Deceased coin-kitty
Maggie – Hostess and manager of the Miner's Pit, ex-spacer
Margaret O'Toole – Forensics department head
Miguel Rodriguez – Sergeant in station security
Olivia Harden – YIPS engineer
Oster Simian – Starlight cantina patron and investor
Pena – Young girl who Toby likes
Terrell "Terror" McKenzie – Ex-corporal in security
Toby – Boy who received BRC surgery
Trent Pederson – Starlight cantina patron and investor

Objects, Terms, and Cantinas

Agri-dome – Dome dedicated exclusively to agriculture

Alliance – Group of races to which the Jatouche belong

BRC – Bone replacement copy, pronounced "brick"

Caf – Drink of artificially grown coffee and cocoa with a mild stimulant

Cap – Transportation capsule

Captain's Articles – Agreement captain signs with the JOS

Coin – Reference to electronic currency

Coin-kat or coin-kitty – Male or female sex service provider

Colony – Entities exiting gate five in the Jatouche dome

Comm-dot – Communication ear wig that relays to a comm unit

Crocian – Alien race, members of the Alliance

DAD – DNA analysis device, sniffer

Deck boots – Boots that hold vac suited spacers to ship decks

Deck shoes – Shoes with patterned bottoms, which allow people's feet to adhere to decks

Dissemination of Assets – Will recorded by a Pyrean in the event of death

Downside – Refers to the domes on Pyre

E-cart – Electric cargo transport

El – Elevator car linked between the orbital station and Pyre's domes

Empath – Person capable of sensing and manipulating the emotional states of others

E-trans – Electric passenger transport

Gasnarians – Original race on Pyre, extinct

Green – Replenishing drink of herbs and vegetables for empaths

Hook on – Expression that means pay attention now, response is "Aye, latched on."

Latched On – Spacer supply house

Messinants – Ancient race that genetically tinkered with species and built the Q-gate domes

Miners' Pit – Cantina owned by Jessie Cinders

Mist mask – Makeup mask

Normals – Individuals who have no empath capability

Plumerase tree – Sweet fruit and an addictive narcotic, streak, from the nut

Q-gate – Jatouche term for transportation gate

Review Board – Judicial body aboard the JOS

Sensitives – Preferred alternate name for empaths

Skins – Preferred clothing of stationers and spacers

Sleepholds – Places for people to temporarily bunk

Slush – Generic term for frozen gases

Sniffer – DAD device

Starlight – Expensive JOS cantina

Stationers – People who live on the Jenkels Orbital Station, called the JOS

Streak – Addictive drug manufactured by the downsiders

Tikar – Jatouche length of time

Vac suit – Spacer's vacuum work suit

Stars, Planets, and Moons

Crimsa – Star of the planet Pyre

Emperion – Pyre's second moon

Gasnar – Jatouche term for Pyre

Minist – Pyre's first and smallest moon

Na-Tikkook – Jatouche home world

Pyre – New home world of colonists

Triton – Pyre's third, outermost moon

Ships and Stations

Honora Belle – Colony ship, also known as the *Belle*

Jenkels Orbital Station – Station above Pyre. Anchors the El car to downside, called the JOS, pronounced "joss."

Marianne – Captain Jessie Cinders' first ship, referred to as the *Annie,* willed to him by Corbin Rose

Spryte – Captain Jessie Cinders' third ship

Unruly Pearl – Captain Jessie Cinders' second ship, referred to as the *Pearl,* willed to him by Corbin Rose

Yellen-Inglehart Processing Station – Mineral and gas-processing platform, called the YIPS, pronounced "yips."

My Books

Messinants, the second novel in the Pyrean series, is available in e-book, softcover, and audio book versions. Please visit my website, http://scottjucha.com, for publication locations and dates. You may register at my website to receive email updates on the progress of my upcoming novels.

Pyrean Series
Empaths
Messinants
Jatouche (forthcoming)

The Silver Ships Series
The Silver Ships
Libre
Méridien
Haraken
Sol
Espero
Allora
Celus-5
Omnia
Vinium
Nua'll (forthcoming)

The Author

I've been enamored with fiction novels since the age of thirteen and long been a fan of great storytellers. I've lived in several countries overseas and in many of the US states, including Illinois, where I met my wonderful wife more than three decades ago. My careers have spanned a variety of industries in the visual and scientific fields of photography, biology, film/video, software, and information technology (IT).

My first attempt at a novel, which I've retitled *The Florentine*, was a crime drama centered on the modern-day surfacing of a 110-carat yellow diamond lost during the French Revolution. In 1980, in preparation for the book, I spent two wonderful weeks researching the Brazilian people, their language, and the religious customs of Candomblé. The day I returned from Rio de Janeiro, I had my first date with my wife-to-be, Peggy Giels.

In the past, I've outlined dozens of novels, but a busy career limited my efforts to complete any of them. In early 2014, I chose to devote my efforts to writing full-time. My first novel, *The Silver Ships*, was released in February 2015. The series, with the release of *Vinium*, now numbers ten.

The Pyrean series relates the tale of a third Earth colony ship and gives readers an opportunity to follow new characters, who struggle to overcome the obstacles of a world tortured by geologic upheaval. Humans are divided into camps — downsiders, stationers, spacers, and the *Honora Belle*'s inhabitants, which consist of empaths and the discarded.

My deep appreciation goes out to the many readers who embraced the Silver Ships and Pyrean series and its characters. I hope you've found the stories enjoyable!

Made in the USA
San Bernardino, CA
16 August 2018